MW01139056

To
Kitty & Elizabeth

~~ This book is dedicated to all of the mothers who suffer
as their children's lives are ruined by the epidemic use of
heroin. We are all sisters. ~~

Thank you for your interest in my story ~ Kim

www.kimcruise.com

1

Part I

THOMAS 1

Betty was beside herself with misery; her inability to comfort her new baby threatened her belief that mothering would come naturally to her. This belief was a key piece in her decision to adopt; she had even mentioned it when convincing her husband that adoption was a good idea for them. *Shouldn't every loving woman be able to reach into her sole and find her way into being a good mother? And shouldn't a good mother be able to make her baby feel satisfaction and well-being?* Betty's heart was breaking. She had been to the doctor many times looking for help but he always proclaimed Thomas to be healthy. She felt her pediatrician was pandering to her when he said her baby was crying only as a form of communication.

But then he did stop. At age 18 months Thomas stopped crying and started screaming.

EARLIER

Betty and Richard Findlay were married in 1974 when Betty was 25 and Richard was 30. Richard was a fairly successful salesman working for a distributor that specialized in tractor-trailer parts. His job included travel, so being gone two or three days of each week was not unusual for him. Betty missed him terribly during the early years of their marriage. By the time five years had gone by, she had taken up a few hobbies and had even gotten a part-time job to help fill the time. She loved quilting and sewing so it was very easy for her to get a job at JoAnn Fabrics. Richard was happy when she accepted the position to work about 20 hours per week but seemed to resent it when work days landed on days he was in town. "I can't ask the store manager to arrange my schedule around yours, Rich." Betty said when Richard complained about dinner being late on a day she worked until 5:00.

"I know that." Richard replied with a shortness that warned Betty about how she should continue with this topic. "But I get the impression that you don't care if I'm sitting here waiting for my dinner."

"Richard, sweetheart, you are the most important thing to me." Betty had heeded the warning. "Would you be happier with our lives if I quit JoAnn's?"

"I'm making enough money so yes, I think I would." Betty noted the selfishness of Richard's answer but she was willing to do a great deal to make him happy. She wasn't going to let the 'honeymoon' end without a fight. She had made a commitment the day they married and she felt very strongly about that. Betty not only gave her two-week notice the next day but she also did Richard an even greater service: she stuffed the knowledge of his grumpy selfishness down into the hinterlands of her heart. She wouldn't pull that knowledge back out to be examined for another 4 years.

At 30, Betty was cute in a natural way. She had sparkling blue eyes and an upturned nose. In the summer, freckles decorated her nose and a spray of them appeared on each side of her face, giving her cheeks a healthy look. She wore tiny pearl stud earrings every day. They were a wedding present so, to her, they represented her married lifestyle almost as much as the gold band on her finger. Her hair was naturally wavy and she wore it cut to her shoulders; a headband kept it off her face most days.

Richard had a slightly more pretentious look; he was very vain about his mustache, trimming it with tiny scissors daily. Following that ritual, he slapped on cologne and then looked at himself in the mirror from several angles. He used a men's hair product to hide his gray hairs and he tried to hide that fact from Betty. She figured it out though because when he would climb on top of her at night, she could smell it - if he had used it recently. Following their love-making one night, Betty went to the bathroom; it was a night when the telltale scent was present. There was a black gelatinous blob on her bathroom counter. Betty wiped it away and bleached the residual stain for him without saying a word. The For Men Only box was peeking out from under the tissues in the garbage can when Betty tossed away the paper towels used in the cleanup. Betty was sorry that he wasn't honest with her about all of his rituals but she liked how he looked so she decided to let it go.

As with many couples, their thoughts eventually turned to having a baby. Betty brought up the idea one morning over coffee. She had been using birth control and changing that warranted a conversation. "Richard, what do you think about us having a baby?"

"Great." Richard didn't put the newspaper down to reply.

"Richard, really?" Betty asked. She wanted him engaged in this conversation as much as she just wanted to take his answer and run with it.

"Yes." Richard said. "Yes, let's have a baby." He set the paper down momentarily to make sure Betty was satisfied. Betty was already hopping up from the table and coming around to Richard's side.

"Oh Rich, this is so exciting!" She picked up one of his hands to try to get him to stand for a hug, "We'll make great parents and I know exactly what I want to do with the baby's room. I'm going to take down the wall paper and-" Richard cut her off.

"Listen, you do whatever you want." He pulled his hand free, "I need to get to the office."

It wasn't possible for Betty to feel discouraged on this morning so she went about cleaning up the breakfast dishes as thoughts of how she would get started turning their extra room into a nursery occupied her mind.

Two years later, Richard came home from work to find Betty crying in the bathroom. "What's going on?" he asked.

"I got my period today..." a jagged breath in, then Betty, sitting on the toilet lid, continued, "I really felt bloated and tired this week so I was hoping that this time I would be pregnant."

"Can you just ask your doctor what it is that's wrong with you?" Richard was impatient with this topic.

"I did, last year." Betty was trying to calm herself so that she didn't upset Richard any more. After a deep breath, she went on, "He said that he can't detect anything obvious and we should just keep trying."

"How long are we supposed to do that?" Richard still hadn't touched Betty or offered any solace.

"If we did anything more..." Betty accidentally let a sob escape, but she inhaled again, holding in the breath for a second, then continued, "it would cost a lot of money."

Richard grunted and left the room. From the kitchen he yelled, "What's for dinner?"

That evening Betty couldn't eat her dinner but she politely pushed it around her plate while her husband ate. When he was done eating, he said, "Maybe we should adopt, that way you wouldn't be getting so upset."

Betty understood his meaning; she said "I realize my sadness is inconvenient for you -"

"What?!" Richard cut her off; he was furious for being called out.

"I'm sorry, I didn't really mean that." Betty quickly tried to smooth the ruffled feathers she had caused. Playing the role of peacekeeper was very hard when she was so heartbroken but she did her best.

"You know I have *our* best interest at heart, right?"

Betty was quick with her reply, "Yes, I know that."

One year later and a lot of paperwork and interviews in their rear view mirror, Betty started sprinting to the phone every time it rang. She had been told by the adoption agency to be ready for the call at any time. Betty had a bag packed for her and one for the baby; both bags sat waiting in the closet near the front door. Finding gender-neutral items for the baby's bag was not an easy task but Betty enjoyed every minute of it.

Betty had also enjoyed decorating the room that the child would occupy. Betty was willing to take in and love either gender, so her decorating choices weren't defined for her. She decided on a yellow room, decorated with balloons as the theme. Betty used a stencil to paint 10-inch tall balloons around the top of each wall, spaced about a foot apart. The balloons were green, red, and blue. The base of the new lamp was a clown holding a bouquet of balloons. Betty used her sewing skills to save money. She bought yellow fabric with large white polka-dots along with white fabric with large yellow polka-dots to make curtains, bumper pads for the crib, and she made a thick, albeit small blanket. The latter was thick and warm with all the padding Betty was able to stuff between the two outside layers.

Her baby projects had been complete for two months before the phone call came in. During that period of time, Betty had a difficult time getting along with Richard. He seemed so short and constantly frustrated. She couldn't help but feel like she had let him down, in a permanent way, by not conceiving his child. She consoled herself by thinking, *just wait till the baby gets here. New innocent life will bring us back together, and I'll be the best mother he could ever hope for in a wife.*

The phone rang; Richard was out of town so Betty knew

she had to race to get it. Her hands were covered with suds from washing the few dishes it took for her to eat when she was home alone. She ran to the phone with a dish towel in her hand. She giggled to herself as she registered the thought that she could *dry on the fly*, and then, *and I'm a poet and I don't know it*...

"Hello?... Yes this is Betty" Betty knew immediately that this was the call she had been waiting for. She started writing things on the tablet next to phone, left there for just this reason. "Today?" she asked. "Yes. Yes, I can do that."

A few seconds later she was calling Richard's office. She didn't know how to reach him where he was but she knew he would have to check in there later, so he could get the news of their new son from the office secretary. Betty then consulted a map of her area; she needed to figure out how to get to a hospital in the next county, an area she had never been to on her own. She was not worried or nervous about this trip. She would get to that hospital if she had to crawl the entire way. It looked like it was about a one-hour drive and she was expected there in about three hours. She grabbed the two pre-packed suitcases and left within about 10 minutes; the idea of waiting at the hospital for her appointment time made her deliriously happy, in spite of the fact that it could be a wait of as much as two hours. It would be two hours of day dreaming of baby powder, little blue onesies, and toy trucks. Richard and Betty had agreed on the name Thomas Andrew if it were a boy; Betty was heading out to get that boy.

It was about 4:00 p.m. when she pulled back into her driveway with their first child. He seemed so perfect, snuggled down into the car seat. He was sleeping so peacefully that she decided to carry in the car seat with him in it, instead of lifting him out of it. Her decision was influenced by her feeling of being inexperienced with all the clips, straps, and buckles that comprised the car seat. She felt if she could set it on the floor, in good lighting,

Thomas would be safer when she lifted him out.

She gazed down at him; he was perfect. He had a thatch of dark hair and round, pink cheeks. She could see the slight rise and fall of his chest as he dozed. When he started to stir, she began the process of getting him out of the seat. She had already warmed a bottle, using the instructions in one of the many books she bought during her long wait. Once she had him freed from his car seat, she carried him carefully to the overstuffed chair in the living room and sat down. She gently introducing the bottle's nipple to her baby's mouth and within a few seconds he took it into his mouth and began to suck. Tears formed in Betty's eyes. This one moment was worth the years of frustration and sorrow. She stared at Thomas as he drank the nourishment she provided him. When the bottle was drained, she held her son up to her shoulder and gently patted his back. Within a few minutes, he released a gentle burp. He fell back to sleep before Betty even lowered him down off her shoulder.

"Good night my sweet baby" she said as she laid him in his crib. She stood over him a few minutes, not really believing that her dream had been fulfilled. Just then the phone rang. She ran for it again, but this time is was so the noise wouldn't wake the baby.

"He's perfect, when can you come home?" Betty asked Richard.

Betty heard a happiness in Richard's voice that she hadn't heard in a few years. "I'll be home by 10 tonight. I've canceled my appointments for tomorrow." Later that night they both gazed down at their perfect son as he slept. Betty got up once during the night to feed Thomas and change his diaper; she let Richard sleep through this new chore.

The next day, Betty jumped out of bed when she heard some tiny sounds from the baby's room. He was just stirring when she got there so she picked him up. "Good morning my sunshine" she said in a sing-song voice. She raised him to her shoulder and headed back to her bedroom where Richard was sleeping. Richard's snores were loud, so Betty changed plans and carried her son downstairs so she could warm a new bottle for him.

Day two of Thomas's life went on like this, sleeping, feeding, gazing, burping, and rocking in the rocking chair. Richard went into work late that day so that he could watch his wife care for his son. By noon though he was gone and Thomas was on his third bottle. Betty began to hope for an opportunity to nap. The excitement of the prior day was catching up with her. When Thomas fell asleep later, Betty dozed in the rocking chair in the baby's room. She felt great when she woke up - those 10 minutes made the perfect power nap.

On day three of Thomas's life, things changed; he began to cry inconsolably. Betty didn't know what to do for him. She rocked him, she walked around, bouncing him against her chest, and she fed him more bottles of formula than the doctor advised. Besides the few hours of sleep he'd get each night, the moments he spent consuming his bottles were the only time the crying would subside, yet tears would still roll out of his eyes. After three days of crying, Betty called the pediatrician. They squeezed her in later that day but couldn't find any cause for the baby's crying. They sent her home with assurances that he'd be fine and the crying would stop. Betty wanted this to be true so she worked through the next couple of days, doing the best she could to keep Thomas comfortable and fed.

After another week of the same things, she called the doctor's office again. She had to be pushy to get an appointment. They seemed to want her to just deal with her baby's agony. Again the doctor looked at Thomas and declared him to be healthy. He did suggest that she change to a different formula, just in case the baby was sensitive to something in the one the hospital had recommended.

Betty felt they were just reaching for straws; she went home again feeling defeated.

Betty had enjoyed two days of having the most perfect child she could have wished for after years of heart ache while trying to conceive. Now Betty was disappointed in herself and sad beyond words.   She hadn't had enough time to fully bond with this baby yet she was tied to him and couldn't entertain the idea that adopting him might have been a mistake. Her life at this moment was not what she had been looking forward to.

Richard was even more clueless than Betty regarding what to do about this difficult baby. His solution was to work more and stay outside whenever possible. Betty was left largely to deal with Thomas on her own. And dealing with Thomas often just meant tolerating the noise and needy requirements of this child. Betty also felt great remorse; her baby was miserable. The doctor continued to be unhelpful. He was 3 or 4 years shy of retirement and his suggestions always implied that Betty was being intolerant of the natural stages of development for a child. "All babies cry Mrs. Findlay, it's the only way they have to communicate." Or "Why don't you just let him cry until he goes to sleep?" She felt like she was repeating herself, saying over and over, "but it goes on for hours" or "but it is an all-day thing." The most encouraging thing the pediatrician said was, "Relax Mrs. Findlay, your baby is healthy and he'll grow out of this."

And so he did; that's when the screaming started.

COREY 1

"Corey you are so dense!" Angela yelled through clenched teeth. She was stomping around the baby's room, hunting for a specific pair of socks that she felt would be suitable for her toddler's outfit.

"Sweetheart, there must be 14 other pairs of socks here that you could use instead." Corey struggled to seem calm. "Eve will not care, I promise."

"You don't understand! You never understand!" Angela's anger was rising. "You think just because something is good enough for you that it would be good enough for me, or Eve."

"That's not exactly true. It's more accurate to say that while we are in this period of our lives when some things are more challenging because our child is a baby, you could maybe feel some relief by letting your standards down a little." Corey continued, "Realistically, in five years, who will know what socks Eve wore on this play date?"

Angela breathed out a jagged, unsatisfied groan. "At some level you're making sense and it's tempting to reduce myself to your logic, but impressions can't be undone." Angela's tone was taking on a superior note. "Eve's outfit today will be perfect or…. or…. we won't go."

End of conversation, Corey said on her behalf, in his head. He had experienced these deteriorating conversations before, they always centered on something that he just couldn't register as important and yet somehow seemed so extremely important to Angela.

"I guess that's up to you" Corey responded. It was fine with him if his 18 month old piece of perfection named Eve stayed home that afternoon. Corey would even change his plans to clean out the gutters and put away outdoor furniture if it meant snuggling on the couch with his daughter. They could read the book that made animal noises. Eve knew the book well; she knew that if she pushed here, or pulled a tab there, flipped a flap over there, she would get the barnyard noise associated with the animal pictured on that page, and she had every page memorized. Corey was always content with reading it as many times as Eve wanted, which was usually 10 or 12 times.

Angela's stomping had become more petulant. Corey could hear drawers opening and then being slammed shut. He retrieved Eve from her crib so that she wouldn't be exposed to this behavior more than was needed. They rocked together in the chair near the window and Corey kept up a banter of softly spoken, peaceful words so that Eve would hear only his voice while Angela was working through her tantrum.

"Found them" Angela said without joy or triumph. "I thought you had taken care of the laundry in the dryer. I should have known. But that's where the socks were." Angela moved to take Eve from Corey. "Let me have her."

"Let me do the socks for you so you can finish getting ready." Corey said, "Then I'll get her into her coat and car seat." Corey wanted to protect Eve from as much of Angela's anger as possible, and that was a big job. Ever since Eve had been born by Cesarean Section, Angela had been angry about something. At first it seemed reasonable. Angela had a lot of pain from the surgical aspect of Eve's birth and then her milk never really seemed sufficient to satisfy Eve. But then there was anger over Eve's sleep patterns and basic household chores like laundry and cooking. Meanwhile, Corey was so in love with his new daughter that he tried to maintain a belief that Angela would eventually settle in and be happy with their threesome. This didn't seem to be happening though and in some ways it seemed to be getting worse. It wasn't just anger anymore; it was also the fact that she was petty, insulting, and she often tried to belittle Corey. Corey could and would withstand this though, because he would do whatever it took to be a good father to Eve. He felt maintaining a solid family structure was his responsibility and he planned to do just that.

Corey had been working as the office manager for an area not-for-profit run by a church diocese, the mission of which was to help area families with things like childcare, health care, adoption, education and parenting. He liked it very much in spite of his one complaint about the organization: they put their religious beliefs into everything they offered to their clients. He would have preferred more open-minded practices where clients could decide for themselves how much of the religion they wanted to incorporate into their experience with the agency. For example, a woman of childbearing age would not be provided birth control as a part of the health care she received from the agency. This to Corey was a poignant example of his silent complaint with the agency. His opinion came from his own experiences.

Overall, he was happy with his job but it didn't pay very well. He worked hard though, not only because that was his nature but also because the organization's position of Executive Director is what he was aiming for; it was currently filled but Corey suspected that his boss had visions of bigger things. Corey was pretty confident that if he worked there for a few years, he would be deemed qualified for that position and the pay would be enough to support his little family. For now, at least he had a job with benefits, and as long as Angela's mother babysat Eve three days a week, Angela could work at her part time job and they would make ends meet, albeit barely. Angela resented having to work however, so this was a detail that fed into her discontent. Whenever she drank vodka, her discontent grew exponentially.

Angela was raised in a family where gender roles were very stereotypical. Her mother didn't work and her father made plenty of money to support the family and enough for Angela to have anything she wanted. Sometimes Angela got new things before she even knew she wanted them; Angela's mother would see something in a magazine and if it appealed to her, Angela possessed it within a day or two. In high school, Angela was considered to be a predictor of fashion. If Angela was wearing straight legged jeans, most of the female population who could afford new clothes was wearing them within the month. Angela's bedroom was the gathering place for the 'popular girls.' Her dressing table was cluttered with make-up kits and bottles of nail polish. Boxed sets of 6 or 8 pairs of earrings could be found, often cast to the side, as if Angela didn't have time to notice that her mother had purchased them for her. In Angela's teenaged brain, she had no need to recognize gifts from her mother; they were to be expected. Her feeling of entitlement was what defined her.

The teenagers on the fringe of this elite group seemed to fawn over Angela, always hoping to be allowed into her clique. This was another thing that, to a small extent, she was oblivious to, and to a large extent, she took for granted. This too fell neatly into her sense of entitlement.

At the end of her junior year in high school, her mother began working on finding a college for Angela. She wanted it to be a place where she could meet appropriate people, especially young men, but since Angela's grades were poor, the options were narrowed substantially. The PASSHE system was going to have to work for them. The Pennsylvania State System of Higher Education would be Angela's home for what they hoped would only take 4 years. Angela shrugged at this news; she just didn't care where she went. She would probably have the best clothes and jewelry of all her new friends. Since she never intended to have a career, college credentials meant nothing to her.

Four years later, Angela was working at the makeup counter in a large department store. She did not enjoy helping people find just the right shade of lipstick or the right scent of hand lotion but she did like the way she was encouraged to take control over a transaction; she earned bonus products by convincing someone to up-size a purchase - suggesting the large bottle of this or that instead of just a medium size package - so this put her in good standing with her boss if not many of her coworkers. It was the day that the in-store training focused on the 'Suggestive Sell' that Angela heard the words, "...you can be in control of your customers if you find a way to earn their attention. This will give you bigger sales and bigger bonuses...." she tuned out the rest and began to find small successes by flashing her dimples, complimenting customers on their clothes, and then boldly suggesting the large size product, or the complementing product which the customer hadn't even considered yet. She did get a nice discount on her own cosmetics but in Corey's mind this wasn't beneficial to his family; it seemed to inspire Angela to buy things they didn't really need. He told himself, if these items gave Angela momentary pleasure, then he would turn a blind eye to the unnecessary spending. It was harder to turn a blind eye to the actual items though, as they began to fill up their tiny bathroom, covering the counter and filling up the cabinet behind the mirror. Angela didn't seem to be bothered by all the clutter, although she was intolerant of Corey leaving things lying around.

"We'll be back in about four hours" Angela said as she walked toward the door with Eve, "it would be like um, really fantastic if you could *really* fold that load of laundry today" she said in her most snarky and venomous tone, "and pick up the house for Christ's sake" she followed that up with a noisy exhale that almost sounded like 'urrrgggg.' Corey let this unnecessary hostility go; she was carrying their child while also leaving so it wasn't a good time to ask her to evaluate - and possibly adjust - her attitude. Instead he hurried outside to make sure the child car seat was fastened into the correct car in the correct way. He was going to have to hustle if he was going to get his list of projects completed along with the list Angela wanted him to complete on his day off.

With a little help from his neighbor, Corey was successful at cleaning the gutters and getting his outdoor furniture put into the backyard shed. A half hour later the house was picked up and the laundry was folded and put away. Angela never put laundry into its intended drawer or closet. She seemed to think that a folded stack on the correct dresser was all that was expected when she was the one completing the chore. Corey hoped that getting socks into sock drawers and pants into pants drawers would earn him a little peace and contentment from Angela but he knew better. He looked at his watch and calculated that there was most likely 45 minutes before his wife and daughter would be back. He asked himself, *what would Angela appreciate the most if I did it in the time left?* He grabbed his wallet and drove to the grocery store, having decided that making dinner was the best plan for pleasing Angela. His favorite grocery store sold a line-up of ready-made meals that were a pretty reliable quality. He was very happy to see that they were offering Angela's favorite crab cakes today and he got meatloaf for himself. For $6 each, the convenience was worth this splurge every once in a while. Back home he plated these meals as attractively as he could and had them warming in the oven when Angela pulled back into the driveway. "Hi Babe!" he said when she came through the front door. "Let me take Eve, I'll get her coat off her."

"What do I smell?" Angela said making a face, as if she had stepped in dog droppings on her way into the house.

"It's dinner honey. I thought you might be tired and would

like to eat early."

Angela exhaled sharply, dropped her shoulders and rolled her eyes to the ceiling as if there were some very fundamental fact the Corey was not grasping. "Did you get the laundry done?"

"Yes" Corey replied as if there were several vowels in the word. He was feeling like a disappointment again.

Angela took in a deep breath as if she needed to center herself. "If you let me know when it's ready," Angela referred to her dinner, "I'll come out and get it."

Corey shoved away his feeling of being defeated. After all, he came up with a dinner for her sake, not his, he reasoned with himself. "Okay Babe, maybe 15 minutes more." Corey turned to the business of getting Eve settled into her highchair. He set her book of barnyard animals on the tray in front of her so that he would be free to get her dinner warmed up.

A few weeks later, Corey was planning a meal for five people; his parents were going to join them for Saturday dinner. Clyde and Rene had a much practiced way of controlling the amount of time they spent in Corey's household. They loved Eve very much but they seemed to be afraid of getting pulled into the work involved in being around a baby, and now, a toddler. Their visits were always by invitation only and always had a clear start and ending time. Clyde once said to Rene, "I never expected much from that kid but I didn't expect him to ruin his life the way he has. I expected it to be a simpler failure." Rene was only mildly put off by this statement. She replied, "Shut up, he is making his own way through this world and you should just be grateful that it's not costing us any money." The couple was united by their selfishness.

Corey made pulled pork in the crockpot. When he could

plan ahead, he could produce this entree for under ten dollars. He took rolls out of the freezer and thawed some corn he had frozen back in August when it was really cheap to buy it on the cob from local farmers. He had spent two hours cutting the corn off the cobs and freezing packages sized correctly for his family. Today he thawed two of those. He also cut some potatoes into French fry shapes so that he could roast those to serve as a side dish. Angela was fixing her hair and makeup so he kept Eve occupied in her highchair with cheerios and puzzle pieces while he cooked. "Daaaddy!" Eve yelled. Corey would never get tired of this, "yes love?" he replied. Eve's answer was predictable but much loved: "daddy." Different tone, same word. And that's how their conversations went for several months. Corey was enamored.

It took Angela 45 minutes to come out of the bathroom to greet Corey's parents following their arrival. Rene had asked twice where she was and Corey just glossed over her absence by saying she was getting ready. It was a small house so the couple didn't risk stating aloud anything about Angela's rudeness. Instead they looked at each other and their son with widened eyes and titled heads. When Corey had the table set and the food ready, Angela came into the tiny living room and said hello. Clyde couldn't resist this opportunity, "I was beginning to wonder if you were really even home."

Angela was not in a good mood on this day. Her usual, acidic attitude was aggravated by having Corey's parents over. "I have a lot on my platter right now Clyde. I'm sorry if my schedule isn't convenient for you." Angela heard her own words and tried to backpedal, "I mean, I apologize for not being ready when you arrived."

Clyde not being one to miss an opportunity said, "Oh, I thought you worked three days a week. I didn't realize your *schedule* was all-consuming." He winked while cocking his head.

Corey inhaled sharply; he knew these were words that would put Angela into her dark place. The very second this thought had formed, his mind shot back, *"dark place??! Hear yourself think that dude. It's a problem."* He decided to address this epiphany at a later date.

Out loud he said, "Hey, let's all move toward the table. Food is ready, and Dad, you can help me put it on the table." Clyde was struck dumb, he couldn't imagine getting food on the table when there were two women present, neither of which had a single broken arm.

Rene cut in, "Let's all work together to get dinner going, okay?" She was now the second person trying to keep their spouse from going to a 'dark place.'

Dinner came and went, Angela didn't say a word to anyone, and Clyde only made short statements all of which included some recognition of discontent. Rene deflected as many of Clyde's comments as possible, and Corey spoke mostly to Eve who was in a high chair right next to him. When everyone was done eating, Corey cleared the table while Rene spent a few minutes playing with Eve.

It wasn't long before Rene reported loudly that Eve smelled like she needed a diaper change. She carried Eve by the armpits over to Corey to report this in a tone which made it seem like a travesty. Her arms were extended out in front of her so that the child with the soiled diaper couldn't accidentally rub against her. Corey had just started scrubbing the inside of the crockpot when Rene entered the kitchen. He called over his shoulder, "Angela, could you get this one?"

Angela's face turned red and then seemed to come to a boil. Angela cleared her facial expression as much as possible but not soon enough. Everyone had seen it.

Angela got up, briskly made her way to Rene, grabbed the child awkwardly, and with no concern for the child's comfort, carried her into the room that contained the changing table. As soon as Angela was out of the room, Rene raised her eyebrows and turned to Corey. Corey shrugged as if to say, *I don't know why you are concerned at this moment*, and turned back to scrubbing the crock pot.

Once the diaper had been changed, Angela handed Eve to Corey and said, "I have a sore throat and I have to work tomorrow so I'm going to bed." It was 7:00 pm. She quietly fixed a vodka and tonic and went to her room.

Clyde didn't speak but Rene expressed her hope that she felt better in time for work. Corey just said good night as he breathed in the scent of his daughter's hair.

Corey's only feeling at that moment was relief. He had no concern for his wife's health since he knew she was faking the sore throat. He had no concern for his loss of an opportunity to snuggle with his wife as she fell asleep; that hadn't happened since the latter days of Angela's pregnancy. The sex had ended even before that.

Two days later Rene called Corey. When he saw 'Mom' on the caller ID he was surprised. She usually let some time pass between their conversations. "Listen honey" she began, "I'm not sure how to say this to you but I'm concerned about your relationship with Angela. And please don't tell your father I called. He thinks this is none of our business and frankly, he's afraid of getting involved."

"Mom, thank you for your concern. I agree that Angela's anger is difficult to be around but I'm hoping it will get better. Please just join me in this hope." Corey's head was swimming. If it was obvious to his parents, it must be something that was real, and hence serious. While he couldn't count on his parents for any type of help, he could use them as a barometer for how messed up his world had become. In light of the fact that he knew they didn't want any meaningful involvement with his life, he had to recognize this conversation as a wake-up call.

Corey started to think about how and when to bring up *the problem* to Angela. In Corey's mind, the term *the problem* was used to encapsulate all that was negative in their relationship and their home. He knew that timing would be key; Angela had so few peaceful moments. The little voice in Corey's mind replied, *few peaceful moments?? How about zero peaceful moments and while we are at it, can we also acknowledge that she brings the misery to the party; she is not a victim of it.* Despite his inner voice, Corey defended his need to find the right time to bring the subject up with Angela. He felt that if he could get Angela to identify the sources of her anger and name some action items that would reduce her anger, then that would be a worthwhile conversation. This hoped-for outcome seemed so reasonable and productive that Corey's spirits lifted. Now he just needed to find the time.

Corey decided that a day Angela worked at the mall would be better than one where she was home all day. Her days spent with Eve seemed to add to her anger, not subtract from it, which was an added mystery for Corey. He spent a week or so waiting to come home to a peaceful household on a work day. After two weeks of waiting, he decided to jump into the conversation he had been planning.

"Hey Angela," he was washing dishes at the time, "can we talk for a minute?"

Angela turned to him with so much resentment on her face that Corey wished he could retract his intro. "Uhh", she stuttered, "I'm really tired, can we keep it brief?"

"I think this is important, maybe even more important than

sleep, but yes, I'll try to be brief. Lemme just finish these dishes."

Angela was miffed that she had to wait while the dishes were finished but she busied herself with getting her own pajamas on and taking off her makeup. She had a few minutes leftover so she poured herself some vodka. While Corey was drying his hands on the towel he always left hanging over the oven door handle he started the conversation, ""I feel like you are not as satisfied with our household as I am and I wanted to talk about how we could improve your parenting experience."   Bam! He nailed his opening sentence. For a split second he was pleased with himself.

"Are you nuts?!" Angela effortlessly destroyed Corey's momentary confidence. She continued, "You got me pregnant in college, I never got to graduate so I have no hope of finding a job I'd really enjoy, and I have to work at a shit job because you can't earn enough on your own even though you got to graduate."

Corey took a deep breath; he still held some hope that his objectives as outlined earlier, could help him make this conversation productive. "I see, so your anger comes from dissatisfaction with your job?" The hope in his voice was pitiable.

"Aaaarrrgh" Angela seethed. "If job dissatisfaction were my key challenge do you think I'd still be working at the damn makeup counter??!"

"Can you tell me please," Corey was humbled, "what else makes you angry?"

"Corey, if you think our situation is something you can fix with your ever-present reasonable voice and your ever-present reasonable lets-all-get-along attitude, then you are wrong!" The last three words spoken with great ferocity.

Angela had verbally stabbed Corey; she knew he valued his own problem-solving skills and his ability to react neutrally to things designed to get a lesser person upset.

"What are you saying?" Corey had to give up his hope of peacefully mediating this topic.

"This thing you call our life is a shipwreck. If you make me address your quality of life, I will tell you to shove it up your ass and that you should take what you are given. Furthermore, if you try to make a change to our marriage, I will pursue and get, complete custody of Eve and you will never see her again *while* you are paying alimony and child support."

Corey fought to stay calm, his thoughts making him dizzy. "Angela…" he paused, in response she turned to go toward their bedroom.

"Don't say my name, and don't plan to sleep in our bed. You have wrecked my life and it's time for you to see it that way."

Corey's jaw dropped open. His thoughts were swimming around and through his feelings, causing him to feel dizzy. He sat down on the couch at the same second that Angela slammed their bedroom door closed. He heard the lock click into place. His natural optimism was replaced by heart break; new words entered his mental dialogue. *Bitch… Selfish… Blaming … Juvenile…* Corey didn't sleep this night; for the first time, he had no hope for his marriage and divorce had become inevitable.

~~~~~~~~~~~~~~~~~~~~~~

THREE YEARS EARLIER

It was a beautiful day on the campus Corey's parents had picked for him. Clyde and Rene's decision was based first on finances; they couldn't risk running short on money when Corey was just the first of two children they'd be paying to educate. Their second criterion, and it was second by a long way, was the programs offered by the school. Corey was enrolled in Business Management which, his parents felt, was close enough to the Non-Profit Management program he really wanted. That program was offered at a private school though, and Corey's parents frequently joked, "you can go to any school you want as long as it's part of the PASSHE system."

Secretly, Clyde thought Corey was too mousey or soft for any type of management job so matching what Corey wanted in a school to what program he actually attended wasn't very important to Clyde.

When he was six, Corey found a baby bird on the ground, abandoned by its mother. He picked it up and ran to the house to find supplies for making it a temporary home. He was certain that with the right help, the bald and fragile baby bird could live a normal life, perhaps even living in a tree right outside of Corey's bedroom window, so that they could stay in touch as it grew up.   But first it needed a place to sleep and some food. Clyde was quick to tell him that this was a ridiculous waste of time. When Corey explained his plan to help this baby creature grow into the feathered bird of his imagination, Clyde guffawed in a way that even at six, Corey knew was insulting. Red blotches formed on his face and tears welled up in his eyes. Clyde growled, "You're such a sissy" then turned and walked away. When the tiny, bony bird died during the night, Corey's wounds were compounded.

By the time Corey was ten, he had learned a trick for getting over Clyde's parenting methods. He took the feelings his father evoked, those of being inconsequential, feeble, and a generalized feeling of being disappointing, and shoved them back into a place in his brain that, at this young age, Corey thought of as a secret compartment. This enabled Corey to feel like he could go ahead and be the person who he felt he was. What his father saw as weakness, Corey felt was kindness. What Clyde called sissiness, Corey called showing sympathy; when Clyde made Corey feel like a disappointment, Corey said to himself, *just you wait and see what I will make of myself.* Corey was blessed with what he felt was an accurate self-image and Clyde was unable to destroy that.

On his way to his 8:00 a.m. lecture, Corey spotted the silhouette of a girl he had recently noticed in his Current Events class. The sun was reflected off a window and that reflection was so bright behind her that most of her details were painted black by the sun's position. The detail that stood out was her ponytail. It was a thin stream of brown hair but it was positioned high at the crown of her head in such a way that Corey felt was a clue that this young woman must be as bouncy and carefree as her hair hinted at. She had exactly the kind of figure Corey was drawn to: about 5'6" or so, medium build, not skinny, not heavy, just healthy and womanly in the right areas. She seemed to have good muscle tone in her arms and he tried to picture how that would translate to her thighs. As he got closer, the sun's effect lessened and he could see she was smiling and laughing with her girlfriend. When he noticed her matching set of adorable dimples, he began to think of her as an angel. This opinion he was forming would last almost exactly three years.

Corey began to wish away the time between his citing of Angela and his Current Events class when he knew he would see her again. He daydreamed a conversation between them where he would say something clever to make her smile or even laugh. Seeing those dimples again would be the objective. When he snapped back into reality, the voice in his head, which sounded just like his father's, told him he had no chance at having a successful conversation with Angela. Corey gave that voice a stage for only about 5 seconds. He might not be loquacious and outgoing but living on campus for the last three years had allowed him to mature and develop a more accurate view of himself. He had a circle of friends that appreciated his ability to speak clearly using few words, spoken quietly. They appreciated his interest in embracing honesty and his concern for his fellow human beings. One female friend told him he was charming and sweet and he secretly agreed with her.

Corey really didn't know if he was attractive or not. He had no obvious physical anomalies, no open sores on his face, or anywhere for that matter. He wasn't short nor gangly. He kept his hair and facial hair neat at all times, due primarily to Clyde's likelihood of harassing him if he didn't. He was six feet tall and somewhere in between thin and somewhat muscular. He seemed to satisfy the criteria for unremarkable, so he only hoped that someone - hopefully Angela - would find him to be her "type."

It was three weeks later when the imagined conversation with Angela became a reality. And while he did get to see Angela's dimples, he didn't have anything clever to say. It took place in the hallway outside the lecture hall following their shared class. On that day, they had come up on opposite sides of a political question the professor was asking. "How much responsibility does a society have to support people who bring problems onto themselves, problems like substance abuse or unplanned pregnancy?" Corey raised his hand and said that taking care of its citizens is a key responsibility of governments. When the teacher asked if anyone disagreed, Angela piped up and said, "Shouldn't people who get in trouble be required to get themselves out of trouble?" A discussion, sometimes heated, ensued. The volume in the classroom rose significantly, and many students picked sides on the partisan dilemma. It was stimulating for everyone and the professor got just what she was looking for. Later, outside the classroom, Corey nearly ran into Angela; it was the situation he was waiting for. They were practically chest to chest when he moved to the right to allow her to pass; she moved to her left, Abbott and Costello would have been proud of them. The same thing happened again when they both tried to undo the awkward first attempt to get out of each other's way. Cluttering Corey's mind was the thought: If only they had been on the same side of the earlier issue. Tapping into courage not yet experienced, Corey said, "hey, any interest in continuing that conversation over tea? or beer? … wine?" Corey, not wanting to sound like he was blatantly asking her on a date, added, "I'd really like to try to understand your perspective."

Angela laughed a quick, self-conscious laugh. "Um… I wouldn't mind meeting you in the cafeteria for a discussion over a Pepsi."

Corey said, "Sold, but, just for the record, if had to pick between tea, beer or wine, which would you pick?" Angela replied, "If you added vodka to the list, it would be much easier to answer."

"Vodka added" spoken as if checking off a list.

"Vodka then." Angela's dimples flashed at Corey.

"Straight up?"

"No, with tonic. And lime."

"Phfshew…. I thought I might be flirting with an alcoholic."

"You're flirting?"

"Ummm, forget I said that." With an obvious smirk he continued, "When can we meet in the cafeteria?"

"My last class today ends at 4:00. How about after that?"

Angela smiled. This flash of dimples nearly paralyzed Corey, his stomach filled with butterflies, he tried to look at her while also looking away.

Corey had a 4:00 class but he no longer cared about Ethics of Management. "I'll meet you at four-fifteen; that work?"

"See you then." She turned to go and that spunky ponytail almost slapped his face. He wished it had.

Corey immediately had a mental to-do list. He wanted to make the most of this opportunity. The list included, shave during lunch break, run to liquor store to buy vodka - just in case, try to find some tonic and if possible, limes, find a clean shirt, double-check need for more deodorant due to stress of most recent conversation, take a shower if needed.

He had a little more than four hours to complete his list while also attending as many classes as possible.

At 4:00 Corey selected the most perfect cafeteria table available: neither located within a cluster nor obviously private.   He wanted to act like he wasn't nervous but the truth was there had been very few girls, or women, who had really caught his eye. He never considered the possibility of being gay, but there were only a few women that really attracted his attention and Angela was one of those few. He did not attend another class that day. Following his interaction with Angela he decided their 4:15 plan was more important than classes. He had a 3.7 GPA so he had some wiggle room with his grades anyway.

Angela arrived right on time, which allowed Corey to breathe a huge sigh of relief. The idea that she wasn't taking this as seriously as he was had crossed his mind. He did register that her arrival did not signify a parallel set of feelings, yet her prompt arrival canceled out the worst of the possibilities.

"Hey, thanks for meeting me" Corey said in his authentic, personable manner.

"No problem. I had nothing else going on."

Corey intentionally did not let this slight register in his brain. The relationship was too new for him to let this bother him. He also did not register the fact that if she had a different response, something like, "wouldn't have missed it for the world!" he would have felt very different, very affirmed.

"Would you like a soda or a milkshake, anything?" he asked socially.

"Ummm, I'll have a cola, but only if they have diet Pepsi"

"I think they do" he said before going back to the zig-zag lineup of counters, all with stainless steel railings in front, comprising a counter one could slide their cafeteria tray across. He didn't have a tray but he was still willing to troll the area for diet Pepsi. And troll he did.

"So, what's your major" he asked as he joined Angela back at the table carrying a large diet Pepsi and a bottle of water.

"I'm in liberal arts for now." She took the Pepsi from Corey and continued, "I don't really know what I want to do with my degree yet so I'm kinda looking around for something that I would like to do."

"I understand that, do you like any of your classes more than the others?"

Angela's response was brief, "No." She shook her head back and forth a little with this answer.

Corey tipped his water bottle toward Angela's Pepsi as if to clink for a toast. "Here's to figuring out what we'd like to do with our lives" he said through a smile.

Angela fulfilled the toast by tapping her lidded, waxed paper cup against his bottle. She smiled thinking, *he's not like the boys from high school but I kind of like him... And Jennifer thinks he's really cute...*

Corey felt like he had run the small talk into its conclusion, "So, on our earlier topic, I'd really like to understand where the line in the sand is between taking care of the less fortunate and, helping people that shouldn't be helped." He cleared his throat, "not to say, or even imply, that I know the answer, I'm just trying to create a starting point for our discussion and I'm umm… well actually, I'm describing a place where I genuinely have a question."

She twirled the ponytail as she considered her answer. She wasn't used to this level of authenticity so she didn't realize he was being genuine.

"Uh… well I'm just kinda tired of people who need things, already have problems going on, like babies and stuff, and, chances are, they have a pretty good cell phone or an expensive tattoo." She continued, "I mean, if somebody gets themselves pregnant, shouldn't *they* find the way to take care of that child?"

"Hmm, well what if the woman in your scenario found herself pregnant, started a new life for herself and that child and the only way her parents had to help her was to provide her with a cell phone so that she'd always be equipped to call for help if there was an emergency?"

With a turn of her head, which caused a very distracting flip of her ponytail, Angela said, "Well if that ever did actually happen, then that would be okay."

"But she'd have to explain to you how she managed to get that phone for you to accept that she was deserving of help?" Corey was trying to get his brain around this while trying not to sound like one-half of a debate.

Then the dimples showed up. "Wow, you are really dialed into to the plight of the needy, huh? I'm really impressed." Angela continued, "I haven't had a reason to think about stuff like this yet in my life but I'm sure I will someday." She took a big drag off the straw in her diet Pepsi.

"So, can you just take a minute and say something about where in your mind, that line is, that one between where we as a government help, and where we don't help."

"I have to admit" Angela said, "I'm not prepared to discuss this with someone so well informed." She continued,"I have to admit I'm a little intimidated by you right now."

Corey thought, *Intimidated? No one has ever been intimidated by me before - to my knowledge - ever. He really didn't want to be the intimidating sort.*

"Wow, well I really didn't mean to be intimidating." He decided to stick his neck out, "how about if we move to a more comfortable location?"

"What do you mean?" Angela asked.

"Well... within the man-code book, I have been studying the chapter called Just-in-Case so I purchased some vodka. And tonic. And well … limes…." He was happy to have woven in some humor while in the act of exposing his motives. "They are in my room."

To Corey's surprise, Angela responded, "okay, let's head over. What dorm are you?" Angela had a lot of experience with guys trying to get her alone and she was not worried. She had always been able to hold her own. Her mother had instilled values of chastity deeply into her and she lived comfortably with the idea that her body was her own and sex with boys would work to produce children when the time was right. In Angela's mind this also meant that even if she toyed with boys, allowing them to feel like sex was going to happen, she had no responsibility for their disappointment, disillusionment or frustration. Their misunderstanding was always their fault and she had no problem with walking away from it.

At Angela's agreement to change locations, Corey had a thought which he had no control over, which was, *wow had I known it was this easy, I might have had a more colorful history.* His actual words were, "Um Parsons, I'm second floor of Parsons." In his new brazened condition he went on, "Are you ready now?"

"Yep, let's go. I can bring this." she gestured toward her diet Pepsi.

It was a brief walk to Parsons and before he knew it, he was working on finding conversation that would occupy them as they used the stairs to get to the second floor. This was harder than usual because he was also busy hoping his roommate of 2 years wasn't home. Corey didn't have enough self-confidence earlier in the day to ask Troy to stay away for the evening, therefore there was a reasonable chance Troy would be there. If he wasn't there at the time of their arrival, no problem, Corey would simply leave a sock over the outside door handle, the way Troy did when he didn't want Corey to come in. In Corey's mind, it was about time he got to be the one to claim that space as his own for a few hours.

Troy wasn't in the room.

"Madame, please allow me…" Corey said with flourish as he waved Angela over to the only chair in the room. "Please give me a minute as I prepare the beverage of your choice." Corey had just now realized he hadn't gotten anything for himself. He had never had a vodka and tonic, beer was his choice when imbibing with his friends. He decided this would be the evening he would figure out if he liked vodka or not. He prepared two vodka and tonics with lime.

"So, where were we…?" Corey cringed inwardly at his own cheesiness.

"Well I really only have my own upbringing to draw from" Angela said. "We are strict Catholics in my family so it's easy when the rules are outlined for you from the beginning."

"My family didn't follow any specific religion so maybe you can start by explaining how Catholicism has led you to your thoughts about people in need."

"Wow, there you go again, being so reasonable and curious and me feeling like I'm only drawing from family teachings, … never actually having to articulate the values behind it before."

"Let's work on that, want to?"

"Uh, sure."

It was the flat tone of Angela's last statement that brought Corey to his senses. *Dude, you've got a hot babe drinking vodka in your room. She's still wearing her shoes along with everything else. Wake up! Get her another drink then change the damn subject to her. Girls love to talk about themselves....*

"First let me get you another drink" Corey got up, he used that moment to think up questions he could ask her. "Where are you from?" he asked as he handed her the fresh drink.

Four vodka and tonics each later, Corey gasped, "are you sure you want this?"

"Please don't stop" her eyes were closed. She had never experienced the feelings that could follow one after the other, like a heavenly chain of events, when the chemistry was right. Angela was startled by the power of it; she was unaware that her body could feel so much pleasure. It started when Corey sat next to her after she had moved to sit on the bed so she could stretch her legs out. When he sat beside her, she became intensely aware of his body heat in a very pleasant way. When he let his hand rest at his side in a way that touched her arm, she felt the need to rub her arm against his. She had never felt a physical reaction like this, where magnets and electricity and a feeling in her belly seemed to be working together to encourage her to get even closer to Corey than they already were, as they sat side by side on a twin bed. Angela had never before felt a signal within her body that made her nipples cry out to be touched. When Corey complied with this unspoken request, the die was cast. There was no going back. Once she had her bra off it was only minutes before she felt she couldn't get her pants off fast enough. She repeated herself, "Please don't stop."

DAVE 1

In 2009 Dave started his own business. He was a contractor and his business serviced people who needed heating, cooling or carpentry work. He owned two trucks, one was a red Ford F-150 pickup and the other was a white Ford E-150 van. A navy blue logo was on the side of each one; the logo depicted the word "Dave's," the jaws of a crescent wrench looked like they were gripping the D, and a screwdriver comprised half of the V. His phone number, including area code, was beneath that. Dave was irked whenever he saw a service vehicle or sign without the area code included in the phone number. *Think of all the times you might just not know an area code, like if you're out of town,* he said to himself. *How about when you're in a region that straddles two area codes?* He continued to himself, *that is a small minded mistake, one which I will never make.* And so when he had his chance to prove that declaration, he did. Beneath Dave's phone number - including area code - were the words, "Heating Cooling Carpentry." There was an image of the head of a Phillips' head screw between each word, serving as punctuation.

The two vehicles served different purposes to Dave so that's why he didn't sell one when he laid off his singular employee. The trucks were equipped with walkie-talkies so Dave could talk to his employee without running up the cell phone minutes. Now those hand-held mics just reminded him of his business woes. Sometimes to cheer himself up, he'd pull one out of its resting place and talk into it, "Hello Dave... come in Dave... this is Dave calling you" This would make him smile inwardly, sometimes he would continue, "Listen buddy, I'm really busy right now but I'll chat with you if you're lonely." There were also times when he would look at a mic and just turn his head in the other direction, as if it were an object capable of mocking him.

Dave's office was located in the basement of his home. It was a walk-out basement so the business had its own entrance, through which his former employee would enter each morning.

Dave held out hope that this would be true again in the future. The office space had one large room and a bathroom - technically a half-bath. The large room had two desks, a large table, and a few filing cabinets. The table was covered with a variety of things: parts that had been pulled from equipment that might be useful on some other job, tools and pieces of tools, and all kinds of papers from invoices to blue prints. This clutter has started to spill onto the now unoccupied desk.

Each day, when Dave would go down the basement steps, he would be careful to close the door at the top of the steps. He would do that for two reasons. First, he wanted an audible warning if someone were coming down the steps, like his wife Lisa or his son Trevor. The second and more likely-to-really-happen reason was that he didn't want his side of a phone conversation to be overheard when it was the bank calling about the truck payments or the suppliers who would also be looking for payments. Dave had gotten pretty adept at spreading out his debt. Like Michael Jackson getting a prescription filled, he would pick up supplies at which ever vendor had the longest time span since his last visit.

By 2010, he had remortgaged his house to raise enough money to keep his business afloat. He was able to do this without Lisa's knowledge because her name wasn't on the mortgage. At the time they had decided to buy this house, she was out of town on business; she traveled a lot for her former employer and they were in a competitive real estate situation. Dave had to apply for the loan while she was gone and it just didn't seem worth getting her added once she got back. At that time, Dave had a good job as a building inspector working for a company he had been with since his college graduation. His credit rating was enough to qualify them for the mortgage.

Lisa was a great wife to Dave. She had a pleasant disposition, she was cute, and she was a great mother to Trevor. She volunteered at his school on the days that she didn't work at her part time job, and she didn't demand any particular amount of parenting from Dave. She seemed to naturally expand and decrease her parenting job as Dave's availability fluctuated. Even though she helped Dave with some of his payables and receivables for the business, she didn't try to get into his business any deeper than the very specific accounts he let her be exposed to. A nosier, more pushy wife would have been a clear problem for Dave at this point in his career.

Trevor was the love of Dave's life. He was eight in 2010 and Dave was certain that eight was the most enjoyable age a son could be. Dave loved the fact that Trevor looked at him like he was super hero, plus, Trevor loved the sports Dave loved. They would watch the Pirates play ball and both would be wrapped up in the game on the screen, but Trevor had enough attention span left over to listen to his dad's running commentary on the game. Dave once looked over and found Trevor practicing the words Dave had just yelled at the screen. His mouth moving and his very quiet voice saying "that guy was so safe, his foot was under home plate!" and Trevor emphasized the word 'under' just as Dave had. Trevor was an average student although he was very intelligent. His teachers seemed to agree that he spent too much time daydreaming and fidgeting, doodling and staring out the window. When asked about this in first grade, Trevor said that he just couldn't wait to get home and play with Dad. Now that he was in third grade, he said "It's way more interesting to do stuff with Dad so that's all I really think about."

Dave was very honored by the love that Trevor returned to him but he knew his parental duty also included helping his son to get a good education. Dave and Lisa decided that Trevor would be rewarded for good reports from the teacher with special one-on-one outings with his Dad. Further, father son activities would be limited - but not by much - for bad reports. Neither Dave nor Lisa thought that depriving their son of parental attention could really be a good idea under any circumstance, so the things they told Trevor they were limiting, were really things that were in question anyway: watching a late movie Friday night, trips for ice cream on Saturday, and things of that sort.

By 2012 Dave didn't know how he would be able to continue

his business; he had gone through all of the money from remortgaging his house. Through his business he made just enough money to pay his family's personal bills and buy groceries. He was working so hard though, that he felt like he should have a lot more money, or luxuries, or something that would make it seem like the effort was worth it. He didn't have any more equity in his home so another mortgage was out of the question. The bank had already turned him down for a loan when they looked into his business and his accounting books. He didn't feel like closing the business was an option; it was too big a part of his life, and he didn't want to appear to be a failure to his wife and son. He felt like if he could just finance an expansion of his existing business, he could be successful.

He didn't currently have the tools to work on commercial refrigeration equipment and there was a lot of this type of business in the area that he had to turn away. Their house was on the outskirts of an area that was growing rapidly so places like Chili's, Friendly's, Outback Steak House, and Applebees were seemingly everywhere. He often had messages on his phone from late at night when an assistant manager who wanted to close for the night would suddenly realize that their walk-in freezer had a big puddle in the middle of its floor and the packages of meats and ice creams were covered with condensation. These businesses had thousands of dollars invested in the contents of their freezers so a contractor's help would be worth top dollar to them. It was always a disappointment to Dave when he'd call them back the next morning and explain that they didn't do that type of cooling. He would much prefer to be using an answering service that would call his cell phone when this type of call came in. He would gladly get out of bed and get on a customer's site, charging three times his daytime rate to fix something.

Dave had done some web surfing to calculate that about $5,000 would buy him the things he needed to add commercial refrigeration to his repertoire. That investment would cover the license he'd need to handle Freon, the gas that was contained in the internal brass piping that kept things cold. It also included the gauges, system analyzers and vacuum pumps he'd need to make routine service calls. If he needed something beyond fundamental refrigeration tools, he could buy them when he needed them. With any luck, he could buy them with his customer's money, the down payment on his services. To Dave right now though, $5,000 was as accessible as $5 million dollars.

The investment of $5,000 could earn Dave over $100,000 more in gross profit per year, maybe even more than that. That increase translated to enough net income that he would finally have a little extra. He could start putting some away for retirement and college for his son. The question of how he would acquire this needed financing became material for his daydreams and night dreams, the latter of which would frequently feel like nightmares. It wasn't only a question of how to earn more, it was also a question of whether or not his business would survive.

A few months of torturing himself over this enigmatic question wreaked havoc on his nerves. He found himself drinking in a bar by 3:00 p.m. most days. While he knew that was not good for his family life or for helping his situation, he justified the behavior with his assumption that it was just temporary. *Just a little stress relief; once things are moving ahead, I won't need this afternoon break anymore*, is what he said to himself over his internal walkie-talkie. *Right Dave? 10-4 Dave. Over and out.*

One afternoon, minutes after he had ordered his first double bourbon of the day, his brother Jay strolled in and slapped him on the back jovially. "What are you doing in here in the middle of the day?" Jay asked. Dave responded, "I guess I'll ask you the same question." Dave smiled through these words to postpone the minute when he'd need to give a real answer.

Dave was sitting on a barstool with a cracked vinyl seat cover; one of the chair's legs was just a little shorter than the others. He was at the VVI, as the locals called it. Those who read from the sign called it the Victory Village Inn. The VVI had a long bar and if asked, the owner, a Viet Nam vet who reliably wore a POW MIA hat, would have estimated that 95% of the drinks enjoyed in his establishment were consumed at the bar. It was a deep, narrow building, so this fact fit well with its architecture. He rarely had to clean off any of the four tables. The regulars there had expectations about where they'd be able to sit when they came in. Dave favored the area past the half-way point but not all the way toward the kitchen entrance. This gave him a chance to recognize people as they entered. Anyone sitting at the first quarter of the bar in the afternoon couldn't see a face on a sunny day until the person was right up to them because of the light coming in the front of the bar. Dave's 'region' gave him a few seconds advantage over someone coming in. Because of the bright lights in the kitchen behind him, he could see a newcomer's face before they could see him. On dark days, the advantage offered by his seat disappeared, but his inclination to sit in his spot did not. On this day, Dave was so intent on staring into his drink, as if the answer to his questions were in the bottom of that glass, that he didn't take advantage of the seat he had claimed. He didn't look up when the door rattled open so Jay had surprised him.

The brothers hadn't spent much time together since their father's funeral four months earlier. Their father's death wasn't a surprise but it was still life-changing for them both. Their mother had passed away 10 years earlier so now they had no parents and that was hard to get used to.

Neither of the parents' passing was startling or dramatic. When their mother passed, she had been in a nursing home for a year, suffering from a painful tumor on her spine. Her pain was never completely alleviated by medications and that was hard for her three men to witness. The Shipway men were not good with things they couldn't fix. When she passed, the family felt a great loss, but they were relieved that she wasn't in pain any longer. Ten years later - four month ago - their father died of multiple system failures; those were the words of the coroner. This soft spoken man went on to explain that old age wasn't an accepted cause of death so they had to use other words which meant the same thing. Dave and Jay's father had died in his sleep at age 85 because his heart and several other organs had just stopped.

Dave took care of the business end of arranging the funeral and later, he administered the will while Jay wrote the obituary and picked the readings and the hymns. The night before their father's funeral, after the calling hours had concluded and all the mourners had been seen to their cars and the thank you's had been said to the staff of the funeral parlor, Jay and Dave went to the tavern down the street and they each ordered a beer. Their thirst was huge. They each took a few swallows before either spoke. It was Dave who broke the silence, "It's weird, it's like I have a vacuum inside me, I can't really describe it."

"I know," said Jay. "This sucks, at least we'll never bury a parent again... I think how busy we are pulling all of this together is keeping us from losing it..."

"What did you do earlier, watch fucking Doctor Phil or something?" Dave said then fake punched Jay in the arm.

"You're an asshole, you know what I'm trying to say." Jay turned away from Dave slightly.

Dave paused a few seconds, thinking deeply and drinking deeply from his frosted glass, "yeah, I do, I am just picking on you right now because I don't have a better explanation."

"Listen to you" Jay replied, "Now you sound like you've been watching Ellen."

The laughter burst from both of them as if it were an overdue belch. It was a much needed moment of normalcy. The interchange had brought them both closer to feeling like they were in control of their situation but there was still room for improvement. Dave made a mental note of gratitude for not having to go through this alone. He was really glad he had Jay to work through this life changing event with.

Four months later, Jay was pulling out a barstool and sitting down next to Dave. "I saw your truck out front so I decided to stop in. It's good to see you, bro."

Dave said, "yeah, you too. I just decided to break from my

routine of work, work, work, and relax in a quiet place for a few minutes."

Just then the bartender approached with Dave's drink. He set it in front of Dave and turned to Jay, "what can I get you? Dave's regular drink is on special, any interest?"

"Uh… just exactly what is Dave's regular drink?" Jay replied with the tone of a man with many questions.

Dave felt like he was busted but before he could say anything, the bartender responded, "double bourbon" spoken as if Jay should have known the answer.

"Um, no thank you. I'll have a Bud Lite, thanks." Jay said and turned to Dave as the bartender went to fetch the beer. "Brother, I didn't know you had a regular drink. Should I be concerned? I mean, apparently, this is a regular stop for you."

Jay was a big man who almost always had a five o'clock shadow so on first meeting, many took him to be a tough guy. The reality was just the opposite. He was often nervous and always thoughtful. Things affected him deeply. He was Dave's younger brother; in fact, he used to be his baby brother since there were four years between them. Dave was thinking of these traits as he decided on his response.

"Well, I guess I'll be completely honest with you" Dave started, "I am working through a big problem and I don't know what the hell I should do."

"I want to hear all about it, but first, is there a solution in here?" Jay said, gesturing around the bar room.

"Probably not" Dave sighed with resignation. "But at least in here my nerves aren't jangling as much." Dave raised his pitch a bit to create a faux-defensive tone, "Don't get your panties in a bunch, I'll be home for dinner"

Jay laughed, "So tell me, what has your nerves jangling?"

Dave took about five minutes to give Jay the overview. About halfway through he was really glad he was telling Jay about his predicament because Jay might have a suggestion for him. Dave didn't have any hope that Jay might have money to loan him. Jay had worked for the town driving trucks for the past five years and he made just enough for his own small family to live on when his wife's paycheck from JC Penney was added in. But Jay was worldly-wise and might just think of something that hadn't occurred to Dave.

Dave began his explanation, starting with when he left his former job as an inspector, including the facts of the second mortgage and the math behind his idea of adding commercial refrigeration to his business services. When Dave finished his summary of the situation, Jay said, "Wow man. I'm so sorry to hear all this." Then out of kindness, Jay continued with a joke to lighten the moment, "Could it be time to find a real job?"

"I'm sure I should consider that idea; I just really don't want to. My company is like a second child to me. By the way, Lisa doesn't know all this, okay?"

"I understand man, but how long can you keep the truth from her?"

"I'm playing that one by ear" Dave replied.

"I wish I had something helpful to offer you" Jay said, "but I can only think that I wish you could have a do-over with the bank, and this time you'd go to the trouble of getting all your assets counted and you'd offload as much company debt as possible, to you as an individual, or something like that. It does seem like your idea for expansion would work if only you could find that five grand."

"Yeah, but realistically, I'm not sure I would still pass the bank's inspection, even after the makeover you're talking about"

Jay had finished his beer at this point. "Hey, I'm gunna take off but let's keep talking about this some other day. Want to walk out with me?"

Dave wanted to say, "Hell no, I'm not drunk yet." but instead he said, "Yeah, ok." Dave put two one-dollar bills on the bar and walked out with Jay.

Dave had a tough time getting a good night's sleep that night. All the facts of his situation kept rolling around in his head, intertwined with his conversation with Jay. Somehow, telling Jay his story made it all even more real. And as something real, it was officially something he had to do something about. Dave felt he had graduated to a new level of trouble.

EARL 1

Earl hurriedly cleared the table used by his two buddies from the American Legion. The spaghetti dinner had been a success, raising over $250 for their post, and Earl loved it when he could combine business with pleasure, chatting it up with his buddies while accepting their $7 each for a plate of food. He would catch up with them at the bar later where they will re-live some of their airborne days while enjoying $1.25 drafts.

Earl had lost his wife three years ago. They had enjoyed a good marriage most of the time. There were some years when they were just simply tired of each other and that seemed to manifest in grumpy, short sentences from Earl to Hope. To Earl, Hope seemed terse, and it seemed she found too many reasons to go to the craft store in town and the fabric outlet in the next town over. Those years finally gave way and a new, slower type of comfort was harvested out of the tedium.

If a death can be good, Hope's was. There was little pain, no surprises, all her loved ones including their 3 children had a chance to say goodbye. It came six months after the discovery of an inoperable brain tumor. Once the children were back in their respective far-away homes and the casseroles stopped showing up in the hands of people wearing forced smiles, Earl became desolate. He frequently paced the floor wondering what to do next. The sadness and loneliness occupied so much space inside of him that he would sometimes go days without food because he didn't feel like there was room in his body for that. All the available space was already reserved for grief. Eventually grief gave way to a sadness and sadness eventually moved aside for a new kind of loneliness, that which one feels when one simply lacks companionship. That's when he started working at the Legion as a volunteer. Earl and Hope had been members for a number of years but working there was a whole new adventure.

Earl's experience started with being trained to use the cash register as well as learning how to properly wash dishes so as to be sanitary. At about the time he mastered the commercial size coffee pot, he took it upon himself to memorize the price list so that he could present an air of confidence to customers who were ordering food or drinks. Earl laughed at himself when he thought, "*I am the Legion*" special emphasis on the 'am,' and while this affirmation was only in his thoughts, the other volunteers, staff and patrons seemed to agree that he was a great asset to the organization.

Earl's coworkers were especially happy to have him on-board. Not only was he capable and gregarious, he worked for free; he was a volunteer. He did not compete with them for the scant resources of this organization. The bar manager, Julie, was always shorthanded since she had to have a paid staff person on premises all hours that the facility was open. She didn't have enough budget to pay anything more than minimum wage and she had to keep each employee's number of hours limited, so that there was no expectation of benefits. This made scheduling her paid employees quite a challenge. She needed to honor their personal scheduling needs while balancing that with the Legion's needs. She couldn't pay them enough to earn her the expectation that they would put their job first. Anyone of them could walk into a TGI Fridays and get a job in a flash, and for more money per hour and more hours per week.

Earl understood Julie's challenge and he tried to make work fun - or at least pleasant - for everyone in order to be part of the solution, versus adding to the problem. One Saturday afternoon, Earl came in to set up for a pig roast to find that one of his favorites was tending bar. Kate was a middle aged woman who worked every-other Sunday but was helping out by filling in on this Saturday. Earl and Kate got along well; Earl reminded Kate of her own dear father, who was 83 years old and living a few hours away, and while Kate wasn't like any of Earl's daughters, she would have fit in to his family nicely. Kate kept this job for a year or so in order to add spice to her life and cash to her wallet. Kate would bring home about $100 each time she worked a Sunday. Kate wasn't silly, like many of the younger bartenders, yet she was able to flirt with the best of them - always in the best interest of the cash register and her tip jar. Earl could tell she had genuine concern for any of the customers who were respectful which was most of them.

On this Saturday, one of the customers appeared to be intoxicated; it wasn't someone Earl recognized. This concerned Earl because it was 1:00 in the afternoon; the bar had only been open for two hours at this point. Earl lingered around the bar chatting up the customers and Kate while watching this guy for any clues that would ease his concern. There would be no easing of concern. As Earl was inspecting the kegs for any that were light and might need switching out soon, this customer raised his head, shook his dirty hair out of his eyes and said, "Barkeep, one more." His tone was gruff and this caused both Kate and Earl to look his way quickly. The Legion was a pleasant place, typically filled with people who liked each other; his tone alone made him stand out. Kate got him another shot of Evan Williams whiskey with a Coors chaser.

Earl went to the kitchen under the pretenses of checking spare beer kegs, once in there he called to Kate in a faked pleasant voice. Kate responded by pushing through the swinging door that led to the kitchen. "Is he a member?" Earl asked without having to specify who he was inquiring about.

"He has a card, it says he belongs to the Palmyron post." Kate said. Earl knew that Kate didn't usually ask for proof of membership and the fact that she had implied she had been suspicious of him when he came in.

"How long has he been here?"

"That is his second drink." Kate told him. "He's been here about a half hour."

"Does he seem more drunk than that to you?" Earl was trying to dig for more information but couldn't think of the questions he wanted to ask.

"Yes, he seemed off when he came in and, candidly, he is giving me the creeps." Kate admitted.

That was all Earl needed to hear. "Okay, I'll get my chores done, then come help you behind the bar - at least until he leaves."

"Earl, no. I don't want to be babied and I'm sure you have other things to do. Please don't worry. I promise I'll call 911 if he gives me any problem at all."

Earl tried to respect Kate's need to feel in charge but as he worked to get his tasks done, the feeling of unease did not dissipate. In the background he kept hearing that coarse voice say, "Barkeep!" followed by inaudible commands or commentary. This man had had Kate change the television channel several times and he bought pull-tab tickets at a fast pace, all while ordering a new drink at least three times during Earl's hour of work.

Earl decided he couldn't just leave but he was torn; he still wanted to respect Kate's ability to run the bar she was currently in charge of. He compromised with himself and took a seat on a barstool, as a customer, once he finished his preparations for the next day's fund raiser. He sat two chairs down from the source of his concern.

Kate walked to Earl's end of the bar and cocked her head and raising her eyebrows at him, "What can I get you Earl?" her tone making it clear that she knew what he was up to.

"I'll have an O'Douls." Earl was not opposed to drinking beer. In fact he loved having one, two, or even more with his buddies - a select group of veterans who had all served in the Korean war. He didn't however, want to start a Saturday afternoon by drinking, especially when his mission at hand was to look out for the well being of someone he cared about, so he ordered this non-alcoholic brew.

"Coming right up" Kate said, but close to Earl's ear, she said, "would you like it served in a bottle with a nipple?" Earl understood from this question that she was aware that he was going to nurse his beer for as long as it took to get this stranger out of the bar. It didn't take very long.

"Barkeep!" He was starting to get loud along with being harsh. Kate looked his way while finishing fulfilling the drink order she was working on. She nodded to him so that he would know he had been heard. A few minutes later, she walked over and asked if he wanted another of the same thing. He said, "You know, I don't mind waiting a reasonable amount of time, you got a nice ass and looking at it keeps me entertained."

Earl snapped to attention, turning his head to the man who was about six feet away from him. The stranger didn't notice Earl's renewed consideration.

"My glass has been empty for a long time now," the stranger continued.

"I apologize, it's busy in here." She gestured at the full bar stools. "I'm not just twiddling my thumbs back here." Kate was starting to take on a defensive tone, doing her best to seem tough. She was starting to feel intimidated though and she wasn't good at acting.

"If you showed off more skin, I might feel more patient."
Kate took in a quick breath at the audacity of this man.

"Leave." Kate stared straight into the man's eyes.

"What?" He responded as if he had never before been
denied anything.

"Leave now or I'm calling the cops on you." Kate
maintained her self-control and her control over the bar but
Earl moved closer to ensure no harm came to his friend.

Earl signaled to Big Mike, a regular who was sitting on the
other side of him. Big Mike was just waiting for his
chance to help so he immediately stood up and moved
toward the door. "Is this yours?" Earl held up a wad of
bills that had been on the bar in front of their unwanted
visitor.

"Damn right!" Aggression, anger, righteousness were
present in equal measures in the strangers voice.

"You gunna tip your barkeep?" Earl asked.

"Yes."

"Good answer." Earl said as he peeled off a $20 bill and
gave it to Kate.

"You have one minute to get out of my bar." Kate, leaning
toward the man, enunciated each word separately.

Mike held the door open as the man turned and headed in
that direction. He was indignant, "this is bullsh-"

Earl walked behind him to the entry door. As he crossed
the threshold, Earl said, "Listen friend, we have nothing
against you but this isn't the type of place you'll fit into.
Please just go on your way. If you come back through this

door, Kate will be calling the cops - believe me, she doesn't make idle threats. And, at least five of us," Earl pointed to the full bar, "will hold you in place until they arrive."

Big Mike gave him the final shove it took to get the stranger out the door. As he turned back toward the bar Kate said, "Mike turn the lock on that door. Let's just make sure he stays gone."

Mike locked up the front door in time to hear Kate ease the tension that remained in the barroom, "A round for everyone on me." The bar gave up a cheer for Kate. "There's just one catch, we're all locked in for a few minutes." Kate didn't want to take a chance that the stranger would ambush anyone leaving but she also knew that they guy didn't have much of an attention span, in his inebriation. It wouldn't take long for everyone to be safe.

Earl's renewed sense of being comfortable with his life was due in part to his success at the Legion but it was also due to his children and grandchildren. One day when he was walking through his usual grocery store he spotted a bin of stuffed animals at the end of one of the aisles. He picked one up and was struck by the feeling that his third granddaughter, Lauren, would love it. He bought it along with his can of 8 O'Clock coffee, loaf of bread, and a package of sweet rolls, then promptly went to the post office and, with a little help from a nice lady wearing a name tag that said Sally, mailed it off to the appropriate household. This was a single-child household so there were no concerns over giving something to just one child. The resulting feeling of having gifted that gift was such a good feeling that he developed a habit of watching for trinkets for his grandchildren He would do his best to send something to one, then another, then another so that they all eventually received something before gifting again to the first child in the cycle.

Earl remembered the importance of fairness in the mind of child. Fairness was given much more importance than was due, in this world where it has nothing to do with who would live and who would die. When he was raising his own three, he always did his best to see that each child had the same number of gifts under the Christmas tree. He and Hope even went so far as to see that the girls all had a fairly equal number of handmade decorations on the tree. As their oldest, Charity, moved into middle school, her handmade contributions diminished making this exercise in fairness less and less important each year.

The girls were spaced in age, as if by magic, by two years each. The so-called magic was really just luck since Earl and Hope's love-making had been a very successful piece of their married life for the first 10 years or so. They didn't practice any birth control until after Felicity was born. They would have loved to have had a son too but the idea of adding to the massive responsibility of caring for three kids seemed to outweigh the value of that one possible enhancement to their happy family life.   So in 1978, Hope went on the pill. In 1983 they had their last first day of kindergarten and in 1987, when Charity was 14, Dawn was 12 and Felicity was 10, they stopped trying to plan the ornaments around fairness. Earl was okay with these benchmarks, and the many, many others, yet he was wistful about them because they marked the passage of time as effectively as any calendar.

Earl's favorite memories were of the summer vacation trips they would take as a family. They didn't have any extra money - although the girls were never aware of a lack of anything - so they bought a pop-up camper and made their way to State Parks, National Museums, National Parks, camping parks and distant relatives' back yards. It was usually Hope who discovered their next adventure; finding a camping park near a historic site was first on her list of possible trips: Williamsburg, VA; Gettysburg, PA; and Niagara Falls, NY were all winners in this category.

To the girls, these trips meant they got to wear sandals and cute shorts outfits, they got to eat a lot more sweets than usual, and they got to stay up late. The very best part of each day, no matter how fun their adventure had been, was the camp fire at night. But first, the dinner dishes had to be washed; they used a Rubber-Maid dishpan set on their picnic table. Each child had a specific piece of the chore: wash/rinse, dry or put away. They would rotate turns at each job; the girl who had to wash and rinse was considered that day's low-man-on-the-totem-pole within their secret hierarchy.

Earl would be responsible for getting the fire built. Sometimes, before sunset, he'd have the girls scatter into the woods to gather sticks, and if lucky, logs. Earl always managed to make each daughter feel like her contribution was very important to their fire.

Hope was their music director. As they were growing up, she made sure the girls knew camp-fire-style songs, and she managed to find and pay for guitar lessons for Dawn, their middle child. The other two took piano lessons but even a station wagon couldn't transport a piano to a camping trip, while a guitar fit nicely between the suitcases in the back.

Once the sun was set, the five of them would sing 'This Land is Your Land', 'She'll Be Comin' Round the Mountain', 'On Top of Spaghetti', all while Dawn did her best to strum along, glancing at her song book to see what chord was next. The very last song was always Taps: *Day is done, gone the sun; from the sea, from the hills, from the sky ; All is well, safely rest, God is nigh.* One summer Felicity asked, "what is nigh?" Hope explained that was a way to say near while rhyming with sky.

Earl and Hope both loved their family life and these adventures. Earl loved "his girls" - of which there were four - so much that he couldn't imagine being happier. He would have slayed dragons or shot heart-breakers if it had come to that. Hope's opinion of their life, if asked, would have been centered around satisfaction and achievement. She would have mentioned the girls' good grades as a way to explain why she felt she had some achievements. Mentally, she would have been ticking off all of the relevant historical sites her girls had first-hand knowledge of, unlike most of their classmates. This is how achievement went hand in hand with satisfaction for Hope.

Hope had a special way of turning American history into a fascinating group of stories. The girls were made to feel like they were involved in a story, versus learning about history, thanks to Hope's gift of presentation. When visiting Abe Lincoln's childhood home in Indiana one summer, Hope suggested that each of the girls take on a role of one of the people they were going to learn about that day. Dawn practically spewed, "I call I get to be Abe!" The sanctity of the girls' system of 'calling things' by means of saying, "I call" followed by whatever the dictate was on that day, left the other two sisters no choice but to find other appealing characters to emulate on this day-trip. Felicity picked Abe's mother, and Charity, stuck with picking last, picked Abe's father.

As they toured the small cabin and surrounding grounds, the girls did their best to stay in character as Hope gently guided them. When Dawn said she had to go to the bathroom, Hope asked her, "Do you need to find an outhouse?" Dawn giggled, nodding. When Charity was pretending she had to leave to go to work, Dawn asked, "Do you need to hitch the horse to the plow or did you do that already?" The girls loved living out the stories Hope introduced them to and Hope felt it opened the door to learning just a little wider. Earl followed a few paces behind his four girls on trips like this. Watching and listening to what to him, was a miracle of education; he thought it would not be possible to be happier. He was filled with love for his girls and a special amount of admiration for his wife.

As each daughter matured and made the move that would put them outside of Earl's perfect world, Earl's quality of life slid down by a notch. The notches weren't in an accurate ratio to his quality of life, but nonetheless, it was a downward sliding scale. Maybe each maturing young woman represented a decline of about 10 percent. Earl would have balked at quantifying his girls like that, but the decline was inarguable.

When the last girl had graduated from college, Hope started to seem a little bit lost to Earl; she had become terse, and more interested in her projects than anything else. This change made Earl's total loss right around 40% which was a big deal. It may have been easier if Earl had seen that this change in his life was a direct result of his family growing up and becoming responsible, happy adults, which is what he had been working toward. If he had seen that he was actually living through a trade-off, trading his loss of "his girls" with his success at parenting, it may have been more palatable. But Earl was not one to introspect, so this factoid never really showed itself to him until much later.

It was something Hope said at the birth of their first grandchild that enabled Earl to see his perceived losses as a trade-off, and eventual prelude to gains.

"This perfect example of humanity is such an achievement for you two," Hope said to Charity and her husband Joey as she lifted her first grandchild from the nursery's bassinet. "And I 'm so proud to have raised you to be the mother of this perfect child, because I know you are going to be a great mother." Earl felt this sounded a bit self-aggrandizing so he stayed quiet, sitting in a plastic upholstered chair in the far corner of the hospital maternity ward room. Just then Hope seemed to realize the selfish orientation of her words. Everyone was exhausted since

Charity had been actively laboring since 4:00 p.m. the prior day. The baby didn't take her first breath until 11:00 a.m. on the same day that this statement was made, and it was currently 2:00 p.m. It's possible that no one but Earl noticed the inward-looking statement Hope had made but Earl's silence alerted her to the need for a rewind/replay of the imaginary tape of this conversation.

Hope decided in that instant that more needed to be said but that her best hope at times like this - exhaustion plus importance - was to strip down her thoughts to the bare truth and reproduce them with no embellishments. This followed by hoping for the best, had worked for her in the past. "I, errr, we are so happy for you two. You deserve so many congratulations and so much kudos. Please forgive me if I want to insert myself into the very most fundamental aspects of this achievement. The achievement is all yours and please don't blame us, errr..., me for envisioning my minor role in this miracle."

Earl nodded to her silently. Hope had managed to explain her prior overstatement honestly while still giving the kids the honor they were due. No one could pull this off as genuinely as Hope, in Earl's opinion.

Just then, he felt he might get to count Hope's 10% back - give or take a point or two - cutting his losses to only 30%.... *Wait,* he said to himself, *you haven't lost Hope! Nor anyone for that matter...* He felt his love and gratitude for Hope at that moment for the first time in a few years.

"Oh Mom, Joey and I are so glad to share this achievement with you and Dad." Charity was exhausted but she continued, "I don't think I would have any confidence in my ability to care for this new person if it hadn't been for the solid parenting you and Dad gave us." Tears formed in her eyes, there was no shame when they slid down her cheeks.

To Earl's way of thinking, Charity had just made the perfect sentence; perfect in response to Hope's restatement and perfect in response to her first statement. His heart was about to burst. He knew he had been honored here tonight too, and he was beginning to see that his losses were also his gains.

2013
ELAINE 1

Elaine Moreland had been a single parent for four years before she could afford to buy her own house. Her sense of achievement soared on the day she signed all the papers at the bank - she felt like she had finally graduated from the school of getting-past-a-bad-relationship. In fact she felt like she had her master's degree from that school and the diploma was in her hand. But the diploma was in the form of keys; three keys connected by a key ring from a Dodge dealership. All three were shiny, at least for now. She picked her kids up at school at dismissal that day and the three of them drove directly to the new house where they ate McDonald's while sitting cross-legged on the bare floor. Sounds echoed around the rooms since there was no furniture or wall decor to absorb the noises. Her oldest, Eric, ran from room to room flipping all the switches, opening and closing closets, and running the faucets as his way of declaring ownership. Danielle, 18 months younger, sat with Elaine and played with the toy that came with her meal, watching Eric and smiling; at age seven, her future beauty was becoming her most obvious quality.

Their new house was a split level but that wasn't obvious from the street. Her house looked a little more cottage-y than the box-shaped typical split levels. The main entrance of Elaine's house opened into the living room so no stairs were needed to get to the kitchen or living room. Off to the side of the living room was the inevitable staircase going down to a den next to the one that went up to the bedrooms. The other split levels Elaine had looked at with her agent Kate, had the choice of staircases immediately inside the front door and one had to go either up or down to get anywhere worthwhile in the house. Kate understood and worked with Elaine on the fact that she just didn't want to walk in to her new house and face steps, yet the neighborhood that fit her budget and was family friendly was predominantly split levels.

previous owners had recently put some money into the ?land family's new house so the kitchen had a new ᴵᵒᵒr made of ceramic tiles in a slightly peachy shade, the den had new carpeting, and most light fixtures were new.

The house also had a full basement - Elaine's first in quite some time. The basement had a washer and dryer, a tool bench and lots of built in shelves. Next to the dryer was a long narrow shelf for folding and stacking laundry. Sometimes, Elaine felt this simple structure was her favorite aspect of the house. No longer would their laundry have to be carried in from the car, still warm from the laundromat, everything they had recently worn piled into massive shopping bags and plastic baskets. Then their clothing had to be sorted on the couch and, if anyone wanted to use the couch, laundry had to be put away immediately; their apartment was just too small. In the new house, laundry could sit on the folding table until its owner wanted it bad enough to retrieve it for themselves.

Eric looked out the window of the room that would be his bedroom, as soon as it had a bed in it. As he peered out over their rural neighborhood, he noticed a man who seemed to be in their new yard, although Eric wasn't yet certain where the boundaries were so he didn't watch the man for long, just long enough to see him turn and head in the direction away from their new domain. The feeling of distrust he felt for the man was easily forgotten due to his new distractions in the house.

All their belongings would be delivered the next day and they could begin the process of settling in. The rest of the day, following their impromptu picnic, was committed to getting the last of their things packed back at the second-floor apartment that had been their home for the last few years. That night, Elaine had each child set aside pajamas for bedtime and clothes for the next day. Moving day was on Saturday and this weekend was not going to be long enough for all the work that lay ahead of them. She had decided to be satisfied with her progress if, by Sunday at noon, furniture was in place, beds were assembled and had sheets and blankets, dishes were in the cupboard, groceries were in the refrigerator and school clothes were identified and laid out for Monday. The rest could be completed little by little.

Elaine was 35 years old. She had auburn colored hair that she wore shoulder-length and styled attractively. She suspected that she was attractive to men since she almost always noticed double-takes in the grocery store or when picking up things at Home Depot. She couldn't assume any attractiveness though, since her former husband put so much work into destroying her ego. Elaine did try to take care of herself, doing her make-up and hair every day that she had to work, and wearing baseball hats and lip gloss on the weekends. She was in good physical condition although she has a pair of jeans from her college years that she would like to be able to wear but dropping 5 pounds needed to happen first. *Someday*, she thought. She spent very little money on clothes - she was a single mother after all - but she only bought items that were high quality and she aimed for classic versus 'in style.'

~~~~~~~~~~~~~~~~~~~~~~~~~~~~~~~~

1993

There was a time when clothes, hair and makeup were the only things important to Elaine. She was very typical at age sixteen. As a teenager, she was beautiful and she knew it. Her looks were important enough to her that she put a lot of time - and a lot of her parents' money - into making sure her hair was perfect and her clothing was of the latest style. She wanted everything she owned to be from whatever the trendiest line was at any particular time. She had a toned body that somehow was slim while being curvey and she flaunted all of her assets. All the straight young men knew who she was and worked to catch her eye.

Elaine was not shy at sixteen, in fact she was a little full of herself until one day during her junior year. It was an overcast day in November, windy and cold as expected in Pennsylvania for this time of year. There were very few leaves left on the trees and the threat of snow was in the air; it got dark by 5:00 p.m. She had missed the bus and didn't want to wait the hour it would take for her mother to get out of work and then come to pick her up so she started walking. The wind was blowing right up her coat sleeves and up her back. She couldn't zip her coat up high enough to feel warm; even pulling on the hood didn't help. She was taking the route that was the quickest way to her house even though it included a few blocks that always seemed unkempt; it wasn't unusual to see broken down cars up on blocks and window screens were often torn. She was half-way down one of these blocks when a car came up behind her, slowed down and came to a stop beside her. The passenger window rolled down and a male voice said, "Want a ride?"

Elaine had been raised to be polite and likable whenever possible, but she also got lessons in stranger-danger and at this moment, these two trains of thought were conflicted. She reasoned, she was not yet close to home, and she was freezing. "Who are you?" she leaned toward the window to ask.

"I'm Thomas, I've seen you in school." He reached for the door handle and pushed the door open from inside. By now, Elaine was really cold from standing still for a few minutes, and she didn't see anything strange about Thomas or his car, so she got in and pulled the door closed.

"Thanks for the offer." Elaine's teeth were chattering, "I live over on Elmwood. You can just take a right up there." she gestured at the stop sign ahead.

"Uh-huh." Thomas said as he stopped at the stop sign then turned left.

~~~~~~`

The weekend of Elaine's move into her new house ended too soon. When Elaine's alarm clock went off on Monday morning, she stirred and stretched and a groan escaped her mouth before she could stifle it. She had selected this clock two years ago because of its available setting which enabled a clamoring noise of two incompatible tones, truly obnoxious, she had labeled it at the time. This morning, such a rude wake-up call was not needed. Elaine knew she was in her new house before she was even fully awake and this made waking up very easy.

Every muscled seemed to be sore. Moving weekend was physically grueling but her enthusiasm was still quite intact. She located some Advil in her purse and swallowed two before waking up the children and starting their carefully choreographed routine for getting ready for school. The kids needed to be at their new bus stop by 7:30. Luckily, the true test of their new routine wouldn't come until Tuesday, when Elaine had to return to her job. On the days she worked, she was expected to arrive by 8:00 a.m. when her first patient was expected. The dentist she worked for was flexible with family situations, but only as long as patients didn't have to wait or be otherwise troubled in any way.

As she pulled her five-year old Honda back into her driveway, after dropping the kids off at the bus stop, she noticed the flag was up on her mailbox. *Curious,* she thought, *I didn't put it up and I'm quite certain it had been down all weekend.* She opened her mailbox to take a look and found it to be empty. It reminded her of her living room just three days ago when Eric was making funny sounds to achieve the cold echo, known only to empty structures. She put the flag down and decided she would check the box again later in the day. According to the clerk at the post office, she had submitted her change of address form in time for the weekend's mail to arrive at its new destination on Monday - today. She was expecting her credit card bill but more importantly, she was watching for a coupon to come from her favorite store, Kohl's. If it came today, she was going to make a quick trip to the strip mall where the store was located and treat herself to some new towels and maybe some placemats. Nothing said home ownership like new possessions and credit card debt. She rationalized by reminding herself that she would be saving 25% with the coupon.

Early that afternoon she saw the mail truck go by, stop at her mailbox, then move on. She was arranging Danielle's clothes in her closet at the time so she made the mental note to retrieve the mail next time she needed to go downstairs for something. Getting Danielle's clothes settled in led to doing the same for Eric's but within an hour and a half, she was done and heading to the kitchen for a cup of coffee. Once her cup that declared her to be The World's Greatest Mom was in the microwave to be warmed, she went out to her mailbox and was very surprised to find it empty. Had she imagined the mail truck stopping at her box? No, she knew herself better than that - she saw it stop. Maybe he only had mail for the prior residents and needed the stop to decide not to leave the mail in Elaine's box. This seemed plausible but what about the mail that should be coming to her, she asked herself. *It should be here by now!* she thought. Elaine decided she'd address the problem the next day. However, she fully expected there to be no problem tomorrow.

Tuesday morning came and the family of three successfully tested their morning routine, ending with Elaine arriving at work on time. "How did your move go?" asked Dr. Spinelli, Elaine's boss.

"It was physically very difficult but it's over. Everything else we have to do, we can get done as time permits." Elaine smiled.

"Do the kids still like your house?" the dentist asked. Dr.

Spinellli was a great boss - thoughtful, fair, and intelligent - but whenever Elaine thought of him as a man she felt a little queasy. His hands were so soft and pudgie, with perfect nails and soft, white skin. And while being pudgie, they were also small when compared to his body. He was about 5' 10" and weighed about 200 pounds, some of which was muscle. His hands however, looked like they belonged on a 13 year old member of the audio-visual club at the local middle school. To Elaine, this feature completely blocked her ability to see him as - or evaluate him as - a man. He was simply her boss. Elaine's attitude toward men was warped as a result of her marriage; she was able to find deal-breakers within minutes of meeting anyone from the masculine gender. Her disinterest in partnering was profound.

"They are ecstatic to be in our own home." Elaine answered, still smiling as she pulled the charts for the patients she was expecting that morning. The office building Dr. Spinelli had moved them into a few years earlier was one of the best in town. The doctor had pooled his funding sources and upgraded everything of importance in the practice. The decor was rich, the technologies were cutting edge and much thought had been put into the comfort of the patients as well as the staff. As Elaine pulled her charts, she placed them onto the designated shelf on her cart. The carts were an investment the dentist had made for each of his hygienists. Each cart housed a laptop, tools, a large screen that could be shared with patients, and access to their practice's computer network.   The practitioners could instantly access medical histories, x-rays, and tutorial videos. It had an integrated wireless receiver so all staffers could instantly and soundlessly communicate with one another, including the dentist, when needed. He also gave each hygienist an allowance for purchasing new scrubs. The scrubs he designated had the name of his practice embroidered on the left side. The hygienist's first name was embroidered above that. Elaine was wearing her favorite lilac-colored scrubs as she wheeled her cart into the area where she would see her patients that day. Her first patient was waiting, reading a People magazine.

The day went by quickly and 4:00, her time to clock out, got there before she expected it. She gathered up her jacket, said goodbye to her coworkers and headed to the childcare center to pick up her kids. She could see her house a few seconds before they got to it and she noticed that her mailbox flag was up again. Her heart rate went up in response; a sense of panic momentarily gripped her. She opened the door to find the mailbox empty. She was expecting three or four days' worth of mail which, fliers included, should be a stack. *Crap* she thought, now she really was going to have to do something about this. She looked at her watch - it was 4:45 - the post office closed in 15 minutes.

Elaine hurried the kids inside and told them to take care of their coats and get their homework out. She Googled to find the phone number for her new post office, dialed it and got a voicemail system. She left a message stating her name, her new address and a request for a call back. She closed by saying that she had completed the change of address before they moved so she was inquiring about how long it should take before her mail started coming to her new address. Minutes later, when she noticed it was after 5:00, Elaine stopped waiting for the call back and focused on making dinner and monitoring homework.

"Can I watch Nickelodeon?" Eric asked.

"Yes you can as soon as your dinner and your homework are done." Eric made a face intended to portray impatience as Elaine turned to Danielle, "Do you have more homework?"

Danielle answered " I am supposed to cut some pictures out of a magazine, is that OK Mommy?"

"Sure, that's fine sweetie. I threw away almost all of them before we moved but I'm certain we can find something for you. What kind of pictures do you need?" She said to herself, *if we had gotten our mail, we have a few to pick from...*

"I need to find family members, like someone who looks like a mom and a grandma, you know, like a baby and a father. That kind of stuff." Danielle continued, "Tomorrow at school we're going to glue them to house pictures that we started drawing today. I want to put a dog in my house too, okay mommy? Cuz I really, really want a dog."

"Okay to the *picture* of a dog, Danelly" Elaine replied. Danielle giggled at hearing her mom use her nickname. Elaine found a JC Penney catalog in her recycle bin and gave it to Danielle to cut up. "You should be able to find most of what you need in here sweetie." Elaine hoped that having their own home would enable them to eventually have a dog; for now though, she didn't have the energy to even think about housebreaking and training a dog. She took pet ownership seriously so until she had extra time and energy, a dog was not a possibility.

Elaine turned her attention back to dinner. She was really committed to providing nourishing meals for the three of them. She didn't have to look far to find a lot of information on the negative impact that some foods - factory raised meats and fish, boxed food mixes, and most grains - have on people. The results included things like inability to lose weight, blood sugar fluctuations, sensitive digestive systems and Celiacs disease, precocious puberty and more. It was the article in Parenting Magazine that suggested how the impact can be exponentially more profound on small, growing bodies that converted Elaine. Granted, she had made an exception last Friday after the house closing when she bought McDonald's for them, but her nutrition conversion caused that meal to be a much more valuable treat to the kids than it would have been even a year ago. Tonight she was making chicken thighs cooked with artichokes and lemon, mashed 'potatoes' made from cauliflower and brussel sprouts wrapped in uncured bacon, the latter being Eric's favorite side dish.

When dinner was done, Elaine didn't ask for help with the dishes since both kids had homework. Once it was completed, Eric went into the family room to watch his planned program on Nickelodeon and Danielle got ready for her bath. "Mommy!" Danielle yelled from the bathroom as Elaine finished putting the dishes in the dishwasher.

Elaine leaned into the stairwell and yelled up to the bathroom at the top, "What?"

"Can you bring me my Barbie, I want to wash her hair."

"Let me know when your hair is washed and rinsed and then yes, I'll get it for you"

"Ok Mommy!"

Elaine finished up the various household tasks she had in progress: dishes were done, kids' homework was done, Danielle was clean, Eric would shower in the morning. All was well as she put the kids to bed, Eric one-half hour after Danielle. Elaine and her son really enjoyed this half-hour they got together as of this school year. They usually spent it watching TV but every once in a while Eric would say something or ask a question which would give Elaine a clue about his world. "Mom, what is a cougar?" was the question this night.

"Well the word has different meanings; can you tell me more about the situation where you heard the word? Was it at the zoo?"

"Mom, I know what a cougar at the zoo is." Elaine thought he was young for this conversation but she didn't want to discourage his questions nor did she want to treat him as if he was stupid.

Elaine replied, "I have heard that word used recently to describe a woman who is attracted to younger men."

"Ohhhh, that explains everything. When I got on the bus yesterday, Joel Connor said our driver was a cougar and that's why she let me sit in front. I didn't want to sit in front but I didn't want to be rude either. I think he was jealous so he was being mean."

Elaine registered the wisdom and politeness of her son, pleased with both. "Yes, that was mean of him, and I'm impressed that you called it jealousy; I think you're probably right. Any other questions on that?"

"Nope; can I have some pretzels?"

"How about baby carrot sticks? I don't think we have any pretzels. You can get them yourself."

Their night ended on a sweet, comfortable note. The next day started almost the same way except for the need for Elaine to be the clock-watching dictator. Her kids just were not mature enough to get themselves ready as second and fourth graders, and her pediatrician assured her that was an age appropriate challenge. She even went on to say that, within her practice, some kids needed a mother's prodding until they went to college. Elaine made a mental note to work out some consequences for dragging teenage feet before she needed to use those consequences. She wanted her kids to be responsible for the things they could reasonably control - when it was "age appropriate."

On Wednesday morning, they had another successful run of their morning routine with everyone ending up where they were supposed to be by their individual deadlines. When Elaine took her first break of the day at about 10:00 a.m., she found a voicemail message on her phone. Ever since having children and returning to work, separation from her phone caused slight anxiety; a voicemail message was something she needed to attend to immediately. It was the post office, "Ms. Moreland, this is Sally from the Victory Post Office returning your call. Our driver is certain he left mail in your box at..." Elaine's head began to swim. She could hear the voice message correctly recite her address but she could only picture that flag. She had never put it up. *What was going on*, she asked herself. Elaine tuned back in to hear, "he thinks he's left mail a few times so we are confused. Please call me back at extension 1236, I'd like to chat to make sure we are all talking about the same house and the same mail. Have a nice day!" The person leaving the message was clearly smiling during that last sentence, just like they told you to do in voice-mail school, or training, or...

Elaine shut her thoughts down, *there's no such thing as voicemail school, just call back, you don't need to analyze the smiley voice*." And call back she did, before her 20 minute break was over.

"Hello Ms. Moreland," said smiley voice. "This is Sally, I'm glad you've called. Could you please confirm for me your new address and your former address?" Elaine provided both. "Ok, please hold for a minute while I check on some things." Additional smiles for this request.

"Ms. Moreland?" Smiley returned to the call, "Our driver has confirmed that he has left mail at your house both Monday and Tuesday, would you like us to hold your mail here for today until we figure out what's going on?"

Elaine replied, "Ummmm yes, please do. When can I get it?"

"We'll hold it at the counter for you. Please be aware," here comes the smile, Elaine predicted, "we close up our window at 4:45." Smile granted.

"And if I don't make it on time? " Elaine was calculating patient schedules, child care routines, drive time, etc.

"We'll hold it one more day before delivering it to your mailbox. But Ms. Moreland, if this continues to be a problem, you may want to get a P.O. Box, that way you won't have any pick-up deadlines."

"Thank you so much for your help" Elaine replied, "and please tell me your name?"

"I am Sally McClullen."

"Thanks Sally. I'll get my mail as soon as I can get there or else open up a P.O. Box on Saturday morning."

After the completion of her workday and the collection of her kids at the day care center, she pulled onto her street and saw that her flag was up again. *WTF?* she said to herself. She pulled over to her box, rolled down her window and opened the mailbox. It looked empty except for one small thing toward the back. She snatched the object and pulled it into her car, then gasped.

"What Mommy??!" Danielle asked when she heard Elaine's emotion.

"Nothing baby, somebody is being stupid." Elaine shoved her new possession deep into her purse for future evaluation.

"What was that?" Eric asked.

"It was an invitation to a junk food party" Elaine lied. "Can you imagine me going to a party that you're not invited to?" She fake-chuckled, "much less one that's all about junk food?"

Elaine had impressed herself with that one. *Jeepers,* she thought, *let's not make a habit of this.* She thought about her new ability to weave tales.

Elaine got the kids into the house and set them up at the dinner table to work on their homework while she cooked.

First, however, she brought her purse upstairs so that she could look at the item from her mailbox in the privacy of her bedroom. She clutched her doorknob tightly so that she could close her door with as little noise as possible. Once she felt she was alone, she sat on her bed and dug into her bag to find the item. Once located, she brought it under the light from her bedside lamp. *Oh my god...* she thought. It was, in fact, what she was afraid it was - a black and white picture of her new house with the Sold! sign in the front yard.

KATE 1

Kate was vacillating between thinking she was done with menopause and knowing she wasn't. For the past several years, she had suffered hot flashes, especially during the night. When they would let up for a week or so, she would become hopeful that they would never return. Unfortunately though, as soon as she registered this hopefulness into her conscience, she would start being awakened by them again. This pattern was really getting tedious for Kate. *Thank the goddess*, Kate thought, she had met and married her big, lovable husband before this all started. They had celebrated their 5th anniversary just this past summer and Tim was very patient with her menopausal symptoms. Since Kate's sex drive tanked whenever the hot flashes increased, Tim's patience was a blessing she counted frequently.

Both Kate and Tim looked younger than their actual ages. Tim was a very big man at 6'8" and 240 lbs. At the time of their marriage, he was the only 56 year old Kate knew whose hair was still black, with very little gray. He was gregarious, a big sports fan and would easily satisfy the definition of a man's man. Kate was tall too, for a woman. She had long brown hair, which she did color. Her gray hairs were very dull and lifeless. Not like her younger sister who had beautiful silvery and black hair, like their mother, which always looked fabulous in her short, styled haircut. Kate's older sister wore her hair very long, much longer than Kate's. She often wore it in a braid or ponytail. She could get away with natural graying because her hair featured many shades of red, brown and even blonde, along with the gray - and it was always pulled back - so the craziness of the aging hairs didn't matter to her and she always looked beautiful. Kate was careful with make-up and clothes and, like her sisters, always tried to put her best foot forward.

Once, several years earlier, before her relationship with

Tim, Kate got a call from a college friend who was passing through town. He was on his way to visit his parents who lived another two hours west of Victory. Kate had a party planned for that night and she was expecting a large number of guests. She invited her friend Ross to stop in and hang out for a little while. As she got ready for her party, Ross sat on a kitchen stool and caught her up on his life. His wife and the mother of his two daughters had come forward with the information that she didn't have any feelings of love for Ross so Ross was struggling to survive a very serious wound. Kate could see this wound very clearly on the face of her old friend; it was as clear as one that bleeds and festers. They talked and talked. Then, when the guests began to arrive, Ross moved into the role of party attendee. Using a charm that Kate always admired, he introduced himself to those he felt comfortable with and ended up having several entertaining conversations before he decided to crash on Kate's couch for the night.

Five years later, Kate opened her mailbox to find an invitation to Ross's second wedding. When Kate arrived at the appointed time, she found it was the sort of wedding that takes place where the reception will also be held. To her dismay, she was the only one in sight without a date. After getting a glass of wine at the bar, she scanned the room for a friendly face. One nearby table held two couples and two empty chairs. One of the women meet Kate's eye and smiled. Kate walked in that direction and said to the friendly-faced woman, "Hi, I'm Kate and I need to confess that I don't know anyone here, do you mind if I sit at your table?"

"Heck no! I'm so glad you asked. I'm Nicole, sit!" Kate slid into the chair with obvious relief. "So, do you know Ross or Sharon?"

"I went to college with Ross. I haven't seen him since shortly after his split with Victoria though." Kate explained.

"Do you live near here?" Nicole asked.

No, I live in Victory."

"How did you happen to see Ross back then?" Nicole inquired.

Kate was beginning to realize she was talking to someone who cared about Ross a lot, or at least knew a lot about his chronology. "Ross was passing through town on his way to visit his parents when he gave me a call. He ended up stopping in and staying for a party I was throwing."

Nicole's face opened up in excited epiphany, "You are the one who helped him so much!"

"What?" Kate was confused

"When he got back from that trip, he felt so much better than when he had left. He accredited a friend from college whom he visited. He said you made him see that he had value and so did his future. You are that friend." She asked knowingly: "Didn't you spend quite some time chatting in your kitchen that day?"

"Yes, we did." Kate was amazed and happy. She had no idea she had made such a difference in her friend's life. His wound had started to heal because of that kitchen chat.

It was about a month later that Kate opened a fortune cookie that provided the words: *You never know who you touch*. Kate taped that paper fortune to her computer monitor and every replacement monitor since then. She vowed to never forget that every person has the power to affect another person.

By the time that small piece of paper was about six years old, Kate was at a point of really enjoying her life, even in light of where she was in her reproductive phases. She had a job she genuinely enjoyed where she worked only about 30 hours a week as a real estate agent. She loved her home and her home life with Tim and their dog Wrangler. She loved that she had two adult children with whom she had a close relationship; their half-sister June was Kate's first step child and Kate cherished her too. She loved her sisters and brother very much and her parents' good health was also a blessing she cited regularly. Tim's three adult children were very important to her along with the two grandchildren his second child had given them. She loved her activities: Zumba 3 times a week, good friends visiting on the weekends, a book club formed by her friend Hap and comprised of special friends that met monthly, and writing her own book.

Kate had started writing a book a few months earlier; a piece of fiction that, for her entertainment only, held slivers of truth. The act of writing occupied her whole mind so it was cathartic; creating subjects and story lines satisfied her creativity. Every once in a while she even thought about getting it published. It was then that she'd say to herself, "What are you, nut??" She said nut, not nuts, intentionally. Kate and Tim shared a love for a morning radio talk show out of Rochester, New York that they listened to on iHeart Radio. The host of the show was a well-spoken, politically liberal guy with a lot of tattoos named Brother Wease. Wease often shared personal stories so Kate and Tim had become familiar with his kids' names and some of their adventures and tribulations. Brother Wease's oldest daughter, Diane, was a vibrant, fun, energetic woman who was intellectually handicapped. Wease would have Diane as a guest on his show every once in a while and that made Kate love him more. Diane would not be shy in front of the microphone and she added a lot of warmth and humor to the show even though her handicap was obvious; the telltale garbled, thick speech would be what the listeners heard - at least at first - then her charm and love for her father became louder than the handicap. Kate wished everyone could accept all of the 'Dianes' of the world the way the Brother Wease show and its listeners did. Diane was the reason Kate said 'nut' in its singular form versus the colloquial term 'nuts' used to imply mental irrationality because that's how Diane said it; Diane had a few reinterpretations of common expressions. Kate, Tim and their friends who also listened in, all got a giggle when one of them would say, "are you nut?" or "what are you, nut?" because it was an inside joke, the use of which cast some coolness on its user and reminded everyone fondly of Diane.

Kate drifted along in her life, peacefully loving her husband, trying to be a good person and succeeding most of the time. They lived in a small house and they lived below their means so that they could have a good retirement. She perceived herself to have a high quality of life, because of, or in spite of, its simplicity. Kate's peace was shattered on a Friday-the-13th during the year 2013.

A few months earlier, Tim's son Tyler and Tyler's wife Janelle, made arrangements for a surprise for Tim's 60th birthday which was in September of that year. They planned a trip to Heinz Field in August to see the Steelers play football in a preseason game. Tim was a Steelers fan down to the core. His family history, maybe even his DNA, almost demanded that he be loyal to that team. Their group for their visit to Pittsburgh was comprised of Kate, Tim, Tyler, Janelle, their two young children - Tim's grandkids - and Kate's daughter Toni, and Toni's boyfriend Bill. They got hotel rooms so no one would have to drive the four-hour-plus trip home after the game; they went out to a nice dinner before the game and the eight of them had a great time.

Tim didn't learn of the plan until Tyler's family of four showed up at their house on a Thursday night unexpectedly. They lived 3 hours away so they had never just dropped in before. Kate had been expecting them since she was a co-conspirator, so she had made sure that Tim was home and the house was fairly picked up. When the two grandkids just strolled in and said, "Hi Grandpa!" Tim almost fell over with surprise. Tyler and Janelle came in next and when everyone was standing in the kitchen, Tim asked in an emphatic staccato, "What is going on here?!"

Layla, the older of the grandkids said, "We're taking you to a Steelers game for your birthday!"

"No way!" Tim said as he turned to Kate to see if it was a joke. Kate nodded her head in affirmation. "Oh my god, really? That's on my bucket list... You spent too much money... It's only August... I'm so surprised" His thoughts and statements were scattered due to excitement. Contributing to his surprise was the fact that his birthday was a Friday that was still a few weeks away, on September 13th.

Later that evening when Tyler's family was out running errands and the two were left alone, Tim said to Kate, "I can't believe this, I have never been so excited about anything in my life." He had tears in his eyes. Tim was not very good at accepting gifts so Kate was relieved that he was graciously accepting this one; especially because they had in fact, spent too much money.

When Tim's actual birthday rolled around a few weeks later, Tim and Kate went out to dinner by themselves; they went to a crab shack-style restaurant and ate too many crab legs. Tim forbade Kate from revealing that it was his birthday. He would have died of mortification if the wait staff had gathered around their table to sing their proprietary version of a birthday song, all the while clapping and inspiring all the patrons to look over to see who was in the hot seat. Hence, dinner was uneventful. When they got back home, Tim went straight to bed because he didn't want their neighbors - who were their best friends - to get any ideas about coming over to celebrate his birthday; he just wanted the day to pass as quickly as possible and be over with. So, Kate was alone when the phone rang. It was Toni, "I have bad news Mom."

~~~~~~~~~~~~~~~~~~~~~~~~~~~~~~~~~~~~

Chandra was a licensed social worker and private practice therapist. Kate had used her services before when she needed help weaving pieces of her life together to create a peaceful household. Kate's second born child, her son Michael had been in and out of trouble since he was about thirteen. He didn't live with Kate at the time she and Tim got married, but needed temporary shelter a few years later. He moved into their basement at that time. Kate needed pointers on how to incorporate step-parenting into a house where they should have been, for the most part, done with the parenting. Even though they were getting more comfortable in their new married life, Tim's temper flared up more often due to the change in their empty-nest status. Concurrently, Kate's patience with the temper flares had diminished. She needed help because a peaceful household was very important to her.

Chandra had helped her to find the things she just needed to accept, work-around or ignore; Chandra herself had personal experience with living with ADHD, which Tim had also been diagnosed with, so she was qualified to help Kate identify the fights worth fighting. For example, when Tim didn't have the patience to put the lid back on the dog food container, Kate asked him to please be careful about that. To Tim, this was so trivial that it seemed like she was nagging. To Kate, this was the only nutrition Wrangler ever got; he didn't have a steady stream of table scraps like a lot of dogs did. She felt that keeping the large container of food palatable and wholesome was important enough to say something to Tim. Chandra helped her to understand that if she could find a work-around, this might become unworthy of Kate-and-Tim discussion time. And she was right. Kate understood what Chandra was suggesting and went to the local big box store and bought a container with a self-closing lid. Sixteen dollars later, there was one less thing causing strife in the Kate-and-Tim household. They were closer to having a peaceful environment. Three years later, Kate needed Chandra to help work through a new challenge.

Kate was overwhelmed with anguish, anxiety, and sorrow. Her son Michael had been arrested for selling drugs while being on probation for the same thing. When Toni had called Kate the night of Tim's sixtieth birthday, she had confirmed something Kate's subconscious was just starting to wonder about. "I have bad news Mom," she continued on that Friday the 13th, "Michael's in jail and they are saying he'll get three years." Toni continued, "I guess he was on probation already, did you know that?"

"No, I didn't." Kate replied, "Hey listen, you have enough going on so don't you worry about this, okay? I'll figure out what's going on tomorrow and let you know." Toni was in Nursing School full time and still working almost full time. Kate wanted her to be able to maintain the focus necessary for this commitment. After taking this worry off Toni's platter, Kate got off the phone and went into her bedroom where Tim had been 'hiding' from the social obligations of his birthday for two hours already. "Michael's in jail."

Tim: "What?!" He was awake.

"Toni called, he was arrested today and apparently he was already on probation."

"Are you okay?" Tim asked.

"Yeah, I think so." That's when Kate's mind began to spin with thoughts of where Michael was at that moment, *what is he feeling? Is he panicking? Is he thinking about how long 3 years could be? What would become of the rest of his life? All his potential was down the drain.* The swirling of these thoughts was so all-consuming; Kate was dizzy and exhausted. She was actually not okay. She lay in bed staring at her alarm clock. It was a clock radio she had purchased before her vision correction surgery, so it had digital numbers that were 3 inches tall so that she could read it back then without having to put her glasses on. Apparently, GE was a very reliable brand because her surgery had been years before even meeting Tim, and that clock was still declaring the time in very large numbers.

On this night she had so much opportunity to observe this clock that she was able to notice how much more light is emitted when the number eight was on the display compared to the number one. Of the 7 LED cells available to display a number, the eight used all seven while the one used only two. She had time to observe that the seven used three of them and that the zero - which was really a rectangle - used six of them, with each change of hour and minute changing the amount of light the time display emitted. *"Certainly someone has noticed and perhaps even recorded this fluctuation in light that occurs simply because time is passing"* she thought.

Kate remembered the days when she was married to her first husband; she referred to him as her 'baby daddy' when she was entertaining herself with her own humor. The two of them had run a contracting company which included electrical contracting and she never forgot how precisely light was measured by the people who designed buildings and wrote the specs that they had to comply with. Candle power was the unit of measure used to designate how much light must be produced by the lighting fixtures designated for each area; a candle power of one was equal to the light produced by one candle. In Kate's mind, one candle produced very little light, therefore candle power was a very precise unit of measure. She had enough awake time during this night to wonder if anyone had tried to measure - using candle power, of course - the difference in the light emitted by a clock at 1:00 compared to 8:56; to her it was a very big difference. She also spent time arranging the possible digits by how much light they would produce: one, seven, four, zero, two, three, five, nine, eight. When she recited this numeric sequence to herself a few times, she realized that she might be going 'nut.' *Can one actually be going nut if that person is aware of the possibility of that happening?... Or does the awareness negate that possibility?...* She let these inane questions fester in her consciousness as the long night wore on. Normally Kate felt very solid in her ownership of her sanity and in fact, the people who knew her well, if asked, would have probably used the word 'sane' to describe her. Repetitious numeric sequences based on things that had meaning to perhaps no one else on the planet was not her style, and Kate knew that.

The next day, a Saturday, her horror became even more real as she had to tell various members of her family and friends what was going on. Her first call was preceded by a text to her sister Liz, her older sister who lived nearby. Her text simply asked, are you up? In response, Liz called her. After a very brief bit of small talk, Kate said, "Michael is in jail and apparently he was already on probation."

Liz said, "Uggghhh, I was so afraid of that when I saw your text."   Liz had known that Kate and Michael had had a falling out, and why. She had been an important part of Kate's support system during the few weeks that had passed since this upheaval, along with their other sister, Sam. Liz's subconscious was apparently on the lookout for the next proverbial shoe to drop, and here it was, fully dropped.

By the time Kate went to work on Monday morning she could barely contain her tears. She would normally tell her very benevolent boss this sort of news because he had shared his own traumas caused by his son's behaviors often enough, but she decided to do him a favor and not mention it until she could do so without crying. The sensation of swirling thoughts along with so many things to worry about at once, had taken on a sound of its own. It was a static-riddled, white noise of sorts that was like a radio station playing in her brain at all times, threatening to distract her from daily responsibilities like driving her car safely, remembering to eat meals, or feeding Wrangler. She needed to call Chandra again.

The last time Kate had seen Michael they had fought bitterly. A few weeks earlier, Kate had uncovered evidence that Michael was involved with drugs while he was temporarily staying in her basement. Kate had told Michael that he needed to stop any such activity . In response, Michael had decided to argue for his right to privacy versus addressing what his mother was saying to him. Ultimately that night, Kate had told Michael to go find his privacy somewhere else. He quickly packed a few things and left.

Within an hour of leaving, Kate had started to get texts from Michael telling her what a bad mother she had been, including how unloving she had been. She chose not to reply. Michael was on drugs and his thoughts were laced with anger and intentional misrepresentations. The texts kept coming. By the fifth or sixth text, Michael's words included veiled threats of suicide. When she still didn't reply, the veil came down and his threat was clear.

Kate was fairly certain that Michael had gone back to his girlfriend's house where he had lived before seeking shelter at Kate's house. His girlfriend, or former girlfriend, was still in love with him in spite of how furious she was with him. It would not take much for him to work his way through Amanda's front door and back into her life. Amanda had kicked him out for reasons Kate was not privy to, nor did she care to be, nonetheless, her confidence in Michael finding shelter there was complete.

Conveniently, Amanda and Toni lived one block apart in the downtown area of Canandesque, a small city about 10 miles from Victory. Kate decided to get in touch with Toni's live-in boyfriend who was a pal of Michael's. She didn't want to involve Toni because of the possible conflict between her feeling of responsibility toward Michael and her need to stay focused on school. Her boyfriend Bill was a good guy, and Kate knew he could be trusted to check on Michael's safety without creating unnecessary drama.

Kate keyed into her phone, Hi Bill, hey listen, Michael and I had a huge fight earlier now he's texting with threats of suicide, I think he went to Amanda's, can you please just get in touch with him and make sure he's ok? I'd be so grateful.

A few minutes later Bill wrote back. He's sitting here having a beer with me. He is no worse for the wear, you don't need to worry.

Thank you, please let me know if anything changes, Kate replied. *Thank the goddess for Bill,* Kate thought.

Despite Michael's apparent safety, Kate was heart-broken. Her beloved son had chosen to take a stance on his right to privacy while living rent-free under her roof and dabbling in illegal drugs. Then he had texted her the words that he knew would be the most hurtful thing he could say to her. That was followed by insincere threats of suicide. If he was anyone else's son, she would have called him a low-life dirt-bag.

Kate was trying to keep Tim dialed into this situation as it evolved but found him to be unable to see it from her perspective. They had been playing cards on the night she and Michael had argued, so he was impatient with how much time she was spending texting Bill. Kate felt that in spite of how much of the situation was manufactured drama and not a real situation requiring her attention, she still needed to do the due diligence and pay attention to what was going on with her son.

Tim had a more clinical perspective, although when situations with any of his three kids arose, he was anything but clinical. While Kate resented this dichotomy, she also understood its value: if they could talk about it enough to harness it, they both could be better parents to their adult children. They could hope to draw from each other's detachment and each other's blinding love to form a hybrid of parenting that long-married couples can't often access. Because of the promise of the hybrid, Kate did not allow herself to lose patience with Tim on this night. Instead, she chose to play cards and put in her thinking time later, when it should be sleeping time.

The next day, as Kate got ready to go to work, she realized she was shaken up. Her fight with Michael, and the reason for it, combined with his horrible texts were registering with her. The last thing she did before leaving the house was to turn to her jewelry box and pull out her "sisters pin." The previous summer, Sam, her husband, and Liz had come up for a weekend of fun. Sam had brought with her beautiful pins that were delicate shapes of colorful metal combined to look like three woman standing side by side, their six legs swinging loosely from the bottom of the metal conglomerate. Sam had bought three; she was wearing one and she gave one to each of her two sisters. By putting on her sisters pin, Kate hoped to summon the strength of the triumvirate the three sisters enjoyed. Her first act once at work was to send an email to her sisters telling them how she was hurting - and why. She copied in her good friends Hap and Linda so they would be at least partially dialed in when she found time to talk to them later in the day.

Kate hadn't attempted to communicate with Michael during the period of time between their fight and the time she learned from Toni that he had been arrested. Instead, within a few days of his leaving, she changed the locks on her house because Michael had a set of keys and because Kate couldn't be sure which of his visiting "friends" had looked around for reasons to "visit" Kate and Tim again in the future. When the time came to discuss bail, she felt no guilt over shaking her head in the widely accepted sign of no.

Guilt and sadness were two different things, though. Even though Kate didn't suffer through any guilt, she still suffered from profound sadness. One day she got a call from Amanda. Amanda had taken on the role of liaison between Michael and the outside world. He would call her when he had access to the phone at the county jail. One time he asked her if she thought it would be okay for him to call his Mom. Amanda's call to Kate was to find out the answer to that question. The first time it came up, Kate simply said, "There is nothing I can do for him so no, I am not ready to talk to him." As time went on however, her resolve to maintain emotional space between them was chipped away by the feeling of loss; she missed Michael. Her heart was hurting.

When it was finally the day of her appointment with Chandra, Kate was feeling better simply because she knew she was about to lighten her burden by sharing it with someone; that proved to be true. In addition, Chandra helped Kate to realize that if she would open the door to communicating with Michael, he may have something to say that would help them both. Kate decided to write him a letter describing how angry and disappointed in him she was and asking him to describe what he was learning from this experience. She was hoping he would say something in response that would allow her to forgive him for how lousy he had been to her when he had last left her house. It would be a bonus if he also offered something that would inspire her to hope that this would be the last time he'd ever get in trouble with the law. She also told him that if they were going to be in communication with one another, she required much more honesty than she had been getting from him. When her letter was ready to go in the mail, she decided to drive it to the post office near where she worked in Victory. She couldn't mail it from her office - her coworkers would figure out where her son was - and she didn't want to mail it from home; their town was too small to contain such a juicy tidbit. She didn't want to be receiving mail from a prison either.

THOMAS 2

When Thomas learned to speak, he used his words as his new ammunition. He also showed a propensity for learning emotionally powerful words more quickly than the standard issue Mamma, Daddy. His first word was 'bad." And he never spoke it softly or in a manner that suggested he was proud of his new power, like the baby that will say "Mommy!" then grin from ear-to-ear. He spoke the word as if it were perpetually written in caps: BAD!

Betty felt this was unusual and it set off her inner alarm. In response to that alarm, she tried to keep negative words out of her vocabulary. When she asked Richard to be equally conscientious, he didn't hesitate to tell her that he thought that would be counter-productive. "After all," he said, "a child needs to live in a real world." Betty thought but didn't say, *yes and a child's father should live in that real world with him.* Richard's habit of being gone was so well ingrained in him now though, that thoughts of influencing the child with his own actions and beliefs never occurred to him.

Richard was capable of flaring up in a way that to Betty, was so unreasonable, and so worth avoiding, that she kept a lot of her thoughts to herself these days.

One time, when Thomas was about to have his first birthday, Richard asked, "Who will we invite to our birthday party?"

"Birthday party? Who is having a birthday party?" Betty was so exhausted at the one-year mark that the idea of intentionally showing other people what her life was like was ridiculous. When she thought about it, she remembered a late-night comedian who used the word, *redonkulous.* So her mental response to Richard's question actually used that word. She thought, *If you think I'm inviting relatives and/or friends into this house, to hear our child cry, you are nuts. That idea is redonkulous.*

What she actually said was, "If you want a birthday party, please go ahead and have one. Maybe I'll get a nap in that day."

Richard's face changed. His reply was quick: "You have got to be kidding me." He was using a very loud voice. "What kind of mother doesn't have a birthday party for a one-year old? You are just being lazy and selfish. You know what my sisters will say? They will say you just don't care about them or Thomas" He grew louder and louder. Betty started to be afraid for her safety, but his inaccurate portrayal of her was more important to her than safety.

"You have got to be the one who is kidding! If you had any idea of what it's like to spend two hours - or even just one - with that child, you would know better." She tried to keep her voice low since she didn't want Thomas to hear the anger.

"You're a bad mother Betty, let's just get that out there. See you later." Then he left. She had no idea where he went and she didn't care. She did, however, decide at a subconscious level, to not argue with Richard when he had his "face-changing-moments." The punishment of being called a bad mother was immediately effective. She even spent a few minutes wondering if it could be true. As time went on, the amount of time she spent nursing that question was not measured in minutes. If it had, in fact, been measurable, it would be measured in weeks, maybe even months.

And so, when Betty wanted darker words to be avoided in her house, she just avoided conversing with Richard. That was the only control she had over Richard's 'parenting' style. Naturally, the further decline of their marriage followed the decline in their conversations.

Two months after Thomas' 5th birthday, she got a letter in the mail from his school; it was signed by his kindergarten teacher. It explained, using a lot of unnecessary words, that Thomas wasn't getting along with his classmates and had been using language they felt was unacceptable. The letter ended with a request that Betty come in for a conference the following Monday at 3:30. Betty was fairly certain she could arrange her day to be free at that time. Richard had abandoned Betty and Thomas two years earlier so she didn't need to tell him about it.

It was September of that year, when Richard left on a business trip; he was due back the next day. When Betty didn't hear from him by 10:00 that night, she went to bed. She had thought it was likely that he would just slip in during the night, but the next morning she found that hadn't happened - his side of the bed was empty. After a cup of coffee, she went back to their room and poked around in his dresser and closet. She found it to be more empty than she expected. In fact, all of his suits were gone and most of his shoes. She quickly figured out what had happened, so she put her screaming child into his car seat and drove to the bank. She used the bank's drive-through so she wouldn't have to move Thomas. Over the microphone built into the drive-through kiosk, she inquired about their balance. The answer was almost what she would have guessed. It was the total of their household bills for a month, times two. *Thank you, Richard for giving me two months to figure out how to get a job and raise a child by myself.* These thoughts were offset by relief that Richard was gone.

Betty arrived ten minutes early for the meeting at the school. She patiently waited outside the classroom until the teacher came out into the hall and invited her in. "Hello Mrs. Findlay, how are you today? … what a lovely day, huh?" The teacher was trying unsuccessfully to sound gracious and Betty could hear that failed attempt.

Betty thought, *oh dear, this is going to be bad.*

"Come in," the teacher directed her to a chair, "I need to

talk to you about Thomas's behavior. It's not very good, but I think you must already be aware of that."

"That's an understatement, candidly" Betty replied.

"Well that's just it exactly. I'm afraid that some of his behaviors are indicative of a greater problem."

"Please be more specific." Betty was frustrated because there was nothing she had been able to do to influence Thomas's behavior, ever. It was like he was able to tune her out completely; but worse yet, it was as if while she was tuned out, he still had a source of information. He knew words Betty would swear he had never heard, and he got ideas that had no identifiable inspiration.

"He put thumb tacks in our hamster's cage, he poured vinegar into most of the student's pansy plant projects, and he flushed another student's drawings down the toilet. The janitor had to snake the toilet after that. Oh, and he has used swear words." She continued, "So we have animal cruelty, antisocial behavior, and damage to property. This is not a good combination. It's confusing because he can be so appealing. I mean, he is extraordinarily good looking and he can be very sweet," she paused. "Mrs. Findlay, we um, I mean me and my aid and other co-workers, we tried hard to not come to this conclusion…" she was stumbling over her words, "well put it this way, we think Thomas needs more help than we can give him. We are not trained for this."

"And he is only 5 years old." Betty finished for her.

"Mrs. Findlay, I'd like to refer you to our school counselor, Barbara Ritzer, she has an idea about some testing that might benefit Thomas or you, or both of you."

"I don't have any health insurance"

"Please mention that to Barb, I'm sure she can help you find services that charge according to your ability to pay."

The resulting appraisal, testing, and diagnosis would be the first of many times Betty was offered the opportunity, as one business office representative eluded, "to illustrate her values" and she would have to do so via her paltry checking account. "What really could be more important than understanding exactly what was wrong with your psychopathic son," they said to her, as they carved out their payment plan with her. She thought, *well, making the mortgage payment and buying food occasionally ranks right up there...* Fortunately, Betty did have a job, but being a secretary in a local insurance agency didn't pave a path to riches; they just got by. And Thomas's behavior just kept getting worse.

By the time he turned 13, Betty was afraid of Thomas. There were no attempts to control his behavior, she gave up on that about five years earlier; now she just practiced avoidance. She knew that meant he was virtually unsupervised and potentially in danger - or causing danger - but the thought of child protective services rolling into her driveway represented a relief; it wasn't something she feared.

COREY 2

As gently as he could, Corey entered Angela's most private area. He was trying not to let all of his weight lay on her, while also trying to be gentle, and he was also very interested in putting his sensitive organ inside her without hurting her - it seemed like an impossible conundrum. *Is this really possible?* he asked himself. Before he had time to answer, he was in and it was over.

"Oh wow," Corey paused, then said, "Are you okay?"

"Uh" her voice sounded wispy. "Yes, I'm okay but I didn't expect all that."

"You didn't expect to have sex? Because for the record, neither did I. Or you didn't expect it to be like that?"

"I'm not sure; I've never done that before."

"Me neither."

Angela was surprised, "We were both virgins?"

"Yes"

Angela started to feel the alcohol, "Oh my god, I'm dizzy, I didn't plan for this." there was a note of panic in her voice which Corey heard loud and clear.

"It's ok, we'll be fine. It might be best if you just settled into my bed and went to sleep. I'll wake you up tomorrow, you just say what time."

When his cell phone rudely reminded the pair of the new day, they both groaned. Angela looked at the time and sat up with a start. *Where was she?* It took a minute for her to remember where she was and why she was still there. Her head hurt and she was queasy. "Oh no!" were Angela's first words that day.

"It's okay, we figured out our timing last night. You'll be okay." Corey tried to soothe her; he thought her dismay was based on her class schedule. "Would you like something to eat? I have some granola bars."

"God no." Angela almost spat out. "I just need to get out of here."

"We had a pretty big evening yesterday. Could we make a plan to meet later? That okay with you?"

"Uhhh, yeah. When is your last class?"

"I'm done at 3:00 today, you?"

"I'm done at 4; can we meet here at like 4:20?"

Corey was relieved, "Yes, great, see you here."

The day dragged for both of them, not only because they both had substantial hangovers, but also because of the memories they were processing - attempting to take what had happened the day before and turn that into a piece of who they were, or at the least, what their lives were comprised of so far - proved far more all-consuming than what their professors and teachers wanted them to be thinking about. Corey was additionally challenged by the fact that he wanted time with Angela to talk; he needed a chance to do his best to make sure she wasn't mad at him or blaming him for anything. For Angela, she was also fighting off thoughts of being a bad girl, someone like that unnamed bad girl she had heard so much about during her upbringing. She was hoping that Corey's reasonable and intelligent manner could ease that concern and guilt from her.

Corey arrived first and left the door ajar so Angela could

just enter when she got there. He sat on his bed with his head resting back against the pillows, much like Angela had done the night before. He felt so happy about having had this experience with the girl with the spunky ponytail; yet at the same time, he was uneasy. He never pictured himself as a guy who would have sex with someone he wasn't in a relationship with and he had no idea if Angela wanted to be in a relationship. As he tipped his head back and closed his eyes for the first time since the alarm went off, he felt a dizzying sensation of needing more rest. Once the dizziness passed, he brought his mind to attention; he only had a few minutes before Angela was due to arrive. As if he was talking to a friend, he said to himself, *'Dude, what do you want to see happen here?'* He examined the self-question for a moment before the answer showed itself. *I want Angela to not feel guilty and I want to be in a relationship with her.* He was certain he could make that relationship work; after all, she had great dimples, she really seemed to match what he had pictured as his ideal girlfriend, and she seemed to be interested in his thoughts.

"Hi, I'm here" Angela's voice was quiet as she ducked in and around the door, ponytail flipping to be in front of her left shoulder. She closed it as soon as she saw that Corey was the only one in the room. "Should I put a sock on it?" She giggled as she pointed to the door. Corey thought her giggle was a good sign.

"Up to you." he replied with a smile. He hadn't realized she saw him do that last night.

Angela walked over to where Corey was on his bed and sat on the edge. "Are you okay?" he asked, touching her lower back. Angela felt a stirring at his touch; she was very much aware of the fact that they were both just inches from each other and inches from where they had been the night before.

She took a deep breath, "Yes," was her reply, "but I'm

really confused and I still don't feel good."

"Do you regret last night?" he asked.

"In some ways, yes; in other ways, I completely understand how it happened. I'm kind of embarrassed to admit that something special happened. I just don't know if it was supposed to happen."

Corey took his time with his response, "So Miss McHenry," he said trying to sound like a lawyer on a cross examination, "You agree that the experience was special, could you go so far as to say it was exquisite?"

"You are so bad!" She yelled at him with a big smile on her face.

"I'm sorry, I couldn't resist. I'll be serious now." Corey adjusted his face dramatically removing his smile and replacing it with a comical straight-face. "If I had a magic wand and could use it on your behalf, what would I do with it?"

"You'd end my hangover, and you'd make it okay for us to do that stuff whenever we wanted to."

"Done!" he said as he waved his index finger as a magician would use a wand.

"I wish." She replied, a little misery in her tone. "Seriously, I like you a lot and I guess I wish we could try out just hanging out together."

Corey thought, *score!* That's what he had been hoping they would conclude. He just wanted a chance to get to know her better, see if his instincts about her were correct. "That's good for me." Corey was elated, "I'd be more comfortable with what happened last night if we tried to see if our relationship with each other could warrant that level of ummmm….. I mean umm… interaction?"

"Let's just refer to it as sex. Want to?" Angela was surprised at her own forthrightness.

"Okay, let's see if the relationship can hold a candle to the sex, okay?" he said with a tinge of sarcasm.

"Oh my god, you ARE so bad, aren't you?" She hit him over the head with a pillow. They were both laughing.

Once the laughter subsided, he said, "In all seriousness, I think we both are saying the same thing and I think that's really good. Let's commit to small things first. What are you doing this weekend? Can we plan to see each other?"

"Let's start small and sit together at dinner in the cafeteria on Friday, then maybe watch TV in the common area, okay?" She asked?

"Should I bring vodka?" he asked with a wink.

"Oh you!" spoken between clenched teeth.

Six weeks later, the joking and playing around was over.

Angela had been feeling exhausted in a way she had never experienced before; she wasn't just sleepy - she also had a feeling of gravity being stronger than usual, by about double. She was hungry but she didn't want to eat. Everything was difficult and therefore, she was grumpy a lot. Every day for the past three weeks, she had taken a nap as soon as her last class was finished. Corey was beginning to worry that she was tired of him, or making up the exhaustion in order to have less time with him.

When the vomiting started, her roommate said the words that were the harbinger of their big change, "You're not pregnant are you?"

"Don't be insane." Angela responded with vengeance. Angela started to count the weeks backwards mentally. She and Corey had had sex one more time after that first time but they had used a condom. Since that second time, they decided to start their romance over with actual dates and much more courtship-ing; sex hadn't happened yet in this new chapter of their relationship. By her calculations, it had been six or seven weeks since the instance of unprotected sex. She hadn't even worried about pregnancy. *How many people get pregnant from their first experience?* She hadn't even really enjoyed that last part of it. Her thoughts must have showed on her face because her roommate set down her hairbrush and walked over to her.

"Oh my god, you are, aren't you? I didn't even know you and Corey had sex"

"We didn't, except twice, and once was with a condom." Angela started crying. "I didn't even enjoy the sex part of it!"

"Your enjoyment is not necessary, silly! Do you know how sparsely populated our planet would be if female enjoyment of the sex act were a prerequisite for pregnancy?"

DAVE 2

Lisa had gone to bed before Dave. Dave had stayed up to drink a wine glass full of bourbon. He hated going to bed and staring at the ceiling so the bourbon had become part of his routine, it was an insurance policy against insomnia. Lisa woke to feel him sneak into bed so she rolled over and ran her hands through his chest hair. A throaty sound of desire came out of her as she moved her hips toward his. "Mmmm hi baby...." Lisa whispered hoarsely. Dave's mind was so occupied by his torturous thoughts about his business and his family's future that he couldn't even fathom the idea of making love to his wife. It was as if he had two people inside his head at that moment; one was saying, *what is happening here? The one woman in the world you want to have sex with and you* can *have sex with is coming on to you.* The other person was saying, *how do I get out of this? I could not possibly have sex at this moment but this woman is not going to understand my inability.* Dave rolled over so that Lisa's hand slid from his chest to his arm; his back was now facing her. His fake snore worked, so Lisa didn't register alarm, only sexual disappointment. She fell back to sleep in seconds. Dave was not as lucky.

Sometime after 3:00 a.m. Dave fell asleep. When his alarm went off at 6:00, he was not refreshed, or even close to it, but one of Jay's sentences was ringing out loudly in his head. "I wish you could have a do-over with the bank…" He couldn't get away from that thought; it kept coming back into his head. Getting in his truck, there was that thought, ordering coffee at the drive through, there was that thought. When he was reviewing one of his quotes with a prospective customer, he realized he had left out an important component so he asked that client for a do-over, so there was that thought, again. By lunchtime, he had a new idea.

Dave and Lisa had picked Victory, PA to raise their son based on the high marks the school system earned. Five years ago, it would have been considered a small town. Five years in the future it would be considered a suburb of Pittsburgh. Right now it was characterized by the fact that much of it was still rural in that area, the houses had big yards, frequently 2 acres or more. Meanwhile, the other side of town was sprawling out at a pace practically notable by the naked eye. One day, there was a plaza with a Safeway, and seemingly the next day, the plaza had a new facade which made it look like a Bavarian village. One of the "village's townhouses" was a Kohl's, one was a shoe store, and the next was a Dollar Tree. The big one on the end was a Wegmans and the Safeway was gone. Dave couldn't even glance toward the new grocery store without thinking about how much Lisa loved Wegmans -- and how much of their money went to that enterprise. He really didn't resent that expense because he knew that his family of 3 was getting locally grown produce when possible, and nutritionally superior food choices -- and it wasn't any more money that he would have spent at Safeway. Lisa loved Wegmans for the same reasons but also because it was, in her mind, the land of abundance: everything she could want or need under one roof.

Both Dave and Lisa were happy with their choice of a place to raise their son. Dave would sometimes drive very slowly down the streets at his end of town, the area that was still spacious. He would play a game with himself where he would try to observe something he had never seen before, yet had always been there. He was trying to absorb his region into his mind, as a way of appreciating it. He wanted nothing more than to be able to stay here until Trevor moved on to his own house following his graduation from college. Today, these thoughts brought Dave back to idea of the importance of finding a way to continue to live here and live in the house they occupied. He needed his do-over.

Dave was usually an honest man but he understood enough about himself to know that his honesty was situational. If he needed or wanted something enough, he could easily move to the less-than-honest side of the road. Today he was on the not-at-all-honest side. Back in his office, he dug around in the file drawer reserved for the things he'd archived when his mother died, and added to more recently when his father died. There were myriad papers that needed to be kept, if only because the two surviving family members didn't know if they would be needed or not. These were all mixed in with documents that were definitely needed.

It took Dave about three minutes to locate his father's social security number and driver's license. He sat at his desk and set these items to the side. He turned to his keyboard and monitor and started to Google credit card companies. He wasn't sure what he was looking for; what does make a credit card company stand out when one is planning to scam them? Maybe it should be neither a big company nor a small one, yet definitely located out of state. He found one that he thought could work, it's not like he cared about annual fees or the like. He started to fill out the form but stopped when he got to the line asking for his address. He couldn't have new credit card things coming to his office address; it was the same as his home address and all that mail got mixed together for Lisa to sort out. He needed something separate for the new mail he'd be getting. That's when he got in his truck and drove to the post office. His do-over with a bank was about to begin, except this time it was with a credit card company.

Dave Shipway, or the reincarnated Weldon Shipway, found it particularly simple to suddenly feel like a resident of P.O. Box 221, Victory, PA. In spite of his address's lack of furniture, rooms and landscaping, utility bills and land taxes, he felt a mixture of excitement and trepidation about this new start. He went back to his office and completed a few credit card applications using his "new" social security number, name and address; when a physical address was required, he used his father's former address. Dave noticed that his hand shook slightly when he was using his father's credentials. He pushed ahead regardless of the message trickling up from his sub-conscience. Once the applications were done, he drove back to the Victory Post Office, purchased stamps, and dropped those applications into a mailbox in the parking lot. All three of the mail collection boxes, sitting in a row at the edge of the parking lot, were made of blue sheet metal, the pull down door of each one bearing a peel and stick label displaying the times when each box would be emptied. Within a few seconds, those do-overs were in the postal system, heading for their corporate destinations.

Dave's hands were still shaking so he decided to stop into the VVI. It was especially easy for him to justify his stop on this day because he felt he had made an important step toward solving the problem that got him making these stops in the first place. He had a second justification too, however, and that was that he knew he had just committed a crime, and he really didn't know much about the possible consequences. *When someone steals someone else's identity, what happens if the person isn't around to press charges? Or if the deceased's family isn't willing to press charges?* The scarier thoughts were about the seriousness of the crime. *If I mailed five applications, did I commit five crimes? Are they felonies or misdemeanors? ... Probably depended on how much money I used -- or misused.* He vowed to himself at that moment that he would not take more than $5,000 from the credit card companies and if at all possible, he would pay it back. *Maybe it would stop being a crime once I paid it back...* These thoughts got him through three double bourbons and two beers. As he stood to leave, he recognized the feeling of being intoxicated, but his hands were no longer shaking. He knew he should call Lisa for a ride but then he'd have to explain so much to her.

As he pulled into his driveway he side-swiped a garbage can. He retrieved the can after parking his truck. As he walked the can up to the house he made another vow to himself: no more getting drunk before dinner; no more drinking and driving - ever. *Imagine how it would hurt Trevor if I got arrested*, Dave thought. *And what if I hurt another person...*

Dave felt like he had to work very hard to seem normal -- or sober -- during dinner. He talked as little as possible and he tried to have food in his mouth at all times to confuse the question of whether or not he was slurring his words. Afterwards, he helped Trevor with homework while Lisa cleaned up. His head started to ache a half-hour into the homework. It was a hangover threatening him before he even got in bed. He needed to drink some water. While Trevor was doing some reading, Dave got up, got a glass from the cupboard by the sink, and, using the refrigerator door dispenser, put some ice cubes in it. He had gotten up for water, but the sound of the ice cubes in the glass reminded him he had other choices. He wouldn't have to worry what his breath smelled like if he were to sip on a new glass of bourbon. And it would postpone the hangover that was knocking at his skull. Before he even completed making the decision, he was pouring bourbon into his water glass. He made his third vow of the day: *I'll just have one, albeit a very large one.*

Later Dave regretted this decision. Usually all that booze would help him sleep, but this night just the opposite was true. When he first got in bed, it made him feel queasy to lay down, so he propped up some pillows and tried to read. After he read the same page three times, he had to give that up; a drunk with a book is still a drunk. He turned off the reading light and tried to just let sleep take over; thankfully, Lisa was sound asleep. His dark thoughts found their entry into his conscious thoughts. When he thought about the possible five felony convictions, his heart rate increased. He tried to will his brain to think about something else. He tried reciting silently the words to a song he liked in high school, "Another Day in Paradise" by Phil Collins. He kept loosing track of where he was and that seemed to invite other series of dark thoughts in. *What if Jay found out, what if Lisa found out? Am I really that dishonest?* If it were possible, Dave would have driven to the Victory Post Office and pulled those faked applications out of the mailbox at 3:30 a.m.

When the alarm went off the next morning, Dave was tempted to think he didn't sleep at all. The sound of the alarm jarred him though, and he had to stir to recognize the source of the noise, so he knew he had at least drifted into semi-consciousness. This was going to be a long day. His head really ached; not the mini-ache of the night before which had convinced him to - yes -

drink more bourbon. When he remembered the water versus bourbon fork in the road, he shook his head from side to side. *What was I thinking?*

His first vow of this new day was formed in his brain: *I will never do that again. I am a responsible adult; I have a wife and an extraordinary child relying on me. WTF...* He made a cup of coffee, poured a glass of water, and headed downstairs with both hands full. He had worked out a way months earlier where he could pull the stairway door closed using his elbow. Carrying coffee and water simultaneously was not new to him.

He set his beverages down and picked up his landline handset; he punched in the numbers on his phone that would play his voice mail messages for him. He also hit the speaker phone button so that he could continue to move about the office while listening to his calls. The first message was a company selling windows. The caller was obviously reading from a script. He canceled the speaker phone feature so that he could hit star-three, the combination that would skip the rest of the message and delete it. The second message held more promise, "Uh, hello." it was a deep, male voice, someone speaking very quietly and slowly, "I need help with my furnace. It hasn't run yet this year but I need it to." He cleared his throat, "My house is very cold." He followed that with a request for a call back, then his phone number. The third message was a vendor looking for payment. He hit star-three again, and then dialed the number left by the slow talking guy with a cold house.

The plan was that Dave would meet this guy who called himself Tom, at 10:00 a.m. at Tom's address. Dave wasn't certain where his address was but he knew it was near the further edge of town. He'd have to drive through his own area and then down the "Miracle Mile," the area with all the plazas and shops that was about three miles long, and get to the outskirts on that side of town. Apparently, the moniker Miracle Three Miles didn't roll off the tongue as well as the name the locals used for it. Dave's GPS showed him that Tom's cold house was really not even within the village limits. *What do I care,* Dave rhetorically asked himself, *a job is a job, as long as I can tolerate all the damn red lights between here and there.*

When the GPS announced his destination to be on the left, Dave pulled into the driveway of a very run down house. He pulled his tool box out with him but he needed to go to the back of his truck to get a few extra things. The heating system he was there to fix was a boiler; most of his calls were for gas forced air, so he needed to grab a few extra things. As he was shuffling through the tools in the larger box in the truck bed, he glanced up to the house and saw a curtain pulled to the side. As soon as Dave noticed the face, the curtain dropped back into place. *Well at least I know someone is home*, Dave advised his only remaining employee.

He carried the tool box up to the front door and rang the doorbell. Dave never heard the bell go off through the flimsy front door, but nonetheless the door opened almost before Dave took the pressure off the button. "Hi.... Come in." his greeter said that deep yet quiet voice; the owner of the voice kept his face directed toward the floor.

EARL 2

When Earl's third grandchild, Lauren, received his spur-of-the-moment gift, she asked, "Can I call Grandpa?" She looked up at her mother, "Please Mommy, this present is so great!" she turned the beanbag style stuffed animal over in her hand. It was pink and frilly, thereby fulfilling the primary characteristics of a desired object. "I have been wanting this one!"

Felicity was skeptical about whether or not this specific toy had made it on to her daughter's radar but she didn't care. She was so happy to have been given this chance to assist in the weaving together of her child's life with her father's. *Wow Dad, great move!* she thought. "Yes, of course you can call him, Lauren. Saying thank you for a present is a very good idea." Felicity dialed the number and handed the phone to her child.

That night Earl fell asleep with a smile on his face. His conversation with his granddaughter Lauren lifted his spirits higher than he thought was possible.

When grandchildren started to populate his world, he and Hope were very happy and proud. When they first started talking to the children, in person or on the phone, they often just shook their heads, unable to understand what the kids were saying. They had lost their ability to translate child-talk. When the kids called, Earl and Hope would set the phone to speaker-phone so they could help each other try to understand, if possible, what the children were saying. Frequently, after listening to a garbled statement heard over the phone line, they would look at each other, both raising their shoulders in a signal that they hadn't understood what the precious child had said. They would then take turns launching a new line of questions. They had learned that saying "What? What?" wasn't the way to go. It only resulted in the child's parent taking the phone from the child to do the translating. Simply asking a new question was a better way to manage the conversation. "What did you have for lunch today?" trumped "I'm sorry sweetie, what did you say?"

Now that the grandchildren were, for the most part, going to school, Earl's ability to communicate with them was vastly improved. His conversation with Lauren reminded Earl that he had it in his power to carve out relationships with these young people. He understood very clearly that Lauren was thrilled that he had thought of her and made the effort to send her something. *And it was so easy... And cheap!* he thought as he was hanging up the phone. Every piece of that transaction was pleasant for Earl, from spotting and buying the gift, to bringing it to the post office, to getting the thank-you phone call. As a whole, it was one of the brightest spots of his recent life. Earl felt he was on to something.

Two days later, he made a point to stop in to the local toy store to pick out something for Charity's two kids. This household had a 7-year old girl, Earl's first grandchild, and a 2-year old boy. He knew he would have to send tandem gifts to this house while the children were so young. He found another bean-bag style stuffed animal for the older child and a 6" football for the younger boy. He wanted each child to have a package to open so he found two small shipping boxes and packed each of them with a gift. He brought these two boxes to the post office. He waited in the line in front of the clerk that had helped him mail his first package. When it was his turn, the clerk, who's name tag said Sally, said, "Hello again!" Her smile was genuine, "Was your package from last week received?" Earl had explained that his first package was going to a grandchild as she had helped him get his address label and postage ready. Obviously she remembered, and Earl was glad.

"Yes!" Earl's smile took over his face. "I got a call the other night from my granddaughter. She was really excited about that silly little thing I sent." Earl raised his shoulders as if to say he didn't get it, but he was happy to go along with it. "So, I'm trying again with another daughter's kids." He looked at Sally, "Do you mind helping me again?"

"Mind? It might be the best part of my day!" Sally was naturally gregarious but she was also truly glad to help.

Earl pulled his wallet out of his back pocket. "I have the address here on a piece of paper." He started to thumb through several pieces of note paper he kept in there. "Here it is," he held up a piece of paper, the kind that is often found on a tablet with a magnet on the back, the top of each sheet might proclaim that "If it isn't on this list, you don't need me to buy it!" It was about two inches wide with a torn edge at the top.

Sally said, "Tell ya what, I'm going to let you write the address on this label, you want regular delivery, right?" She held up the white label with a blue border as she asked.

"Yes." Earl, the new student of postal protocol, answered crisply.

"Okay, so stick one of these on each package and then fill out the 'To' information and the 'From' information. Then I'll weigh them and we can talk about postage."

"Gotcha." Earl bent his head down to complete his task. He adjusted his glasses so that he could read the address he had recorded on his torn piece of tablet. He felt he was under pressure because of the people in line behind him and he started to fumble. In his moment of loss of composure he put the city name on the line meant for street address. He felt humiliation threaten to take over his feeling of pleasure. "Oh Sally," he said referring to her name tag, "I've messed this up..."

Sally noticed his change in demeanor and a tremor in the hand he was holding his pen with, "No problem! I wish I had a nickel for every label I had to re-do" She moved to clear off the far end of the counter. "Here, slide down here and have your own piece of postal real estate."

Earl glanced at the spot Sally was referring to, "Great." he glanced at the people behind him apologetically; "Sorry." he threw out to the group.

The woman immediately behind him smiled warmly and said, "No worries." Earl inhaled deeply as he slid his items to his new spot. He nodded thankfully to the smiling woman.

At his new spot at the end of the counter, Earl found a few extra labels that Sally had left for him, in the event of another mess-up. He didn't need them though. Now that he wasn't holding anyone else up, and Sally was free to help other customers, there was no pressure and Earl was able to transcribe the address written on the note paper onto the label. He completed the From section from memory. *Who can't write out their own address?* he said to himself when he started to feel glad that completing that part of the label needed no reference materials. *Foolish man.... Wasting this nice lady's time...*

Sally was back, "How are you doing?" She glanced at his packages, "You're doing great!" she answered her own question when she saw two completed labels.

"Sorry to hold you up, Sally." he used her name almost experimentally.

"Don't be crazy!" she shot back, "Mr. Ummm... Mr...." Sally was trying to garner his name by reading his label upside down.

"I'm Earl." he said as he reached his hand across the counter to offer a handshake introduction.

"Earl, hi, I'm Sally." she was smiling widely while moving his packages to the scale. "It's going to be $6.95 to mail these." Earl reached for the dollar bills in his wallet. "I hope you keep sending these packages Earl," Sally said. "The USPS needs the business and it's fun for me to help you."

"Well it does my heart good, so you'll probably see more of me." Earl replied.

"You are welcome to bring a pile of blank labels home with you, I mean, only if you'd be more comfortable filling them out there." Sally processed his transaction as she continued, "If not, you are welcome to write them out here. Just be sure to get in my line." Sally winked as she said this last part.

Earl had been particularly sensitive to human kindness since Hope's passing. His life prior to that time had allowed him to frequently overlook it simply because his life was easy. Once he had to face the loss of Hope, he was put in the position of counting on and hoping for instances of kindness. He had thought he had moved past this phase of vulnerability, but Sally's simple and easy way of making him comfortable hit home. He swallowed. In spite of his feeling of gratitude, his smile was a rictus, a mixture of happy, grateful, and very, very sad. There was a lump in his throat as he replied, "I'll see you soon, Sally. Thanks so much." He hoped Sally didn't know him well enough to recognize the thick emotion in his throat.

Two days later, he went mall-walking, something he did once a week for exercise. A handful of friends from the community center typically met up at an agreed-upon time, at the Starbucks kiosk near the mall's main entrance. The number of participants seemed to ebb and flow, as one would drop off, two would join in, or just the reverse. Earl's attendance over the past six months was about 85%, yet 100% of the participants were acquaintances of his. He made a point of ensuring that.

When he had first started mall-walking, he realized he needed socks and rubber-soled shoes, and felt some dismay when he didn't know where to go to buy these simple items; Hope had always taken care of that kind of thing. His daughter Dawn called Earl later that day though, so he asked her, "I need socks sweetie, and sneakers. Where should I go?"

Dawn heard the sound of a potential set-back in his recovery from grieving behind this question. She decided to keep it light and hope to help her beloved father to feel empowered. "You have a Kohl's right there, don't you Dad?"

"Yes I do, it's right in the plaza."

"I think you should start there. If you sign up while you're there, you'll start getting notices of their sales." Dawn offered. "What else do you need?"

"I don't need anything else and I probably won't wait for a sale on sneakers, I have walking to do now." Earl smiled and Dawn heard it.

Dawn giggled, "Okay Dad, I'm glad you're walking." She added, "but sign up anyway so that you can be picking things up as you need them. Okay?"

"You got it." Earl responded. The next day he went to Kohl's and found a pair of tan colored, rubber soled shoes that had a Velcro closure. He liked the color because he felt he could wear them as shoes or as athletic wear, and the Velcro made it so he didn't have to bend over very long; it was much quicker than tying laces. He tucked the box under his arm and headed toward the sock display.

There were so many options that Earl felt confused and a

little astounded; self-doubt threatened his buying experience. *Hold on amigo... Having choices is good... Just stand still and look around for a minute*, he instructed himself. There were white socks that came just to the ankle, white socks that came half-way up the calf, white socks that came up to the knee, and colored socks to match each of these options. Then there were trouser socks, *what are trouser socks?* ribbed socks, argyle socks, and there were still two racks he hadn't looked at yet. Just then, a white-haired woman with an energetic pace walked by. It may have been Earl's expression that inspired her to stop, as if on that proverbial dime. "Can I help you find something?" she asked with a smile. Her pink lipstick was an exact match to her turtleneck.

"Welp..." Earl pronounced 'well' as if it were spelled 'welp,' "my daughter suggested I get some socks here." He cleared his throat and pressed on, "I need some to wear with these shoes." he held the box out as if it could explain what type of socks he needed.

"You have a lot of choices." said the pink lipsticked lady.

"That's my problem." Earl replied.

The sales clerk began to understand the situation. "I recommend these." she said as she pointed to black socks sold in a package of three. The label touted a cushioned sole. "By choosing black, no dirt will ever show." again the smile.

"Sold!" Earl was so grateful that he didn't have to make the sock decision. Later that day, he thought, *gosh, good thing pink lipstick lady didn't work in the furniture department or someplace where things were expensive. My wallet might be suffering right now.*

When Earl got home from his successful shopping trip, he had a message on his recorder. He hadn't made the switch to voice-mail yet because he didn't understand where he would retrieve his messages from. His device that had Play, Rewind, and Erase buttons made perfect sense to him, and it had always been reliable. He saw the blinking light indicating a new message.

Earl didn't know it, but his girls had gotten a private three-way chuckle out of his use of a message machine. He was apparently reading its instructions intently when he made his outgoing recording. It went something like, "Hi, this is Earl and I can't get to the phone right now. Please leave me a message and I'll call back." then in his whisper-to-himself voice, "press star when your message is complete..." This last quiet sentence was followed by the tone that meant the outgoing message was complete, just as the instructions he was reading had promised.

Earl hit the Play button on his device, "Hi Grandpa, it's Linda," a young and happy voice pierced the air; Earl leaned closer to make sure he didn't miss a word. "I got a package from you today, please call me back so I can say thank you." Earl thought the message was over; he reached toward his recorder to hit a button just as the message continued, "I'm so excited about my new Beanie Baby. Thank you!" then a pause, "but please call me back even though I already just said thank you." He heard a quiet giggle "Bye!" He knew the message was definitely over at this point. Earl, smiling from ear to ear, reached over and hit Stop. He wasn't ready to use the Erase button for this message.

Earl pulled his wallet out of his back pocket and fished around for the piece of tablet paper that had his girls' phone numbers on it. It was especially dog-eared, so he looked for those rough edges. Once located, he turned to the phone and punched the one key followed by a 10-digit phone number.

The phone rang twice before it was picked up in Charity's

house. Before the phone's handset was up to the mouth of the answerer, Earl could hear Linda's voice saying "It's Grandpa! Mom! Caller ID says..." Linda seemed to realize that the handset was up to her mouth and ready for use, "Hello?" she had switched from yelling into the background to using a more mature tone for speaking on the phone.

Jokingly Earl said, "Is this Miss Linda?"

Giggling out loud now, Linda replied, "Yes Grandpa, it's me." Earl knew she was smiling.

"I had a message from your secretary, or was it from you..." Earl pretended to wonder.

"Grandpa! It was me!" Linda's laughter took on the tone of one who knows they're being teased.

"Oh! Okay, well how can I help you?" Earl continued his mock professionalism.

"Grandpa, I got a package from you and I love it!" Linda inserted a lot of drama into the end of this sentence. Earl was picturing her pirouetting around the kitchen.

"I am so glad you like it, Sweetie. I just saw that pink pony on the store shelf and it practically told me that it wanted to be yours."

"Grandpa, I did really need this one for my collection, and Nicholas loved his present too."

"Oh good," Earl had almost forgotten about Nicholas's gift. Nick didn't talk on the phone yet so Earl hadn't hoped to hear from him. "Has he played with it?"

"Oh yes, and he screamed when Mom made him put it down to eat his lunch."

Earl laughed out loud. "Well Sweetie it just makes my day to talk to you. I'm so glad you called."

"You're welcome Grandpa, ummm... I mean, thank you!" She burst out in another laugh. "Mom wants to talk to you, is that okay?"

"Oh I guess...." he tried to sound like he had been asked to go talk to the school principal.

Another giggle, "Here she is, bye Grandpa! I love you!"

Earl's throat filled with that thick feeling of emotion and his eyes filled with tears. He loved his grandchildren more than he had ever expected to, back when Charity announced her first pregnancy. And now that some of them were old enough to talk with him, he felt their love for him - this was something he had never thought to hope for. He tried to swallow and blink but Charity was on the phone talking to him before he was able to adequately shift gears. He was afraid she would worry if she heard his current emotional state in his voice, even though it was all good; it was a lot of love being felt by a vulnerable man. Earl coughed as if to make it seem like he had a tickle in his throat. He was buying time.

"Dad?" Charity questioned the noises she was hearing. "Are you okay?"

"Sorry honey,"" two forced coughs, "something went down the wrong tube." He continued to fake the clearing of his throat.

"Get a drink of water." his daughter demanded. Some panic was showing up in Charity's voice.

"I'm okay." Earl's charade had worked at buying him some time. His moment of being overwhelmed with his granddaughter's love had passed. "How are you, Sweetheart?"

"I'm fine, Dad. Dad, thanks so much for sending the gifts to the kids." She paused, "It was such a great surprise to find them in the mailbox... and one for each of them."

"It was my pleasure." The overused sentiment was entirely true for Earl.

"I am especially grateful that you picked gifts that were small yet definitely chosen for the individual kids." Charity's voice cracked, "It made them both feel very special."

"I'm glad it worked out, Charity."

They ended the call a few minutes later. Earl took in a few deep breaths as he walked around his living room-dining room area. He looked at pictures on the wall and in frames on the side tables. He felt euphoria but having no one to share it with seemed to truncate that. *Hope, our grandkids are so great!* he thought while looking at a picture taken of the two of them at their 20th wedding anniversary. His eyes were filled with tears again. He was sad that Hope hadn't gotten the chance to experience this while also still being so happy about his recent interchanges with his kids and grandkids.

His reverie turned into a fantasy conversation with Hope. "I'm going to sew some tiny outfits for the ponies and the Beanie Babies," Hope said, smiling in his imagination. "Pretty soon some of the kids may be interested in Barbies and then my sewing opportunities will multiply." Her imagined smile widened. "Maybe some of them will want me to teach them to sew, and then they can stay overnight; one at a time so that we can spoil them individually, Earl!"

Earl was jarred out of his thoughts by the phone ringing.

Who is calling me? His question contained some impatience. He wiped tears off his face.

"Hello?" Earl's phone voice didn't reveal any emotion.

"Hi Dad!"

His girls always knew they could count on Earl to know who was calling by their voice. The only other person who could do that was Hope. In fact, during their teen years when they went diving for the phone every time it rang, no outsider could accurately guess who had answered with any reliability.

"Hi Dawn!" Earl was instantly happy again.

"I just wanted to check in to see if you had been able to find socks and sneakers today."

"Nice of you to check in, although unnecessary..." Earl wondered if he seemed like he had become one of those doddering old people who had to go into a 'home' because they couldn't buy their own socks or otherwise care for themselves well enough.

"I just wondered, Dad" Dawn quickly followed up, "I was glad our conversation yesterday gave me a reason to call again today." She had found the right thing to say, just as her mother would have, and Earl stopped worrying about being doddering.

"As it turns out, I did get sneakers and I did get socks."

"Great! Did you have any trouble?"

"Nope. There was this nice lady with pink lipstick...." Earl intentionally dropped off at the end of his response.

"Dad! A lady with pink lipstick helped you buy shoes and

socks??!" Dawn was trying to not sound like she was smiling. "Was she an employee of the store?" She finished with an audible laugh.

"I'm not sure." Earl joked. "She was wearing a name tag but it's possible that she was another customer just roaming around looking for single men who needed help shopping."

"Well... I must say... I ummm... I think I'm glad I called you tonight." Dawn laughed.

"I'm doing just fine sweetie and I'm glad you called too. I think I'll go put my new sneakers on so I can walk around and break them in a bit before I meet all those young ladies at the mall tomorrow." Earl deadpanned.

Dawn hadn't realized she was being toyed with, "Your walking group is all young women?" as she asked it, the improbability registered with her. "Dad, you are so darn cute."

Earl changed the subject, "How are the kids?"

"Good!"

"What kind of things are they into these days?" Dawn's two were next on his list for gifting and Dawn didn't know it yet.

They chatted about her six and four year old, exchanged I-love-yous and got off the phone.

Earl tore into the package of new socks and pulled some on. Then he pulled his tan sneakers out of their box and, sitting in his recliner, pushed his feet in, one at a time. These purchases represented Earl's path to exercise and the socialization that came with that. He stood up and walked around his living room, looking down at the way his pant leg fell on top of the new shoes. He walked over to the sliding glass door in hopes of seeing a reflection of his lower legs from the same angle another person would see it. *Hmmm* he thought, *Hope, what do you think?* He asked the room. He waited but there was no answer. He felt the ache of loss trying to reenter his heart and he shut it out. *I guess I'll just have to see how the mall-walking ladies like my new foot wear.* He forced the joke onto himself. The fact that he had made a similar joke to Dawn earlier enabled him to enjoy his own humor. His shut-out was effective against that most recent insurgence of sadness.

ELAINE 2
1993

"No, I said turn left." Elaine wasn't afraid yet; she was just annoyed because he wasn't following her instructions. Thomas did not reply or even seem to have heard her. "Hey, you are going the wrong way Tim, or Tom or, what did you say your name is!?"

"Shut up" Thomas replied.

Elaine felt a palpable surge of terror slide down her torso and settle into her gut. "Where are you going?! What are you doing?! My father will kill you if you hurt me.... Stop the car!" she finally screamed at him.

"Shut up bitch or I'll hurt you right now." He sped up the car and took the next left which would lead them out of town. Elaine started pounding on his arm and shoulder but it didn't faze Thomas; he eventually raised his arm and backhanded her in the face. Elaine was so shocked that she fell silent, tears rolled down her face and she clutched the place where his hand had connected.

"Your pretty face looks a little different right now." Thomas chortled cruelly. He pulled the car over to the side of road. They had gotten far enough out of town that there was no other traffic. "Quit whimpering, you know you love attention, I can tell by the way you flaunt yourself all around that school - now you are getting some attention - from me."

"Please. Please don't hurt me." Elaine moved herself as close to the passenger door as she could. She could feel the handle against her back, it was an old car and the lever-style handle stood out from the upholstery of the door, it wasn't housed within an arm rest like the cars that were manufactured more recently. The smell within the car also indicated its age. The odor was almost tangy or pungent, a mixture of old rubber and old leather with an undercurrent of decay. There was an aspect of the odor that for a fleeting moment made Elaine wonder what might be in the trunk. The car's steering wheel was a circular ring with a smaller silver ring within it that Elaine thought was the horn. The wheel had a round wooden knob affixed to it - Elaine had seen a steering wheel accessory like this knob at an antique car show she went to with her father a few years ago - it was that knob that Thomas used to steer the car using only one hand, freeing up his right hand to provide the attention to Elaine that made her cry.

Just then, Elaine heard a car behind them; she resisted the urge to turn and look because she didn't want her captor to be aware of it if he wasn't already. Her instincts took over and she reached behind herself and pulled and pushed that handle until she tumbled out onto the ground. Thomas lost a second as his mind refused to accept that his hostage had gotten out from under his control. In that lost second, Elaine scrambled to her feet and ran to the middle of the road and waved frantically at the car that, by now, had gone past them. The driver, who happened to be looking in his mirror because of a debate he was having with his passenger over the make and year of Thomas's car, saw her wave and recognized her as the girl from school whom he wished he had the nerve to talk to. Brake lights came on, followed by white tail lights. They were backing up. Thomas opened his driver's door to try to block Elaine, she ran around the door as he got out of the car. "Bitch, get back here." he yelled in a tone that only a murderous madman could produce.

"Fuck you!" Elaine shouted over her shoulder as she reached the car of her saviors. "Help me!" she screamed toward the two high school seniors in the vehicle.

The newcomers did not realize that they had come across a crime in full swing. So the driver's first reaction was to laugh in order to play along with whatever the popular girl was trying to do. "Help me!" she screamed again, this time it was more fear-filled and husky; Elaine's throat would be sore the next day from that scream, but she'd be alive to experience that. The new tone was what made it clear to the rescuers that they were, in fact, going to rescue Elaine. Their switch into savior mode was instant. The driver got out and pushed Elaine into his car. Thomas was just feet away now but the two heroes were not afraid of him; they outnumbered and out-sized him, and there was no gun or weapon in sight so they ignored his orders to stop. Their car - since it had been manufactured within the current century - had power locks, which they deployed as soon as all three were inside. Elaine was clumsily straddling the center console as the driver hit the gas pedal. Elaine collapsed with relief and shock onto the passenger. "It's okay, you're okay. You're Elaine right?" Every male knew her name. "I'm Ted and you're going to be okay. Where do you want us to take you? Home?"

This was a rational question but Elaine was not yet able to be rational. She put her face into Ted's chest and cried. While patting her back and stroking her hair, Ted said, "Matt, let's just drive toward town. We better hide the beer though, just in case." Elaine's appearance on the road had interrupted their plan to get drunk on Genny Cream Ales outside of town.

"I'll pull over as soon as we are sure that fucktard isn't following us." Matt said as he continued to speed down this country road, checking his mirror frequently. A few minutes later, he reduced his speed to the posted speed limit. He pulled the car over to the side and stopped. Matt reached into the backseat and lifted out the twelve pack. He got out of the car and put it in the trunk. As he got back in, he extended his hand to Elaine and said, "Hello, I'm Matt." He smiled to try to help her calm herself; she was now sharing the seat with Ted, the two tightly wedged into the bucket seat. Elaine accepted his hand and she shook it. In a shaky voice she returned his greeting. Matt asked,

"Elaine, what was going on back there?"

The simplicity and validity of the question brought Elaine back to reality and her crying began again. Through her sobs she said, "He was going to hurt me... he hit me... he's crazy." her words formed a jagged sentence and the realization of the seriousness of the event registered to the three of them. Matt and Ted looked at each other over the top of Elaine's trembling head. Matt enlarged his eyes and tipped his head slightly in order to wordlessly ask Ted what they should do.

"Let's take her to her house," Ted suggested. "I really feel like we have to find her parents."

An hour later, Elaine was sitting on her living room couch being interviewed by a soft-spoken police woman. Elaine's father was in the kitchen talking with the woman's male counterpart. "How did you end up in his car?" she asked Elaine.

"I was walking home from school... I was freezing... He offered me a ride"

"Was this at school?"

"No I was on Prescott, on my way home, he pulled over and rolled down his window." Elaine was crying again. She felt so stupid and so afraid.

"So you voluntarily got in his car?"

"Yes." Elaine was wringing a tissue into shredded knots with both hands. In the kitchen, two male voices murmured quietly. Elaine's father was making an argument for an immediate arrest.

At the completion of her interview, the police officer joined the men in the kitchen. She said "We can't pursue kidnapping, but we've got unlawful imprisonment and aggravated assault."

"What about attempted murder?" Elaine's father asked in an elevated tone.

The male cop replied, "Mr. Simmons, we will be as aggressive as we can with charges, please don't worry about that. We do, however, have to stay within reason in order to be taken seriously by a judge."

"That's right ,Mr. Simmons." The female cop continued, "Now that I have the details nailed down, I'm confident that we will have an arrest tonight. We will call you once he's picked up so you can rest more easily."

Later that evening, Thomas was taken into custody. Elaine didn't sleep well that night, but Thomas's mother Betty slept well for the first time in many years. It was very hard for her to watch her son be handcuffed and marched to the backseat of the waiting police cruiser, but her sadness was buffered by a feeling of inevitability. Her subconscious was aware that it was only a matter of time before he would be caught doing something illegal. She even had a moment of relief as her conscious mind registered that at least no one had died. Yet.

KATE 2

When Kate was pulling up to the plaza that contained the post office, she noticed that the flag they were flying was much larger than the usual flag found at a post office or typical federal facility. Then she remembered that the building used to be a Perkins Restaurant. Perkins always flew such gigantic flags, and Kate made a bet with herself that this post office was flying a flag that 'came with the building.' She pictured the real estate listing and laughed at herself when she thought, *Free flag with every building!*

Kate went inside the former Perkins building to buy a stamp and arrange to rent a P.O. Box. Looking around, she was surprised at how many people were at the post office. *I could do everything required to mail anything I want, from my office. Why do so many people use the brick and mortar USPS structure?* Kate wondered, *Do they not have internet access? Maybe they don't have a printer....* Kate's only reason for driving to the post office was privacy; she didn't want her coworkers to see where she was sending mail. *What are the other reasons people need to physically come here??* Kate was curious in spite of her all-consuming distraction.

As she waited for her turn, she looked around at the other patrons, trying to get some insight into their need to be there. The number of senior citizens seemed to be about the same as in the general population, so it wasn't just a simple lack of technical skills that populated this facility. In fact, the other people milling about seemed to be a cross-section of society in general. When it was her turn, her hands shook as she completed the paperwork necessary for renting a P.O. Box. Her curiosity about the other patrons forgotten; thoughts of Michael taking over, causing the white noise in her head to increase in volume. A few minutes later, she was a tenant of P.O. Box 220, Victory, PA, and she had the stamp she needed to mail her first letter to Michael; one that had a jail address on the front of the envelope.

A few days later, Kate started getting phone calls from a number she didn't recognize. It was an 800 number and she thought it was probably Michael. She didn't answer. She didn't want to talk on the phone with him; she wanted to get a letter from him. Kate got confirmation from Michael's girlfriend that the number that had been showing up on her cell's caller ID was in fact, the inmate phone call service used by the county jail where Michael was. During their conversation, Amanda asked Kate again if she wanted to talk to Michael. "I sent him a letter and I want to know his response to my questions, but I am hoping to read his answer."

Later that night, Kate was lying in bed trying to read but the knowledge that Michael had been reaching out to her began to haunt her. The memory of each call seemed like a ghostly tentacle reaching for and sweeping over her heart. The weeks that had gone by since the day Michael had been arrested had allowed for feelings to accumulate in the same place, so her heart was overloaded. She started to cry, and one tear lead to three tears, three led to nine, and within minutes the tidal wave of sorrow she had been denying was making its way out of her eyes; her lungs and vocal chords were caught up in the surge.

Tim heard noises he didn't recognize as he sat in the living room of their home watching football. He got up and went into the bedroom he shared with his wife; he found her doubled up, knees to chin, in their bed with mascara running down the rivers that had formed on her cheeks. "What's wrong?! What happened?" He was terrified.

Slowly rocking her body forward and backward, she said between sobs, "It's Michael."

"What happened?!" Tim's eyes were wide, mistakenly thinking something had happened to him.

"I just miss him SO much." Kate choked out.

Tim sat down beside Kate. "I think you should plan to visit him." Chandra had suggested this too, so Tim's suggestion meant that two people Kate respected were giving her the same advice. The thought of being in the same room with Michael, even if it was in the county jail, made Kate start to feel a little better. Her sobbing slowed down and she made herself take a few deep breaths. One of the reasons she hadn't wanted to visit Michael was because she didn't want to offer him her support, at least not yet. The last words between them were still the words he texted to her the night he left her house after Kate confronted him with evidence of his drug use. But thinking about visiting him for her own sake was different.

Kate finally fell asleep considering the possibility of visiting Michael. The next day, the inmate phone calling system number showed up on her caller ID and she decided to answer it. By now, Michael has her letter and he must be trying to respond to her questions. She pushed the green button on her phone's screen. "Hello?"

An automated system informed her that she was getting a call from an inmate named Michael. The word Michael was spoken in Michael's voice, dubbed into the mechanical speech of the phone system. Kate started to shake all over. The recorded voice was giving her instructions on how she could accept and pay for the call. Kate started to walk toward her purse, assuming a credit card was going to be needed. She pulled her wallet out of her purse with her free hand and as she turned to go back to the other room, she knocked her purse off the counter, spilling its contents all over her kitchen floor. Coins, lipsticks, breath mints, and ibuprofen tablets went rolling in all directions. For a moment her kitchen sounded like a pinball machine: ping, bang, clatter-clatter-clatter ... cha-chiiiing-pop.... The final sound was made by a tube of chap-stick that was both spinning and rolling when it came to rest at the base of her refrigerator.

When Kate turned her attention back to her phone, the Stepford-Wife voice planting instructions into Kate's ear was saying, "Key pound one to indicate that you will pay for this call, pound two if you wish to stop receiving calls from this number. Kate's phone had a virtual keyboard that appeared when she shook her phone so she gave it a shake. *Key pound one,* she reminded herself, and as she followed these instructions she remembered that her virtual one key hadn't worked in quite some time. Instead of functioning as a number key, it shut her screen down and today was not going to be the exception. She shook her phone again to bring the keypad back up. She knew there was a sweet-spot in the square representing the number one but she had to tap it very lightly for it to work as a number key. Her hands were shaking badly, and the sweet-spot was right next to the line between the number one and the number two. If she hit pound two, she would be telling the automated system that she didn't want calls from this number again. *Focus Kate!* She made herself stare at the spot on her keypad that she had to try to tap ever so lightly. She was very glad no one was around to see her trying to use her shaking hands. She tapped the spot in the upper right corner of the one's square. Her screen shut down again. Kate shook her phone and tapped again; no luck. After the fourth set of shake-taps, Kate was told by an emotion-free voice that her call had timed out. Kate sat on the edge of her bed and cried. She had crossed the emotional hurdle of deciding to talk to Michael and then was unable to complete her piece of the work to follow through with it. The sorrow from the night before came back quickly. It was as if sadness knew the route to her heart now, so making its return visit was very easy, perhaps even convenient. Adding to her sadness was not knowing what her attempt to take Michael's call had sounded like to Michael. Was he hearing the same instructions she was? Or was he being told that the target for his call wasn't fulfilling instructions after having picked up the call? Was he hearing tinny music intended to help him stay patient in his knowledge that the call was still connected?

Just then Kate's phone rang again. It was the same number. Kate answered and the mechanical voice began its instructions again. This time Kate had her credit card in her hand so she stayed sitting where she was. Instructions she hadn't been able to listen to before, because of the cacophony of purse contents spewing about her kitchen, gave her information on how to register with a certain website where she could prepay so that she could accept a call without all the work of keying in numbers. She hunted for a pen and paper and was successful with the first drawer she opened. She noted the website address just as the voice was telling her to key pound one to indicate that she intended to pay for the call, pound two to stop receiving... Kate hit pound one and it worked this time. Kate exhaled. The voice continued, "Key one if your card is a Visa, key two if your card is a MasterCard, key three..." Kate looked at her card with renewed, unnecessary panic, *oh, thank the goddess for MasterCard.* She wasn't going to need to key a one. She hit the two and the voice continued, "Please enter your sixteen digit card number." Kate's hands were still shaking but she was able to enter her card number. Next the voice asked for her card's expiration month and year. Kate looked back to her card. The date was stamped into an area of the card that had a decorative picture on it. It was a particularly busy area of the picture and Kate couldn't make out the year. She looked around quickly for her reading glasses but couldn't find them. Afraid of timing out again, she took a guess. She knew the month was 09 and she followed that with two digit year of 14. The voice: "Please hold while we process your card." Now Kate was listening to tinny music. It was roughly eight measures of music that played in a loop; over and over she heard the same tune before the voice came back. "We are sorry, your card has not been accepted. Good bye."

129

Kate slumped where she sat. *Do you even believe that?*!
She said to Tim, who wasn't home. Kate breathed deeply.
She decided to focus on the website address she had
written down. To key that into her laptop's browser, she
would again need her glasses, so she headed toward her
purse where she always kept a spare pair. As she entered
the kitchen, a loud crunch reminded her of the mess she
had left the last time she was there. Kate had stepped on a
breath mint. She raked up the former contents of her purse
then grabbed her dustpan and whisk broom. After using
that to sweep up the white powder that used to be a mint,
she found her glasses and went to her laptop to browse to
the web address she had noted.

Kate was much more comfortable working with a website
than she was with the humanless voice of monotonized
instructions with time-out time bombs planted who-
knows-where. She filled in the blanks using her Tab key to
jump from the Name field to Street Address and on to
Phone Number, noticing that her hands weren't shaking as
much now. When she came to the point where she needed
to plug in her credit card number and select the number of
minutes she wanted to prepay for, she pulled her card back
out of her pocket. With her glasses on, she keyed in her
card number and then looked at her expiration date. Her
card expired 09/15. She had guessed the expiration date
incorrectly earlier. She keyed that in and within seconds,
was rewarded with a pop-up telling her that her card had
been accepted and she was now free to receive calls from
prison inmates. *Woo-hoo! I can get calls from prison
inmates!* Kate joked with herself. *Inmate. Singular. I wish
they had said inmate,* she jokingly poked at herself.

Now she wanted Michael to call again. Again she was
wondering what Michael's side of these calls had sounded
like to him. She wanted to explain the various flaming
hoops she had jumped through to speak with him, but even
more so, she wanted to hear his responses to the questions
and statements she had mailed to him.

It was a few hours later when Michael made his next attempt to call his mother. When Kate saw the number she started to shake again and she hit the wrong button for answering a call, accidentally hanging up on it. This time Michael was able to call right back, so as Kate steadied herself, she got the next call and correctly answered her phone. "Mom?" it was Michael's voice.

Kate felt the tears flood her, "Hi baby." She crumpled into a chair in her dining room, her face instantly wet.

Michael started the conversation, "Hey, I umm... wanted to say hi and let you know what's going on with me."

Kate was emotionally overdrawn, but she couldn't accept Michael's introduction to their conversation. He had been shitty to her the last time they spoke and now he was selfishly offering to bring her up to date on *his* situation. "Michael." She interrupted him, "Is that really what you want to say to me right now?"

"No. It's not." Michael paused. "I need to tell you that I'm really sorry for how I spoke to you."

"Anything else?" Kate asked.

"Yes. I love you and I miss you and I was really wrong to talk to you that way. Please tell me how you are. I'm worried about you."

Michael's concern for Kate melted the ice she had been trying to protect herself with. "I'm okay but I am not good." Kate was trying to be honest and informative. "I worry about you all day, every day. I don't even dare hope this will be the last time you get in trouble." She finished with, "What the fuck were you thinking?! You were already on probation for selling drugs??!"

"I wasn't really on probation, they just said that."

"Michael, stop. Did you get my letter?" Kate was getting

angry.

"Yes." he said.

"Then you know I'm insisting on absolute honesty if we are going to try to have a relationship." Kate felt sad but strong. She knew she had to restart their relationship on terms she would be satisfied with.

"Well I wasn't going to be on probation until after my next court date." Michael explained.

"Michael, you had been arrested and then got arrested again, right?"

Michael murmured an affirmation.

"The rest is splitting hairs. I need honesty from you if we are going to be speaking with each other." Kate wanted to finish this necessary piece of their conversation so that they could use their time to talk about how her son was holding up.

"Okay... Okay." Michael wanted to be finished with this too.

"Okay then. How are you doing?" Kate let her love for her son be heard in her question.

"I'm okay. I'm looking forward to the 31st when I go back to court. I hope you can come that day."

"It's a little too soon in our new relationship for you to ask me that." Back on defense, she said this as if the word 'new' were in sarcastic finger-bending, air-quotation marks.

"Okay, but it would give me a chance to see you and see how I think you're doing." That melted the rest of Kate's ice shield.

"I'll think about it." she replied. "How are you doing? Is

there enough to eat?"

"I'm okay; and no, there isn't enough food. We eat dinner at 3:00 and that has to last until breakfast."

Kate groaned. For some reason that she was never able to identify, the thought of her children being hungry or not getting needed nutrition pushed her emotional buttons. "Is there any fruit? Or vegetables?"

"No, there's a lot of starch. I get 2 pieces of bologna most days at lunch though so I guess I'm getting meat." He added, "Sometimes at breakfast there's a little cup of fruit cocktail, the kind of cup you get from a restaurant when you order your salad dressing on the side."

Just as Kate was about to lament this inhumane treatment, a voice cut into their conversation, "you have 30 seconds left on your call"

"Oh my god, you're kidding! How long do we get?" Kate was balancing a lot of emotions at this moment - relieved to hear Michael's voice, dismayed at his circumstances, glad that they were on their way to being able to talk to each other again, joyous at his ability to say some of the things she needed to hear - but now it all had to get wrapped up in 30 seconds.

"Twelve minutes. I can call you again though."

"Can you call me tomorrow? I need to know more things about your situation." Kate tried to not sound desperate.

"What time?"

The next day would be Sunday. "Morning is best but any time is good."

"Okay, I'll call you as soon as the phone is free. Mom?"

"Yes?" Kate was crying again and trying to hide it.

"I love you. You have been such a good mother to me and I am really sorry for what has happened."

"I love you t --"

"Your call is now complete. Good bye." Kate stared at her phone. Looking into its glossy surface, she tried to make sense of her feelings.

Kate was sitting in her dining room trying to mentally swim through the emotions that felt like river currents swirling around in her head. One emotion percolated up to the surface of her awareness - it was relief. Her need to keep a distance between herself and her son was over. The very unnatural separation of mother and son was over. Kate went looking for Tim to tell him she had spoken with Michael. That night she fell asleep easily but was awake by 2:00 a.m. Kate's subconscious was forcing her to face the reality of Michael's future, both near and distant. She sat up in bed, desperate to think of what her son might be able to do for a living with his felony convictions on his record.

Kate recalled a very helpful tip from Chandra; she had said, "when you are at peace or seeking peace and Michael's situation threatens to change the place you are in, picture him as a cloud that passes over your peaceful picture." Chandra was very genuine with her interest in helping Kate, "Do you know what I mean?"

Kate replied, "When I need peace, I can picture a sky or a horizon. If thoughts of Michael," she paused, "...or his situation, try to invade my thoughts, I'll encapsulate him into a cloud and let that float on by, in my imagination."

"Right!" Chandra encouraged. "And even if you're at work or just trying to watch TV and the thoughts try to enter your conscience, do the same thing." Kate nodded as Chandra continued, "Because you acknowledge being unable to do anything to help him, so you should be able to be guilt-free about letting him float over in a cloud, in order to take care of yourself." Kate looked at Chandra, breathing deeply.

"I really can't do anything for him at this point." Kate said almost to herself.

"That's right, you can't. But you can take care of your daughter Toni by taking care of yourself." Chandra knew how important Toni and Toni's education were to Kate. "Michael can be your clouds and Toni can be your horizon... for now." Chandra looked directly into Kate's eyes, waiting for agreement, or questions, or rebuttal.

Kate sat back, absorbing the words, wanting to think of what her challenges to this concept might be before her hour was over. Kate trusted Chandra to accept any possible response. She glanced at Chandra's filing cabinet while she thought through this new suggestion. On it was a magnet that in a fancy scroll said, *Don't believe everything you think.* Kate appreciated Chandra's suggestion and she told her so. She appreciated the magnet almost as much; she thought about people like her nephew and one of her childhood friends, who suffered through paranoia, which was a very real fact of life for them.

"I think I can use that visual. Thank you." Kate stood to leave, knowing her time was up. She shook Chandra's hand with both of hers. She tried to infuse warmth into the handshake so that Chandra would feel how much Kate valued their time together.

Now that Kate couldn't sleep, she called on the suggested visual. Kate lay back down and pictured a mountain range with a blue sky behind it. She pictured Michael's situation wrapped up neatly into a cloud and before Kate could watch it pass into the left side of her mental image she was asleep again.

The next day around 9:00 a.m., Michael called again. "Hi

sweetie" Kate said when she answered the phone.

"You are getting a call from," pause... "Michael." again in Michael's voice dubbed in. "Please stay on the line if you wish to speak with this inmate." Kate was only a little embarrassed to have personally and incorrectly greeted this mechanical system. Kate was driving home from a Zumba class so she pulled off the road at the next safe spot, so that she could focus on her next 12 minutes with her incarcerated son. She was putting her transmission in park when she heard the next directive. "You will be connected to your caller now."

"Hello?" Michael's voice.

"Hi sweetie." Kate settled into her car's bucket seat.

"How are you today?" Michael was making conversation as he waited to see if his mother had an agenda for their second chat.

"I'm a little better than yesterday." She smiled at her own awareness of improvement. "How are you?"

"I'm okay, thanks. A little bored but I am safe and I'm okay."

Kate followed up, "What do you do with all your time?"

"I read as much as possible but I've read almost everything they have here." Michael cleared his throat in the same way his father always had.

"Are you allowed to get books?" Kate asked.

"Why yes, I can. They have to be paperbacks and they have to come directly from Amazon but I can get them." Kate was trying to make the mental note to consider sending him some books when Michael followed with, "It would be great if you sent me one or two." She could hear Michael's manipulative smile.

"I might." Kate said. "Hey, can you exercise at all?" Kate wanted to know but, even more, she wanted to duck the manipulation.

"I've been doing pushups in my cell. I've gained 20 pounds since being here."

"Wow, that's good, I think. You were getting pretty skinny." Kate observed. At the same moment, she wondered why she hadn't worried about that before. That should have been a clue that her son was involved in drugs. "So tell me what you know about your legal situation."

"Well," Michael began, "as I told you yesterday, I go to court on the 31st. I'm not sure what will happen that day; I'm hoping to hear from my lawyer before then."

Kate thought *Lawyer? Must be a public defender.* Aloud she said, "I see, and how often can you make phone calls?"

"As often as I want, I just have to wait for the phone to be free."

"And what kind of things can you have sent to you there besides books?" Kate asked.

"That's all." Michael replied. "We have to get money through commissary, then that can be used to buy anything else I need. Amanda has put money in that for me so I bought snacks so I'd have something to eat at night."

"What did you buy?" Kate wondered.

"I'm starving all the time here, so I bought packages of cookies because they had the largest number of milligrams in each package for the same amount of money as everything else." Michael went on to tell her about the other things available for sale; all the food was junk food.

Kate felt anxiety rising up inside her. Thinking about her child being hungry and being given foods that only made a small contribution to his nutritional requirements was torture. She wrapped that up in a cloud and sent the thought on its way toward stage left as she listened to him talk about the personal care products that were also available. Apparently he went several weeks without having shampoo and soap. *He is being punished and he deserves to be punished,* Kate reminded herself. She took her thoughts about dandruff and body odor and wrapped those in another cloud.

"I told Amanda that I would help to take care of Bruiser, financially speaking." Kate told Michael. Bruiser was a 100-pound pit bull that Michael had had for almost ten years. Kate was unwilling to help Michael financially, but she felt that helping with Bruiser fit with her values, therefore, that made her feel better.

"Oh great, thank you," Michael replied. "and so, if I really do get three years or something crazy like that, I'm going to apply for this thing they call shock, it's a six-month program that replaces three years of prison time. It's for non-violent offenders whose problems are around addiction."

"You have 30 seconds left on your call."

"Oh my god, that went by so fast, I need to hear more about this thing you're telling me." Kate said in desperation.

"When can I call you again?" Michael asked.

"How about Wednesday?" Kate replied.

"I'm very busy that day, Mom" Michael joked. A single laugh burst from Kate. Michael continued, "I'll call you Wednesday after you get out of work."

Kate's laugh had made her feel better, like steam had been released from the pressure-cooker of her emotions. "Okay sweetie. I love you."

"Mom?" Michael's tone was serious.

"Yes?" Kate was all ears for the next sentence, her laughter forgotten.

"I love you so much and I'm just so sorry about how I treated you." Michael choked up on the last few words.

Kate's heart broke, "Let's talk about that more on Wed-"

"Your call is now complete. Good bye."

Again Kate looked at her phone as if it were the rude, offensive object causing her frustration. She shook her head as she gazed into its shiny face. She was beginning to understand that once someone was in the criminal justice system, that person and their loved ones lost control over the situation.

Kate did not know how she would have survived this loss of control if it hadn't been for Toni. Toni had always been a mother's-dream-come-true. When she was first born, Kate wondered how the other mothers managed to settle for having regular babies when babies like Toni were possible. At about the time Toni turned one, Kate learned she was pregnant for their second child. She was thrilled and she knew enough to be grateful for two pregnancies that were not accidents; indeed, they were very much wanted pregnancies. She did however, say to herself, *I'm happy about this second child, just don't expect me to love it anywhere near as much as I love my daughter. It's just not possible.* Of course she did love this second child just as much, but it was a different love. Kate grew to believe that if she had ten children, she'd have ten brands of love. Kate's love for Toni was an exquisite brand while her love for Michael felt gigantic, and undying - defying her sensibilities.

Thirteen years later, Michael required more of Kate's time than Toni did. Starting with meeting with the principal, then school administrators to discuss his pot smoking, then, within a year, she was attending substance abuse programs, and that transitioned into meetings with county workers who helped her to get Michael into the PINS program. Soon, Michael had graduated to intense outpatient drug treatment which required Kate to drive him 20 miles away three days per week after work. The program lasted two hours each day, not enough time for her to return home, yet too much time for her to sit in the car and wait. Kate saved up her money and bought a bike and bike rack. This saving took longer than it should have because when she was putting the sixth twenty dollar bill in her jewelry box, she found her $100 had been reduced to twenty dollars. Her thief wasn't smart enough to take all five bills, making her think she may have misplaced her stash. Instead, in a distorted example of kindness, her thief left her one of her saved bills.

Kate did eventually buy a bike and a bike rack, the latter clipped into the trailer hitch of her red VW Jetta. She started riding her bike during Michael's two-hour sessions; she rode about 20 miles each time. One of her friends had loaned her a gauge that monitored her speed and mileage; she would use that to challenge herself to increase her average speed each time she set out. By the time Michael failed out of this program by means of dirty drug tests, Kate had lost 10 pounds and was well on her way to having defined muscles in her legs and arms. Meanwhile, Toni kept her nose to the grindstone and was working part time and finishing high school with honors, with very little help from Kate.

As Toni graduated from high school, Michael graduated to inpatient treatment. Kate took him out of school and transported him to a program outside of Philadelphia where he would live for six months under the supervision of trained drug counselors and educators. Toni stayed strong and reliable and loving, making it easier for Kate to survive what, in hindsight ten years later, would seem comparatively very simple, yet at the time, was very difficult.

As Toni grew into a young woman, Kate was proud to see that she had a very clear sense of justice, and she possessed wisdom beyond her years. Kate enjoyed every single minute of the time they had together. Once Kate had gotten to a point of financial comfort - meaning she was able to pay all her bills, had no credit card debt and sometimes had a little extra cash at the end of the month - she and Toni would go the local Clothing Bug. At this store, stylish clothes could be found for not a lot of money. They would play a game called DPM, which stood for dollars per minute. It would start by Kate stating how much they could spend. Then the two of them would each enter the store and as quickly as possible find, and try on when necessary, desirable items that would cost a total of half of Kate's declared amount. Sometimes when Kate didn't need anything new, she would let Toni spend all of the declared amount. Once they were finished at the register, Kate would check the time, do the math and announce the DPM. They always tried to top the results from the previous time. Since Kate hated shopping and Toni loved new clothes, this game suited the two of them perfectly.

When Toni moved out and lived on her own, she would visit Kate at least once a week. At first, Toni didn't have a washer and dryer so she would pack up all her laundry and go to Kate and Tim's house. On these evenings they would cook together, developing new ways to make low calorie, nutritious, yet tasty dishes - or they would play card games or board games. Kate hoped Toni never got her own washer and dryer, but inevitably she did. Kate was filled with joy when she saw that their weekly visits did not change as a result. Toni still visited, sometimes with her boyfriend Bill and sometimes solo.

It was during the solo visits that Toni would confide in Kate the things going on in her life. She would lean on

Kate's sage side. Finding Kate to be uplifting and helpful, Toni would tell her friends, "You should really talk to my Mama about that," when her friends needed advice or just to talk. Toni called her mother 'Mama' even after she herself was an adult woman and she seldom missed a chance to say, "You are the best Mama ever."

Toni was Kate's rock, and Kate was Toni's. Kate wondered about the other mothers who had to settle for having ordinary adult daughters.

THOMAS 3

Thomas had forgotten one of the rules of experimentation: don't take chances if there are circumstances you can't be in control of, and especially not if they have potential serious consequences. This was a second cousin to his rule about cleaning up after an experiment - but the former was a rule of the 'before' sort, and he didn't yet have the maturity to control all of the 'before' pieces. His pathetic, spur of the moment attempt to abduct Elaine in high school, as an example, had serious consequences for Thomas.

After a not very speedy arraignment, which was highlighted by a court appointed lawyer's advice to plead not guilty to aggravated assault and unlawful imprisonment, he was returned to the county lock up. His stay there lasted until his even-less-speedy trial which was punctuated by adjournments and postponements. All in all, his mother's initial break from her adopted reality named Thomas, lasted six months. When the judge pronounced the 17 year old guilty, she watched him walk away in handcuffs again; this time a one-year sentence defined her second break. He was sentenced to a year in the Montgomery County Youth Center.

The county transport bus delivered Thomas to a backdoor of the facility. He was handcuffed, and the white lettering on his shirt still declared him to be an inmate of Alleghany County Jail. The next days were a blur for him because, since the facility prided itself on its psychological evaluations, that came first. The testing and interviews were one of Thomas's least favorite ways to spend time. A very patient man explained to Thomas that this was in his best interest. If there was something going on with him that could be treated either therapeutically or medicinally then that would make the rest of Thomas's life much better, once figured out. Thomas sighed deeply in acknowledgment while thinking: *I'll never let you in*. His need for control, included controlling what he revealed of himself. *You can look inside me but you will find nothing.*

The MCYC, as the staff referred to it, often recommended transfers of its inmates to more appropriate treatment facilities, once more was known about them psychologically. In Thomas's case, it was determined that he would serve out his one-year sentence with them. He was put in an area that housed about 30 other young men. No one involved in placement decisions ever admitted that they just didn't know what to do with Thomas.

Thomas, along with most of the staff of the MCYC, was just watching the calendar for the completion of his 12-month sentence. During the eleventh month, social services contacted Thomas's mother Betty to request a meeting. The topic was, what to do with Thomas on his release. Betty arrived at the appointment 5 minutes ahead of time. After speaking her name through a small stainless steel grate in the large glass window, she sat with her purse on her lap, staring at the floor. She could not imagine how she could go back to having Thomas live in her home. She was still jumping at sounds and worrying each time the phone rang. A door opened and a woman holding a manila folder close to her chest spoke her name.

Betty followed this tall woman into her small office. "Mrs. Findlay, we need to talk about Thomas." Betty nodded in acknowledgment of the topic at hand. The social worker continued, "He'll be released next month. Have you thought about that?"

Betty cleared her throat; she held one hand with the other in the event they were shaking, "Yes, I've been watching the calendar."

"Have you been in communication with him during his incarceration? They allow visitors there on Sunday."

"No I haven't. We did not have a very close relationship when he was arrested." Betty said.

"Well, I need to dig into a potentially uncomfortable subject, Mrs. Findlay."

Betty thought, *I'm very used to being uncomfortable so just get going.* The words she spoke aloud were "Please, go ahead."

"Mrs. Findlay, I know that Thomas was adopted, and I can see by the records provided by Catholic Charities program that you've needed help with him from a very early age." Betty nodded her agreement with the facts, so the social worker continued, "If you don't object, we would like to help Thomas start the process of applying for the U.S. Army. He will not have a criminal record when he is released. He will have served his time and his record will be erased, so we see this as an opportunity for him to live a normal life while still having the benefit of a structured lifestyle."

Betty's relief at hearing this suggestion was huge. She started her response, "Is it possible that he could go straight from the youth center to the Army?"

"Thomas is a unique case for us Mrs. Findlay, so we don't really know that answer. In a best case scenario, yes. But it's possible that it will take longer than the 6 weeks we have." Betty took a deep breath; her concern was obvious. "Please allow me to ask a blunt question."

Betty shook her head in agreement, "Please do." So far Betty had appreciated the more blunt points of this conversation.

"Would you recommend that we look for a half-way house for Thomas, for the period of time between his release and his potential induction into the Army?"

Tears slid down Betty's cheeks as she nodded, indicating yes. When Thomas was pronounced guilty a year ago, she thought that was the final stage of her failure as a mother, but there was one more step. She was moving her head up and down, in an indication of an affirmative answer to the social worker. Her question was yet one more opportunity for Betty to fail, and she was doing it.

The social worker was on the more astute and kind end of her group of colleagues. "Mrs. Findlay, there is only a certain percentage of a child's development that we can influence. In some cases, that percentage is very small. From what I have seen of the world, you have done a great service to our community by raising Thomas to the best of your abilities."

It was hard for Betty to speak; she was still trying to swallow the failure of the prior minutes. "Do I need to sign anything?" Betty choked out.

"No, I'll get in touch as soon as I know anything more." The social worker touched Betty's arm in a gesture of kindness, "You can rest well knowing that we will do all we can to transition him as quickly as possible. If anything changes in his location or disposition, I'll call you personally."

Betty picked up on a potential hidden sub-topic. She turned quickly to the woman, "If he's released before arrangements can be made, you'll let me know?" Betty's fear and panic were ineffectively veiled.

"Yes. I will personally call you if anything changes."

More tears escaped Betty's eyes as she realized that this woman was clearly aware of how pathetic her situation was.

DAVE 3

Once inside Tom's house, Dave tried to create a tone he himself would be more comfortable working around, "Hi, I'm Dave let's get a look at that boiler." Dave smiled directly at the face of his customer.

The customer turned and started walking toward the back of the house without responding. Dave stood in his spot unsure of whether or not he should follow. Tom stopped and turned back, "It's this way." he said coldly, almost harshly, emphasis on the word 'this.'

"How 'bout if I follow you then." Dave said as he started in that direction. Dave felt that this was one customer whose personality he couldn't match in the way he usually did. Dave had a natural gift for sales and often that made him chameleon-like, people often felt comfortable with him very quickly. In the case of this customer, there was no hope of quickly gaining his confidence. Dave felt he had nothing to lose so he just stayed with his slightly facetious, whatever-you-say-man demeanor.

Tom opened a door that was in the kitchen. Dave noticed that when he opened it, dust balls swirled around the kitchen. There were marks on the floor that matched the path of the door's swing. This half-circle mark must have taken 50 years to make. The door knob hung limply in the round metal plate affixed to the door. It was a porcelain knob set into a dark metal base on a matching spindle. Tom had to rattle it a bit to get the mechanical parts to match up; so the turning of the knob resulted in the releasing of the latch.

Tom stepped aside and pointed down the staircase. "Watch your head at the bottom there." he gestured toward the basement. "The boiler is on the left. You got no reason to go to the right. Understand?" He was looking down at the floor again.

"Gotcha." Dave tried to sound cheerful. "I'm only interested in getting you some heat." He headed down the stairs.

When Dave got to the bottom and looked around, he didn't

know if he should be amazed at the collection of possessions, or the amount of dust, dirt and cobwebs covering everything. He went to the left, making sure to make noise on the left side of the bottom of the staircase, loud enough for his new customer to hear. The floor was covered by a blanket of dust; it all swirled around with every footstep. There were no signs of anyone having walked through this layer recently.

Once he located the boiler, it didn't take long to determine that the ignition mechanism was not working. This was a very old boiler, and the ignition was a vulnerable part even on boilers half its age. Dave manually lit the boiler and it roared to life. He could hear the sounds rattling and pinging around the house as the heat made its way through the pipes that transported it.

Dave straightened up and collected his tools. He hitched up his blue jeans and headed for the base of the staircase. Without intending to, he looked over to the opposite side of the basement. It looked like just a lot more dirty junk. He took a few seconds to look around; that was intentional. The floor on that half of the basement had a clear path through the dust on the floor. The path led to a wall made of plywood and two-by-fours. The outside wall was another ten feet further away. This plywood structure was two-sided, Dave could easily envision how the remaining 2 sides necessary to make an enclosure were actually the inside walls of the foundation.

Dave headed up the stairs. "I have good news and I have bad news," he said when he got to the top to find Tom waiting for him.

"Go on" the word 'on' spoken as if it were the latter part of the word lawn, 'go awnnn.' Somehow Tom managed to sound hostile with just those two words.

"Well," Dave began, "the bad news is that your ignition mechanism is shot. I really can't believe it's lasted this long because it does appear to be original equipment."

"No idea." Tom replied, apparently indicating that he had no knowledge of his heating equipment.

"The good news is that it can be started manually but I don't recommend you rely on that." Dave went on, "If something goes wrong with your timing, your pipes could freeze or worse, there could be problems with carbon monoxide."

"What the fuck..." Tom said in his flat yet bitter tone. "Can you fix it today?"

"I'll try. I have to locate the part that will work on your boiler." Dave finished, "It is running now so you'll be warm soon."

"Get the part and then call me." Tom sounded like he was hiding fury yet his actions were jerky; he didn't know where to look or how to hold his arms. He was moving his feet yet not going anywhere. Dave was looking at a large, nervous-looking, angry man. Dave did not really like nervous added to angry, so some warning flags went off in his head.

Dave reminded himself that a job was a job, so he headed for the front door. "I'll call you as soon as I know anything." As he pulled out of the driveway he started to think about the odd situation he had found himself in. He didn't really know how to categorize what he had seen in this strange man's house, but he knew he was going to have to put some time into thinking about it. He didn't want to over think it, since it was possible that it was harmless, but the chance that it wasn't was also present. He decided to go back to the office to make the phone calls needed to source the old ignition component. That way he could also check his phone for any other customers who may need him to work in a less creepy, more profitable environment.

Dave had no new calls; he made a mental note to get in touch with the yellow pages company. He had been advertising in the penny saver and newspaper, but he had just started to realize that most of his work was emergency repairs, and people don't pull their penny savers out of their recycling bin when they have an emergency; they go to Google or the yellow pages. *Note to self,* Dave thought, *cancel yellow page advertising and penny saver ads*. After a few more minutes of web surfing, he found the part he needed at a place that didn't have him on credit hold. He was almost disappointed by how easy it was going to be to fix the reclusive and anti-social guy's boiler. He called Tom and arranged to arrive back at his house in 45 minutes.

The strange man was in the front doorway when Dave pulled up. He motioned for Dave to go in then said, "I'll be right back, I need gas for my log splitter." Again, he was looking down and using as few words as possible. Dave was relieved that he wasn't making the jerky motions and doing the frustrated feet shuffling. Remembering that he was not going to be able to be social with this guy, Dave himself put his head down and headed for the stairway door in the kitchen.

When he was about half-way down the steps, he heard a large motor start up in the back yard. Once Dave was in the basement, he heard it rumble down the driveway. The basement lost a little light as the vehicle passed by the window on that side of the house. It rumbled like an old, eight cylinder vehicle that hadn't had a tune up in quite some time. Dave hadn't seen it yet but he was betting it was pickup truck.

Without thinking, Dave glanced to the right side of the basement as he turned to the left. The noise of the truck leaving - going down the driveway that was on the boiler's side of the house - made Dave realize that he didn't need to manufacture a noise to illustrate where he was to any listener; the potential listener was gone. In fact, he was free to be on either side of the basement. That old truck was going to be like the door to Dave's basement - an audible warning of someone arriving. He didn't really care about what was on the other side of the space so he moved toward the boiler and started to pull his tools out and get the new parts out of their packaging. His mind however, weighed the two sides of the question of whether or not to take a peek over there. It was strange that the weirdo upstairs only used that side of the basement, and used it frequently by the looks of the pathway in the dirt. And it was weird that he warned Dave against going over there. The turning point for Dave was when he registered that he had a limited amount of time to take his peek, but it was a very safe amount of time in light of how loud the vehicle was.

Dave stood up from his squat in front of his tool box. He straightened himself and wiped his hands down the front of his blue jeans; he was thinking about what he was about to do. Whether he was being impulsive due to curiosity, or maybe it was bad judgment caused by his hangover; regardless, he was at the entrance to the plywood enclosure before he concluded this line of thinking. Dave's cautious inner voice said, *Be careful, you don't know if he set up a means of checking to see if you'd come over here.* Dave retreated to his tool box and found his flashlight. He shined the bright beam on the door latch and all around the door to this enclosure. The door itself was unusual. It had drywall nailed to it. He used his tee shirt to grip the latch handle. His inner voice took on an edge of sarcasm: *Do you really think that man can detect fingerprints?   Good point,* Dave complimented himself. *I'd better be on the lookout for more simplistic tricks or traps.* He shined his flashlight around the room, side to side, at first just above the floor, in the event there was a trip wire. It was clear within a few seconds that he was in a room used to develop black and white photos, a dark room.

Dave raised his beam higher. Hanging from the ceiling were several clothes line-style ropes, all weighted down by pictures held in place by clothes pins. Across the room, beneath the rope lines, was a counter top with several shallow trays and various instruments. He swept the beam across the lines of pictures. They were pictures taken from various distances and with varying degrees of focus but they seemed to be mostly shots of a house, all the same house, and then a few that were pictures of a person. Dave's intelligent voice reminded him that his time wasn't unlimited. Dave's sense of intrigue piqued as he confirmed that yes, these were all the same house and the ones featuring a person, were all the same attractive brunette woman. He pulled a picture of the woman toward himself to get a closer look without unpinning its clothes pins. It was a picture of her starting to get out of a car. She was in the most awkward part of the actions it took to get out of a car that was fairly low to the ground while carrying a purse. She was wearing a camel-colored coat; it must have been windy because a strand of her hair had blown into her mouth. It was clear that she was not posing for this picture. A small label affixed to the bottom said 'Elaine 9-5-13' in scratchy handwriting. Dave assumed that was her name and the date, but he started to sense something weird. He pulled another one closer; it was approximately the same scene but the subject was turned away. It appeared she was the same person since she wore the same coat and was standing in front of the same car. This sticker also said 'Elaine 9-5-13.' He looked closely at one more. This was a picture of the same woman, this time she was opening a mailbox and peering inside. The house number 5791 was on the side of the mailbox and the flag was up. She wore a denim jacket with the hood of a navy-blue sweatshirt hanging out over the back of the collar and her hair was in a ponytail. The sticker on this one said, 'Elaine 10-8-13.' The three pictures were grainy and blurry. Dave looked at one of the pictures of the house, it had a For Sale sign in front of it and it was labeled, 'Elaine's Future House.' He didn't dare to investigate further but he was feeling pretty sure that if he had the time, he could use these pictures to develop a chronology of this 'Elaine's' recent life, whoever she was.

He left the room as he had entered, using his tee shirt to control the door's latch. When he got to the bottom of the staircase, which he now viewed as the basement divider, he looked back to see if he could detect his own footsteps into the forbidden region. He didn't think so.

Dave forced himself to immerse his mind in to the task at hand - that of repairing weird guy's boiler. He needed to get busy in order to get done so that weird guy got the impression that his work was speedy, or at least reasonably timed. He did not want to be perceived to have had extra time. Further, he needed his mind to be immersed so that his face didn't give away his feeling of having discovered something bad; not to mention the invasion of privacy which had just occurred. He needed to be fully occupied by his task so that he could pull off this deception. He would give himself the luxury of really contemplating his new knowledge after he was paid and safely off of the property.

Dave was putting his tools back into his Craftsman tool box when he heard that identifiable motor roll past the basement window. Perfect timing; he manipulated his timing a bit further by making sure he emerged through the kitchen door just after Tom had entered through the back door. "Oh hello." Dave feigned mild surprise.

"Done?" Tom's tone was so flat it barely revealed the question that it was.

"Yep. Here's your bill, we got lucky on the parts and the timing. I need $185 then I'll be on my way. I can take cash or a credit card."

"Fuck." there was that barely hidden fury again.

Dave wasn't going to participate in any argument. He had invested money in materials and driven to Tom's house twice today. He was familiar with the type of customer who argued when the bill was presented; in his experience they usually backed down when their next move was outlined for them. "I can take MasterCard, Visa or American Express."

"I'll get you some money." Tom left the room. Dave could tell he had gone upstairs due to the noises coming from the ceiling. Dave had a few minutes to look around the kitchen. The sink was empty and so were some of the counters. The empty counters were clean, not a paper towel scrap nor pasta remnant in sight. The other counters however, had a variety of things - one had jars and lids, one had a stack of magazines and one had hand held kitchen tools, mostly knives. Dave looked at this last one a second longer because it struck him as unusual that its contents were all lined up with precision. These tools were laid out on a tray like the trays in the dark room downstairs. Behind the tray, bumped up against the back-splash was a small blow torch. Something about the blow torch made Dave feel there was a question that he couldn't quite identify. *For a guy that doesn't know how to light an ignition switch to get heat, that's a weird tool...*

The counters and sink were incongruent with the dirty floor because they were recently cleaned. Yet, there was an odor. Before Dave could attempt to pull his thoughts together as a conclusion or theory, Tom came back to the kitchen. "Here's $190, if you don't have the five you can keep it." He nodded toward the front door as if he could nudge Dave in that direction like a mother cat does to a kitten, except without the cuteness.

"I must have a five, hang on." Dave set down the tool box and pulled his wallet out of his back pocket. He really did not want to carry around the feeling of owing this guy money. He sorted through his wallet and again noticed a tremor in his hand. "Here's a five." he fished it out and handed it to Tom.

"Good." Then, "Bye." It wasn't like he was saying goodbye with a hiccup in between. He was ridding himself of Dave the same way Dave wanted to be done with him. The nod toward the front door was not necessary a second time.

That night, after dinner and homework - and a large glass of bourbon - Dave lay in bed putting together the pieces of his strange day. *He's just a customer; ...let's call him a former customer,* he thought. Dave was trying to relieve his brain of the burden of thinking through the mystery Tom represented. After all, he wasn't responsible for the guy. *But what if he was the only one aware of "Elaine"... Was he responsible for that?*

You got no reason to go right... The words, spoken with an acidic, angry tone bounced around in his mind as he woke shortly after midnight. It was a sentence that seemed to summarize the reason he might want to put some thinking time into evaluating his prior day. *Why did he say that? Why would he care enough to throw out a warning that would change an everyday darkroom into a mystery that's interrupting my sleep? And at a time I don't need any help with sleep interruption,* he added to justify his sleepy indignation. He was able to recall the face of the woman in the pictures. She was clearly the kind of woman who would cause heads to turn: large eyes, pretty hair, full, red lips. She was curvy yet athletic looking. All of her features were proportionate yet unique. She had a look that could inspire a long gaze from a man - even men who thought of themselves as above that. Dave was halfway through his second night of sleeping badly when he started to wonder who Elaine was.

When the alarm went off the next day, Dave was startled out of a deep sleep. He had fallen fully asleep, but not for long enough. He turned off the alarm clock and rolled over. He didn't hear Lisa's cell phone alarm 30 minutes later. When she rolled over to get up, she was surprised to find her husband still in bed; the only other time he had slept longer than her was when he had pneumonia two years ago. She shook his shoulder gently, "Are you OK?" the concern in her voice was explicit.

"I think I'm sick." Dave lied.

"Oh no, what's wrong!? Where do you hurt?" Lisa's concern hijacked her tone of voice completely.

"It's nothing serious. I just feel ill; dizzy, achy, you know." his voice trailed off. He was trying to satisfy her curiosity so that she'd leave him alone; he needed to convince her quickly, while falling back to sleep was still a possibility.

EARL 3

The next morning, he found his group of fellow mall-walkers milling around the Starbucks meeting spot. As he approached the group, to his own surprise, he did a quick demographic assessment: six women, four men. Within the 10, there were three couples. That meant that 3 women and one man were single for a total of 2 single men and 3 single women. He liked these odds. For a moment his mind turned to the guy who did their taxes. *Would he allow the cost of the new shoes to be used as a tax deduction since they could be a necessary tool to eventual happiness?* Earl did the shut-out again. This time for different reasons; he knew this tax deduction was a silly stretch - but more importantly - he realized that no one would be doing *their* taxes. This year, it would be *his* taxes.

His walk that day took the group in a different direction, one they infrequently took. As they passed by a store called Baby Bird, Earl saw a display of small play things for toddlers. He had never been into that store before so he decided that was where he would go when the stores opened for the day in 20 minutes.

Twenty-five minutes later, Earl passed through the entrance. He was promptly greeted by a 20-something woman, "Good morning!" She cheerfully greeted him. Earl nodded respectfully. "Can I help you find anything?"

"Well, I'm looking for two small gifts for my grandkids." Earl was wishing this sales clerk were older and wearing pink lipstick.

"How old are they?" the sales clerk prodded gently.

"Two, he's a boy, and 4, she's a girl" Earl complied.

"You said 'small gifts' so let me point out this table of toys that is intended to be for that age group" she walked toward the center of the store as she talked and Earl instinctively followed her.

"Thank you, this is perfect." Earl was looking at a collection of rubber duckies, small trucks with large wheels, and other assorted toys made of compound plastics.

"Just give me a yell if you need more help, my name is Abby."

Again Earl nodded respectfully. He replayed in his mind what Dawn had told him the night before about what things the kids were interested in. He bought a colorful dump-truck that promised to 'offer bath-time fun with wheels that allowed it to float' for two-year old Jesse. For his granddaughter, Hope Junior, he bought a 'Princess Mirror' that also promised to float in the bath tub.

This four-year old beauty was born before Hope's diagnosis; her naming was an honor for the original Hope. At the time of the naming, Earl's three adult daughters lamented the fact that girls were not given the suffix of Junior or Senior, nor did they use II or III after their name. *What could possibly be the origin of that tradition - or lack of tradition,* they wondered. Dawn did some research on the question and came back with the hypothesis that girls simply were not important enough "back then" for the family lineage to be demarked by the use of these suffixes. The three women immediately, and practically in unison, decided that Dawn's first born would be called Hope Junior.

Hope Junior never questioned her nickname. Fortunately, shortly before her passing, Hope Senior did get to witness the child's surprise at other people's quizzical responses to her name. The child's innocence about prejudice was clear, and Hope Senior was proud to play a role in banishing unfair and incorrect preconceived ideas about a female's worth to a family. When Earl was back home, he paused to think about this blessing of timing when he wrote out the name Hope Junior on one of the labels Sally had given him at the post office. His eyes didn't fill nor did his throat close, he only smiled as he raised his head to see birds flying in to and then later, back away from the bird feeder he had lovingly filled earlier that day.

COREY 3
June 2013

Corey needed to focus on work. It was very hard though, in light of the fact that major changes were afoot for him as well as for his daughter and his soon-to-be ex-wife. His future however, was contingent on his ability to keep his job during this trying period, if he was also able to work toward his eventual promotion, which would be icing on his cake. For now though, he needed to take a one-day-at-a-time attitude toward his responsibilities at work.

Today, he needed to get ready for the United Way dinner that was going to honor his agency on Thursday night. The event committee had asked him to share a story or two about how his organization had positively impacted the community they shared via the programs they offered. Corey was scanning through case histories that were filed with the code 413 which represented Adoption Support and Preservation, a service for parents of adopted children. The mission for this service was *To support and perpetuate parent child relationships created by adoption.* He picked this code because he wanted to be presenting stories that had a positive spin for the community and one that embraced the fundamental principles of his Catholicism-based agency. He found about 5 stories that would work for the audience he expected on Thursday.

Corey moved on to another code to scan stories. Next up was code 514, After School Programs for At-Risk Youth. This group worked to keep kids busy after 3:00 p.m. on weekdays. There were a lot of clients listed under this code, probably because there was no criteria for qualification, only that the client be a youth and that youth needed to be available to participate after school. Corey pulled up 5 case files from this group too. His last search for this day was on code 219, Closing the Gap in Student Performance. The mission for this service was, *Providing a Playing Field on Which the Exceptional Student Can Perform at*

Their Best. This mission statement was due for review, since the board of directors correctly observed at a recent board meeting that it was overly euphemistic. While the agency was not opposed to euphemisms, they didn't want to sacrifice clarity of intent for the sake of palatable labels. It would have been more accurate for the mission statement to read, *Giving Kids One More Chance to Make the Best of School When They Probably Really Aren't Going to Make it to Graduation.* Clearly, this as a mission statement would not be approved at any board meeting any time soon. There would need to be discussion, including what the casual observer would call excruciating detail, on the subject of what this service was really achieving. And then that would be compared to what they were trying to achieve. Lastly, the result of these comparisons would be examined next to the national average, blah, blah, blah. Corey could barely stand to think of the tedious data he would have to provide in order for the board and it's sub-committees to feel like they were doing their jobs when they devised the new (and improved!) mission statement for code 219. Corey's inner voice said *Ugh!* This was definitely the one thing he didn't like about his chosen profession. He valued the work of the committees and sub-committees, these people were all volunteers from the community, but their progress was so slow. As a paid staff member, he found himself chasing around for details and statistics that later frequently got lost or ignored when the various committees would meet to discuss or debate the issues at hand. Meanwhile, as the person who really did see everything going on within the agency, his voice didn't count for much during these debates. Corey remained proud of his job and his agency, but he was past the honeymoon phase of his employment.

He had pulled case history samples from the three service codes he felt the United Way would most want to hear about and he sat back to begin the process of digesting the contents in order to regurgitate it in a form that would be appealing to his audience. The output he was looking at was on an Excel spreadsheet. The fields of data he had selected included case number, date of entry, completion date, success code and a few other things. Corey's plan was to go through these data and then pull the full file on his selections in order to get the details people would want to hear about. When he started sorting the spreadsheet by the various columns, he found an unexpected coincidence. The sort he ran on case number showed three examples where the case number started with the characters FINDL followed by the service code; there was one for each of the three codes he had done a search on. *What are the chances of that?* He asked himself. Then when he thought about it for a minute, he realized the chances were not that slim.

If a client family had an adopted child, and subsequently had problems raising that child, they very well may use the exact services Corey had decided on for his presentation of stories.

He went to his monitor and keyboard and pulled up all the details for the case numbers starting with FINDL. The three histories he read comprised a fascinating story - unfortunately it wasn't going to be useful for his United Way speech. The story was too frustrating, too futile, with no happy ending. This family named Findlay had adopted a boy; later, at the insistence of his kindergarten teacher and the school counselor, they sought help for anti-social behaviors. A few years later, the mother - Corey was reading between the lines now - didn't know where else to turn for help with her out of control child so she made one more call to Catholic Charities. *Wait, one more?* Corey asked himself.

He went back to his database of service recipients and searched on the Field Service Code. He entered FINDL and got five hits. The three he had originally searched on weren't everything the Findlay family had experienced under his agency's roof. The two additional codes were 213, or Socializing your Child, and 622, or Teenagers

Looking for Christ. The first of which was usually used by families who lacked opportunities for their children to play with others prior to entering school. The latter program, 622, had the nickname of Please-Fix-My-Baby, among the staff, since it was usually used by parents who had no control over their adolescent or teen, yet their 'baby' was about to 'age out' of the system. This was a service that was on the chopping block currently. When responding to budget cuts, the success rate of Teens Looking for Christ was embarrassing to Corey. It just didn't pull its weight; in fact, it sometimes was a predictor of failure. It offered help at a point in a child's life that was just too late to claim to make a meaningful difference.

Corey's interest in his agency and its services was genuine though, so he read through the files of Betty and Thomas Findlay even though he knew they were not going to provide content for his speech. His hope was to find a theme or a commonality that might help another family in the future. His reading uncovered stories of anti-social behavior, divorce, cruelty, loss of parental control, and sociopathic episodes. Corey found himself shaking his head side to side as he read. His files, once sorted correctly, portrayed a very sad story for Betty Findlay and a very interesting, albeit scary, story about her son Thomas.

Betty would be 64 and Thomas would be 37 right now, thought Corey, *I wonder where they are now...* Corey shook himself to attention. Caring about people was a liability to him right now. He needed to focus on his United Way presentation. There were a lot of happy stories ready to be harvested from his database and that thought reinvigorated his interest in his search.

It didn't take long for him to find a family to focus on. The Robertsons had adopted a girl 14 years ago, and three years later, they had a child biologically. This family of four had used Adoption Support and Preservation, and Closing the Gap in Student Performance. The latter service had a completion code of SUCF which meant that the child enrolled was considered to have completed the program successfully; in this case, she had graduated from high school. Corey's decision on what family to talk about during his presentation was made; he began to dig into the computerized files to get the other little details that he would use to expand his presentation.

ELAINE 3
October, 2013

Elaine took Sally's advice and rented a P.O. Box that weekend. She also picked up the mail that they had been holding for her. There was no Kohl's coupon and no credit card bill though. She did get a Penny-Saver, a utility bill and lots of other things that she really didn't want. She planned to stop in again on Monday after work to get any new mail. She decided that she could probably be okay with getting her mail two or three times per week until the delivery problem was worked out.

On Tuesday, she drove straight home after picking up the kids. Her heart began pounding when she saw that the flag was up on her mailbox again. She pulled into the driveway and got the kids inside before walking back to the box to see if there was anything else noteworthy about her mailbox. She put the flag down and opened the drop-down door. There was a full size piece of heavy weight paper with a black and white image on it. She started to tremble; she knew what it was a picture of before she got it all the way out of the mailbox. It was a picture of her, taken at the moment she found the first picture. She could tell when it was taken because she knew what day she wore which scrubs to work - that, and the look of shocked surprise on her face was a look she didn't display very often, thankfully.

Elaine had agreed to let her ex-mother-in-law pick up Eric and Danielle after school on Thursday so that they could work on Halloween costumes together. Maria was very good at crafts and she went all out for this October holiday every year. It had been a while since the kids had spent any time with Elaine's former in-laws. When Maria called to ask for this date with her grandchildren, Elaine had been trying to think about what she was going do with her kids while she was at a 5:00 appointment she had just scheduled. This impromptu plan was going to work out very well. Elaine and Maria always had a mutual appreciation for one another, so Elaine agreed to the plan after securing the promise that they'd be home by 6:30 to work on homework. Maria would of course feed them. Elaine could plan on her kids getting all kinds of things that she would not normally give them, including snacks before dinner and dessert afterwards.

Elaine's 5:00 appointment was at the sheriff's department. She was going to show them the picture of herself that she had found in her mailbox two days earlier. Elaine made arrangements to leave work at 4:00 to accommodate the appointment. She had been really confused about what to do about her mail being missing ; she grew further confused when photographs showed up instead of mail. At work the day after she found the first picture, Wednesday, she brought it up to Jo, a coworker whom she trusted. Jo's response was adamant, "Are you kidding me? You haven't called the cops yet?" Her voice was too loud for the office.

"Shhh" Elaine admonished. "I just think someone is playing a game with me; I am pretty sure it's Donny." Elaine named her ex-husband. "I'm going to be so embarrassed if the sheriff discovers it's him. I mean, he shouldn't have any power to scare me after all these years."

"Embarrassed my ass!" again Elaine put a finger to her lips to quiet Jo, "You are being stalked. Hear me say that word again - stalked." Jo paused, "And I don't care if it's Donny, or Donny Osmond. You need police involvement."

"Okay.... Okay. I'll call them on break."

Jo continued, "The picture thing is really creepy, but let's not forget that your mail is missing too. Do you have any idea what may have been in your mail?"

"My Kohl's coupon!" Elaine said with mock shock and sorrow, "And my credit card bill."

"You should probably call that credit card company too and get a new account." Jo advised.

"Thank you for your help, Jo. Your clarity and common sense is really what I need right now."

As planned, the next day, Elaine left the office at 4:00. She drove home first to change. She didn't like to be around strangers in her scrubs; she felt they revealed personal information about herself that she might not want those strangers to know - like where she worked. She stopped to look in her mailbox, as she did every day, and like almost every day before, it was empty. She did this more to confirm that there was no mail in the box than to see if she had gotten any mail. She had been using P.O. Box number 222 at the Victory Post Office for 3 days now. Elaine felt 222 was a lucky number. She wasn't very superstitious but she loved even numbers as well as repetitive numbers and this offered both. When the clerk at the post office handed her a card with instructions for setting the combination to the lock and told her the box number, Elaine felt it was a sign that her new house and new life were all going to work out. Elaine would do almost anything to feel good about her new house again.

After pulling on a pair of blue jeans and a long sleeve cotton shirt, she grabbed a pair of low boots and stepped into them. She put her clogs away in the closet and grabbed her denim jacket while she was in there. She headed back down the stairs and stopped in the kitchen to confirm that the picture was still in her purse. It was, so she pulled her keys out and went out the door, locking up as she left.

She climbed into her car; she was in a hurry now because

only 15 minutes were left before she was due at her
appointment. She put the car in reverse and backed down
the driveway; she shifted into drive and started down her
street toward the main road. She reached behind her left
shoulder to grab her seat belt and looking down, she
plugged it in to its receptacle. Not buckling her safety belt
until she was underway when she was hurrying was a bad
habit that she was trying to kick; she never let her children
see her do this. It took her attention completely off the
road and it meant that for a few seconds she was driving
while being unsecured - and it only bought her three
seconds at best. She was scolding herself as she raised her
head back up to the windshield. She looked ahead then
checked her rear view mirror - just then a head appeared,
blocking the majority of that mirror.

Her scream was involuntary. There was a man in her back
seat. Not only was she startled by the surprise appearance
but she was also instantly terrified. The terror struck at the
core of her body; it wasn't necessary for her to think
through the implications of someone - an unshaven
someone - having hidden in her backseat and remaining
hidden until she was underway. She immediately knew she
was in trouble and this man was menacing looking; her
terror was debilitating. She stomped on the brake in
response to the electrical horror that was jumping across
her nerve endings. The man was wearing a black and red
plaid wool coat that was frayed at the cuffs and speckled
with wood chips and unidentifiable dried matter. He
smelled of dirty oil and wood smoke. His beard was
straggly and thin, like the kind of facial hair where a true
beard would never be possible.

Within seconds of discovering she had a passenger, she
felt the sharp edge of a blade against her throat. "Keep
driving and shut up bitch or I'll kill you right now." he
growled at her.

Elaine's brain lit up; she recognized those words and that

voice. Thoughts were ricocheting around in her mind. *No... Could it be him? It has to be him...* Long-ago memories that had been locked away successfully were now flooding back into her conscience. *Wait, don't assume it's him, it could confuse the situation... Who are you kidding, it IS him...*

Elaine had lost track of Thomas during the years since high school. Her parents had convinced her that he was gone; she didn't need to worry about him and she had acquiesced to that comfort. Once, when she thought about him as an adult, she had decided that, as his first victim, she would be notified if he was back in the community.

She glanced into the mirror, took her foot off the brake and allowed the car to roll forward while she waited to see what would happen next. She mentally straightened herself up; she now knew who her adversary was, and she was transitioning to fight mode. She physically straightened at the same time, causing the knife to scrape the skin that covered the cartilage in her throat. She didn't care, she was using every available piece of energy and attention to respond to the threat of Thomas. The only weapon she had was her intellect and using that to get away from him would be her only chance to get back home to see her children.

An icy calm washed over her. She would see her children again and that was all there was to it.   "Where should I go?" she asked, looking him in the eye using the mirror.

"Take a left at the stop sign." Thomas said as he looked away. Having that second of eye contact made him feel less powerful. He wouldn't let that happen again.

Elaine noticed his discomfort. She was trying hard to remember everything she knew about Thomas from high school and the encounter that changed her life. *What do I know that I can use? How can I exploit whatever it is that makes him uncomfortable?* She looked at him in the mirror as frequently as she dared. She was pretty certain that he wouldn't look at her if she was already looking at him. She was waiting for an opportunity to grab her cell phone. She felt she only needed three or four seconds to reach into her purse and pull out the device slowly enough that the activity didn't catch his eye. If she could get the phone, pull it to the side of her leg close to her hip so that he couldn't see it without leaning into the front seat, then she might be able to dial 911. Maybe the operator would be able to hear enough to know that an abduction was in progress.

She could see the stop sign ahead where she was to turn left. Her plan would have to wait until after the turn because of the amount of time she needed to spend looking in the mirror to keep him from looking at her. She needed to be looking at the road as she approached the intersection. She turned on her blinker, "Where are we going?" she asked.

"Shut up bitch." There was that voice again, "You'll find out when you need to know." They were on a straight stretch of county road. Elaine decided she had to take a shot at her plan soon. The internet was full of stories of abduction and advice for dealing with it; the advice was always to fighting where you are, even if you have to take chances. Most murder victims are murdered at the location an abductor moves his victim to. If at all possible, do not allow yourself to be taken to a new location. *Maybe that's why Thomas chose my car, I'd already be on my way somewhere, he used his advantage to change my direction to the location of his choosing...*

She started to move her right arm toward her purse while glancing in the mirror as often as she dared. Without turning her head or leaning her body in that direction, she found her purse with her hand. She reached up under the flap that crossed over the top of her bag when her purse was closed. When the flap was properly aligned with the front of her purse, magnets clicked to announce closure. Elaine didn't want to unfasten the magnets because it could make a noise, so instead she fished her hand up under the cloth flap and reached down into the bag. Inside it, she identified her wallet and her makeup bag by feel. Without shifting these items, she stretched her fingers as far as should could and gained just enough reach to feel the smooth surface of her phone. She would need to push her hand further into her purse to be able to grip the device.

Elaine looked in the mirror and tried to wear an expression of fear and submission. She didn't have to act much to come up with the fear piece of that - she was terrified. But the look of submission would be replaced by determination if she wasn't careful. She pushed her hand further and grasped her phone. Now she only needed to get her arm back to where Thomas would feel it belonged.

"Hey!" Thomas spat at her.

Fuck, I've blown my chance... Elaine thought.

"Turn right at this next road." Thomas still held the knife against her throat. Elaine looked in the mirror to signal the acceptance of his order while also making her final move. She was trembling from head to foot with relief at not being caught, and with fear that the boldness of her plan might backfire on her.

Her phone was now wedged between the right cheek of her butt and the seat of her car. She would plan her next move after the upcoming right-hand turn.

Elaine was familiar with the road they had turned onto. She knew they had about a half-mile before any other turns were going to be possible. She flipped open her phone using only her fingers; her shoulder and arm did not move. She thanked the goddess of dental hygiene for her dexterity. As she faked focusing on the road, she felt her way around her phone's keyboard. *Was the nine at the bottom of the vertical column of numbers that had the three at the top?* No. *Think Elaine, think! The three had the six under it and the nine was under that. I don't care what is in that bottom row of numbers right now, I'll friggin' check out that pound sign some other day*, she thought. *Right now I need to press the key that is third from the top in the right-hand column.* And she did. The phone obliged with a confirming vibration. Now, top row, far left - twice - to complete the three-digit sequence.

"Nine-one-one, what's your emergency?" The device was set to speaker-phone. Somewhere within her struggle, Elaine had accidentally pushed a very important button.

"What the fuck?!" Thomas spewed his words as he used his knife-wielding hand to reach toward the professional sounding voice. He grabbed the phone and threw it out the car window. He returned the knife to Elaine's throat and allowed it to sink into her soft flesh. A drop of blood appeared at the knife's edge. Like the leader of a marching band, that first drop led the way for all the other droplets to follow. The path went down her neck, between her breasts and into the waistband of her blue jeans. Elaine could feel the warmth of the parade.

Tears rolled down her cheeks. She had broken her own heart.

Thomas's fury was palpable. "I'm sorry..." Elaine tried.

Thomas hit her on the left side of her head. "Fuck you bitch!" he screamed. Fortunately he didn't have much wind-up room so the blow didn't threaten her consciousness. "You have ruined my life and now you are not even respecting me."

Her seat belt helped Elaine to stay upright after the blow

and keep driving. "I'll do whatever you say..." she sobbed. "Where do you want me to drive?" Her trembling had changed from head-to-toe shaking, then to shudders that rocked her entire body. It took everything she had to keep her car going in a safe trajectory.

Thomas increased the pressure of the knife against her throat. Elaine could feel a surge of warmth follow the parade route down to her waist. She tried to look down to see if she could see blood in her lap but that made her contact with the knife even more threatening.

"Bear right up here." He pointed ahead of them. Then growling directly into Elaine's right ear, "If you try anything at all, again, you are dead. You will never see your house or kids again."

Elaine nodded; sobs escaped her mucous-y mouth. She tried breathing deeply through her nose; she knew she had to get back on solid ground with her own self or her intelligence would not be available to her. When she opened her mouth to try to speak, a bubble formed from the thick lining that all of her emotions had summoned to her mouth. She blew air out of her mouth to break the bubble. Her nose was dripping when she said, "I'll do whatever you want."

A few minutes and a few more harshly-barked directives later, Elaine was driving slowly down a residential driveway. She couldn't see much but she got the impression of a run-down two-story structure. The driveway wasn't paved. She allowed the car to roll toward a broken-down garage that was included at the far end of the scope of her headlights. Thomas jerked the knife upward and into her throat further. Elaine eyes opened wide as she started to wonder if she was going to survive the next few minutes. She could tell that she was bleeding heavily now. The marchers in her parade of blood had turned into a mass of marathon runners who had all achieved their fund raising goals and were within striking distance of the finish line.

"You will live a little longer if you follow my directions closely." Thomas's voice sounded like he didn't open his mouth very wide when he spoke, and he had a trachea half filled with gravel.

Elaine was frozen in place. The reality of her injuries along with his control over her very near future was making headway within the thoughts she was entertaining. She stared back at him in the mirror.

"Put the car in park, lean forward and put your hands together behind your head."

Elaine did as he said; raising her shaking arms, she clasped her hands behind her neck and bent forward at the waist. Thomas moved the knife out from under her right arm as he grasped her hands with his other hand forcing them into a palm-to-palm position. Before she could detect his momentary compromise of control, he dropped the knife and, while continuing to use his left hand to hold her hands together, reached for a stretch of rope he had in the back seat with him. He roughly wrapped the nylon rope around and around the narrowest part of the intersection of her two wrists. Elaine groaned. His methods were so crude and rough, she could feel the ropes tearing her skin. He had pulled her arms back behind her head, in his haste, pulling further than the usual person's range of motion included.

"Shut. The. Fuck. Up." she felt his spittle hit the side of her face. He was still busy doing something while holding her arms behind her head. Tears continued to roll down Elaine's cheeks. Elaine heard a strangely familiar sound, a ripping or tearing sound. *What was that?...* She was working hard to regain her interest in finding some footing and naming that sound might help her to know what was going on. *Think Elaine!* She urged herself again.

Thomas started to wrap something new around her wrists. It pulled at her skin and reduced her ability to move her wrists from a possible ten percent down to zero. *Is there such a thing as zero percent,* she dizzily wondered, her head swimming, *or is it just simply zero...?* Duct tape. *Duct tape!* He was wrapping duct tape around her wrists and the sound was him tearing the duct tape off the roll. The rope was just a temporary restraining measure.

Elaine was alert to her situation again. Her motivation to overcome the events of the last 10 minutes was, however, counter balanced by her understanding of duct tape. Her stomach roiled anew as he kept wrapping and wrapping the tape around and around, moving from her wrists to her hands, around and around. When he finally used his teeth to separate the roll from what he had dispensed, she couldn't wiggle a finger.

Thomas opened the backseat driver's-side door. He maintained a grip on Elaine's silver bundle of hands as he opened her door. He reached in and pulled Elaine out of her seat by her hair. He dropped his grip on her hair and moved her bundled hands to the front of her, pulling her toward the back door of the house.

Elaine screamed. Her earlier thoughts on abductions and victims being brought to a new location had taken over her thoughts. She was not going toward that house voluntarily.

Thomas backhanded her before her scream was finished. "That is your last chance bitch. You have a chance to live but you are not respecting that." He pulled her hands down to her knee level and started to pull her again, intentionally throwing her off balance. "Cutting your throat seems like a good idea right now."

Elaine was sobbing and staggering and she was afraid of what he'd do if she fell down. She struggled to keep up with him. She was coughing and crying and trying to live. A picture of Danielle and Eric claimed the forefront of her mind. She inhaled deeply. She had no choice but to be led to his next destination but she had manufactured some hope. While she stumbled along after this demented man, her thoughts of her two precious babies had renewed her determination. She decided then to resume her role of submissive abductee. Statistics about abductions didn't have to predict her future; she needed to keep trying. Thomas dragged her up back porch steps as she carefully tried to look around, gathering any available clues about her situation.

175

THOMAS 4
August 10th, 2013

Thomas was driving through the area to deliver a face cord
of wood. He often picked up extra money by providing
wood to people who were having labor day bonfires or,
much less likely, those who were getting ready for the
return of cold weather. On this day, his customer lived in a
small aging neighborhood. If one were to drive from the
center of town and head toward Thomas's house, this area
was the last area that could be called a neighborhood
before you got to the very rural region that Thomas lived
in. The house had been his mother's, until her death; she
had lived there since marrying her self-centered husband
39 years earlier.

As Thomas drove down these winding roads, he looked to
his right and involuntarily hit the brakes. He quickly
corrected himself though, because he knew he needed to
go unobserved. It had been a very long time, but he had
never really stopped looking for the girl who had scorned
him in high school, the same girl who was the reason he
spent a year in The Montgomery County Youth Center.
And there she was, walking with another woman down the
driveway of a house less than a mile from where he lived.
He looked for the house number and repeated it over and
over to himself so that he would be able to find it later and
do a better job of examination. Later, he'd be able to take
more time to figure out if this was an opportunity being
presented to him. For now, he kept his truck rolling down
the road.

Elaine had noticed the truck and was curious about why it
had slowed so suddenly. It was a loud, old truck; in the
back window was a sticker that said FUBO. She chalked it
up as just a redneck who wasn't used to seeing two woman
walking down a driveway together; maybe he thought they
were a couple. All thoughts of the truck and its driver left

her as soon as her real estate agent asked when they could reconvene to put together the purchase offer. The excitement of finding a house that she could afford, and within which she could easily picture herself raising her kids in a happy environment, made it easy for her to turn her attention back to her agent.

"I can meet you at your office in 20 minutes" Elaine said hopefully.

"Perfect. There is a distinct advantage to being the first in with an offer," her agent Kate said, "we can knock out the offer and I'll still have time to deliver it tonight." Kate climbed into her car, "See you in a few."

Thomas delivered the load of wood and decided to drive around for a while, kill some time so that he could go back to that house on Clover Meadow and look around a little. Half an hour later, he headed for the street he had been on earlier. *Number 5791... 5791...* It had become a chant in his head. There was no one around this time, so he slowed down and crept past the house. There was a For Sale sign in the front yard. On the sign was a picture of the second woman; she was wearing a gold-colored blazer. Her phone number was as prominent as her smile. Is it possible that the woman he hated as much as he loved was moving into a neighborhood near his house? Over the years, he had looked for her in the phone book, and more recently on the internet, but he was never able to locate her. Now it seemed she had been laid at his feet. He felt the stirring feeling that he enjoyed when he was doing his special projects. He had to adjust the crotch of his jeans to remain comfortable, pulling down on the front of one of his pant legs and shifting in his seat.

How could he confirm what was going on here? The situation seemed obvious to him but that wasn't enough. Sometimes the human mind had the ability to make a situation seem like the situation the individual was seeking.

He learned that lesson when he was a young adult serving in the military in the Middle East.

He briefly considered pretending to be interested in buying the house, getting in touch with the smiling agent for a walk-through, but his social skills were less than poor. He was never comfortable talking to another person unless he had control over them and he was the only one doing the talking. He would not be able to 'shmooze' the agent to make her think he was a prospective buyer. Once the purchase transaction was complete, he could check public records to see who the new owner was, but what if it wasn't a transaction and she was there for some other reason, *how would he find Elaine again?* And, what if it was someone else who just looked like Elaine? *Looked exactly like Elaine, walked exactly like Elaine...* he thought.

These thoughts stayed with Thomas. When he lay down to try to sleep, the thoughts became even more active. Elaine had haunted his thoughts every day since the first time he saw her when he was a sophomore and she was a freshman in high school. He watched for her every day, working equally hard to hide the fact that he was watching. Each new school year he would skip as many classes as it took for him to figure out at least one class period in her new schedule when he could anticipate where she would be. He preferred to find a place that he could stand around unnoticed, so that he could also observe her arrival to that spot. He perfected a stance where he could watch from a distance, holding his head at a very specific angle that allowed his hair to hang in front of his eyes. He had grown his bangs long so he could peer through the ragged ends without anyone being able to detect what his stare was pointed at.

The second September of his "interest" in Elaine, he noticed that her breast had grown since the prior year. He thought about measuring them with the calipers they used in shop class. He spent hours picturing how he would do that. First, he would tie her hands together behind her. The coupling of her fists would make her back arch when he laid her down on top of her own fists. Then he would tie her ankles to the legs of the table or bed or whatever the surface was he was using. Her legs needed to be tied separately with a few feet in between them, so that he could monitor any physical reaction she might have to his advances. He was fairly confident that her body would react in a way he would want to see. Then he would carefully measure the size of her breasts, recording the dimensions of the right and then the left. He would also measure her areolas and her nipples, carefully noting all measurements. He wanted to be able to detect and record any changes. He spent hours on this fantasy, making small changes to the setting and the order in which he'd do things as time went on. Elaine would never speak in his fantasy; she was his and his words to her were the only ones that could register as audible. He would stroke himself as he worked through this play he had orchestrated. Sometimes Thomas would climax as Elaine, in Thomas's mind, would arch her back and coo as he moved from the right breast to the left, gathering statistics. That early climax would postpone the completion of the 'play' by only a few minutes since, as soon as his mind went back to the job of measuring Elaine in her tied-down position, he was also back to dominating her. Stroking himself was the natural byproduct of his ownership.

Right now, though, Thomas needed to confirm that it was Elaine he had seen. He decided to leave a message for the real estate agent before the office opened the next day, that way he wouldn't risk getting into an awkward conversation. Early the next morning, he used his cell phone to call the number on the for sale sign. "Hello, I need to confirm that Elaine has seen a house on Clover Meadow Drive umm... number 5791. I am a building inspector and as a favor, I was supposed to see it with her but I didn't make it in time. I've lost her phone number so please let me know if she is all set." He left his number then hung up.

Ninety minutes later, the office secretary picked up the message. She scanned the appointments for the prior day and saw that Elaine Moreland had seen a house on Clover Meadow. In the interest of being the most helpful real estate office in Victory, she called the number left on the message and left her own message, "Elaine Moreland did see the house on Clover Meadow yesterday. Thanks for checking and make it a great day!"

Thomas was looking for Elaine Simmons but 17 years had gone by since he last saw her. It was easy for him to assume that Elaine Simmons was now Elaine Moreland and that *his* Elaine was trying to move into his neighborhood.

~~~~~~

There was a time in Thomas's life when his fantasies of Elaine were enjoyed while using other props. In fact, even before he had an interest in girls, he found excitement in capturing and dominating creatures. When he was seven, he grabbed a neighbor's kitten that he found in his yard. He was feeling angry that day because his teacher had made him sit away from his classmates because he was pinching the girls that were near him. Once he got home, he was walking around his yard swinging a stick through the fallen leaves and yelling at his teacher during an internal conversation he was having with her. Just then the kitten appeared from behind a bush, it made a small mewing sound that could have been mistaken for a squeak. "Shut up." Seven-year-old Thomas said as he swung his stick in the direction of the cat. When the cat acted afraid of him, he was glad. That was when he scooped the cat up and brought it down into his basement. He didn't know exactly what he was going to do with the cat but he felt empowered to experiment with some ideas.

Thomas cleared an area of the workbench in the right-hand

corner of the basement by sweeping his forearm across the area. First, he had to find a step up, so he grabbed a bucket and turned that upside down. When standing on that, he had enough height to clear and then use the bench. The workbench had never been used for its intended purpose so there wasn't much to move: a roll of scotch tape, wadded up pieces of paper and some styrofoam packing peanuts. He set the cat down and held it in place with one hand pressing against its chest, pressing its bony back against the surface of his work area. With his free hand he reached for some rubber bands that were hanging on a nail. He tied the kitten's front legs together by wrapping a rubber band around and around, he got so caught up in the act of looping the band around, that by the time he registered what he was doing, the band just wouldn't stretch any further. Now the cat was franticly scrapping at his arm with its hind legs. One of the scrapes was particularly effective and, in response, Thomas cried out then pulled his arm up to look at the damage. When he saw blood, without thinking, he pounded the cat with both fists together.

The kitten was a long-haired gray cat with white markings on its face and on each foot; it had white on its chest as well. It dropped over on to its side when he pounded it. Thomas thought it was dead. *Wow, that was pretty easy,* he thought. He was equal parts disappointed in the experiment being over, and excited at how simple it was to have this experiment take place. Just then his mother called down the steps, "Thomas, what are you doing down there?"

He was startled back to reality. He knew that his mother would not think that his experiment was okay, even though he would not be able to articulate himself what was wrong with what he was doing. His knee-jerk reaction was to reply to her with any response that would keep her from coming down the stairs.

"I just needed some scotch tape." he yelled back up the steps. He grabbed for the tape that had hit the floor only moments earlier, holding it out in front of him, he went running up the stairs, forgetting about the kitten. At the top of the stairs, he said, "See?"

"What do you need tape for?" his mother inquired.

At seven, Thomas was very clever and quite skilled at manufacturing stories to cover lies or actions. This question from his mother caught him off-guard, however, because he was still recovering from the surprise of her appearance at the top of the stairs. His "experiment' with the cat had put him in a trance-like state. In his mind, he had been in a bubble of secure space. He learned a lesson on this day: never let your guard down. When you are doing something important, always be on guard.

"Ummm... I'm building a fort out back." Thomas knew his mother had a soft spot for boys doing boy-like things. Even this early in his life, he knew that if he said he wanted to go play with trucks, she would approve, even if he had misbehaved earlier.

"Oh, okay." She let him pass as he theatrically carried the scotch tape through the kitchen then out the door that led to the back porch. He was holding the tape as if it were a rare specimen, using only two fingers and keeping it held aloft in front of him. His mother turned and closed the door to the basement.

It was the next morning before Thomas remembered that he had left the kitten in the basement. He didn't have any time to go down there. *Besides*, he thought, *Mom will never believe that I need to go down there before school.* His mother was in the kitchen putting together his lunch as she reminded him that he was 10 minutes behind schedule. Thomas finished dressing; he put some toothpaste in his mouth so that he would smell like he had brushed his teeth.

He walked out to the curb with his mother and two minutes later he was on the bus heading toward school.

When he got off the bus later that day, as usual, his mother was waiting for him. What was unusual was that she didn't seem glad to see him. They walked toward their front door and Thomas decided to remain quiet, waiting for her to give him a clue about what was happening from her perspective. "Thomas?"

He looked up toward her as his response.

"I had to go into the basement today to get a box of craft supplies." Her words informed Thomas of what the up-coming topic was going to be. He hadn't even thought about the cat since that morning.

"There was a dead cat with its legs tied together on the floor."

Thomas thought, *On the floor? Was it still alive when I left it down there on the bench?* He said, "What? How did a dead cat get in our basement?"

"Thomas, this is very important!" They were inside the front door now and his mother had squatted down to be at eye level with him. Thomas had never been able to maintain eye contact with anyone so he was squirming and trying to turn his head away. "Look at me!" she said, shaking him slightly; she was using the harshest voice he had ever heard her use as she held him by both of his upper arms.

"What?" Thomas shot back in a bitter, angry tone.

"Thomas, I need to know if you hurt that cat and I need you to tell me right now."

"You're hurting my arms." he whined. Thomas twisted

himself to try to get free of her grip.

"Thomas! You tell me!" she shouted, but the tail end of her shout sounded like a crying voice and Thomas's decision to use denial was reinforced by the knowledge that his mother was not going to be up for a full-fledged parental attack on him.

He stopped squirming, "Mom, I don't know anything about a cat, so stop squeezing my arms." He made himself look at her face. He saw her tears well up before he looked away.

Betty dropped her grip on her adopted son's arms. "Go to your room."

"Why am I being punished?" he said indignantly.

"Go. To. Your. Room." She spoke through clenched teeth.

After that, Thomas was more careful to take care of any evidence left over from what he would start to think of as his "*special projects*."

He learned several things from the cat incident; he learned about the importance of clean-up and he learned how exciting being in control was. He didn't yet know about the concept of passion at age seven, but he understood that he felt excited, energized and focused when he was involved in his *special projects*. Later in his life it would be described as his passion.

By the time Thomas was feeling called to experiment with humans, a more intelligent form of life, many cats, squirrels, one puppy, and a woodchuck that was already almost dead but still able to cry out, disappeared from his neighborhood. He lived through a sort of transition period where he would still be working with animals but he was thinking about - planning for - a human experiment. He was 12 or 13 and developing a fascination with girls when his sexual curiosity seemed to naturally align with his interest in his special projects.

He first saw Elaine when he was 15. She was a freshman and he was a sophomore in the local high school. The pieces that fell together in his mind made an almost audible '*clink-clunk*' in his head when his special projects and Elaine were both, for the first time, occupying his thoughts at the same time. He felt the excitement of one who discovers a mission that was going to be very meaningful to them. Later, when he was thinking over his kinship with his new mission and enjoying the feeling of electricity running through his extremities, he thought, *Wow, I bet Neil Armstrong felt like this when he got his first rocket as a child... I bet John Lennon felt like this when he started to play his first guitar...*

Thomas recognized that hurting other people was wrong. His understanding of that principle was on an intellectual basis only, and only because it had been drilled into him. He didn't have an emotional understanding of it - that feeling that most people call guilt. Every teacher, counselor, baby sitter, had, along with his mother, drilled the concept into his head; but it was only a concept. If asked, Thomas would have admitted that he gave them reason to focus on this principle when teaching or guiding him. At the time his sexual interests collided with his experimentation, he knew that it would be wrong to persue this new chapter. But the plan began to develop anyway, little by little, as if it had its own life. Perhaps it was the gradual yet slow development of his plan, or perhaps it was Thomas's inability to feel guilt - either way - there was nothing within his conscience that was working against this new idea. In fact, there were gears turning that promoted the concept of human experimentation. Like most young teenagers, his body was sending him all kinds of signals that seemed to say, *Sex... find a way to have sex... or see sex...* while Thomas's more personal tangents included, *See what woman's bodies can endure...* And, *find ways to do things MY way....* among other things.

Thomas felt he deserved to have what he wanted. He felt that he was always targeted by authority figures who just didn't want him to be the person he wanted to be. After many years of being told to stop whatever it was he wanted to do on any particular day, or being accused of something that, in his mind, was just a way to get by around people who were nothing like him, he had formed a mental image of himself. *I think I'm above all this bullshit....* His self-image was that of someone who was different from everyone else. Thomas stopped expecting to be understood and approved of. He stopped measuring himself against others in his age group. He stopped caring if his mother was happy with him. He started feeling like he deserved to do whatever it was that would bring him satisfaction.

When Thomas entered his senior year of high school, the elevation of his opinion of himself ran parallel with his feeling of an impending deadline. There were hundreds of girls that would be able to help him fulfill his sexual interest in experimentation with control, and he was certain that many would enjoy being chosen for the experiment. However, no one was as fascinating as Elaine. Aside from her looks and her please-fuck-me body, her demeanor in the school hallways made her an undeniable target in Thomas's mind. She seemed to be able to orchestrate other peoples' reactions to her. She would giggle at the right moment for the football players, and she would poke at and play hide-and-seek with the popular smart guys - using locker doors, or other people to hide behind and then peek out from - in the cutest possible way. She deployed delight, chagrin, and an air of superiority to maintain her status as the one girl everyone should be paying attention to. Elaine's version of control was so different from Thomas's that he needed to know more about it, the way a child captures a lightening bug in a jar in order to observe it and delight in its unique qualities. Elaine controlled her audience; Thomas controlled the things he chose for his special projects. *Whose power to control is more real? More effective?....* These questions tortured Thomas and threatened to pull the rug out from under his ability to justify his special projects. This year was probably his last year to observe and learn from Elaine's special qualities. Time was, in fact, running out.

Two months into this school year, he would have the feeling of having Elaine laid at his feet for the first of two times in his life. He was driving home from school in his own car; it was a 1965 Chrysler. He had had to save for a year and a half to afford this vehicle that barely ran at the time of the purchase. Thomas's mother approved the purchase for three reasons: first, she felt that men should be able to do basic car repairs and she had no way to teach her son that skill herself; second, having Thomas busy tinkering with an inanimate object seemed like a good idea to a mother who had lost the feeling of knowing her son about 16 years earlier; last, she was done trying to raise this child, and if he had his own transportation she could be done with appearing like she was parenting him.

On this cold, autumn day, he was driving home from school, going slowly down each stretch of road on his route home, enjoying the noisy muffler noises of his car and surges of power whenever he pressed on the gas pedal. He wasn't excited about getting home. His life had been what he considered to be boring for the past few weeks. He had none of his special projects going on and his biggest challenge was avoiding his mother. Just as he turned onto Prescott Street, he saw the very recognizable shape of his target, and in spite of the briskness of her pace, Elaine was walking as only Elaine could.

KATE 3

Kate's book and her book club became very important to her as she tried to remain calm during the most difficult time of her life so far. She had gotten pretty far into her writing before she revealed to the club that she was working on a book. She knew this group would want to read it so she wanted to be sure it would eventually be read-able before she told them about it. Hap, of course was the exception. Kate made sure that Hap stayed dialed in to her situation since Kate relied so heavily on her kind honesty and opinions. Kate would end up with a feeling of being cleansed with the bonus of having material to think about whenever they would get together for what they called a 'wine night.' Wine nights were best when Kate had a driver to and from Hap's house, since the name of the event was derived from the thing that massive amounts of were usually consumed.

Over the years there had been many interesting things for them to tell each other about. Boyfriends, lovers, employment situations, so-called friends who had shown reason to be cut from the list of true friends, family, parents' health, children, parenting, and sex were all common topics, with the latter item always being the most interesting. Hap and Kate shared a generous sexual appetite at certain points in their lives. Some years wine nights were monthly. The year of Michael's arrest, wine nights were roughly quarterly. This reduction was due in part to the advent of Book Club. As a play on words, and a nod to the Wine Night and the group's love of wine, this club called itself, "Read Between the Wines." Hap even found T-shirts displaying these words which she bought for the six members the club had at that time.

After a few initial meetings, the club settled into a protocol where the hostess would do her best to serve food that was somehow relevant to the story. The first time this happened was when the group had read *Modoc*, a story about an elephant that spent much but not all of his life in a circus. It was Hap's turn to host and she served popcorn out of red-striped cardboard containers, like those found at the circus. She also served animal crackers, peanuts, and fresh fruit and the tradition was born.

When telling others about this tradition, Kate's favorite example for describing it was when they read *Strange Case of Dr. Jekyll and Mr. Hyde.* This book had absolutely no mention of food and again it was Hap's turn to host. On the table in her downstairs sunroom, she set a table with the usual snack-sized plates and paper napkins. At one end of the table she placed a plate full of walnuts and blueberries - examples of 'super foods.' At the other end, she put a plate of bacon and one of cookies and chocolate, quintessential examples of the opposite. The group admired Hap's cleverness.

One of the best treats was served when it was Lisa's turn to host. They had read a book that featured a French meal served in Amsterdam. Lisa spared no effort when she provided a very fussy French dessert that followed delicate asparagus and other indulgences from that region.

Another great example of food served based on a story was the first time Patti hosted. Her inaugural fare was harvested from the book, *The Unexpected Guests.* In this story, food was scarce and treats almost nonexistent. The cook for the family was still somehow able to provide a birthday cake for the character named Emerald which featured green roses made from frosting, to honor the character's favorite color. The night the book club met, Patti served a cake decorated with green frosting roses. As the club members entered her dining room and spied the cake on her side board, they all remarked instantly on Patti's great idea. The cake in the book was mentioned in only one or two paragraphs, yet everyone recalled it and complimented Patti on her resourcefulness.

Kate and Tim's granddaughter, Layla, was apparently

listening to Kate's stories about book club because when she was allowed to have her own email address, one of her first messages was to Kate and Tim asking if they would like to join her book club. She also extended her offer to Kathy, Kate's neighbor, whom she adored. Kate was very happy that Layla and Kathy loved each other because Kate loved both of them as well. Tim - Grandpa to Layla - was more than happy to read a children's book in order to have a new connection to the granddaughter he adored.

Kate and Layla went to the Victory library to pick out the first book for their new club. Layla picked a book called *Rump*. The story was a prequel to the story of Rumpelstiltskin and featured a favorable twist on the tale. Like Read Between the Wines, Layla wanted to serve food that was somehow related to the story, so this presented a new challenge to Kate: the characters in Rump didn't eat anything that existed in the real world.

The characters did however eat a muddy, slimy mixture called sludge; it was sustenance for an underworld of trolls and was teaming with crawling worms. Kate translated that to chocolate milk blended into mashed bananas with gummy worms mixed in, served in plastic see-through cups. Layla was delighted. It was a snack that looked truly disgusting but, to a nine-year old, tasted delicious. Layla led the discussion since the book club was her idea. Her first question was, "What one word would you use to describe Rump?" The group took turns answering.

At Kate's next book club meeting with her grown-up friends, it was her turn to lead the discussion about a book that promised to reveal the realities of a person pictured in a famous painting. Following Layla's lead, she asked, "What one word would you use to describe Mona Lisa?"

DAVE 4

Dave was unable to fall back asleep so he abandoned his claim of being sick. While Lisa was showering, he rolled himself into a sitting position, legs over the side, and scratched his chin. He leaned forward into a standing position then pulled the back of his boxers out of his butt crack as he walked toward the bathroom.

"Are you better? Are you okay?" Lisa asked from the shower stall when she saw his shape through the cloudy glass of the shower door.

"I'm not great but I think I'm okay. I just remembered a customer that I have to go take care of today so I'm at least going to go do that." Dave braced for Lisa's argument against this plan.

"Are you sure? I can drive you as soon as Trevor goes to school" her sentence dropped off as she waited to hear Dave's response to her suggestion.

"No." Dave was at the sink looking at himself in the mirror. *When did I get this old?* He turned toward the shower, "If I'm not well enough to drive, I'll let you know or I just won't go."

"If you can just-not-go, why don't you simply just-not-go?" Lisa was often able to use logic against him.

"It's an elderly couple who have no heat, they're using space heaters that aren't very safe. If I can't go finish their job, I'd have to call one of my competitors and have them do it." *Good job Dave, you pulled that right out of the ol' hidey hole.* He patted himself on the back mentally.

Lisa was toweling herself off, "Oh. Is it that adorable Les and Eve you introduced me to at Wegmans?"

Dave had been watching his wife dry herself off then wrap her hair in the damp towel. He was starting to lose interest in everything except his wife. He reached toward her placing his hand in the center of her lower back; she recognized the look on his face. "I thought you were sick." she smiled, "I guess I'll stop worrying about you." He reached further around her waist to pull her to him; her arms were up over her head trying to manipulate her towel into a stable turban so his attempt was successful and she fell into his chest. "Our son is in the next room waiting for his turn to be in here." she said as she kissed her husband's neck.

Dave enjoyed the momentary feeling of normalcy he just had with his wife; he didn't want it to end. He really missed the relationship they used to enjoy. As Lisa pulled on her robe, he forced his thoughts back to his agenda for the day. The minute he remembered his post office box, he was back to feeling like the Dave-of-late - all thoughts of his wife's curves gone. He felt disgust with himself but at the moment Lisa opened the bathroom door and let Trevor in, he vowed to make it past this current situation. He vowed he would get out from under his illegal maneuvers and work hard to be a profitable, honest businessman. For now though, he had to finish what he started.

Dave wasn't certain what time the post office opened, but it was located near a McDonald's, so if he got there and had to wait, he knew he would at least be able to get a cup of coffee during the wait time. He showered, dressed, and left; it was only a few minutes later than if he were following his usual schedule. He arrived at the post office a little before 8:00 a.m. He read the sign on the door and learned that the doors would be unlocked at 8:30. He climbed back into his truck and idled over to the McDonald's drive through. He ordered a large black coffee and on impulse added hash browns to his order. Fatty foods sounded like a good idea. Once back in the parking lot of the post office, he took the lid off of his coffee to let some heat escape, hoping that would make it a tolerable drinking temperature a little sooner. As he contemplated the swirling steam that was rising out of his cup, filling the truck cab with the quintessential scent of morning, he peeled the paper back from his oval-shaped hash brown. Before he was even aware that he was eating it, it was gone. He looked at the empty wax paper envelope it had been served in and felt a loss. *I ate that so fast, I didn't even realize I was eating it. Now it's gone.* Dave made a mental note to cruise through that drive through again once his P.O. Box had been checked.

When Dave saw the uniformed employee unlock the door from inside the building, he climbed out, pushed the button on his key to lock up his truck and walked over to the entrance. Butterflies started hopping around in his stomach, *I didn't know butterflies could hop...* he made himself think of something unrelated to his task at hand. He focused his thoughts on Trevor, imagining what his day might include. Dave walked up to his assigned box, peered into the window and saw that there was, in fact, something in there. Thoughts of Trevor were replaced by thoughts of identity theft and mail fraud. The butterflies were now square dancing.

He opened his box, stuffed the contents into his jacket's inside pocket and left without looking at what he had received. Once back in his truck, he looked around, locked his doors and pulled the contents from inside his jacket. *Dave, you are not cut out for this, you just locked your truck doors before looking at your mail...*

He held three envelopes in his hand. All three were from financial institutions. He opened the first one. It was from one of the companies he had applied with. It contained a congratulatory letter and three temporary checks. Dave registered this as a win, but it was a win with some huge catches. The second was from a company he had applied to; they were acknowledging his application and outlining the other possible ways that they could help him achieve his financial objectives. The last piece of mail was from a credit card company he had not applied to. He rechecked the front of the envelope. It was correctly addressed to Weldon Shipway, Dave's father, and it included the correct P.O. box address. *How could this company know about me - or who I'm pretending to be - when I didn't reach out to them?* he asked himself. It seemed pretty clear that one of the companies he had applied to must have sold his information to other companies. *Man, I do not get this industry. What have I gotten myself into? I'm fucking with an industry I don't even understand - that's pretty freaking stupid.* Dave's plan to get out from under his foray into criminality was reinforced by this unnerving piece of mail. Dave shoved the first letter back into his pocket and tore the other two up into tiny shreds. He shoved the shreds into the empty hash brown envelope and then shoved that swollen mess into the two inches of coffee remaining in his throw-away cup and put the lid back on the top of the cup. He started up his engine and drove the 100 yards back to the fast food drive-through. He was no longer hungry for another hash brown but he sidled up to an outdoor trash can and tossed his now-heavy coffee cup into it before heading back home.

He entered his home through the downstairs entrance reserved for the business. Lisa wouldn't stop his progress with questions about his health that way. She understood that she needed to behave like he was at work at a remote location. They had established that expectation within his first year of working out of their home. Dave's intention was to spend some time in front of his computer confirming what refrigeration equipment he could buy and for how much, then making predictions on what types of work he would be able to accept and the value of that work. He wanted to make sure that his original plan and calculations could justify his cashing of the first check - a turning point that couldn't easily be undone. He glanced to the left and saw the light on his voice-mail indicator.

Seeing that red light caused his stomach to lurch again. Voice-mail messages had evolved into something bad for Dave. He picked up the handset and pushed the message button. *You have three messages,* a bodiless voice informed him. *Press One to....* Dave cut off the voice by pressing one. The voice informed him that the first message had come in at 7:45 a.m. "Hi Dave, this is Don at Quarts Equipment, I need to hear from you today or unfortunately I'm going to have to put you on credit hold. It's going to take 1,500 dollars to get back to good. Please call me." Dave silently shook his head and he hit the delete button. The next message came in at 8:01. "Dave, this is Corrine calling from Wards. Give me a call today please. I need to get a payment plan into place with you." Corrine followed up with her phone number before hanging up. Dave was feeling his nerves tingle and his butterflies were again dancing as he hit the delete button, inviting the third message to play. "Dave, dammit buddy, I'm in an awkward spot here. My boss says he has to see some cash from you before we can sell you anything else." Dave recognized his old friend Paul's voice. Paul worked for the auto parts store that Dave preferred to use. "Please put me out of my misery by dropping off five hundred bucks or so. More would be great." He heard Paul's handset hit the phone base as the message ended.

Dave felt his stomach convulse; he couldn't deny the inevitable. He ran back to the outside door, threw it open and while clutching his gut, he threw up his hash brown; it was swimming in brown liquid. Most of the expulsion landed in a potted plant that Lisa had placed there to add dignity to his "corporate entrance." *Coffee is good for plants, right?* Dave's sickened mind inquired. When the convulsions were over, he stumbled to a stuffed chair that was in the corner of his office room. He dropped into it as he wiped sweat off of his face. He was shaking badly. He took a few deep breaths, stood back up and walked to his bathroom. There he splashed water on his face and swished water around in his mouth. As he toweled off his face, he heard the door open at the top of the stairs.

"How are you feeling honey?" Lisa called down the stairs. She must have been worrying or she wouldn't have violated their understanding about the meaning of that door.

Dave opened the bathroom door and called back, "I'm okay, just a little dizzy and tired."

"Oh, sorry honey," Lisa replied. "Was it Les and Eve you needed to go see? You didn't answer me before..."

Dave was confused, *Les and Eve? What is she talking about?* "Huh?"

"The old people who needed heat?" Lisa reminded him.

Dave had forgotten the story he had made up to explain why he needed to leave the house in the midst of his not feeling well. "Yes it was them and they are fine now," he looked up the stairs into his wife's face and then added, "Snug as a pair of bugs in a rug."

"Oh honey," Lisa replied, "I am so proud of you. It makes me so happy that you do important things for people in our community." Lisa's earnestness was palpable.

Dave forced a laugh. "You just take that attitude and go get wifing." Dave tried to make a joke that would get Lisa to close the ever-important door and go about her business so that he could think about his business and his plan. When her comment registered on his conscience, it made his self-loathing ratchet up a few more notches. Dave went back into his bathroom and heaved up the last of his coffee. Bile was in his mouth and he tried to spit it out but the taste seemed to be trying to take up residence. He took a mouthful of water from the sink, swished it around and spit that into the toilet before flushing away the brown mucousy swirls, spinning clockwise as he watched the bowl empty.

Dave moved over to his desk, wiping his mouth with his shirt sleeve. *What to do next?* At least there weren't any more messages on his phone. Although, that meant he also didn't have any service calls to go on. He started a tabulation of the cost of things he'd like to buy to expand his business. Again he came up with roughly $5,000 of expenses. He replayed his phone messages in his mind and decided that he also needed to make a list of companies he owed money to and how much. He had made about three entries when he decided he needed to do something more about the taste of bile in his mouth. Just then he heard the front storm door slam shut. He decided Lisa must be going out to the mailbox and that this would be his chance to use his bathroom upstairs without explaining himself. He bolted up the stairs and hurried to his bathroom. He found the bottle of 'Fresh Mint Flavored Rinse' under the sink; it promised to whiten his teeth while freshening. The freshening part was irresistible to him at this point. He twisted off the cap and drank straight from the bottle. He mixed the contents of his mouth around for a few seconds before spitting it into the sink; he needed to disengage a few stretching strings of mucous with his fingers. After wiping his hand off on the towel Lisa kept on the small towel bar to the right of the sink, he stood upright and looked at his watering eyes in the mirror. *Man, you are not cut out for this.*

He made his way back downstairs before he heard the front door reopen and close. As he turned back to his spreadsheet on his computer's screen, he still tasted bile. *Maybe this is part of the new life I've carved out for myself.* He continued to make his entries into his spreadsheet that listed his debts. His brain was swimming; the column of numbers was getting so long. *Relax man, pretend this is someone else's problem for now.*

Dave ended up splitting his debts into three columns - the first one represented those that had to be paid before any additional purchases could occur; that one totaled $3,250. The second column represented vendors that would probably extend a small amount of credit but would need some money within the next month; that column totaled $2,200. The final column listed vendor accounts that he owed money to but weren't yet aware that he should be monitored closely; that column totaled $1,035. He had some decisions to make, but whether or not to use the checks from the credit card companies was not among them. Should he use the money from these companies to pay off his debts instead of expanding his business? Or, buy the supplies he needed to expand his business and pay off some debt? And, what to do about that feeling that he really didn't want to cross the line into the criminal world? *Pretend this is someone else's problem....*

Dave put himself in the mindset of an accountant giving advice to a small business owner. *I suggest you take this one step at a time*, he said to himself in a paternal tone. *If you plan to rip off more than one credit card company, why not start by stealing only $3,000 from your first target. Use $2,000 of that to buy equipment and $1,000 to satisfy a debt or two. Email all your commercial customers to let them know you now have the ability to service their commercial refrigeration equipment and cross your fingers for a week or two.* He was hoping he'd get a few new jobs right away and those jobs could help him pay off more debt and maybe even fund more of the equipment. If that plan didn't pan out, or didn't pan out enough, he could consider cashing a check from a second credit card company. *One step at a time.*

Dave noticed his hands were shaking, yet he also felt some relief in having the first part of his plan laid out. He stood up and walked over to the old recliner in the corner of his basement room. He slumped into the chair and kicked out the footrest. Within minutes he was asleep, but his rest was punctuated by startling dreams. Ugly faces would appear suddenly in his dream's mind's eye; bile filled his mouth in his dreams and even though the dream-Dave would spit it out, his mouth remained full. Worst of all was seeing his son Trevor walking away. Dave called to him in his dream but Trevor never turned around, he just kept walking away. An hour later, Dave woke up because of an involuntary jerk of his body. He was covered in sweat; his mind was reeling because of the Trevor dream he was having at that moment. As he stood up, he smelled his own sweat mixed with another bitter odor. He needed a shower. He started up the stairs, hoping he could get into the shower before Lisa realized where he was.

While the hot water was pounding down on Dave's head and shoulders, he was working through the question of how exactly would he turn the temporary checks from credit card company number one into actual cash. He worked through several ideas, shooting holes into most of them. By the time he had drained most of the hot water tank, he knew he was going to need his father's ID and needed to find a non-local branch of the bank that still had some of his father's money in it. Both of these would be found in his office. He quickly put on clean clothes and brushed his teeth and hair.

By the time he was back in his office he felt a little better and a lot cleaner. He pulled his father's driver's license and ATM card out of his filing cabinet and slipped them into his back pocket, glancing at the staircase in the event Lisa had somehow made her way down the staircase without his knowing it. Then he turned toward his monitor and keyboard and googled R&T Bank. He clicked into the page of branch locations and found one in a town on the western outskirts of Allentown. The drive would take about an hour. He got in his truck and headed in that direction.

As he drove, he weighed out the risks of what he was about to do. His plan was to use the bank's drive-through, wearing a baseball hat and sunglasses. The picture of his father on his driver's license showed him wearing glasses that had some tint to the lenses due to the bright lights inside that DMV where the picture was taken. He would turn up the collar to his denim jacket before he got there. His hope was to drive up to the kiosk, put his license, ATM card, and one check made out to 'cash' for $3,000 into the plastic, hinged tube, and just grumble responses to anything the teller might say to him over the microphone. If it didn't go smoothly, he could just tell them to cancel the request and give him back his ID and then he'd drive away. *What if the bank had some system for knowing who was alive and who was dead.* Dave was fairly certain that neither he nor Jay had notified this bank of their father's passing.

Dave pulled his truck over to the side of the road. It was a rural stretch with few other vehicles. He climbed out and made his way into the ditch about five feet from the edge of the pavement. There he worked a handful of muddy dirt up out of the wet area. He went to the back of his truck and rubbed his handful over his license plate. He had only about 5 more miles to go and he hoped the impromptu camouflage would cling to the plate that long. That way, if he had to abandon his plan to acquire cash at the R&T drive-through, no cameras could prove his felonious intent.

Once back into his truck, he felt his stomach butterflies take wing as he shifted his transmission into drive. His phone's navigation was telling him to turn left in one-half of a mile. He knew from seeing the branch location on the map on his monitor back home that there wasn't much navigation to work through, once he got off this stretch of state road. It was now-or-never time.

Is there any way I can make my business work without breaking the law? Dave pictured the three columns he had created earlier on the Excel spreadsheet. The voice-mail messages replayed in his head as he did this last minute evaluation. Suddenly, a horn blared to his left - he turned quickly and saw a driver jerk his wheel to the left to avoid a T-bone collision with Dave. He had driven through a stop sign without noticing it. *Dude, get a grip. And, while you're at it, leave this scene. There was no accident thanks to the skill of the other driver and you have an obvious problem with your license plate right now.*

Dave mimed an "I'm sorry" message to the other driver; hands and shoulders raised up, mouthing the words of apology. The smoky dust, created by the skidding turn of the other car, was rising up and around the intersection; making eye contact difficult between the two drivers. Dave pushed down on his gas pedal and left the scene as quickly as possible. *Just go and get this done,* Dave said to his Weldon self. *You are not Dave right now. Just rise above it and watch yourself get this done.*

Within minutes Dave was following arrows that directed him around to the side of the bank that had the drive-through. He flipped up his collar and got behind one car that was in the process of a transaction. He leaned forward in his seat so that he could pull his ID out of his back pocket, as his father would have done. *You are an actor right now, you are working a scene in a movie.* He paired up his 2 forms of ID with the check he had filled out earlier. He shrunk himself down into his jacket as he thought of himself as an old man, his head hunched slightly forward. He saw the tail lights of the car in front of him flashing past reverse then showing no rear lights - indicating it was in drive - as it pulled away from the kiosk, that driver's turn complete.

Dave put his truck in drive and took his foot off the brake. He rolled his window down as he pulled up to the tube station.   He pressed the button that would lower the Plexiglas window that was in front of the cylinder he needed. Once it was exposed, Dave calmly pulled the cylinder into his lap and placed the three life-changing items into it. He replaced the cylinder into the tube station and pressed a button that would send his items into the bank and its attending authorities.

"Mr. Shipway?" a voice from the tube station asked. Dave jerked his head up and toward the window where a young male bank teller was looking at him.

"Yes?" Dave grumbled in his best old man's voice. His heart was racing and he held his own hands to keep the shaking from being obvious.

"Do you want large bills?" the teller asked.

Again Dave tried to be as brief as possible, "Yes." He turned away and sunk back into his jacket, looking straight ahead. Soon he heard the tube return to his side of the vacuum system. He pressed the button one last time to reveal the transporting device. He pulled it into his lap again, opened it and pulled one of the bank's envelopes out, stuffing that into the inside pocket of his jacket. He replaced the plastic tube and put his truck in drive. He rolled out of the bank parking lot and got back on the road he had followed to get to the bank. Once back on the straight-away of the state route, he accelerated and allowed himself to think about what had just happened. *Holy freaking shit. That was so easy.* He replayed it in his mind. Wait! His ID, *where is that right now?* Flares and red flags went off in his head. The shaking started over again. There is no way he could pass himself off as his father in person, if by chance he had to go back to the bank to request the return of his ID. He pulled the truck over to the side of the road and pulled the bulging envelope out of his pocket. He slid the stack of bills out of the end of the paper pocket. His ID was there, on the top of the stack. He took a deep breath and pushed the two plastic cards into his back pocket for the second time that day. He returned his

attention to the cash in his hand. It was all one hundred
dollar bills. He flipped through the stack, counting the
number of bills. Thirty. He held 30 one-hundred dollar
bills. Feelings of amazement fought for dominance over
the feelings of guilt. Amazement was winning as he pulled
back out onto the road.

Dave came to a full stop at the intersection he had almost
died at earlier this day. When he confirmed no vehicles
were coming on his left and on his right, he crossed
through, feeling like this crossing marked his passage back
into the safe part of his world. *I am Dave again, father of
Trevor, husband of Lisa, brother of Jay, son of...* He
stopped himself there. He could not proudly claim to be
the son of the man he was pretending to be so that he could
steal money from credit card companies. As shame
flooded his consciousness, he noticed that the sky had
turned cloudy and dark, almost as if it were in sync with
his feelings. He pulled off his sun glasses and put those
and his hat in the passenger seat. He made his way back
home. Later he would not be able to recall any of the trip
home that followed his crossing of the intersection with
the two-way stop.

As he entered the town where he lived with his wife and
son, he glanced at the clock on his dashboard. Three
o'clock. There was still time to do more with his plan. He
turned his truck in the direction of the auto parts store
where his friend Paul worked. Once in their parking lot, he
peeled eight fresh bills off of his stack of money. The
remaining bills went into his glove compartment. Dave
walked into the store and spotted Paul behind the counter.
Paul was on the phone but he nodded and smiled at Dave,
directing him to get in his line as he finished up his phone
call. As Paul was hanging up the phone, Dave reached
across the counter to offer a handshake, "So sorry my
friend, I did not mean to put you in an awkward spot here."

"Hey, all is well that ends well, right?" Paul spoke as one

who wants to assume a problem is about to be resolved; the obvious question just below the surface.

"That is my motto today, my friend." Dave said magnanimously. As Dave handed Paul the cash he was carrying, he repeated, "All is well that ends well."

Paul took the cash to the counter behind the cash registers. He keyed a few things into the keyboard there and printed out a receipt for Dave. The bottom of the receipt indicated the balance that was still due. "Here you go, buddy," Paul smiled as he handed over the paper. "I appreciate you responding to my message."

"No problem. I'm sorry you had to prod me." Dave was thinking about his own words, 'no problem,' and was astounded at just how much of a problem it really was - a problem of his own making, though.

Dave stopped in at The Victory Village Inn on his way home. Today he would be having a very personal, albeit small, celebration. He moved toward the back of the bar, to his usual seat, nodding yes to the bar tender who offered him his usual request. He replayed parts of his day as he swirled the whiskey around in the shorter of two glasses in front of him. The fact that he had committed a felony registered with his conscience on every available level. He was shaking his head back and forth minutely as the bar tender approached him. Preemptively, Dave said, "Yes, another round please."

"Beer too?" The bar tender asked.

Dave looked down to see that his beer was full but his shooter glass was empty. "Uh, no," he laughed at himself, "just another bourbon, please."

Dave headed for home about an hour later. His hangover was gone but he was working on a new one. Dave felt better for having paid off most of one of his many debts. Tomorrow he would plan the best use of his remaining hundred dollar bills.

The next morning Dave woke up feeling happy. His head wasn't aching and if it weren't for his dry mouth he wouldn't have known that, again last night, he had drank more that the 'old Dave' would have. As he placed his feet on the floor next to his bed, the memory of the bank drive-through came back to him. His stomach lurched, *I am a criminal,* he thought. No longer was he just contemplating becoming a criminal. He had crossed that line. His feeling of being happy didn't last a full minute.

He showered and went downstairs. As he registered the sounds of his family's other two members rising above him, he booted up his computer. He knew he wanted to spend at least $2,000 on new equipment, but it didn't make much sense to do that before he had a customer who needed him to do refrigeration work. His plan was to find a safe place to stash the 22 bills he still had and take a day or two to drum up some new business. When he got the first request for his new specialty, he would go buy whatever he needed for that job. For now, he booted up the program he used to create documents. The program was billed as a free way to enjoy the benefits of Microsoft Word.

He started to key in the benefits he had to offer to his commercial customers. His intent was to write down everything he could think of that could be perceived as a benefit to his customers - adding onto that, anything that would appeal to a customer who was experiencing a refrigeration emergency. He eventually honed these ideas into a bulleted list of ten items. He arranged these things into an order that made sense relative to how many people they would have meaning to, how much of an emergency it might represent, and how much money could be lost or saved.

Once happy with his list of reasons to use his company for commercial refrigeration service and maintenance, he crafted an introductory paragraph and a closing paragraph. He sat back and looked at his screen. He had his first piece of marketing material done. He was ready to turn that into an email and get it out to his commercial customers. He felt like he had had an accomplishment and that felt good. *Look at me, I can bring home the bacon and fry it up in a pan....* He was allowing himself a small amount of enjoyment. He went to his database of customers and started to click through those he had email addresses for.

After pasting his new message into emails for about sixty contacts and hitting send on each one, he realized he was hungry. In fact, he was really hungry. Dave clicked to save his document and turned off his monitor. Back in his truck he headed for McDonald's and the post office. McDonald's was first, at this point Dave couldn't think beyond the growling, wrenching feelings in his abdomen. Hunger was causing his head to swim as he looked at the menu: Sausage Egg McMuffin? Egg and Cheese Biscuit? The only thing he knew for sure was that he didn't want an order of hash browns. "May I take your order please?" a voice came from the screen he was looking at.

Dave tried to hide the fact that he was startled. "I... Uh... Yep. I'll have two Sausage Egg McMuffins."

"Two Sausage Egg McMuffins." the voice confirmed back. "Would you like a cup of coffee or some hash browns with that?"

Dave's mind flashed back to the prior morning, "No. Uhhh... No thank you. I'll have a small cola."

"That will be eight twenty-five. Please pull ahead to the first window."

"I'm on my way." Dave promised the voice.

Soon Dave was pulling to the far right part of the post office parking lot. He wanted to be able to sit still and eat his breakfast. It was almost 11:00 and he was suffering. He put his truck in park and pulled the warm bag of food onto his lap. Before he realized it, he was pulling out the second of his two breakfast sandwiches. A few swallows of soda marked the transition from sandwich one to sandwich two. After he popped the last bite of breakfast into his mouth he leaned his head back against his headrest and felt a rush of primal satisfaction. He breathed deeply a few times. *Wow, man you needed that.* He picked up his cup of cola and discovered it was empty.

Deciding to just get this second stop over with, Dave walked into the post office; he pulled his head down into his jacket as much as what was reasonable, and walked over to the area that housed the rented mail boxes. He peeked into his box's little window and saw a few envelopes. He opened the door, reached in, and pulled out the envelopes and stuffed them into his jacket. He really didn't even want to know who they were from, yet.

KATE 4

When Kate first started to communicate with Michael by phone, he was in the county jail near where they lived. They got into a somewhat comfortable routine of talking on the phone and exchanging letters. Kate was forced to learn about the policies of this institution regarding mail, phone use, visiting times, and commissary. Commissary is the word used to describe how inmates could buy things for themselves if their loved ones provided money to do so. The county lock-up that Michael was in provided only enough food to keep a person alive and that's why he had been buying cookies. He also needed money in his commissary account to buy soap and/or shampoo and if possible, deodorant. Kate didn't want to contribute to his commissary at this point, but she did send him books; she felt providing books fell into the category of building his brain while he couldn't do anything else. To the best of her knowledge, no one had died of body odor or dandruff. Books had to be paperback, however, and they had to come directly from a seller who had clearance, Amazon was one of these. She learned of the rule regarding paperbacks versus hardcover the hard way. In one of his phone calls Michael told her that a guard had mentioned that he had gotten something from Amazon that would be put with his personal possessions. The guard explained that was the procedure when someone received a hardcover book. *Great,* Kate thought, *he'll get that $24.00 book in two to three-and-a-half years.*

Kate and Amanda went to visit Michael a few weeks after Kate had started to talk with her son. The clerk checking them in seemed to be intentionally treating them badly, even though both women had above average social skills in full deployment. They had arrived five minutes early and although there was no one else in competition for this clerk's services, she scolded Kate for not having her identification out and ready for her. She scolded Amanda for some equally small error. Kate was not used to having to acquiesce to this type of veiled abuse so accepting it for the moment increased her anxiety about attending a visit within the county jail. After getting past the check-in phase with the person Kate was mentally referring to as the power-hungry bitch, PHB for short, they moved to an adjacent room which held a few rows of 12 chairs each; about half the chairs were filled when they entered.

Kate tried to listen to what Amanda was saying as she chattered endlessly, but Kate was so fascinated by the Petri dish of this particular subculture - her county's incarcerated families - that all she really wanted to do was look around and attempt to eavesdrop on conversations. As each new group entered, Kate observed them as innocuously as possible, silently adding to her new database of facts related to the families of the incarcerated in her community. Soon all the chairs were filled and new arrivals had to remain standing, lining the walls. So many seemed to know exactly what was going on, laughing with the people they arrived with - many of which were children - and occasionally glancing at the clock. For a moment Kate wished she could laugh too, but the casual acceptance of the majority of people in this waiting area led Kate to the belief that her discomfort was an acceptable burden to bear for the time being.

At one point, many of the visitors moved toward the far side of the room in unison, forming a line, as if following a directive that Kate was unable to hear. Minutes later, the institutional clock on the wall marked the hour just as a door at in that area opened. Kate and Amanda got into this new line. Kate's heart started to race. *What am I doing in a jail house?!* she asked herself. She worked on calming herself as the group was herded into a hallway with nothing but a heavy door at the far end. Once everyone was fitted into the small square footage of this tiled hallway, the door behind them was locked, the metallic sound of which made Kate's stomach lurch. She felt like a lab rat. No going forward or backward until someone in "power" deemed it so. A guard appeared at the door at the end of the hall; he used his key to open the door to Kate's next experience.

The next room was set up for visitation; the built-in, room-sized fixture was shaped like the letter C. The outside of the C was comprised of cubicles made primarily of Plexiglas. Each cubicle had two metal stools secured to the floor on the visitors' side and one stool on the inside side of the C - presumably, this is where Michael would appear and sit. The Plexiglas was about five feet tall and it included side walls to delineate the elbow room available to the two stools on the visitors' side of the configuration. The group of people there for the visit moved around the C-shape until all the people were seated in stools around the edge of the room. Once everyone was seated, another loud door was opened and the inmates, all dressed in navy blue, faded cotton coveralls, entered the room single-file. They each looked around, spotted their family members, and headed to the stools opposite them. The room filled with the smell of unshowered people.

Many of the guests clearly knew the rules and Kate was trying desperately to learn the protocols in this snap-shot of time. The others hugged the inmate they were there to see over the top of the Plexiglas structure before sitting and starting into a conversation that seemed to pick up where the last one had left off. When Michael made his way over to Amanda and Kate, he hugged his girlfriend first. Kate realized that meant she could hug her son next, albeit briefly. She gripped him tightly, closed fists pressing into his back. Michael's way to start their conversation was to say, "How are you?" Kate was programmed to answer honestly, so her answer was, "I'm mad at you!" She took a breath, "Look at where I have to talk to you!" With a small gesture, her right arm indicated the institutional room with armed guards at every entrance.

"I know Mom." Michael's tone was intended to calm her.

"Let's just try to talk nicely for now."

"I plan to be nice but I can't just not be mad." Kate replied.
As these words left her mouth, Kate felt her immense love
for her son. She melted slightly and sat down. In spite of
feeling somewhat patronized by her son, who didn't want
a scene, she tried to focus on the reasons this visit could be
good for her and productive for him. Kate had a few things
she needed to discuss and she allowed these to the
forefront of her thoughts.

About half-way through the 60 minute visit, Kate
experienced anxiety to the degree that she had to center
herself. She folded her hands in her lap and stared at her
clasped hands; they were the only thing truly familiar to
her in the room. She stared at the point where her hands
met and thought about her favorite peaceful place, a spot
on a wooded trail where she and Michael and Toni would
pass away Saturday afternoons when the children were
much younger. They would pack a lunch and just go
explore for hours during those years. Often Kate's sister
Liz and her son would join them. These were probably the
most peaceful days the five of them had spent together,
and Kate called upon this memory now in order to endure
her visit to a place where she did not feel she belonged.
She didn't want her son to belong here either but she had
no control over that. She could hear Amanda and
Michael's chatter in the background of her momentary
meditation; they were not aware that she had this need to
be removed for a few minutes.

Their departure from this visit was pretty much a reversal
of the procedure for the entry except that Amanda was
crying. Loud locks locked and unlocked, guards avoided
eye contact and guests were expected to move in an
unspoken choreography toward the exit.

After this visit Kate went home exhausted. Her Saturday
energy was expended and she needed a nap.

The rest of the court dates went by in a blur. It amazed Kate how tiny the steps toward conclusion were within the local court system. Without fail, each time she entered the court house, her chest filled with anxiety; she trembled and was dizzy for the duration. In one appearance, the judge instructed Michael that if he chose to plead not-guilty, he would be facing more severe charges that would be pursued against him with even greater vigor. To Kate, this didn't seem just. She thought everyone had the right to plea not-guilty without risk of making their situation worse. This county's practices seemed to slant the justice system substantially in favor of the prosecuting side. She learned later that this county channeled petty criminals into the state prison system at a rate higher than the other counties in the state. *How lucky are all of the rest of the county's population who don't need to be aware of this....*

When Michael finally pleaded guilty to the two felony charges he was facing, there was some relief. At least now they were moving toward the inevitable sentence and, hence, ultimately the completion of that sentence. On the day the judge sentenced him, Kate sat in the courtroom accompanied by Amanda, Toni and June, Kate's precious step-daughter from her first marriage and Michael's half-sister. Michael knew he was going to be sentenced to either three or four years, based on what his public defender had told him. Although on a calendar it's a difference of only one year, in the PA court system, it was a greater difference than that because a three year sentence or less would qualify Michael for the program called Shock Camp that Michael had told Kate about. In this program, six months of successful participation is a substitute for three years of prison time, and the six months were not in a maximum security prison, it was a minimum security facility. Michael and Amanda had written letters to the judge asking him to consider a three year sentence.

It was finally Michael's turn to speak on his own behalf prior to sentencing. He outlined the fact that he had a very employable skill group, a supportive family, and he identified Amanda as his fiancé. He spoke for about four minutes before it was the judge's turn. The judge spoke clearly and with some vehemence. "These things you list off as reasons why you deserve a light sentence are all things that were present in your life before you committed these crimes. You have taken everything that this county has to offer you and you have made an art form out of seeing how far you could take this, how much you could get away with." He went on for five minutes or so. Kate was astonished at how informed and accurate his appraisal was. At the end he split the difference and sentenced Michael to three and one-half years. Michael left the courtroom shuffling to avoid tripping on his shackles. He glanced at the women there to offer support and raised his shoulders in a sign of, 'oh well, I tried.'

Kate was amazed at his coolness. When she spoke with him on the phone the next day she said, "You should be shitting your pants! I do not understand why you are not shitting your pants!" Her son was going off to a state prison for roughly three years, *had he not seen or heard anything about what this will be like?*

"Mom, calm down." Michael replied. "I think I can still get shock camp because I have learned that the time qualification is based on 'good' time. Three and half years of good time in a prison is the same as three years. The word 'good' referred to good behavior; as long as he didn't cause problems for the guards, get in any fights, or test positive for drugs, his sentence would be considered three years.

A few days went by. Kate's stomach was churning because she knew any day her son would be transported to a maximum security prison with a reputation for being a really bad place. Chandra had agreed with Kate when she made this observation during one of their meetings. Chandra had done some work with parolees released from there earlier in her professional career. Kate was also tormented by the lack of information. No one owed her the courtesy call saying, *"ummm, Kate, we plan to move your son tomorrow, we'll feed him first and let you know when he arrives safely."* The complete lack of control over the situation caused its own version of stress. Michael called her on day four. "Any idea when they'll transport you?" she asked.

"I've heard that they wait until they have a full bus, but they fill it with people from a lot of county lock-ups so I really don't know when that will be." Michael was sounding upbeat. "I can't wait to get out of here though." Michael finished.

"Really? I've heard that Arimle is going to be hard on you." Kate was probing to try to get a feel for Michael's state of mind and level of awareness.

"I'll be okay. My sentence doesn't start until I get there so that's why I want to get going."

"Listen sweetie, when you get there I want you to keep a low profile. Speak to the guards only when they've spoken to you. Okay? At least until you feel like you understand your surroundings." Kate was trying not to sound desperate.

"Don't worry Mom, I have no plans to kick off a prison riot or join a gang." Michael was joking and that made Kate fear that he wasn't taking this seriously.

"Michael, again, why aren't you shitting your pants??"

"Mom, I am actually shitting my pants. I know it's going to be a rough place, but I want to keep the faith that I'll be able to get into a shock camp quickly. I can take a few weeks of almost anything." This was Michael's first admission that he might be nervous about his next step. That was all Kate needed to let the topic go. She didn't need to goad her son into being fearful sooner than necessary. She only needed him to be aware and alert to his next challenges. So since she knew that he accepted that his next stop was not at, *sound the train whistle...* Petticoat Junction, it was in fact more like, *sound the slamming metal doors...*Shawshank Junction, she could stop this line of questioning.

On day ten following his sentencing, Kate got a call from Amanda. "He's in Arimle."

Kate slumped back in her chair. "What else do you know?"

"He has what's called a DIN number, that's how inmates are identified. I'll give it to you so you can write him. But anyway, his ends in zero... and that is an even number." This last phrase was thrown in as if Amanda didn't think Kate would know if zero was even or odd. Amanda continued, "So he can get visits on any day that is an even date, so I'm going down there tomorrow."

"Please call me on your way back." Kate practically begged. They chatted a bit more about how Amanda would get there - she had no running vehicle of her own - and what the rules were for visiting for this institution and then got off the phone. Kate took a deep breath and tried to channel her son to see how he was feeling. That didn't work for her though, it never did, so she gave that up and instead, sent out thoughts of strength and peace into the universe, asking that they be delivered to her son if at all possible.

The next day came and went with no phone call or text from Amanda. Kate felt like Amanda had no idea what it was like to be a mother. But how could she, Kate rationalized. She was so young and she wasn't a mother.

Understanding Amanda's parameters didn't make them easier to accept. Kate slept badly that night.

The next day Amanda called. "I'm so sorry I didn't call yesterday. I was just so upset."

"Upset? Upset by what??!" Kate demanded.

"That place is so awful." Amanda choked up as she tried to explain. It was clear that she was suffering too. Kate realized she needed to be gentle as she sought information on her son's well-being. "I got there, I climbed all the steps." Kate and Amanda both knew that one of the things this prison did to be foreboding was to keep the 100 plus outdoor cement steps one had to climb in order to visit an inmate. "Then they told me I couldn't go in because I was wearing leggings. They said leggings were intentionally sexy. I had to go back down the step and drive around the town until I found a store where I could buy some cheap pants, but they couldn't have any metal, no metal snaps or buttons. And they were just so mean to me about it."

"Oh sweetie, " Kate consoled her. "I'm so sorry." Kate was frantic to hear about Michael so she tried to be patient during this part of Amanda's story. "Were you able to find some?"

"Yes, I did, so then I had to go back, climb the steps again, and go through a metal detector. It went off so they made me go in a little room and take off my bra. Then I had to go through it again. That time it didn't go off so I had to go get redressed then get in a line for the visiting room. It was about an hour before I saw Michael."

"How is he?" Kate asked quickly before Amanda could talk more about her own experience.

"Ugh, I don't know. I don't think he's very good, Kate. His eyes kept filling with tears." Amanda started to cry again and this time Kate joined her. This was really bad news.

"Oh honey... " Kate tried to sound soothing, "what else can you tell me?"

"He gets one roll of toilet paper for two weeks. If he runs out before then, he supposed to use his sock."

"You are kidding me?!" Kate was astounded. This was both cruel and unusual in her mind.

"No, and there's not enough food, and he says there is screaming all around him 24 hours a day." Amanda sniffed and swallowed hard. Both women were trying to stay composed during one of their most difficult conversations yet. "He has to be in his cell 23 hours a day, and he can't get books there, did you know that?"

"No." Kate was feeling desolate. Her son couldn't even read. No wonder his eyes were filling with tears. What could possibly occupy his mind all day and all night long with crazy yelling everywhere and hunger pangs at all hours? How did they expect anyone to rehabilitate themselves in a situation like this?

The next day, Kate sent off parts of the book she was writing in a letter to Michael. The rules said he couldn't have a book, but she decided he could have a letter that contained a book. The excitement of this idea made her light hearted for the first time in several months. After mailing the letter from the drop box at the post office she had been using since Michael's incarceration - the former Perkins - she went home and sat at her keyboard. Giving her son reading material became her new objective. Her interest in writing her book was amplified; her prolific side was refueled.

On the day she mailed her third installment, three days after the first installment, she received a letter back that contained paragraphs from Michael with comments on his surroundings and day-to-day schedule, which Kate could tell had been told through a soft lens of his thoughts. In addition to the euphemistic paragraphs, she found the first installment she had sent to him with his hand-written mark-ups. His edits were very helpful to Kate. He would write such simple things as, *If you would describe how this character looked before revealing her inner thoughts, I could "hear" her thoughts a lot better because I'd be picturing her.* And, *You said Corey was going to a SUNY school yet the book is set in Pennsylvania.* Kate said to herself, *Duh*, followed by *thank you Michael! Let's rock and roll on this together!*

Kate's writing became her number one mission. As soon as she got home from the real estate office each day, she'd sit in front of her laptop at the dining room table and hammer out more characters. Eventually she ended up with six characters, of which she herself was one. The rest were figments of her imagination, but they all needed to be using the post office. That was the connecting link within her book.

Tim was glad and supportive. He was grateful that his wife wasn't crying or worse, shaking and crying, throughout the day. When he got home from work he would find something to fix for dinner so that Kate could continue to sit in front of her keyboard. Kate found much catharsis in her new routine of writing for hours each day for two reasons: the first was that she was creating lives that she had complete control over, unlike her own real life. The second, though, was because she was writing about her real life in one of the six characters in her book, the character she called Kim. In putting Kim's feelings and experiences into words, she was packing them up into what Chandra would call a cloud, and then she would send that gliding across her mental horizon as soon as she hit Save on her word processing software.

The next time Kate met with Chandra, she told her she was feeling much better. Her nervousness and anxiety had reduced to a minimum. Chandra mentioned that Kate seemed to light up when mentioning her therapeutic writing. Chandra had a sabbatical on her calendar and Kate assured her she could travel to California to see her sons with no worries about what Kate was facing. Kate really felt like she held the key to her own peace of mind. Chandra, in turn, was very happy for Kate.

When she left that appointment, Kate shook Chandra's hand with both of hers. "Thank you. As before, you've really helped me to find my own way." Kate walked down the three flights of stairs back to the parking lot where she had left her car. It was easy for Kate to picture Chandra as a friend.

Each one of the people Kate held dear to her heart would gladly accept Chandra into their circle of 'jewels.' Jewels was what they called themselves - the group of women Kate embraced. Membership to which required a love of life, a valuing of diversity, and a quest to help others see the beauty in our world. Toni had become a Jewel recently, as had Linda' daughter Chloe, Sue's daughter SW - a name she earned for her raven hair and beautiful white skin, just like Snow White - had joined at the same time. Hap's oldest daughter was a hopeful new member for the next year; she was younger than the other daughters. When the Jewels first identified themselves to each other as a subset worthy of distinction from their larger group of friends, they were on the deck at Linda's summer home on Yockhon Lake. At that time, they hadn't imagined their daughters joining them in the years to come. The fact that the most recent meeting of the Jewels was comprised of four original members and three of their offspring was a blessing they didn't see coming. They did recognize it when it was in front of them though. There were tears and much chatter over this blessing when it became a reality in Kate's living room.

Suzanna was an elder, original Jewel who didn't have children. As such, she served as the voice of wisdom. She was held in a place of honor because she was their "see-er." She was able to look past much of the emotional clamor in society and identify the meaningful things worth their precious discussion time when they met. Her first words on this special day welcomed the new Jewels. Champagne was on hand so eight glasses were raised. It was a good day for Kate.

Kate slipped into a routine of mailing new pieces of her book to Michael and watching her mailbox for fat envelopes containing marked up pages. Michael's letters always contained little notes about how he was doing "just fine" but still hoping to get transferred to a shock camp. Kate knew he wasn't doing "just fine" because Amanda had told her that he really hoped his mom wouldn't visit him while he was there. Meanwhile, Amanda visited him almost every day that had an even date. Michael didn't want his mother to see him in this horrible situation.

By the time two hundred pages of the book had passed from Kate to Michael, and then from Michael back to Kate, he had started to reveal some details of his stay. The thing that troubled him the most was the violence of the guards against the inmates. The guards would try to entice the inmates into arguments and then enter their cells and beat them with their clubs, calling the argument an act of rebellion. Later on she would learn that there were also inmates of a lower class who got a different treatment. These were the inmates involved in hurting children or sexually abusing a person of any age. In the case of these inmates, the guards would open the cell doors and let other inmates enter; leaving the fate of the first inmate up to those who were allowed in. Michael was left to just listen.

Kate got one letter where her son was explaining how he was being treated as an admired person within the prison population because he could spell anything. Someone down the row of cells would yell, "Hey Phillips, how do you spell 'Dear Mom?' " And since he would always know the answer to this type of question, he had earned a place of honor. When Kate wrote back, she told Michael that maybe he was living through a unique opportunity to extend kindness to people who didn't know what that was like. Michael responded with a stark truth, "Mom, I am kind to anyone who asks but these people are crazy. This is not a good place for me to extend myself beyond what is asked of me." Later in his letter he continued, "So many people here are literally crazy. There is screaming all day and all night, and most of the screamers seem to like it here."

After Michael had been in Arimle for four or five weeks, Kate got a call from Amanda. Michael had been moved to a shock camp. Amanda had gone to visit him at Arimle and after waiting in the waiting room for a few hours, someone came out and told her that he'd been moved. A quick internet search had confirmed he was on his way to Lakeside one of the state's shock camps. The next day Kate got a letter from Michael, the last he'd sent from Arimle, telling her that he had been put in isolation because the next day he was being moved to a shock camp. He was very excited. Kate learned months later that inmates were moved to isolation so that none of those being transported could use the knowledge of a transport to arrange for an on-road ambush. Sending a letter was allowed because of the time delay.

Kate was both relieved and anxious. Her son was out of state prison's hell but he was moving to an unknown situation, being transported by unknown means by people who didn't care about him. Kate recalled the days when she knew her son's school bus schedule and she knew the school bus driver; she could count on a phone call if there was anything amiss in the planned schedule.   There was no one calling her now to say, "Mrs. Phillips, Michael wasn't on the bus this morning so we are calling to check on him." This call had actually happened 20 years earlier when she had forgotten to report her son as absent from school for sickness once; his fever was so high that Kate's only concern was getting him to the pediatrician. Her current situation was such a far cry from this fading memory that Kate had to sit down as she worked through it, her head involuntarily shaking from side to side.

A few days later Kate received a letter from Lakeside, the red stamped star on the outside of the envelope confirming that it came from a state incarceration facility. Michael had landed at shock camp and was now waiting to be assigned to what they called 'a platoon.' His six-month program would not start until he was within one of these. Lakeside was a 'reception facility' which meant that all shock camp inmates would start there then be assigned to a platoon which may be at a different shock facility, Michael explained. As soon as he was assigned to a platoon, the six-month countdown to his return home would start. Michael said in his letter that he was hoping to be assigned to a camp called Moriah; only the inmates who had no violence in their past and only those who had been deemed to seem trustworthy could be assigned to Moriah, so he felt it would be the most tolerable place to live, eat, and breathe for six months. When Kate located this camp on a map she was skeptical of whether or not this was worth hoping for - it was six or seven hours away. Kate's car was leased, so she was careful about the number of miles she drove; she couldn't picture how she would be able to visit her son very often during his stay, and she missed him very much. It had been about seven weeks since she had seen him during the less-than-intimate visit to the county jail back in their hometown.

Kate thought back to the visit to the county jail where she had seen her son for the first time since seeing him in the court room; it was also the last time she had seen him. She had wanted to use some of that visit to make sure that

Michael understood what the situation was doing to her.
She felt that knowledge might work as a deterrent to
Michael for the future as well as allowing her the feeling
of standing up for herself. It didn't work out that way
though. The decorum Kate expected of herself in public
precluded crying, plus Michael's need to appear to be cool
in front of the men he currently shared his life with led
him to saying things like, "It's okay Mom," and, "Let's not
talk about that now Mom...." Kate would have had to
make quite a scene in order to make her point and dump
her load of trauma into Michael's lap during that visit.
Even though the demographic that comprised the audience
did not include anyone Kate expected to send a friendship
request to via Facebook, she was still unwilling to make
the scene that would have been necessary.

Once Michael's letters had started to arrive from the least
severe of the Shock Camps where his platoon would be
formed and his six months would begin, Kate was
noticeably calmer. Between working on her book and
knowing that her son was safe on a daily basis, the white
noise in her mind has gone silent most of the time. The
fear that Michael still didn't really understand how his
actions had impacted his mother still troubled her, though.
She couldn't really do justice to the topic by mail. And
when she had her first visit to Michael at Moriah following
a brutal seven-hour drive, it was evident that those
opportunities were not going to provide fertile ground for
the needed discussion either. Kate decided that it was more
important than ever that the book she was writing capture
her feelings.

Amanda had already visited Michael once, at a time that
Kate was not free to go. It was the first opportunity that
Michael had had to have a visit, since visits had to be
earned, and earning took some time. When Kate was able
to go, she felt she had no choice but to include Amanda.
Amanda had never missed an opportunity to visit Michael.
Maneuvering around seemingly insurmountable obstacles -

like not having a car - she even traveled to Arimle each possible time, which was every other day. Visiting opportunities at Moriah were on alternate Sundays.

Amanda's most profitable work opportunities were on Saturday nights when she worked at the bar until close early Sunday mornings. Kate and Amanda worked out a plan for Kate to drive to the house Amanda had shared with Michael to pick her up at 3:00 a.m. after she closed the bar. They drove from there into the parts of Pennsylvania that seemed to define the term 'hinterlands.' Their goal was to arrive at a time that would come as close to the 9:00 a.m. start of visiting hours as possible. While it was winter in Victory, Kate headed out on clear and dry roads. Almost as soon as they had gotten off the expressways that comprised the first one-third of their trip, they ran into blinding snow and roads with slush frozen into the shape of the last traveler's tire tread.

As they passed through the various counties that comprised this hinterland, Kate noticed signs that said 'Rough Road Next 10 Miles.' When ten miles had passed under them, there would be a sign that said, 'Rough Road next 8 Miles,' and so on. When crossing county lines, she saw, as Amanda slept in the passenger seat, signs that said things like, 'Cameron County a Salt Experimentation Region.' Kate quickly figured out that the so-called experiment was whether or not people would and could drive on roads where no salt was used. During the blizzard Kate found herself in, the difference between the experimenting counties and those counties not participating in the test was as clear as day and night. Her stomach began to roll at the sight of these signs. As the sun was beginning to rise on the day of Kate's first visit to Moriah, the new light became very important. They were on roads where if cars met, one would have to pull over in order for them both to pass. Hairpin turns, rocky drop offs, and frozen bodies of water within feet of the crumbling blacktop defined these roads. A mistake would likely be fatal.

To say the least, Kate was uptight as she woke Amanda
and readied herself to enter the largest of the buildings on
the Moriah campus. A life-sized plywood cutout of
Smokey the Bear directed them to one specific door.
Smokey was holding a sign that said, 'Visitors This Way.'
The sign was shaped like an arrow and it pointed to the
door that was used as a funnel for the guests that were
expected on visiting day. Smokey seemed friendly to Kate
and in spite of the gray sky that hung a mere few feet over
her head, her spirits lifted slightly. After all, the county jail
had no friendly bears, visitors had to figure out for
themselves which door to use.

When it was Kate and Amanda's turn to check in, the
deputies and guards were jovial and almost friendly. When
they completed the required paperwork, one particularly
fresh-faced and soon-to-be handsome deputy asked who
they were there to visit.

"Phillips? You're here to see Phillips?" was his reply when
Kate told him. "I just had him in my platoon for two weeks.
Please tell him that Steve hopes he didn't hurt his pretty
face when he shaved this morning." He winked as he
finished his sentence. It was unexpected camaraderie and
Kate was instantly relieved. She wanted to sit down to
allow the relief to wash over her but Steve was directing
them to the door to the room where they would wait for
Michael to enter to begin his visit.

Kate and Amanda had been seated for fifteen minutes
when Kate saw Michael enter the room. She was as
surprised and she was glad to see him. He was wearing a
white button down shirt, navy blue pants, a tie, shiny black
shoes, and his head was shaved. Amanda hadn't
mentioned any details like this to her. Kate cried as he
wrapped his arms around her and hugged her tightly.
"Don't you cry now Mom." Michael said as he unwrapped

himself from her.

"When can I cry?" she asked sharply, involuntarily.

"Mom, I'm fine here, and safe. We try to act like this place sucks to bust on the DIs but trust me, it's so much better than Arimle."

Trust me? Kate thought, *did he really say that.* Instead of following up on that thought she said, "I had no idea you had so many freckles on your head."

Michael scrubbed his head with his knuckles, "I know, right? Some of them are scabs from my scalp rash I get when I have no shampoo."

Kate replied with a thought she had much earlier in Michael's incarceration. "No one has ever died of dandruff, to the best of my knowledge." She was feeling the need to exert some tough love almost in retaliation for Michael's attempt at controlling her emotions. "And what is a DI?"

"It stands for Drill Instructors. This place is very military-oriented so guards are called DIs." Michael explained.

The four hours of their visit went by quickly. Kate left 15 minutes ahead of the designated ending time so that Michael could have a few minutes alone with the woman he planned to return home to at the end of his six months. As she passed the lobby where she had signed in earlier that day, Steve said, "Hey you need to sign out."

Kate turned, "Oh, I'm sorry, I didn't know."

Steve pointed to the book where she had signed in, his finger on the spot where she needed to enter the time of her departure. Kate couldn't see very well. Her eyes were full. "It's 2:45 Ma'am; if you could just put that here."

Kate did her best to work with her shaking hands and vision impairment. She finished the task of filling in the time and started to head for the door. "I hope you have a nice holiday." Steve said, referring to Thanksgiving which was the next week. Kate looked into his face, surprised.

"Thank you," her eyes could no longer contain the amount of liquid in them. "You too." She tilted her head and blinked rapidly but was committed to looking straight into his face. She thought again, *you never know who you touch.* She had been touched profoundly by his kindness, partly due to the contrast to the others she had been exposed to since Michael's arrest. "You have such an important job and I thank you for doing it." There was no pretending that she wasn't crying at this point. He opened the exterior door for her.

"I'm just a country boy doing a job that's available up here. You drive safe now." Kate shook her head in denial of this humble response but she had no more words. She exited quickly and went to her car.

Once locked inside of her Honda, she let go of the modicum of control she was still working with. Tears flowed freely, mostly because after spending four hours with her son, it was already not enough time. She missed him already. Steve's kindness had simply thawed another piece of her heart, enabling her to feel all of the emotion the day had called for.

By 11:00 that night, Kate was climbing into her bed. Tim had fallen asleep on her side so that when she got home, there would be a warm spot for her. "How did it go?" he asked sleepily as he slid to his own side of the bed.

"Oh... There's so much to tell you. We can talk tomorrow but for now, I feel so much better now that I've seen where he is."

"Okay baby, I'm glad you're home safely. Love you." Tim kissed her cheek before turning on his side and returning to sleep.

Kate slept well that night and woke only when her alarm went off the next morning. She had more than six uninterrupted hours of sleep for the first time in several months.

THOMAS 5

Eighteen months after his failed attempt to get to know Elaine better on a dusty country road when he was a senior in high school, Thomas was released from incarceration. He had a layover at a halfway house that lasted one day, then went on to Fort Jackson for basic training. He had a mixture of feelings upon his entry to the halfway house he was assigned to; he felt apprehensive since he felt like an inmate while being almost in the free world, and he felt the freedom that the proverbial bat out of hell feels. These conflicting feelings made him feel agitated as the woman, Donna, showed him around on his arrival. Her job was to provide a tour and explain the rules he'd need to know prior to the Welcome Class, a class that would be more like here-is-our-extensive-list-of-rules class.

Rules   were very important at the Charles Henry Transitional Home for Men. They had a wide range of people staying there, from paroled rapists to non-violent drug dealers, so they could not assume anything about the manners or civility of their guests. They needed to define manners and civility *for* their guests.

Donna was walking Thomas through the kitchen, reciting a litany of kitchen rules. "Wash any dish you use if it's not meal time; no eating after 9:00 p.m. Be sure to dispose of waste in the proper "Thomas!" Donna sharply interjected into his thoughts, "You need to listen to me if you plan to make your reentry a success."

"I am." Thomas lied.

"Lying is not a good way for us to start the cultivation of your relationships with the community."

Reentry... Cultivation of relationships... Did she really just say that in her oh-so-superior voice? Thomas thought. As he replayed it in his mind, while Donna stood staring at him, waiting for a response, something snapped inside him; he heard the noise and he felt the effect.

"I am going to reenter and cultivate *you* if you don't get on with this and show me where I can sleep tonight." Thomas growled at her.

Donna stepped back and gasped. "I will not be spoken to like that. I'm calling the house warden right now. You go sit in that chair." She pointed at the dining table. His surge of anger seemed huge yet just as quickly as it had come on him, it was gone. Thomas's time in the Montgomery County Youth Center had taught him that niceness didn't get anyone ahead in this life, so without any attempt to 'make nice,' he just sat down as instructed. He could hear Donna's voice in the next room; her side of the phone conversation didn't give him any clues about what to expect, but her tone implied that she was shaken up.

Damn bitches, they can't take a joke, Thomas thought. He noticed a staircase then, and decided to find his own way to the bunks or bedrooms or whatever they had to offer him.

Thomas found three large rooms, each with two sets of bunk beds. One of the lower bunks in the second room seemed unused so he threw his backpack at the foot of that and stretched out to try to take a nap. He felt like he had just started dozing when he was shaken violently by a strong hand.

"Get up." A demand from a very insistent voice.

Thomas's internal system had been trained to hear voices like this. It would have been incorrect to say that his inner barometer had forewarned him that this was coming, Thomas was completely free of any inner barometer, that unspoken ingredient that drove the majority of people to react based on the prediction of the behavior of those around them; and most people would have predicted a harsh follow-up to the scene in the kitchen. For Thomas though, it was much more like a trained reaction. Being shaken to an awake status was something that he had, in fact, been trained for. He was standing at attention before the shaker had a second chance to shake.

"Identify yourself, what is your DIN?" The person who had awakened him was asking for the number that was Thomas's identification since he had been in the state's system of incarceration.

"13B1380." Thomas responded from rote.

"Name!" The shaker insisted.

"Thomas Findlay." Thomas's tone was neutral now. All emotion was gone because this interchange had brought him back to the environment in which he had grown comfortable most recently.

"Findlay, you're out of here." The man continued, "The best news you may ever hear is that we have a place you can stay tonight, some call it a lock up, but tomorrow you are being transported to Fort Jackson. Grab your backpack."

The next morning, Thomas was again woken by a rough shake. "Get up, the bus is here." He didn't recognize where he was but it didn't seem to matter.   This man held handcuffs connected by a chain to some shackles.

Thomas's stomach was rumbling. He hadn't eaten since early the prior day. He followed the direction of the man leading him toward a small-sized bus. Thomas's velocity was limited by the shackles on his ankles. In his experience, guys like that guard had the ability to provide food - snack bars, juice boxes, packets of peanuts - once the vehicle got rolling so Thomas wanted to be on his good side. He tried to follow the guard's directions to the best of his ability while still just waking up. "You're lucky Findlay" The guard said, "I've been told to take off the shackles and cuffs once we're underway. Apparently you're not really a ward of the state, just a sleep-over guest that needs a chauffeur."

Within 24 hours of getting on that bus, Thomas was at Fort Jackson in South Carolina, learning how to be in the Army.

Thomas found the Army to be easy. It was very much like jail, minus the imprisonment. Basic training was, to Thomas, all about learning to appear to be obedient, and Thomas had mastered that while he was in the Montgomery County Youth Center. He found it very easy to follow his drill instructors' demands and schedules because the what they led to was marching for hours and standing in straight lines for meals as well as other mundane activities, all things that gave him the time he needed to think about Elaine and how he would 'catch up' with her.

'Catching up with Elaine' was how he described to himself, his endless planning and fantasizing about reconnecting with her in the future. During basic training, he had a few hours each day to commit to this. Once he was moved to Kuwait, he had days where he could spend hour after hour working through his plans. He thought about controlling her - since that was what his initial attraction to her was based on: her ability to control others in a way that was different from his way. He thought about getting even with her for the year and a half of his life he lost because of her. He also thought about her body, what she would look like naked. He pictured her hair and her skin. He imagined that her scent would be light and clean with maybe a slight tinge of something flowery. He thought about loving her and how he would show his love. He thought about how she would squirm under his control and beg him for his kindness. In his mind, she would eventually accept his way of showing his love.

As time went on, Thomas's thoughts seemed to find focus. Controlling Elaine in a way that made her feel controlled while getting retribution for the wrongs against him was his objective, once boiled down. He was sure Elaine would understand his need to seek retribution. In his fantasies, sometimes she would thank him for the opportunity to cleanse herself of the wrongdoings that were her responsibility. He began to feel ownership of Elaine during these sessions. Ownership meant he could do whatever he wanted.

Kuwait was a dangerous assignment about 3% of the time. Many of Thomas's platoon members were genuinely committed to the safety of Kuwait's residents as well as the members of the military they were there with. Only occasionally did the forces working against them in Iraq pose a threat. It was a peacekeeping mission, so this commitment was appropriate. The fact that Iraq did, however, sometimes threaten safety contributed to a sort of brotherhood among both the men and women who took their jobs seriously.

There was a core group of the committed bunch that formed an actual club in 1996. Thomas was not invited to join. Thomas didn't consider the fact that he did not share their commitment; he only considered the fact that, yet again, he had reason to think of himself as different from ordinary people. This newly formed club named themselves The Angels of Forbearance, and one creative member came up with a logo that cleverly depicted the initials TAF entwined with stars and stripes of red white and blue. One night when the club's members were out on the town for several hours, one member suggested they get tattoos of the club's logo. The next morning, 10 of the 12 members had a sore spot and something new to show off on their forearms. "Ow, it feels like a cat scratched my sunburn" one woman complained.

A few of the men were nearby. "Toughen up, Bowerman," one teased her, "I hope you never experience an actual injury."

"Shut up, Gillis," the female cadet shot back, "I'm just commenting on it because I feel proud of it."

Thomas could overhear this interchange. He had noticed the logo of the club he was not welcomed into, and it irked him each time he saw it since TAF were his initials: Thomas Andrew Findlay. When the tattoos showed up all around him, he felt like he couldn't get away from it. His initials, everywhere, *What the fuck... They must know that's me they are wearing on their arms...* He felt himself involuntarily leak out a slow rumbling growl. He kicked his foot locker in anger and turned to leave the room.

"What the fuck Findlay?" Gillis asked, with his disdain clearly showing.

Thomas swung his head around quickly and faced the man. "The Angels of Forbearance???" Thomas asked, cocking his head to the side and squinting at the man. "Whose brilliant idea for a name was that?" His deep voice added malice to the question.

"Why do you care?"

"Because I think your brilliant P.R. representative who came up with that, really just wanted to use my initials." Thomas replied, continuing in his almost-monotone growl; his body language was threatening Gillis, but either Gillis didn't care or he didn't pick up on that.

"What? Is your middle name Alice or something?" Gillis smiled a fake smile while batting his eyelashes in mock feminity.

Thomas lost the last remaining fragment of his self-control and took two quick paces toward Gillis. His forearm in front of him like a shield, he nailed his antagonist to his locker with those 18 inches of his muscular arm. Gillis's head snapped back, making a loud bang of skull against tin. Surprise was clear on his face. He regained his composure instantly.

The consequences of a fist fight could be substantial within a military peacekeeping unit; fortunately, Gillis still had control over himself. He raised both arms over his head, palms facing Thomas, "Findlay," Gillis was speaking through clenched teeth, "you will pay for that but it will be off site." The ferocious promise was delivered with his head leaning aggressively forward toward Thomas.

"Hm." was Thomas's response, his chin pointed directly at Gillis for a second. He inflated his chest and turned and walked away. Later that day, Thomas located the tattoo parlor the club had used. Before entering, he went into the tavern two doors down and consumed three shots of Jameson and a beer. He then backtracked to the tattoo parlor and had the TAF logo permanently inked into the left side of his chest. He owned those three letters and now he had proof of that. He also had an idea about how those letters could prove that Elaine belonged to him - still.

Part II

THOMAS 6
October 2013

The wheels had been set in motion the minute Thomas put the picture in Elaine's mailbox. By his best guess, he had a maximum of two days before law enforcement would be involved. It was improbable that they could ever tie the black-and-white photo to Thomas, but it was very likely that they would keep a close eye on Elaine and her house. For this reason, Thomas was furious when he went to the post office to collect the contents of P.O. Box 219 and found it empty. His supplier had guaranteed delivery on this date and his whole plan was based on the timeliness of the various steps. Could he go back and retrieve the picture from her mailbox? He looked at his watch and decided that that would be too risky. Could he go ahead with his plan without the key ingredient he was expecting in his P.O. Box on this day?

Two days earlier, Thomas had contacted a supplier in Russia whose website promised speedy delivery. When he called them directly, they obliged him at an added fee of only $120 by arranging for a delivery from 'an associate' in New York City. This cut the shipping time substantially. Thomas provided the destination address - Thomas's P.O. Box, and his credit card number. No other details were discussed. Thomas made his phone call at 6:00 a.m., 3:00 p.m. in Moscow, to purchase a single vial of chloroform from his new vendor; his guaranteed USPS delivery date was two days later.

Thomas's quest for new ways to embark on a special project, using a person for the first time, led him to the library a few days earlier. He learned the fundamentals of internet searching by watching television shows like NCIS where they used Google to answer questions about seemingly anything. He saw the very reliable Abby Scuito key in search words like, *what brands of carpet use polyester fibers* or, *what is a local source of parchment paper that includes zinc chloride.* Abby always got several answers to each question. Thomas started his relationship with internet browsers in the library; he not only searched on Elaine's name but he also searched for details on the use of Propofol; he had heard of this drug during the widely publicized investigation of Michael Jackson's death. He keyed in, *how can I buy Propofol.* Within a few seconds he learned from WebMD that this drug was injected into a vein. Thomas scratched that off his mental list of experiment aides. He expected his subject to squirm and perhaps fight him. An intravenous drug was not going to work within his plan.

His second search was more helpful, *what will make a person unconscious.* Again, answers were provided immediately. Thomas felt a surge of power from this new resource. He had been half expecting Google to come back with, W*hy do you want to know?!* The way his mother would have or any of his teachers in school. He clicked on the first entry and found it was an advertisement for something called 'Better Living Through Chemistry.' He clicked on the second link and found information on Nitrous Oxide and Chloroform.

Thomas felt that he should hurry. He did not know what to expect of the library staff; he didn't know if it was possible for them to determine what he was there for. He kept looking behind himself but all he could see was an elderly woman looking down through the reading glasses on the end of her nose as she looked at her computer monitor. Nonetheless, he read the paragraphs of information quickly. Nitrous Oxide, he learned, was also called laughing gas. He didn't really want his subject to be laughing; he wanted something with a nickname more like sleeping gas, or completely-knocked-out-gas. He moved on to reading about Chloroform. He learned that it caused immediate unconsciousness but that the level needed to cause that was considered to be a dangerous level. He skimmed through the dangers but those notes didn't cause him to reconsider. Thomas noticed that the right hand margin of his search screen was a box titled 'Related Questions.' One of the suggested questions in the box was, "Where to Buy Chloroform." His love for Google grew exponentially.

Minutes later Thomas was walking out of the library with a piece of paper with a phone number written on it stuffed into his shirt pocket. The number started with 011 7 495 and Thomas wasn't sure if he should dial one first, but he didn't care. He would just keep dialing different combinations until he reached his target. He planned to do that the next morning.

Thomas had really enjoyed making plans to do a special project with Elaine ever since he discovered she was buying a house near him. His favorite way to fall asleep at night was to work through fantasy plans for restraining her somewhere within his house. He took pleasure in meticulously considering each of the possible rooms in his house. His bedroom was the first room he mentally examined for his experiment. His room offered bed posts that would be convenient for holding her in place. *Did he want blood on his sheets, though? Did he want her to feel like a queen, as he expected his future wife to feel when he allowed her to share his bed?* No. He wanted Elaine to feel controlled, as someone who needed to be punished should feel. Elaine had tormented him during the last three years of high school. And when he created time for them to be alone together, she freaked out in a way that was not necessary. She even made him hit her. Later, she was responsible for him having to go away for a year. His life was not the same again after that - ever. No, Elaine needed to be punished and that meant that there would be blood and she would need to be uncomfortable.

Next up on Thomas's reconnaissance of his own home was

his mother's former sewing and crafts room. This was on the top floor, like his bedroom, and featured many stacks of boxes, some labeled "Mom's Fabric" or "Sewing Tools" and some not labeled at all. The stacks were very untidy and some had fallen over completely. Since returning to this house after his mother's death, whenever Thomas needed something, like scissors, he would go up there and just tear through boxes until he found what he wanted. He never took the time to close them back up or return them to their stacks. He ruled this room out fairly quickly because it would take so much work to even make the space needed to experiment with the punishment of his subject.

By the time Thomas had graduated to surfing the internet at the library, he had come to the conclusion that Elaine would be punished in his dark room in the basement. He had also decided that the way she would repay him for the damage she had done to his life was by bearing a scar, a scar of his design, for the rest of her life, be it short or long.

Thomas began to plan his next step. Getting her to his house would be essential.

SALLY

Sally McClullen had worked at the Victory post office for 15 years. She got the job when her youngest child entered high school. She had overheard one her friends tell someone else that the post office was hiring in their town. She said, "Hey, tell *ME* about this job opening!"

Her friend said, "I didn't know you were looking for a job!"

Sally laughed and said, "Well I wasn't until just now."

About two months later, Sally showed up at the designated time and was trained on the ins and outs of selling postage, weighing the packages, and the various rules of international mail. She became a master of the cash register, and within a year was also sorting mail. She put in 25 hours a week for the US Postal Service.

The next years flew by as her children, one by one, graduated from high school and went on to college. When her third and last child left the house she went full time with the post office. Her schedule matched her husband's now. They would both leave the house at 7:30 and both return around 5:15. They always made sure that at least one of them would go straight home from work to let their beloved dog out as early as possible. Ranger was a Bernese Mountain Dog with a lot of love and a lot of hair. He had been an important part of the McClullen household since their youngest son turned 11 and was ready for the responsibility of helping with a dog. Ranger was eight years old himself now. He slept almost the entire time Sally and Brice were at work, so waiting until shortly after five to get back outside was easy for Ranger in these later years.

One Friday morning, Sally forgot her cell phone; until she

realized what she was missing, that day was like any other work day. She stopped her car in the driveway as Brice continued on his way to work, not realizing that she was setting a chain of events into motion that would change the lives of many people. Sally went back inside to find her phone. She passed Ranger sleeping at the foot of her bed and ran her hand along the line of his back as she walked to her side of the bed. She looked around her bedside table for her phone but it wasn't in its charging stand where she usually left it. She walked back to the other side of the room and again touched Ranger. That was when she realized he had never responded to her first touch. She stopped right where she was and turned back to Ranger, "Ranger! Wake up!" she cried out.

Ranger had passed peacefully onto whatever comes after the worldly life for dogs. Sally sat on the bed, petting Ranger and crying. She was saying "Oh Ranger, I'm so sorry," and "Thank you for being such a good dog to us all these years. You were the best dog we could have ever asked for."   Eventually she came to the realization that she needed to do something about his body being on her bed. She resumed her search for her cell phone. If Brice had been home, she would have had him call it so that she could hear its ring and then locate it from there. But that was exactly the problem: Brice wasn't home. Sally couldn't picture herself moving Ranger's 100 plus pounds of weight herself. She probably could have dragged him to the garage, but she wasn't ready to do anything that would have been jarring or painful to an alive Ranger. She started crying again.

Eventually Sally wrapped Ranger in the comforter he was laying on. She left him on the bed and went to work to call Brice. When Brice answered, he launched immediately into an apology for taking her cell phone to work with him. "I don't know how I did that but somehow I have my phone and yours." After explaining the sad news, they made a plan to meet back at the house at 10:00. Sally used the hour she had to sort the   mail that had come in that morning; there seemed to be more than usual. Tears kept forming in her eyes, and the only thing she could think about was the very large bundle that was on her bed at that moment. She knew Brice would be upset too, and that thought just made her tears more plentiful. At one point, she had to stop her sorting to blow her nose. When she returned to her task she was still rattled, but her muscle memory kicked in and she resumed the task of picking up mail and inserting it into the next box. She didn't realize she had skipped a box. Patron of box 201 received mail addresses to 200. And so on.

COREY 4

Corey had acquired a P.O. Box about three months earlier. He had decided that it was in the best interest of his daughter to divorce his wife as early in the child's life as possible since divorce was inevitable. He had to get the arrangements in place, at least as much as possible, before letting his wife know that this was in their future. Angela was vengeful, angry, and conniving. Corey needed to make sure there was no question that he would end up with the house and at least 50% custody of their daughter Eve, and this required some planning.

Corey was still the assistant director at the Catholic charity organization he worked for, but he was shooting for the Director's job so he was very careful that his employer remained in the dark about the plan he was working on. Divorce was still very much frowned on among the Catholics who had been running his organization - especially when there was a child involved. The child made it impossible to position a divorce as an annulment - a distinction Corey felt was silly. When he was talking about it as a representative of the organization, he found the distinction to be embarrassing.

Corey was using a Divorce-Yourself service he had purchased online for $200.00. That provided him with access to all the forms and a description of the steps for the state of Pennsylvania. He had the starter package sent to P.O. Box 224, Victory, PA. He also had to be in touch with a real estate appraiser. He needed an estimate of the house's worth to be already established when it was time for Corey to offer to buy Angela out of it by splitting the equity between them - the equity minus his down payment of $20,000 anyway. He hoped that half of the roughly $10,000 remaining in equity would be enough to get the attention of Angela's greedy side. She would probably think that $5,000 would go a long way for a young woman living in a small - but stylish - apartment while bearing only half the expenses that it took to raise their daughter. The appraiser was also using the P.O. Box to communicate and schedule the necessary inspection.

Corey checked his P.O. Box about twice a week. This week, Corey made an additional stop on Friday because his work had put him in that neighborhood and he could make the stop without taking time out of his personal schedule. He walked up to his box - it was bigger than the ones next to it so it also cost more than those smaller boxes. He could tell by looking through the small glass peep-hole that there were some things in there. He dialed in his combination and when he swung the door aside, he could see he had two small packages. *Strange*, he thought, everything he had gotten to date was in envelopes, albeit large ones at times. He couldn't imagine what had come to him in a box so, in spite of there being other people around, he started to open one right away.

It was soon clear to Corey that he had opened someone else's mail. He turned the package over and looked at the mailing label. It was addressed to Thomas Findlay. He looked at the other customer by the P.O. Boxes, "Hey, are you by any chance Thomas Findlay?"

DAVE 5

Dave was in the Post Office to see if there was anything from any of his new credit card companies. These stops at the post office always made him nervous because the reason he was using a P.O. Box made him nervous. His box appeared to be empty, but he opened it to make sure. Just then a guy a few mail boxes down spoke to him, "Hey, are you by any chance Thomas Findlay?" Dave looked up at the guy talking to him. "If you are, I apologize for opening your package. I didn't look at the mailing label first."

Dave replied while still processing why that name was more to him than just not-his-name, "I, uh... Um, no, I'm not Thomas Findlay, but I feel like I do know him." Dave's head was running through a mental Rolodex. He had a lot of names in his system, but not many of them had an impression attached to them. This name definitely had an impression, and it was coming to the surface of his consciousness. Like a diver swimming upward toward the surface after a particularly deep dive, he felt like he had just broken through the surface of the water, "Wait! I know who you're asking me about." *...Deep breath in...* Almost dizzy from the epiphany, Dave walked closer to this stranger and looked at the contents of the package he had opened. "Are those scalpels?" Dave asked incredulously.

"Looks that way, weird, huh?" Corey replied. Corey was trying to pull together his thoughts too, so that he could explain why scalpels seemed like an unusual find. "I mean, the guy's name didn't say Doctor, and it seems like these should have been going to a hospital..." Corey trailed off; he was explaining only to himself; Dave was working his own thoughts.

Dave's mind was working very fast since he had realized that scalpels were intended to be delivered to that very creepy guy with the forbidden darkroom in his basement. "Is that another package for the same guy?" Dave asked while reaching for the package in the other guy's hand.

"Um yes," Corey's tone included surprise at having the second box taken from him. In almost anyone's book this was a truly rude gesture, and the abruptness of the snatch was profound. Yet Corey somehow understood that Dave was on the brink of putting together two or more important pieces of information so he looked into Dave's face. They were roughly the same height so eye contact was quick and almost startling. Corey could see very clearly that Dave, the package snatcher, was intensely working through his thoughts on the situation; it was possible that he was also calculating a response. Less than two minutes had gone by since Dave's question of whether or not Corey could be Thomas-what's-his-name, yet the world seemed to have shifted on its axis. *Was it possible that a thick cloud had just passed in front of the sun, making it darker outside?* Corey reined in his thoughts so that he could stay mentally present for the moment at hand.

"This might sound weird, I'll try to give you the short story: this guy Tom, errr Thomas, is an unusual guy - very creepy." Dave continued, "I have some reason to think he might be stalking someone, and so yes, those scalpels are probably even weirder than you are thinking. I need to open this other box. Sorry." Dave started to open the second box. Soon packaging materials were falling to the floor in his haste.

Just then Dave overheard a conversation taking place at the counter around the corner where the stamps were sold and packages weighed. "... her name is Elaine" The name Elaine is what got his attention. It was hard for him to accept that a snippet from an over-heard conversation could be related to the events he was having to evaluate at that very moment but he couldn't ignore it so he turned his head to point his ear in that direction, trying to collect as much sound from that corner of the post office as possible. Then a woman's voice, "She just didn't show up? Is she a pretty young lady?" Then the first voice again, "Yes, and she's very nice too."

Meanwhile, at the mention of the words 'creepy' and 'stalking,' Corey started to remember that he knew the Findlay name, and his associations with it weren't good either. Dave's brief shift of attention gave Corey all the time he needed to pull together his own set of facts. Corey felt responsible for whatever it was that was going on right then. Not responsible in the way that would make it his fault, but responsible for the knowledge, having recently sewed together the story of Thomas's life for reasons that bordered on his own entertainment. He pushed the negative aspects of the feeling of responsibility - guilt - backwards into his brain where he also stored all of his father's unfair admonishments. Corey decided then that his insight into the creep's life could be an important asset to the situation that was unrolling in front of him.

Dave had the second box open and both men looked at the contents and then each other. "Holy crap." Dave said.

KATE 5

Kate had written a letter to Michael that she wanted to mail. As she wrote out the address, she was again sickened to be putting the words Moriah Correctional Facility on the envelope beneath his name, so she shoved the envelope deep into her handbag before driving to the post office. She had been using a P.O. box to receive mail from him for a while now.

Kate's head was swimming. Although her good days outnumbered her bad days now, this was one of the bad days because she had been thinking about how her son could possibly ever earn a living with a felony conviction on his record. There was a loud horn blaring at her, *What?* she asked herself as she looked around. Kate found herself in the middle of an intersection that had a four-way stop sign. She was intending to turn right into the post office parking lot but somehow, while waiting, she had rolled past the stop sign. She began to mouth the word 'sorry' to the other drivers while also raising an index finger to indicate just one minute please. She tried to back up so that she could take the right she had been trying to make, but it was a tight intersection, and reversing for 10 or so feet was going to be necessary since there was a car waiting at the stop line to pull out of the area Kate was trying to pull into. The truck behind her didn't understand why she was trying to back up. She looked in her rear view mirror to see why he was continuing to blow his horn. It was obvious that he was angry; he was pounding on his steering wheel and sitting forward in his seat as if he wanted to get his face as close to Kate's car as possible.

Kate cut her wheel and put her car in reverse. This allowed her to back up about half as much as she needed to. She pulled forward and got as far into the intersection as she could without hitting the sedan that was trying to pull out of the post office parking lot. She needed to do this same move again to get into the lot, but the driver of the truck behind her was too impatient. He had already pulled into the new eight feet that Kate's maneuver had allowed him. Now she was stuck. The truck was at the rear corner of her car and the sedan was at the front corner.

The driver of the sedan that was leaving the post office, fortunately, was a patient and smart woman. She could see what was going on and she put her car in reverse then backed back into the parking lot to allow Kate to swing wide into the parking lot.

Kate waved her thanks to this smart woman as she drove in and pulled over to the right hand side of the parking lot. Just then the pick-up truck roared around her on the left. Kate looked up to see a FUBO sticker on the rear window before she went back to the business of worrying about her son. She put her car in park and got out. She needed to buy a book of stamps, so she walked inside. The pickup truck and its angry driver had headed for a parking space on the left, which was closer to the entrance to the building than Kate's choice on the right, but finding them all to be occupied, he circled around and ended up parking in the same area as Kate. He was putting his truck in park as she was walking into the building. A man exiting the post office was holding the door for Kate as he clutched two small packages to his chest with his other hand. "Thank you." Kate said; he nodded and kept going.

DAVE 6

Dave and Corey realized that while scalpels were weird, scalpels plus chloroform were worthy of action. Corey was glad he had taken a minute to get his knowledge into play. "You know, I know this guy's family," he paused, "or I know of them at least. There's been some serious trouble in that house."

Dave didn't need to hear any more; he started toward the door. Corey moved in that direction with him, "Dude wait. I'm coming too. Couldn't you use some help?"

"Hell yes, thanks man. Let's go." Dave answered. Corey had planned to go regardless of Dave's response so his agreement saved a few seconds.

In about five quick, yet long steps they were at the door. Dave paused only to hold the door for a dignified looking 50-ish woman coming in. As they cut across the parking lot, Dave saw his customer Tom heading toward the building. *What are the odds of that?*! He asked himself. Dave answered himself, *Pretty good odds actually. I mean, if you were having scalpels and chloroform delivered to your P.O. Box, wouldn't you pick them up as soon as possible?* He said to himself, *Dave, you hit the nail on the head again.* He replied, *Thank you Dave.*

Dave knew they had just been given a window of opportunity where they could be certain that Thomas Findlay would not be home, for at least a few minutes. Once he and Corey were both in his truck, he pointed Thomas out to Corey and explained their opportunity and why this chance really wasn't a coincidence. Thomas was going through the entry doors and they could see him from the back. Thomas was wearing a red and black wool coat and faded navy blue cotton pants. His hair was brown, sprinkled with gray, and there was a patch at his crown that was bald. He wore heavy, old, black work boots.

Corey said, "Are you shitting me!? That is Thomas Findlay?!"

PART 3

THOMAS

Thomas went over to his P.O. Box and opened it. Inside were a few envelopes all addressed to Weldon Shipway. He emptied his box and slammed the door closed. He was taking them up to the counter to do something - he hadn't thought of what yet. On his way there, the woman causing all his problems in the parking lot got in his way again. His anger burst out of his mouth.

KATE

Kate headed in the direction of the counter to purchase stamps. Just as she made the corner to head to the right hand side of the building, she bumped into a man who had come from the left side where the P.O. boxes were. He looked at her and said, "Bitch, get out of my way." Every word was emphasized and spoken with such anger that she immediately stepped out of his way. Kate was horrified at the amount of anger he was hurtling at her, but it was then that she realized he was the driver of the pickup truck behind her during her debacle of a four-way stop sign move.

EARL

Earl had developed a nice friendship with Sally over the past year. She had been very helpful to him as he learned how to mail packages to his grandkids. It could have been argued that he mailed more packages than he otherwise would have just simply because his contacts with Sally were some of his best moments. He had learned the names of her children and husband, and he had heard all kinds of entertaining stories about Ranger, their dog. Earl didn't hold any hope of their friendship ever being more than that. In fact, Sally's marital status was a relief to Earl since he would never have to worry about anyone getting the wrong idea. On this day, he was leaning against the counter - Sally was behind it. He could tell Sally was upset because what little eye makeup she had on was smudged, and her eyes were red. "You okay Sally?" He asked gently.

"Ranger died this morning, Earl." Her breath caught and a fresh wave of sorrow swept over her due to Earl's kindness. "It was so much harder than it needed to be because I couldn't find my cell phone to call Brice. I had to leave his body on my bed and come to work to call him."

"Oh Sally, I'm so sorry." Earl saw that Sally was fighting to keep from crying. He started to talk more just to fill up space and give her time to swallow her sadness. "This must be a bad day, I had an appointment to get my teeth cleaned earlier and my hygienist was a no-show. They told me she didn't even call in." He continued, "A substitute did the job, so I'm okay," he smiled to show his shiny teeth, "but that seems so unlike her."

"Really, what's her name?" Sally asked.

"Her name is Elaine." Earl replied.

"She just didn't show up? Is she a pretty young lady?" Sally felt like she might know who Earl was talking about.

"Yes, and she's very nice too." Earl concluded.

They chatted for a few more minutes, covering the usual topics of weather and kids and each other's health. Earl kept the chat going until he could see that Sally had settled back into the role of friendly postal clerk. He felt it was safe to leave her to take care of whoever may need her services next. He said, "Keep your head up kid, I'll see you again soon."

"Bye Earl." Sally said as she touched his hand briefly. Earl was a rare breed and Sally knew it. His ability to discover what was going on with Sally on this day, and to help her maintain her composure while at work, was a gift that Earl used to the advantage of his friends. Sally was grateful that she knew him and she cherished their professional friendship. She even spent a minute wondering if she could somehow incorporate him into her personal life at home. Maybe she and her husband could invite him over to play cards, *What card game allowed for three players?*.... Voices shattered her momentary lapse into social planning.

The same voices caused Earl to swing around more quickly than he would have normally, because just then he heard a deep voice say, "Bitch, get out of my way." Earl was a chivalrous gentleman and never tolerated the mistreatment of women. Without thinking, he headed to the central area of the small building near the entry doors. The woman being denigrated was his old friend from the American Legion. Kate hadn't worked there in a long time, but Earl and Kate understood each other. Like an additional daughter to him, she always took time to ask him how he was doing and what projects he might be working on. In turn, Earl would ask whatever questions he had that assured him that she was safe and her life was moving ahead as planned. Earl always volunteered to work on the every-other Sunday that Kate would be bartending. They both felt that they made a good team.

He didn't take time for small talk right then, though. He put himself in between Kate and this stranger, facing the man. He used his favorite technique for diffusing a potentially volatile situation. "Sir, can I help you?" he said as he pushed his chest toward the man a far as he could without actually touching him. Earl looked straight into Thomas's face.

Thomas was still dealing with the fury that was rattling around inside of him. He knew he was in public and that meant he couldn't respond to this old man the way he wanted to. "No. I'm fine." Thomas moved to step around Earl.

"I just have a quick question for you before you go." Earl said, still piercing Thomas with his stare. Thomas was unable to withstand Earl's stare. He looked away, defeated for the moment.

"What?" Thomas said, making it sound like a statement, not the question that was in response to Earl's statement.

"Can I please have your word that you will never speak to this woman again," he gestured toward Kate, "and that you will never go near her under any circumstances?" Earl thought he was talking to a sane man.

Thomas's only interest was getting this little chat over with, "Yes."

"Yes what?" Earl sought clarification.

"Yes, I will not go near her and I will not speak to her."

Close enough, Earl thought to himself as he stepped aside to let Thomas pass and head toward the counter.

Earl wanted to catch up with Kate, it felt so good to see her, but he had just released the angry man so that he could go speak with another woman he cherished. "Hey Kate, listen, I need to oversee this conversation," he used his face to point toward the counter, "let's catch up soon."

Kate realized that Earl would probably take care of any woman who was put in a compromising situation by a man, but she didn't know that Earl and Sally were also friends. She turned toward the direction Earl was heading back into.

"Thanks SO much Earl for having my back just then, don't worry about it. I really don't want to go to the counter right now, but I need stamps." Kate had a memory bubble to the surface of an unpleasant scene at the legion a year or so earlier. She had seen, *or smelled,* that rude man before.

Earl needed to get up to the counter; he could see Thomas holding envelopes and flapping them in the air. He saw Sally's face change in response. He turned back toward Kate and said, "Listen, go use that machine. If you have a debit or a credit card, you can get stamps even quicker using that." He pointed back toward the entrance at what Kate had thought was an ATM machine.

"Oh! Good idea, thank you!" Kate was relieved to get away from the very angry man. Because Kate used the stamp vending machine, she ended up pulling out of the parking lot long before Thomas exited the building.

Earl had moved back up to the counter to pretend to read an informational brochure about getting your passport. He had missed the first part of Sally and Thomas's interaction but he could tell that Thomas had gotten someone else's mail, and that Sally needed to have him fill out a form regarding the mail he felt he should have actually received. Thomas was enraged over the idea of filling out a form for lost mail.

"Are. You. Kidding. Me?!" Thomas said in his deep, flat tone of fury.

Earl moved a little closer to Thomas. "Hi Sally, is Joe out back?" Earl was trying to make it clear that he would be making sure that everyone was safe while he was in the post office.

Sally turned toward Earl, a question on her lips, "Joe?" Earl winked, "Oh yes! Joe is out back. He's meeting with our security director." Sally was bright, and she had caught on to Earl's charade. They both knew there was no such thing as Joe-out-back.

"I'm really sorry sir, but it is required." Sally turned her attention back to the angry man, "I'm happy to do the writing if you just tell me what the answers are. What is your first name?"

Thomas said, "Forget it." He turned and headed for the door.

"But sir," Sally started.

"Let him go," Earl advised, "there's something about him that I just do not like. No sense in you pushing your services on him if he's willing to just walk away."
Sally was relieved. This had been a very difficult day and she felt like her sadness was a bubble rising to the surface of a bad burn. It wouldn't take much to pop it, and then the puss would run all over the post office in the form of tears and an inability to complete her shift.

DAVE

Dave drove as fast as he could to Tom's house. He didn't know that other people: Earl, Sally, and Kate would all be unknowingly adding to the amount of time he and Corey had been given to figure out what was going on.

ELAINE

Elaine was so thirsty. She didn't know how long she had been in this dark, cold place, but she was certain that a day had gone by. The room was filled with absolute darkness. Even after hours of opportunity for her pupils to adjust, there was still no sign of light anywhere. She had drifted in and out of sleep. Her arms were still bound together by the duct tape handcuffs, and the floor beneath her was hard concrete - only a thin mat was between her and that hard flat surface. The last time she woke up, she tried to shift her position to be more comfortable, but when she closed her eyes in an attempt to ease the sharp pain in her head, she slipped back into unconsciousness.

Now she was stiff from being slumped over in a propped-up sitting position in a cold environment. She still had a sharp pain in her head and her shoulder joints ached. Her guess about how much time had gone by was simply based on her perception that it had been a lot of time. She tried to explore her surroundings with the senses available to her. She discovered that her hands were no longer bound. *He had been in here while I slept?!* She pushed the thought of intrusion aside to make room for feeling grateful for this small freedom. She felt around herself by patting the floor in semicircles that grew larger with each pass. She had started very close to her own body by exploring in this crude fashion with her right arm. She was afraid of what she might find, so she proceeded carefully and slowly. She didn't know if she would be able to maintain control of herself if she came across something furry or mysteriously wet or sticky. When she reached as far as this arm could reach, using tiny tentative pats of the floor, she started again, close to her body, using her left arm. On her third semicircle, she felt something. She was grateful that it felt like it was made of a hard plastic, something with a shallow rim. She carefully explored the shape of this object. Its rim was a consistent height of about a half-inch around the edges she could reach. When she felt up and over its edge she found the hard plastic continued as a flat surface, like a tray. She stretched her arm to feel further and felt a something cold and wet. Gingerly she explored this new shape. It was a glass and the glass was on a tray! She picked it up and brought it to her nose. She was very thirsty, but she wasn't going to drink just anything. It smelled like water and had a small amount of condensation on the outside of the glass. She tipped up the glass and

tasted a small amount of it; it was delicious. Within
seconds she emptied the glass. Quickly she reached back
toward the tray to feel around for anything else that may
have been 'served' to her while she was unconscious. She
found only a small puddle of water where the glass had
been sitting. She raked her fingers through that in
frustration. Her vexation leaked from her mouth. After a
minute, she pulled her fingers through the water again then
licked her fingers, repeating the process until the tray
squeaked when she dragged her fingers across it.

The water had revived Elaine a little. She squirmed herself
into a more upright position. The muscles in her buttocks
cried out in relief as well as pain. Elaine started to feel
sorry for herself; she thought, *What the fuck... I'm so cold
and so sore... I'm hungry, thirsty, the scab on my throat
stings, my head really hurts...* But then she remembered
her kids. *Buck up bitch. Remember, you are not a POW in
a Japanese concentration camp. You are one person being
held by one sick man; use your f-ing resources.* Elaine had
shifted into mother-mode and felt gratitude for the fact that
she knew her former mother-in-law would keep her
children safe, even as she most likely assumed that Elaine
had run off in a fit of irresponsibility.

Elaine moved into a hands and knees crawling position,
discovering that her ankles were bound together. Just then
she heard a sound from above her. The cold concrete floor
made it easy for her to assume she was in a basement but
the creaking sound of movement above her confirmed that.
She cocked her head to get the most of this audible clue as
possible. It was clear that someone was walking on the
floor above her as the sound moved from her left to her
right. She heard squeaking next, with additional shuffling.
Her instincts told her this was a door - *theeee door?* the
door at the top of the stairway that divided her from her
captor. The sound of footsteps on the stairway treads
confirmed this. Without thinking, Elaine moved back into
her slumped, sleeping position against the wall next to the

tray. He would know she had been awake because the water was gone, but with any luck, he would believe that she had succumbed to sleep one more time due to whatever drug he had given her. She would buy time and perhaps even information about her situation if she could play the sleep card one more time.

Within seconds of getting back into her sleeping place, a door quite near her on the right opened. She heard footsteps approach in her direction. She made her facial muscles slack, like a picture Eric had once taken of her when she had fallen asleep on the couch one exhausting Saturday. She had made him delete the picture because her vanity couldn't allow for its existence. She nonetheless learned that she was capable of a loose and drooling mouth. Her split second of opportunity was used to recreate the face she remembered from that picture.   A beam of light crossed over her relaxed face, she assumed it was a flashlight.   It hurt her eyes even through her closed eyelids. She controlled the urge to react to the pain.

Elaine felt a boot push at her hip, a nudge intended to get a response from someone who might be near consciousness. She gave no response.

"You got lucky bitch."

Elaine's sensory receptors lit up like a Christmas with the Griswolds. He was speaking to her!

"Fools working for the United States Postal Service bought you one more day before the fun starts."

Elaine heard the footsteps turn away. As the entry door opened again he spoke one more sentence, "I think you'll like the plan once you get used to it. It's so necessary." The door closed. Elaine's mind reeled. *What does that mean?* Just then, the door reopened and a quick phrase was added to the nightmare, "It's my turn to be in charge Elaine, you will like that." The emphasis was on 'will.' The door closed for a second time. She heard the clack of hardware: a clicking lock, then she heard the footsteps go up the stairs, followed by the sound of the door at the top, then the footsteps across the floor.

Elaine thought her heart might explode; it was beating so hard she was certain she'd be able to see it beating if she looked down at her chest, and if she could see. She was still in mother-mode so she knew she had to calm herself. She moved into a slightly more comfortable position: she placed her hands at her sides, palms up as they had taught her in Yoga class, and forced herself to breathe deeply. Deeply in as far as possible, then - with much more difficulty - breathing out as far as her lungs would allow. She repeated this three times before allowing herself to assess her new information.

The most important fact she could garner from her new knowledge was the time line. She had until tomorrow to get herself out of this situation. She didn't dare assume it was a full 24 hours. Tomorrow could be as soon as even eight hours away - or less. For the sake of not doing anything prematurely, Elaine decided to work with a ten-hour time frame. This would most likely include a period of sleep for Thomas, and would give her the time she needed to understand her surroundings. It's not like she needed time to repair the Apollo 13 like Jim Lovell did, so she might as well keep her time line within the limits that matched her crude situation. If she needed more time, she'd give it to herself - if that was within her power.

She felt around her ankles to try to figure out how they were bound. It was a small chain like what swings hang from on a child's back-yard swing set. There was a padlock connecting the two ends. *Well, I can't do anything about that.* She got back into her hands and knees crawling position and began her exploration. Elaine was forced to drag her legs behind her in tandem since they were secured tightly. She made progress though, as she crawl/scooted along the side of the wall she had been leaning against earlier. She reached ahead first with her hands, and when she found nothing she'd scoot the rest of herself into the space she had just reconnoitered. She found nothing on the floor accept a predictable layer of dust the stirring up of which caused her to feel like sneezing. She covered her mouth and nose and sneezed silently into them. *Crap, an additional challenge.* Elaine stopped moving her hands flat-palmed against the floor, and started just placing her finger tips in tapping spots across the floor in front of her so that less dust would rise up into her breathing air. She waited expectantly to find something - something awful, something unacceptable in her normal life. It was then that her mind filled with the possibilities of what she might stumble across in this freak's basement. She had watched the first three of the Saw movies and was regretting that. She slumped onto her haunches. *This sucks!* she shouted at herself. Tears rolled down her face. *Where am I??!!!*

After a few minutes of feeling sorry for herself, she remembered what her job was and how much time she didn't have to do it. She straightened herself up again into the crawling position she had been using. She wiped wetness off her face with the back of her hands, then checked out the next area in front of herself and found it to be clear. The next crawl/scoot brought her to the door way. She knew that because she was confronted by a wall that had a rubbery, flexible mopboard-type of thing where the floor met the wall. If she pressed against it, she could make it concave away from her up to about an inch from the floor. Above that, it had a solid backing. Feeling upwards and finding hinges on the right near the wall confirmed her discovery. Elaine suspected that she might have found the single most important aspect of the room - the way to get out - before even figuring out what else occupied her space. *Wow, a smart woman would have set out to make this particular discovery immediately since you knew the direction he entered from. But no, you had to*

*act like the whole room needed to be understood before
you could possibly work at your escape.* She admonished
herself briefly before she shut down this unproductive line
of thought.

Elaine hadn't heard any noise from above her in quite
some time. Would she be able to hear if he had moved to
the second floor? Her memory of the house as she drove
her car down the driveway so long ago made a second
story seem likely. The house was old and had a fairly
small foot print. Like so many houses built in the early
1900s, it seemed likely that the scant living area on the
first floor was strictly kitchen, living room, dining room,
and all sleeping took place one story above that. She hoped
he had moved upstairs but she didn't want to take any
chances just yet. She decided to take some time to quietly
familiarize herself with this door.   She would pay special
attention to anything she heard above her while she did
this exploration.

She identified its edges first. It seemed to be a standard
size door, yet it didn't feel like a door that was selected and
purchased from the local Home Depot, sized to fit within a
standard-sized opening. It felt like it had been made for
this purpose. The surface facing her felt like a wall except
for the rubber gasket thing at the bottom, the hinges at the
side, and the crude hardware on the left about half way up.
She could feel indents where nails held the surface to what
she pictured as a framework beneath it; the surface felt like
drywall. She moved herself into a standing position by
hopping in a way that got her feet underneath her; she
leaned on the door and pulled herself upright. This action
proved that there was some give to the door. She could
move it back and forth in the open and close direction a
fraction of an inch, but she didn't test this boundary further
for fear of making noise; she noted it for later exploration.
Elaine moved on to make a greater study of the knob and
closure hardware now that she was on a level that made
this easier. It felt like the kind of latch from days gone by,

that when lifted, it raised a metal slat above a notched metal piece that held the slat in place, thus also holding in place the door it was attached to. She remembered her grandmother's shed had a latch like this. When the metal slat was raised on one side of the door, it also raised a mirror image slat on the outside of the door, so it could be operated from either side. Elaine tried to silently raise the latch. It worked as it was intended to, but that only changed the amount of give the door offered by a little bit, maybe a half-inch. She put her ear to the door near the latch and wiggled it as much as she dared. It sounded like the outside mechanism was working along with the inside mechanism. The fact that the door's operability didn't change could only mean one thing: there was another device in play on the outside of the door. Perhaps even something as simple as an additional latch which offered a place for a padlock to do its dirty work.

She felt around the surface of the tall and narrow edge, the surface that is hidden within the door frame when the door is completely closed. She had pulled the door toward herself, taking advantage of its give, to do this piece of her manual examination. She felt a rough, unfinished edge that was papery and also chalky; it was about a half-inch thick. Then beyond that was a splintery, wooden surface that was maybe an inch thick. She mentally confirmed that it was in fact drywall nailed to a old wooden door. The edge she was feeling was apparently the edge that had been cut to downsize the standard width of drywall to the width of the door. She pulled the door a little harder toward herself to see if she could feel beyond the rough wood. She gained a fraction of an inch and found that on the other side of the wood was more of the chalky/papery surface. The wood was sandwiched between sheets of drywall.

Elaine finished her exploration of her exit by running her hands across the top of the door. There was another rubber gasket type of thing up there, running along the top of the door. *Why would he do that? Using a makeshift door in a room that was utterly and completely dark....* Elaine turned herself so her back was to the door and slid down into a sitting position. She mulled over this new information, she felt like there was some pieces of the puzzle that she was failing to put together. *What am I missing?!* She took three more deep breaths and forced herself to think of all the things she did know. She ticked off her list:

- ✓ Homemade door
- ✓ Old latch that doesn't release door
- ✓ Some give to door but not much
- ✓ Gasket things at top and bottom of door
- ✓ Drywall nailed to wood on both sides
- ✓ Complete darkness
- ✓ Cement floor
- ✓ Basement setting

She decided she had no choice but to explore the room further in spite of her fear of the unknown. She began to follow the wall to the left of the door. It wasn't long before her exploring fingers ran into a metal case; she ran her fingers up the side of it and decided it was something like a locker, so she moved to the front of it to explore more It was about 12 inches deep and had the type of vents near the bottom that a gym locker would have. She guessed there would be more of these vents near the top, but so far there wasn't enough reason for her to stand up to prove that. She found three such vent openings, so she decided this was three lockers standing side by side. She reached up to find their latching mechanisms, which felt familiar. She got up on her knees to try the latch and was rewarded when she lifted the latch straight up and pulled. Just like in eighth grade gym, the locker opened! She again hopped herself into a standing position and began excitedly feeling around inside locker number one. At her eye level, she felt clothing hanging on hooks. The smell implied that these were work clothes reserved for particularly dirty jobs. *Nasty!* She thought. The shelf above the hanging clothes contained loose hardware, nails, bolts, screws and the like. She started a mental inventory. Who knew what she might need before this night *-day?-* was over. Before closing door number one she felt below the hanging clothes. Something was sitting in the bottom of the locker. It was hard to determine what it might be exactly but it felt neither evil nor useful. Maybe it was a headset designed to protect the hearing of someone operating loud equipment. It had that curved, padded feel to it. Elaine moved on to door number two.

Nothing hung on the hooks of the second locker. She reached up to the inevitable top shelf and found what had to be several pieces of sand paper. *If there was anything on the planet that was designed to be identified by feel, it just might be sandpaper,* Elaine thought. After feeling around to make sure that was all that was up there, she felt around in the bottom of locker number two. Sitting on the floor but leaning against the side wall she found a saw that seemed to be shaped like a stretched out letter D. Her dad had one of these. *What did he call it?* The blade was very thin and flexible and about a half-inch wide. *Was it a hack saw?* she asked herself. Her mental inventory registered it as such. The accuracy of her name for it didn't really matter. She knew there were more items here that needed to be "inventoried," so she moved on. She found what felt like a very large nail file. It had a wooden handle and was about 14 inches long - all told. The filing surface had a very large grain to it. Elaine didn't really know the words for describing this file, but she did know for sure that she would never use it on her fingernails. The next object was a screw driver. To her it seemed extraordinarily long, with a flat head at the end. Its handle was plastic, and she could easily picture the word Craftsman stamped into it. She set this aside thinking it might be handy later. The last item on the floor of locker number two was an oily plastic funnel. *Eww*, she held it aloft only long enough to confirm that there was nothing else behind door number two.

She started to scoot toward door number three when she remembered the long screw driver she had set aside. She started to slide that into the back pocket of her pants as she reviewed her mental inventory. *Wait a cotton pickin' minute! Elaine! You just found a hack saw.* She frantically went back to door number two, sat down with her bound ankles in front of her. As quickly as she could pull that saw back out, she was working at the chain that bound her ankles. More than once she nicked her ankles. The saw was long and awkward for holding with just one hand and she needed the second hand to hold the chain away from her skin. She slipped a few times and that would cause the saw to land on her ankles. She tried to stop the momentum of the sawing motion before it landed on her. As it turned out she didn't have to work very hard at this, she broke through the first spoke of the chain link after two dozen or so strokes of the saw. Instead of trying to saw through the second half of the link, she used the screwdriver to twist the link enough to offer an opening. *Bingo!* The chain fell free. She set the chain and the screw driver down, setting them back in the direction of her "sleeping spot" in the event Thomas returned and she needed to pretend she was still imprisoned and unconscious. She inspected her ankles with her fingertips and inwardly declared them to be just fine. The truth was there were several small cuts created by the jagged blade when it landed on her skin a few times; one of the abrasions had blood trickling out of it. Two days ago, she would have run for the first aid kit - today she shrugged it off thinking of it as nothing.

The blood on her ankles reminded her of the blood that had run down her chest on her drive here, she reached up and gingerly touched her neck. *Ouch!* There was a spot that was very sore and she could feel the raised crusty track of dried blood sealing off the wound. *Wish I could have forgotten about that a little longer.* As she felt her skin below the cut, she realized her shirt was open in front almost down to her navel, and it was torn. *Pervert.* Elaine put this line of thought to the back of her brain. *C'mon woman, we have more work to do*, she reminded herself. Carefully, she stood up and took tentative steps toward the third locker. She moved very slowly, keeping her hands in front of herself, feeling around in the air for anything that might surprise her.

Door number three was right where she expected to find it. She lifted and pulled the handgrip to open it. She felt toward the clothing hooks first and found a scratchy-feeling piece of attire. Based on how thick it was, she guessed it was a coat. That was the only thing on the hooks. She reached up to feel the top shelf and carefully felt around. She found a small cardboard box. It reminded her of gum from her childhood: Chiclets packaged two to a box. She doubted it was gum, however; it smelled only of dirt and oil and the feel of the cardboard wasn't sleek and waxy like she remembered the gum's packaging was. It was more dry and coarse like the type of package that would absorb a drop of water instantly. She moved on to find a handle of some sort. After a thorough manual examination, she decided it was a paint roller handle. The third and final item on this shelf was a roll of tape. She guessed it was masking tape and that there wasn't much left on the roll. She felt around the bottom of the last locker. There was a used, dried up paint roller adhered to the tin floor. Next to that was a plastic-wrapped package. She quickly figured out that it was an unopened package of two paint rollers. Elaine stood up and reviewed the useful things on her inventory list: sand paper, saw, screwdriver, file, Chiclets... Chiclets? Why did she feel like she should know what this really was, she really didn't think it was the type of gum given out at Halloween in 1979. Most of her handy-woman knowledge came from her father. She started to think about his workshop back in her childhood home. Just then, she heard something - it was the door at the top of the stairs. Elaine froze; a feeling of both freezing cold and extreme heat paralyzed her, and a prickling feeling tortured her whole body. By the time the first stair riser squeaked, she had come back to life, quickly moving herself into her sleeping spot. She hid the screw driver under her butt and put the saw behind her back, holding it in place with her weight. Then she draped the chain across the top of her ankles, and just as she heard noise on the outside of the door that held her captive, she made the sleeping face she remembered from Eric's picture. Listening intently, she heard a small amount of shuffling on the floor, then she heard the sound of the door being pushed inward against the latch, moving that small degree she thought of as the door's give. It held in that position for a few seconds; *was he listening at the door?* Just then the give gave back and the door returned to its natural position. A few seconds later she heard the door at the top of the steps swing closed then latch, followed by footsteps moving toward the back of the house.

What the fuck?! Was he trying to determine if she was still unconscious? She needed to rethink her plan and do so quickly. Just then, she heard a new sound. It was unmistakable: a loud engine was rumbling down the driveway. Then, complete silence.

~~~~~~

Elaine's heart was still pounding from the threat of Thomas reentering her space. She leaned her head against the wall to think through the more recent events. *Is it possible that someone else was here and that someone else just left?* Elaine decided that her best bet was to assume that Thomas had left after reassuring himself that she was still sleeping. She stood up. If she only had some light this would be so much easier. She decided to invest one or two minutes into finding light. She moved in the opposite direction of the door and the lockers, hands outstretched, frantically swirling the air in front of her in search of unknown obstacles. She was operating under the assumption that it would be okay if she accidentally made some noise now. Something hit her forehead, surprising her. She had been braced for finding the unknown with her hands, not her head. She instantly squatted. *What the hell was that?* It didn't hurt, but it landed squarely across her forehead; it was something lightweight. Slowly she rose up a small amount, using her hands to explore the air over her head. She found a thick piece of paper, when she gripped it she was able to pull it down toward her for about six inches, then it slipped out of her hand and bounded upwards. Elaine hadn't expected there to be a limit to how far she could pull it since it seemed pretty loose, but the second time she gripped it, she held it tightly. She was standing at full height again, so she only had to reach just above her own height to determine that the piece of heavy paper was attached to a loosely strung rope - *a clothes line?* - and held in place with clothes pins. *Okay, to the best of my knowledge, pieces of paper hanging from clothes line rope have never killed anyone.* She cajoled herself, then, *This is a dark room!* The pieces fell together at that instant, and they all fit together perfectly. So many things made sense now, but the things that still didn't make sense were what threatened her life.

She moved past the clothesline carefully and soon found another one. She worked her way past that and found a countertop of sorts. This wasn't granite or even Formica, it was rough wood, but it was counter height. She reached to the back of it and felt the cold stones of the house's foundation. If there was a window in this room, it would be on this wall. She followed her way to the right to see if the counter ended, allowing her to be closer to the outside wall. That was a dead end, so then she moved to the left. Another dead end. She thought about Eric and Danielle and decided to get up on top of this makeshift counter top. She swept her hands across it first to clear any objects that might hurt her or slow her down. She turned so her back was to the counter; placing her hands on it, she hoisted herself up onto it. Elaine pulled her legs up and turned herself back toward the wall. She reached up and felt high up on the wall. Score! The wall recessed to accommodate a window. Finally some luck! She felt the surface of the window and found it to be covered with something. She worked at the edge of this 'something' to try to peel it away, but it held fast; it wasn't just taped in place, maybe it was wall paper or the kind of shelf paper that had the peel-off backing. Maybe it was paint. *Fuck this shit, it's still gotta be glass underneath it.* She felt around the counter top for something she could use to smash the window. She found something that felt like a short piece of a two-by-four. Using that, it was easy for her to break the glass. The first ray of light hurt her eyes and caused shards of pain to go all the way to the back of her head and down her neck. Elaine gasped; turning away she covered her eyes with her hands. She understood that her pupils had been opened probably further than they had in her entire life. Yet, she had no extra time. She made her eyes adjust by parting the fingers in front of her eyes in small increments. She did this as quickly as she could, using her ability to bear the pain as her speedometer.

While she was coaxing her pupils back to a more normal position, she was facing away from the window. It wasn't long before she saw the two clotheslines of pictures dangling in front of her. The white side of the paper was facing her, but she had no doubt that the other side of each piece of paper would be an image of something - or someone. She turned toward the window, swallowing the pain of that change in exposure to the light. With one quick movement, she used the block of wood once more to enlarge the hole in the glass; cold air blew in. She examined the window to determine if it might be an exit for her but it was only six or eight inches tall and maybe 18 inches wide. Elaine hopped down off the counter.

Her next target was the door. She ducked under the clothes lines and ran to it and pulled on it to add her sense of sight to what she already knew the door. It was indeed wood sandwiched by drywall with gasketing at the top and the bottom, no doubt to block light. She wanted more light for examining the latch, so she turned and looked around for a light switch. It was then that she came face-to-face with a picture of herself.

Elaine already knew that she was dealing with a seriously sick individual, but this was a harsh reminder. In this picture, she was climbing out of her car, her hair was blown into her face and a section of it was in her mouth. She looked at a few other pictures; most of them were of her house. Directly to the right of the picture of her was one that looked like a tattoo, someone's upper chest baring the image of three initials: TAF. She didn't have time to waste on looking at pictures, in spite of it being as sickly fascinating as watching a train wreck. She turned away to seek out an additional source of light. She located a bare bulb hanging from the ceiling. She yanked the chain and, with no miracles needed, it lit up, lighting the whole room. Elaine moved back to the door and again pulled it toward herself as hard as she could as she peered at the latch and whatever was stopping her from opening the door. She could see a sliver of the metal piece that she was betting flopped over a loop which was - she guessed based on a thunking rattle- secured by a padlock.

She grabbed the hack saw that was still leaning against the wall in the area she thought of as her sleeping space. *Was it thin enough to fit through the very narrow opening she created when she pulled very hard on the door? Maybe she could force it through that tiny slit...* No, not even close; it was too wide at the tip where the blade was held in place by some type of bolt. It was too wide by at least a third of an inch. Elaine was starting to feel like her time was running out. Feeling some panic, she grabbed for the long bladed screw driver and starting gouging away at the drywall on the far side of the door. It looked like the drywall might be thicker than the space she would need to push the saw through the crack. Just then, she heard a vehicle in the driveway.

~~~~~~

Dave arrived at Thomas's house by the quickest route he knew. Corey held tight to the fold-up handle located above

272

the passenger door so that he wouldn't bounce around the front seat; he didn't want to complain or sound the unsafe-driving-alarm so he held tight and kept quiet. Dave pulled into the driveway much faster than he normally would - knowing every second counted and not knowing that other Victory denizens were buying him more time.

Corey was gazing up at the house, remembering everything he had read in the files at work, files all bearing labels that began with FINDL. It was easy for him to picture the disappointments, unrewarded efforts, and traumas taking place here. He looked up to the roof and back down to the foundation, registering the gravity of this family's circumstances. He noticed something and looked closer, "Hey, there's a broken basement window there," he said as he pointed out the passenger window.

"Seriously?" Dave replied. He was trying to picture the layout of the basement so that he could determine if a window on this side of the basement was a key feature. He didn't want to waste any precious seconds when they might only have two or three minutes.

"Yes. And there seems to be some light inside there." It was a day that lacked sunlight, as October days often did in Pennsylvania, making sources of light more noticeable.

Dave hit the brakes of his truck. He had been in that basement; the idea of light emanating from one of its windows was strange enough for him to decide that investigating that opening was worth the time it would take away from their brief span of opportunity.

They both jumped out as soon as the truck was in park. As they ran toward the tiny basement window, Dave remarked that the broken glass was outside the window, sitting on top of what looked like a leaf salad. "If it had been vandals busting this asshole's balls, the glass would be on the inside."

The two men had to lay on their bellies to look into the opening. The window was below ground level and it was outlined by a semicircle of corrugated metal that held the earth back away from the window opening. Nonetheless, dried leaves, lawn mowing debris, and branches threatened to fill the opening. Corey scooped out as much of the debris as possible with a few swipes. Dave tried to shout through the opening. "Hello? Hello?!"

~~~~~~

At the sound of a truck in the driveway, Elaine froze. In her mind, she knew she needed to move, but she was unable to pull the screw driver away from the door crack she had been trying to enlarge. She was unable to turn her body toward the window where she heard the sound of a truck.   She felt her body begin to shake, but she was unable to do anything for herself that would be a response to this new occurrence. She was frozen in place while her brain shut her body down in self-defense against the worst fear - a fear that she'd held at bay until she heard the sound of the truck motor. Eventually, she turned and slid herself down into a sitting position on the floor, knees against her chest, succumbing to whatever would be the eventual outcome. Rocking in place and moaning, she waited.

"Mama?... Mama?!" a voice in Elaine's head was inserting itself. "Mama!!" It had turned to a shout.

"Shhh Danielle... We need to be quiet." Elaine responded to this voice silently.

"No Mama! Get Up!"

Elaine started to peel away the layers of perceived reality from the things that were real; she felt this was the hardest thing she had ever done, but her precious daughter was urging her to do this. She registered the cold concrete beneath her buttocks and the room that had once been dark but was now dimly lit. She looked between the hanging photographs toward the window and saw gray daylight. "Okay Danelly," her pet name for her beautiful daughter sprang to her mind, "I'll try to do something more for us."

Elaine, in a quest for clarity, shook her head and looked around. Danielle was nowhere to be seen. Elaine was, in her state of panic, both relieved and frustrated that her daughter was not with her. Just then there was the noise of a scuffle outside the broken window. Elaine froze again. A male voice: "Hello?"

~~~~~~~~~~~~~~~~~~~~~~~~~~~~~~~~~

Dave turned to Corey, "In the truck bed, there's a tool box. There's a flashlight on one of the top shelves. Grab it."

Corey did as he was told and within seconds was back with a flashlight. Dave grabbed it and immediately started to fan a small amount of the room with its beam; it was all that the miniature window allowed.

~~~~~~~~~~~~~~~~~~~~~~~~~~~~~~~~~

"Hello?" Elaine belatedly replied, questioningly, to the male voice. Danielle's momentary presence had given her a dose of bravery.

~~~~~~~~~~~~~~~~~~~~~~~~~~~~~~~~~

Dave and Corey heard her response at the same time; they both stiffened. It was at that point when they took the very small step into hero mode. "Are you Elaine?" Dave asked. They heard only whimpers in response. Corey frantically raked more debris from the window well.

When enough yard leavings had been pulled from the small opening to allow both of them to get their heads in front of the small window, they spotted fragments of a trembling, curled up figure. She was on the floor in the direction the voice had come from.

"Elaine, we are here to get you out of that basement."
Dave spoke boldly. "Please come over to this window." He
paused, "We are here to help."

Elaine wanted to trust this voice. She urged her voice box
to reply, pushing sound out of her throat, drawing from the
now vanished presence of her daughter, "uhhh...." it was a
quiet sound. She put more strength into it, "Who are you?"
the end of this question dropped off into a sob.

Corey sensed Elaine's mindset and realized that the
flashlight was not helping Elaine; it only helped them. He
pushed away the end of the flashlight that Dave held,
moving it away from the window opening, and nodded
toward Dave to indicate that he wanted a turn at coaxing
this woman toward them. Dave clicked the flashlight to off.

"Elaine, this may sound scary, but we think you may be
being held against your will by a man named Tom who
plans to harm you." Corey spoke clearly through the
window opening.

The simplicity of these sensible words struck Elaine's core.
"Ya think?!" she replied, sarcasm being a remnant from
her visit from Danielle.

"Elaine, please come over to this window so we can see if
we can get you out." Corey said.

"That window is too small." Elaine said as she struggled to
stand and head toward it.

Dave joined the conversation, "Do you know of another
way out?"

"Well, I've been trying to get my saw out the door, to saw
through the latch." She paused, "It doesn't fit yet." Elaine

explained.

Corey turned to Dave, "You know your way to the basement, why don't you go see if getting her out that door would be any easier than out this window." Dave instantly took off in the direction of the back door.

Dave returned quickly, "No go. There's a deadbolt on that door." He continued, "There is a window into the kitchen we can break, if need be, but let's first make sure we can't make this opening work for getting her out."

Corey looked at his watch; they had been there approximately eight minutes. "Let's call the cops and use the time it takes them to get here to get her out this window." Corey continued in his efficient manner, "She's safe now no matter what," he pointed his voice toward the window opening in hopes she would overhear what he was saying to Dave. "There's no way he can hurt her now that we are here, but for her sake, if we can help her out now..." he didn't get to finish his sentence. Dave was back down on his belly.

"Elaine, please come over to the window." Dave asked as gently as he could. "Elaine, you need to do it now." He emphasized as much as he dared. While he waited to see if she responded, he turned to Corey and went on, "Dude, please go to my truck; my cell is in the console. Call 911." that's all he needed to say before Corey was heading toward the truck. "Just tell them it's possible that a woman is being held against her will." Dave shouted at Corey's back.

When Dave turned back to the window he saw a pale face looking up at him through the window. "Hi Elaine." she nodded in response. "I promise I won't hurt you, I only want to help you get away from this creep." Elaine's face crumpled, her words of gratitude were too large to be vocalized. Dave's instincts took over, "I know, this sucks,

but you're going to be okay." Tears ran down Elaine's face.
"Please just climb up to this window so we can see if there
is any way..." Dave was using the largest stick in his reach
to clear away the remaining glass shards from the window
opening. Elaine had to turn her face away from the
opening to protect herself from the pieces of glass falling
toward her. "Sorry!" Dave half laughed, half barked. "This
stuff would cut you up pretty bad if..."

"FREEZE!" Dave recognized Thomas's gravelly voice
immediately. Elaine scrambled back at the sound and
climbed under the table she had been standing on. Dave's
heart sank, yet adrenalin lit up his body. He rolled away
from the sound of the voice while shouting to Elaine, "Get
away from the window!"

The sound of a loud crack filled the air. Dave felt his leg
heaved away from his other leg as if a giant had flicked it
with his middle finger and thumb, as one would do to an
insect found one's pant leg. It was a full second before he
felt the bullet hole in his leg. *Oh man, this is going to make
rescuing the pretty girl a lot harder...* He rolled himself
toward an overgrown bush for the scant coverage it would
offer, then grabbed the place on his calf that felt like it was
on fire. The logical part of his brain assessed the damage:
no pulsating streams of blood, no hanging chunks of flesh.
The other side of Dave's brain took this information and
used it to decide he could ignore the fact that he'd been
shot. He could see Thomas coming down his own
driveway, a long gun visible at the end of his right arm, his
old truck parked on the street. Dave attempted to stand to
move in the other direction, but pain prevented that. So
much for ignoring the bullet wound.

As Dave was attempting to swallow the pain he was
experiencing and clear his head, Thomas caught up to him.
Standing over Dave, he pointed his rifle directly between
his eyes; the front sight at the end of the barrel was so
close that Dave couldn't focus on it. "What. The. Fuck.

Are. You. Doing. At. My. Fucking. House?" Thomas growled with enormous, barely controlled anger. Dave smelled oily metal and gun powder. Spittle rained down on his face like the petals of a fireworks flower on the Fourth of July. Thomas harshly kicked Dave in the soft spot of his side, below his rib cage. "I'm talking to you!"

"Man... Wait. It's all okay..." Dave held his hands up in front of him as he deployed his gift for blarney in a desperate attempt to survive.

Thomas screamed between clenched teeth, "Fuck you asshole, you are going to die!" The final word was expressed using every bit of air in his lungs; the anger was palpable. He lunged toward Dave, too angry to use his rifle. As he reached for Dave's throat to shake him to death, the gun, forgotten, fell to the side. Dave rolled to the other side; using the momentum of his roll he propelled himself up onto his good leg. He started to hop toward his truck, and in doing so, found he could use his injured leg, he just didn't want to. His survival instinct overruled his interest in avoiding pain, but he still didn't move quickly enough.

In a split second Thomas was on him, tackling him roughly to the ground. He used his huge fist to pummel Dave's face. Dave tried to move out from under Thomas, but Thomas had the advantage of being on top and being free of bullet wounds. As his punishment continued, Dave caught a glimpse of color moving past the back of his tormentor. Thomas then grabbed Dave's throat with both hands, and started to shake him like a rag doll. Just as Dave was blacking out he heard a familiar voice.

"I'm sending you to hell right now if you don't let go of my friend." Thomas froze with his hands still dug deep into the flesh of Dave's throat. Corey's voice held many years' worth of maliciousness, a tone used for perhaps the first time in his life. As Dave's vision cleared he could see that Corey held Thomas's gun even closer to Thomas's skull than Thomas had held it to Dave's. Corey's chest was puffed out and his stance exuded confidence. Thomas's fingers dropped away from Dave's throat.

~~~~~~

When Elaine heard Thomas's voice in the driveway, she felt complete loss. In that one second, that one word, *freeze!* she felt she had lost everything. She climbed under the table, frantically pushing random objects out of her way so that she could make her way to the outside wall. She planted her back against the cold damp rocks that comprised the foundation as she clutched her knees to her chest. She held her eyes tightly shut as she rocked herself slowly. She hummed a lullaby from her childhood as she sunk into a self-protective cocoon, woven with memories of feeling secure as a child on her mother's lap.

~~~~~~

Dave used his good leg to push himself out from under Thomas as Corey held the rifle steady against his head. As he worked himself into a sitting position a few feet away from Thomas, Dave asked, "Dude, did you get to make a phone call?" He raised his eyebrows in exaggerated fashion to imply the question contained special meaning.

"Sure did." Corey replied, never taking his eyes off Thomas nor lessening the pressure of gun barrel against skull. As if on cue, the faint sound of sirens could be heard in the direction of Victory proper.

Thomas heard the sirens too. His reaction was unexpected by Corey. Feeling like he had nothing to lose and a very large score to settle, Thomas jerked himself out from under the barrel of his own gun and in less than a second, was on his feet facing Corey. He kicked at the rifle, dislodging it from Corey's left hand, the index finger of

Corey's right hand was still on the trigger. As Corey struggled to regain control over the weapon, the gun went off.

Elaine was wrapped in a cloak of her memories of childhood. She repeated the same lullaby over and over, never tiring of the simplistic melody and comforting lyrics. When she heard the gun shot, she urinated where she sat, never pausing her song.

PART IV

The stray bullet from the rifle went straight through Thomas's right foot and lodged about four inches into his gravel driveway. The two seconds he spent being stunned was all Corey needed to regain possession of the weapon, as well as solid footing and a stance poised defensively toward Thomas. The rifle was again pointed between the evil man's eyes.

The wind shifted slightly and Corey unintentionally breathed in the air surrounding Thomas. Corey's mind filled with images of anger, hatred, filth, and decomposition. Just then, Thomas lurched toward the gun. Without thinking, Corey lowered his weapon enough so that when he fired, he splintered Thomas's left knee. Thomas descent to the ground was instant and not at all graceful.

Dude!" Dave yelled. "Way to go!"

Corey replied without forethought, "The olfactory sense is the one most closely related to memory, right?"

"Huh?" Dave was lost.

"Never mind." Corey followed with, "I have some experience with hatred and anger. Let's leave it at that."

Police cars were on the right street now; the blue and red flashing lights could be seen between the trees in the distance. Thomas was screaming in pain and clutching his leg. "I'm going to keep my gun pointed at this piece of shit, why don't you greet the officers." Corey offered just as two patrol cars pulled into the driveway. Dave started limping toward the police cars.

As the marked cruisers came to a skidding halt, the officers in the first car, jumped out, guns drawn, using their car doors as shields; they squatted pointing the guns at the three men. Someone in the second car made an announcement using a speaker of some sort, "Drop your weapons immediately, hands where we can see them." The tone surprised Corey; he felt like a hero so the seriousness of the cops was a surprise. "Drop your weapon now." This time the voice was more than serious: it was a voice that needed to be listened to. Corey set the rifle down in front of himself, very gingerly, realizing then that the cops wouldn't know yet who the good guys were and who the bad guy was.

Thomas shouted out, "They are trying to kill me!" Four officers hurried toward the three of them; one used a radio attached to his shoulder to call an ambulance, then snapped on a pair of disposable rubber gloves and squatted beside Thomas while his partner trained his weapon on him.

The remaining officers moved toward Dave and Corey. "Down on the ground! Keep your hands where we can see them," one cop repeated. The three men were all in handcuffs within seconds. Laying on their bellies and succumbing to a pat-down, Dave and Corey both sputtered information about the hostage in the basement while the cops made sure they had no additional weapons on them.

A cop with a name tag reading Sergeant Russell stopped them, saying, "Wait, slow down, where is this hostage?" Corey and Dave pointed at the illuminated basement window. Corey interrupted, "She is scared to death, please let us go down to get her, we've already been talking to her."

Russell said, "I can't do that. Technically, you are a trespasser at this time." Then, with more kindness in his voice he continued. "What else do you know about this situation; make it short."

Dave jumped in, "Her name is Elaine, we don't know how long she's been down there, but it's been at least a day. She had been talking to us through that window so we know she's there against her will. We also know he had been stalking her and planned to hurt her."

"You guys have a lot of knowledge," Russell said with a hint of sarcasm. "Hang on, somehow I believe you." He turned and yelled for the officer who had summoned the ambulance. "Kruse, come over here. Keep an eye on our informed friends here for me while I take a peek in that window."

Russell used the flashlight attached to his belt to peer into the low opening. "Hello?" Dave and Corey held their breath while they waited for Elaine to reply.

"Hello, Elaine?" Russell tried again. For a moment there was no breeze, no rattle of fallen leaves, and no one screaming in pain. It was during that moment of silence that Russell heard what sounded like a child singing a song very quietly; it was a sing-song voice fading in and out. "Hello, my name is Alan and I'm here to help. I'm Alan Russell and I work for the Victory police department." He heard just a few notes of the song again when Thomas renewed his screaming, drowning out the childish song.

Russell stood up, "I heard someone ... or something down there until this one started screaming again." He turned toward Thomas, "The ambulance is on its way, do you think you could keep it down for another minute until they get here?"

"Fuck you." Thomas snarled.

"Kruse, I'm going to try to get to her through the house. You hold down the fort out here." Kruse nodded his understanding.

"There's a deadbolt on the door," Russell reported back three minutes later.

"I should have mentioned that to you," Dave interjected. He was standing again, "But listen man, she's a really nice lady and she's really scared. Is there any special way cops have to get into locked houses when there's a hostage inside?" Dave shifted his weight onto his uninjured leg; doing so put him at eye level with Russell and Russell looked him straight in the eye. Their eye contact held for a few seconds. Finally, the officer looked away and toward his colleagues.

"Hey, you guys have any glass cutters?" He shouted as he walked toward the police cars.

"I do!" An officer from the second cruiser replied as he pulled his Billy club out of a back pocket. "I never met a piece of glass I couldn't cut," he said, proudly brandishing the polished stick as the two men strode back to the rear door. As the ambulance noisily pulled into the driveway, Sergeant Alan Russell and his fellow officer entered Thomas's house.

Inside the house, as he sensed the presence of fear and long-forgotten failures, Russell's training kicked in. "Victory Police Department!" He shouted clearly as he entered. He and his glass-cutting associate both started scanning the room for any dangers that might present themselves. Russell noticed the counters were very clean and tidy, yet the floors were filthy.

They called clear on the room and checked all connecting rooms, each time declaring loudly who they were and each time getting no response. While fulfilling this safety procedure, they located the stairs going down and that's where they headed next.

"Stay behind me," Russell said - he felt like he was the right candidate to help a scared woman and he didn't know the other officer well enough to know how he would handle her - he wanted the lead role. Russell's kind, intuitive, and professional manner was well known within the Victory police force so cop number-two was happy to take the rear as they descended the old staircase. At the bottom, they identified themselves one last time as they scanned with their flashlights, again, doing their best to make sure there were no unforeseen sources of danger.

They turned to the right and quickly came to the end of that route; a hot water tank and a furnace were backed up against the stone foundation. They backed up and went to the left of the staircase, and soon found a very odd door with a padlock dangling from a homemade hook-and-eye type closure. Russell knocked gently. "Elaine, I am Sergeant Alan Russell, are you in here?" No answer.

"Elaine it's very important that you say something to me so I know to get you out of here." No answer.

Elaine was rocking and singing. She thought she might be on her mother's lap on the front porch of the house she grew up in, or on her grandmother's lap in the sitting room of her old house. She felt wrapped in something protective. These women would never let anything bad happen to her. Just then, Danielle came up behind her and shook her. "Mom!" The sensation and sound didn't make any sense to Elaine, she tried to sink back down into her comfort zone. "MOM!" Danielle shouted very loudly directly into Elaine's ear. This jolted Elaine, she looked around herself, startled, not recognizing where she was.

"Danielle, you don't have to be so rude..." Elaine's voice trailed off as she looked around: Danielle wasn't there. Just then, she heard another voice.

"Elaine, please answer me, we are here to help, my name is Sergeant Russell." The training this officer had received taught him to continually articulate who he was and who he was representing, in the event that prior declarations had gone unheard and so he would always know that he had been as clear as possible.

Elaine became aware of the coldness under her and against her back; she again was aware of her intense thirst and the aching in her bones. She smelled mildew, dirty oil, and urine; she sensed the loss of time. Fear surged through her veins and threatened to shut her consciousness down for good when she heard one word.

"Elaine?"

Elaine attempted a reply: "Yes," but there was no sound. She heard a voice in the back of her head, *Mom, you really try hard, do you hear me?! Give this your best so we can be together again!* Elaine tried again; "I'm here," still no sound came out of her throat. *Mom!* Elaine filled her lungs with air and really pushed out her words; she wanted Danielle to be proud of her. "I'm here..." This time some sound came out.

Alan Russell felt a wave of excitement wash over him. "Great Elaine, we are with the Victory Police Department. You sit still and we will be right in to get you. Don't worry about anything."

DAVE 7

Dave and Corey spent the next hour at the local hospital. Elaine had been transported there right after her rescue, so by the time she was wheeled into the brightly lit building, Thomas's entire driveway and hundreds of feet around his house had become occupied by VPD vehicles and cop cars from surrounding departments; all with lights spinning. Dave's wound was attended to by one of the ambulance crews and deemed superficial but worthy of additional attention; he was taken to the hospital under the rules of abundant caution. Corey followed along in Dave's truck; the fact that Corey's car was still at the post office and Dave was going to need his truck soon, contributed to Corey's plan to follow the ambulance. The delay in their departure allowed them to witness the obligatory crime scene tape going up, which cordoned off a large section of the rural street; uniformed officers were everywhere they looked. Later, by comparison, the VPD interrogation rooms seemed peaceful. The two men spent no less than two hours there.

First the two men individually explained the events of the afternoon at the Post Office and the events that followed. Later they explained their foreknowledge with Dave describing working on Thomas's boiler and sneaking a look at the forbidden dark room and the pictures labeled with Elaine's name found inside of it. Corey revealed that he was aware of Thomas through the adoptive family's use of the agency he worked for, many years before. It was really just the name he knew, he explained, not the person.

Alan Russell led these interviews with Kruse's help. They knew that the criminal was not in this interrogation room, yet they had to work to unearth the details that would be needed for the sake of a seamless prosecution later.

When Dave finally lay down in his own bed that night, he

pulled Lisa to him and let her warmth invade his body. "Mmmmm.... Honey, you're so late..." Lisa mumbled.

"I know, I'll explain tomorrow, it's all good." He smiled at his own understatement of the truth and dropped off to sleep within a few minutes.

The next morning, Dave woke before the alarm went off. *Wow, if it weren't for this bandage tape tearing out the hairs on my leg, I'd feel like million bucks,* he thought. He made the coffee quietly so that Lisa could have a few extra minutes of sleep. As he counted the scoops of coffee he poured into the waiting filter, he realized, *I don't have a hang-over. Yesterday was the first time in I-don't-know-how-long that I didn't drink any alcohol.* He felt embarrassed momentarily because of this realization. He replaced that feeling with one of determination: *My son will have a sober father.* He drank the first, of many, cups of coffee that day with a feeling of understanding his mission.

Once Lisa was up and the morning's efforts had skipped ahead to the routine which resulted in Trevor getting to school, Dave went downstairs with the agenda of righting a few wrongs. Even if he had to go bankrupt, he would repay the credit card company he had defrauded. Bankruptcy was not illegal, so his family could survive that. He opened the file drawer that contained all his father's documents. Lifting the entire file out took both hands; Dave hadn't realized it had swelled so much since his father's passing. He and Jay had gotten in the habit of just dropping documents in as they came across them in straightening up their father's final affairs.

He laid the hanging file on his table and started looking for the remnants of the credit card applications he had sent in. He decided his first task was to somehow cancel the applications he had sent in but hadn't heard back from yet.

Once that was done, he would find the remit-to address of the one he had gotten money from and send in as much money as he had in his business checking account. Screw everyone else he owed money to.

One manila folder within the green hanging folder contained things Jay had found when cleaning his father's desk out. It was labeled simply 'Checking Accounts.' Jay had dropped the entire manila folder into Dave's cabinet once he confirmed that the checking account statements within it were all accounts that they were aware of. Dave set that folder aside since it had nothing to do with the credit card applications. He stopped thumbing through the drawer when he heard papers crash to the floor. *Shit! I set it too close the edge of the table.* Dave stopped his search to turn and collect the contents of the spilled folder. His lack of a headache made it possible for him to laugh at himself. *You idiot...* he thought, and cracked a half-smile. As he picked up the pages of bank statements and the windowed envelopes that had contained them, he found an unlabeled nine-by-twelve inch white envelope. It was sealed and the fact that there was nothing printed on it, no 'to' or 'from' address, and no postage, caught Dave's attention. He looked at both sides to confirm that there was nothing written or printed on it that would explain its presence in the Checking Accounts folder. It seemed as good as empty, so Dave fanned it to see if he could detect any weighty contents; his clear mind allowed for the presence of curiosity.

Taking the white envelope with him, Dave returned to his coffee cup and sat down. He took a sip of the luke warm brew and began to tear the sealed end open. He pulled out a single sheet of what felt like fancy paper; it had a raised seal on it. One word caught his eye: "Bond."

COREY 5

Eve was staying with Corey's former wife Angela on the night he ended up in the VPD interrogation room, so he arrived home to an empty house. As much as he missed Eve on this night, he was still not done feeling the relief that coming home to an Angela-free house presented him with.

There had been times when Corey chastised himself for the mistakes he had made with Angela: first impregnating her while they were in college, then later for tolerating her abuse. He did, however, find a way to forgive himself and move forward in his new life. It wasn't the type of forgiveness advertised by the agency he worked for. Instead, it was the kind that had meaning to - and effect for him. Corey, the quintessential user of introspection, started with naming the benefits that came out of the mistake. In his case, that was the easiest step. In one word, it was Eve. The second step was harder; he had to identify each thing he had done wrong. He named them to himself, starting with having sex with a person he did not really know at a time when child-bearing was not in her best interest. As much as child-bearing was not part of his objective on that one night, it was still a known possible outcome. Over the next months, this led to more self-discussion on how this had led to their marriage and subsequent discontent.

The next step was the most difficult step for Corey because he didn't want to - nor could he - forgive himself for doing something his body was designed to do. It took a great deal of hair-splitting and introspection for him to find the statement of fact that he wanted to forgive himself for. The one he ended up really focusing on was, *In my immature, inexperienced, alcohol-laden desire to relate to a woman, I went too far too soon.*

Corey spent several months meditating on the two truths:

the good that came out of his mistake, and the crux of the mistake. Before long, his self-forgiveness gave way to a self-acknowledgment of the wonderful aspects of his new life as a single parent to Eve.

Corey pulled down the bedding on the bed that had once been a place of misery. He snuggled under the covers that smelled like his choice of fabric softener and was seemingly, within minutes, turning off the alarm that informed him it was time to get up for work. As his feet hit the floor, he felt refreshed. It was going to be a good day.

KATE 6

In June of Tim's 61st year, Kate and Amanda went to
Moriah to witness the graduation of the institution's 67th
graduating platoon, of which Michael was a part.
Graduation was at 9:00 a.m. on a Thursday so they did a
slight deviation from what had become their mid-night
routine. This time, they left Amanda's home in
Canadesque at 8:00 p.m. when Amanda got out of work.
They drove 80 percent of the way to Moriah before
stopping at a charming-looking motel they had spotted on
other trips to the facility. This motel investment was
intended to be a treat Kate was bestowing on herself and
Amanda, the two people who had tirelessly visited, written
to, and otherwise supported Michael throughout his
incarceration. The treat wasn't actually much of a treat
however, since they arrived at midnight and had to depart
by 7:00 a.m. Nonetheless, they would have Michael in the
car with them as they drove past this quaint motel the next
day, heading in the opposite direction. There was no way
to dampen the spirits of these two women.

The graduating ceremony was comprised of two main
components; the first was a marching drill. Michael's
platoon of 46 young men completed an incredibly complex
set of maneuvers in a medium-sized parking lot in front of
a deck that the attendees were invited to stand on. The
deck was sort of like a balcony but really was just an
extended loading dock behind the building. The
maneuvers included counted-off steps that went not only
north-south and east-west, but also diagonally. All the
while, flags were held high and held low, and no one
bumped into another participant, nor was anyone speared
with a flag pole. Kate, Amanda, and almost everyone else
observing were slack-jawed at the intricacy and perfection
of the routine. It was clear that hours of practice were
involved.

After that performance, attendees were invited inside to witness the actual graduation. Five young men were recognized for outstanding achievement. These achievements included things like quitting smoking, weight-loss, or completion of a GED: all things that had been achieved during the 6 months of the program. Kate expected Michael to be recognized for something, but he wasn't. She realized after some thought that Michael had arrived at Moriah so much further ahead in the world than the other men, that there was not reasonable room for him to achieve anything within their limited expectations. Kate did learn on the way home that Michael had written the acceptance speech for some of the men receiving the acknowledgments. That explained why those men didn't know how to pronounce some of the words within their own speeches. Kate, not for the first time, was saddened by how much potential her son had, that was to date, going to waste.

Kate and her two passengers hit the road to head home to Victory by 11:00 a.m. that Thursday. They drove as far as they could before hunger forced them to stop for food. Their lunch took place in a small town Kate had not stopped in before, so they didn't know what to expect as they walked up onto the front porch of a place that advertised 'Food' in fuchsia neon.

Michael politely ordered a Coke from the waitress after Kate had asked for ice water. Amanda said, "Can I just get a shot of Jameson?"

When the waitress returned with the drinks, Amanda tossed hers back. This was the first time Michael had been within 500 feet of alcohol in many months, yet he seemed nonplussed. The terms of Michael's freedom prevented him from drinking alcohol for at least one year after his release, but apparently Amanda had no real or implied restrictions.

Kate encouraged everyone to order whatever they wanted to eat; she was feeling magnanimous. Michael ordered the largest burger they offered and when it was set in front of him, accompanied by a generous amount of fries, he almost drooled. Kate made him wait the three seconds it took for her to take a picture of her shaved-headed son with his burger. Amanda's selfishness could not steal this moment of joy from Kate nor Michael.

While Michael was finishing the last of his meal, Amanda sneaked away to the bar to get one more shot of her preferred whiskey. Kate pretended not to notice in the hope that that would make it easier on Michael.

The remainder of the drive home, Kate's mind continually festered over the fact that her sober son was going home to a house occupied by a woman who needed to drink shots of whiskey within easy smelling distance of him - the first chance that she got. These thoughts led to other things like, *What will he do to earn a living? Can he ever expect to find a job that will provide health insurance? Will he ever be able to get out from under the debt he built up while he was living 'high?'*

Kate was bringing her son home, but there were many things left to worry about.

DAVE 8

Almost ceremoniously, Dave slipped the piece of paper out of the white envelope. After seeing the word "Bond," the next thing he noticed was a number. Preceded by a dollar sign, there was a number printed in numerals, followed by the number written in words: Fifty Thousand.

At first Dave felt the jaded feeling one gets when reading that Ed McMahon has stated, via a letter, that "You are one of twelve to qualify for $250,000! You just only need to consider subscribing to Publishers Clearing House publications. But even if you don't, send in this form because you are still are qualified! The smallest thing you could win is an RCA Color Television!" Exclamation points are everywhere within this letter and your name appears at the top as if it's written in cursive by Ed himself.

Dave chuckled at himself for the fact that his attention had been captured for a second by this document. Since he was already sitting in his favorite chair with a cup of coffee within easy reach, he leaned back and put the piece of paper to his nose. He inhaled deeply as he thought his way through this recent moment of foolishness. The scent of the paper didn't give him any additional information but the extra moments of feeling the paper did. In fact, Dave was stopped short by the feeling that this wasn't ordinary paper. It felt more like cloth. It really was parchment.

He examined the paper in detail now. It was an EE Bond, made out to the bearer. The name of the purchaser was Weldon Shipway, on a date that was roughly five years ago. Its face value was $50,000.

Dave picked up the phone and dialed Jay.

KATE 7

Michael did his best to settle into a new life with Amanda. Kate got the feeling that she was not privy to the details that were under the surface, but she remained available to Michael, without asking questions or even wanting the answers, as he made his re-entry to the real world.

With Michael being 26 years old, Kate was working hard to not be in charge of his success. He had to do it on his own, and she needed to be done being responsible for it.

After Michael placed a Facebook page advertising handyman work, he called her to ask, "How does somebody get business cards?"

Kate replied, "They ask their mother!" Kate was happy to help him if he was helping himself. Creating business cards and paying the online vendor $25 dollars for them was something Kate was very willing to do. She came up with a cute design that depicted a house made up of a screw driver, a paintbrush, a light fixture - all kinds of things that represented tools that fix up a house - formed into the shape of a house. The tag line read, Let Me Fix It! followed by a brief list of Michael's skills and his phone number. She delivered them to him four days later.

Michael was genuinely grateful and excited. He felt like the business cards validated his attempts to make a living on his own. Michael's father and Kate had done the same thing some twenty-five years earlier so it was easy for Kate to understand his vision.

For his birthday one month after his release, Kate bought Michael an 18-volt tool set that included a power drill, a skill saw and several other snap-on options. In addition, Michael had tools that Kate and her 'baby daddy' didn't have back then. Tools like Facebook, Craig's List, and a website to generate business. Kate kept her fingers crossed.

Michael did give Kate lots of reasons to think positively. He looked her straight in the eye when they talked. He made a point of talking to her, or least texting every day. He kept most of the plans they made although he was almost always later than he would agree to. The tardiness problem was something his father's entire family suffered from; it was called 'Phillips Time' by family insiders. The event that shored up Kate's confidence more than anything else was when Michael ended his relationship with Amanda.

Michael had found himself needing to get away from Amanda quickly. He had discovered that she had a $100 per day drug habit that she had been hiding from him. When he found needle marks on her arms the same day that she had spent her entire paycheck, he became very upset and called Kate asking if she would talk with him while he calmed down. Kate was at work but she instantly put on her counselor's hat and talked quietly about how nice his life would be once he got this big change - and move - behind him. When they hung up, Kate hoped Michael felt better about his new path. Kate was definitely relieved to have the wild card named Amanda on her way out of her son's life.

EPILOGUE

Saint Theresa's Carnival was expected to have a great turnout this year. The temperatures were predicted to be in the high 70's during the day and in the high 60's during the four evenings this fund raiser would take place. The early October air smelled fresh with hints of dried leaves making it clear that fall was underway.

As executive director of the Catholic charity that was the primary sponsor, Corey planned to attend each night. At least part of the time he would work the dart-throwing booth that displayed their logo; his assistant director and a few other employees planned to work the rest of the time. Blowing up the balloons to replace those punctured by the last players used up a lot of his energy and attention when he worked, and he enjoyed that.

As Corey was playing the role of the carnie, calling out to passers-by to entice them to play, Dave, his son on his shoulders, approached the booth, "Hey man," they high-fived each other then Corey high-fived Trevor. As they started to chat, Dave's wife Lisa approached from the other direction; Eve was cheerfully holding her hand and skipping along beside her.

"Hello Gentlemen," Lisa said smiling. "Anyone want to join a few ladies for a corn dog and hot cocoa?" Eve giggled and Corey reached down to tickle her belly.

"I can meet you there in 20 minutes," Corey replied.

"I want to wait with Daddy!" Eve cried out cheerfully.

"That okay Corey?" Lisa asked.

"Sure, jump on over here, little one," Corey answered as he lifted his daughter up and over the counter and into his side of the carnival game booth.

Lisa finished their conversation for now, "Okay, see you two at the food court in 20 minutes."

"Bye Aunt Lisa!" Eve called out. "See you soon!" Eve was excited, "Daddy, Daddy, look at my new bracelet! Aunt Lisa got it for me. I just love it, don't you Daddy?" Eve held up a bracelet made of loops of small elastic bands. Corey admired it with exaggerated attention. He nodded and smiled as he kissed his daughter's forehead.

A few weeks before the October date that St. Theresa's carnival was expected to start, the calendar for volunteer shifts was passed around a meeting of the Sons of The American Legion. At the urging of the Women's Auxiliary, The American Legion planned to take a booth at the carnival this year. They planned to sell hot dogs, corn and chili dogs, and a few assorted beverages, along with packaged snacks such as chips and pretzels.

Earl's life was busy, but he still enjoyed his role with the Legion, so when the calendar passed in front of him, he wrote his name in the time slot for Friday and Saturday night. He would work from 4:00 p.m. until 8:00 p.m. each night. In his mind, he would get the best of the family time visitors and he would get home before anyone had too much time in the beer tent.

Friday's weather turned out to be better than anyone had dared to hope for. The sun came out early, and by 5:00 p.m. the temperature had reached 80 degrees. The sun was bright, the sky was blue, and the air smelled good. Selling sodas and hot dogs was a really good idea for any organization that wanted to raise money in Victory, PA.

Earl was enjoying bantering with his steady stream of customers. "Would you like to supersize that order ma'am?" he joked with a woman with three kids in tow. A gentleman older than Earl was the next one in line, "Sir, I can sell you two hot dogs for merely twice the price of one, if you'd like to take one home with you."

Before long, though, the line was long, and those waiting weren't as cheerful as they were at 5:00. Earl felt bad for the people waiting because there was only him working. There was no one to call for help.

Kate and Tim were strolling through the carnival, Michael and Toni close behind. They had already eaten so they hadn't planned to stop anywhere except maybe the beer tent. Kate noticed the very long line before she saw Earl behind the counter. "Oh honey, look at poor Earl," Kate looked up at Tim.

"Want to help him?" Tim asked.

"Oh, yes, that's exactly what I want and it would be so fun if you helped too." Kate's voice was filled with love for her husband. This was an example of one of the things she loved about him the most: his willingness to help people that she loved.

Kate and Tim walked to the end of the counter and lifted the gated edge, letting themselves in. "Stay in touch by cell, we'll meet you in a little bit," Kate said to her two kids as they walked toward the rides.

"Hey, what's going on here? Kate! It's so good to see you!" Earl turned toward Kate and Tim for a scant few seconds when the next person in line shouted at him.

"Hey old man, it's my turn."

Tim side-stepped down the counter to respond to this rude customer. "Hey, I'm your old man now, what do you want?" Tim leaned toward this customer as he asked, all six feet, eight inches of him working in Earl's favor.

Kate said, "Hey, we're going to help out here just long enough to get this line down to a manageable amount of people. We didn't have anything else to do, so we thought this would be fun!" Kate was making sure Earl's pride couldn't be damaged.

"Aw Kate, you're the best." Earl was as pleased to see her as he was to have the help.

The three of them worked out their division of duties and behind-the-counter choreography quickly. Within a short time the line was down to a few people, but those few people were consistently replaced by other people. After another half hour, Earl finally felt like he could take a minute to sit down on the stool at the back of the booth. Kate and Tim stood at the side chatting. The sense of achievement was uplifting, and all three were smiling. A pretty lady came out of the shadows with two kids. "Still open?" she asked as she peered in.

"Elaine?" Kate asked. "Elaine! It's me, Kate! How is your new home working out?" The two women hugged awkwardly across the counter.

"Kate! I haven't seen you since I closed on the house, how are you?" Kate introduced Tim, and then Elaine introduced Eric and Danielle. The group chatted for a minute before Earl interrupted.

"Hey, I know you! You used to clean my teeth." Earl smiled widely at Elaine.

"Oh my goodness I did. How are you?" Elaine asked, genuinely interested yet feeling overwhelmed by needing to speak to so many people only 16 months after her second traumatizing abduction.

"I'm just fine," Earl sensed that she didn't want to explain why she didn't work at Victory Dental any longer. "I hope you are well too." He walked away smiling and waited on the next group of customers, leaving her to speak with Kate.

"Kate, Tim, you are relieved of duty! Thanks so much for your help!" Earl shouted over his shoulder.

Kate and Tim ducked back under the counter, they took seats at the table next to the one Elaine and her children chose. Kate chose the side where she could keep her eye on Earl for the last few minutes of his shift. Danielle and Eric squirmed with excitement at the idea of eating this rare meal of carnival food.

Earl's last customers of the night were two men, a woman, and 2 kids, all laughing and talking together comfortably. Earl couldn't tell who was married to whom, if anyone; they were a contented group. He would have guessed, if asked, that the two men were brothers.

"Hey Eve, what do you want to drink?"

"Corey, is it okay if Eve has lemonade"

"Dave, do you have a ten? I only have twenties."

"Lisa, please have Trevor grab some napkins."

Lisa: "Dave, Corey, where do you want to sit?"

Their banter was natural and fun. The last thing Lisa had said though, had caught Elaine's ear. ... *Dave, Corey... How often do those names go together?...*

Elaine glanced over her shoulder and she knew right away that it was her rescuers. She turned back around immediately, feeling the blinding sensation of jangling nerves that was always there, just below the surface, always ready to remind her that she was a victim. Her heart started to pound and her ears filled with a roar. Her hands were shaking and she was sweating while feeling cold. She turned again to get another look at the happy group.

She *was* a victim. The word in its past tense rang back into her ears loudly. These men deserve credit for making the past tense a reality. They put their lives on the line for her when it would have been so much easier to turn a blind eye to the complicated situation that brought them together. Because of them and her own indomitable spirit, she was a survivor instead of a victim.

"Danielle, give me one of your special hugs please," Elaine turned to her daughter unexpectedly. Without letting any time pass, Danielle set down her sacred corn dog and squeezed her Mom in a way that only she could, and one more time, Elaine was given needed strength by her daughter. She stood up and walked over to the hot dog stand.

Interrupting a chatty conversation about lemonade and chili sauce, Elaine said, "Excuse me, Corey? Dave?"

As if it has been practiced, both men's jaws dropped in unison; Corey's corn dog hit the ground as Dave's soda slammed on the counter. They turned to the woman who had united them in their fierce friendship. They had agreed between the two of them previously that they had to allow Elaine her privacy; therefore, they would never seek her out or expect to hear from her. Having her show up during a happy family time and openly greet them was more than they had thought to hope for.

Elaine put one arm around each man's neck and squeezed them both to her as they both embraced her too. The three hugged in a way that seemed never-ending When that initial feeling had worn off enough for them to remember that there were important others looking on, they pulled apart, enough to see each other's tears.

Dave was the first to regain composure. "Elaine, I want you to meet my wife," he pulled Lisa into the circle. "Lisa, this is Elaine."

Lisa, grasped each of Elaine's hands as she looked into her eyes. Elaine met her gaze and held it as Lisa worked out what she wanted to say. "You are my hero, Elaine. I am so glad to get to meet you." The two women embraced in a way that women who understand each other can. Tears ran down both of their faces before the hug was finished.

Choking on her words, Elaine said, "I want, umm... I mean I *need* you to meet my children. Eric, Danielle, come here." She motioned them over. "You know these names, this is Corey and Dave, and this is my new friend Lisa."

Eric and Danielle looked up at their mom to wordlessly ask, *thee Corey and Dave?* Elaine nodded yes. Eric bolted toward the closest man, Dave, clutching him around the waist, almost knocking the wind out of him and holding his head against his chest. "Thank you." Eric choked out.

Danielle was shyer than Eric. Corey reached out to her and pulled her away from the group a little bit. "Hi Danielle, I'm so happy to know you. Do you know why?"

"Uh, cuz I'm her daughter?" Danielle thumbed toward Elaine.

"Yes, that's part of it. But also it's because you and your

mom have such a strong bond, I wanted the chance to meet you so I could be sure to get the chance to tell you how special that is. It's not like everyone else's, it's more." Corey looked into Danielle's eyes to see if Danielle understood this at all. She was pretty young still and may take her special bond for granted.

"Oh I know," Danielle replied lightly, smiling. "Can I play with your daughter?" Corey laughed and nodded his approval.

Kate watched this scene develop, and when Tim asked if she needed more napkins, she held up an index finger to silently ask for some time. Tim looked around for an explanation for this request. When straining his neck to the left, he saw a group of people that had to be Kate's focal point. Kate knew some of the details of Elaine's ordeal via the Victory grapevine, but she really wanted to observe what was clearly a joyful and healthy gathering of people.

As the group was enjoying the carnival sounds and smells, mulling around the picnic table, kids darting around and playing with one another, they didn't notice the slats coming down, closing the hot dog stand they were sitting in front of. Many tears had been shed, but smiles remained in abundance. Before anyone had a chance to think about making their way home, Earl came up carrying as many corn dogs as a person can carry.

"Hello all! Dig in! I brought treats! Everything left over is for us to share!" His words were cut off by his own big laugh as he handed out the corn dogs between the two tables. When he finished laughing, he continued, "And if anyone needs a lemonade, I have a key." He winked at Eve as he finished his sentence.

Elaine took a deep breath and sat down on one of the benches. "Hey pretty lady, can I buy you a drink?" Earl winked as he asked while pointing to his waxy soft drink cup. He was a little concerned but didn't want to push himself on her if she just needed to sit quietly for a minute.

"I... am... I am fine." Elaine finished her sentence sounding solid. "For the first time in a long time I am completely okay." She took a breath, "This is such a big deal that I hadn't planned on - I'm sorry, it's a long story - I'm just taking a moment to breathe it in."

Danielle's voice drifted in from the kid-pile "Mom! Come play with us!" Elaine looked at Earl and Earl nodded in a silent 'go.' He knew he didn't need to understand.

Kate sat alone, observing Corey and Dave excitedly talking to Lisa about Elaine and Elaine's kids, as well as all the kids playing together. She saw Earl smiling at her and nodding toward the kid pile with pleasure. She saw Elaine smiling widely at the adults as she walked past them and toward the kid-pile so she could join in that fun at Danielle's request. And then Tim was behind her, taking her hands and lifting her up off the bench. He put his arms around her and hugged her. Her love for him was never greater.

Kate's heart swelled with the feeling that life was good.

~~ THE END ~~

ACKNOWLEGEMENTS

I wrote The Post Office when I found myself buying stamps and arranging for a P.O. Box so that I could communicate with my son who was in prison on drug-related charges. I didn't want my co-workers to see where I was getting letters from and sending letters to. Standing in line I couldn't help but notice how many other people were using the facility and I began to wonder, *Why do so many use the brick-and-mortar building when I can usually complete all my postal tasks from my desk at work?*

This is the story of six people who need to use the post office in the small, fictitious town of Victory, PA, all for different reasons. One person is me, and in The Post Office my character, Kate, is writing this book as a means of catharsis. The other characters are fictitious. The Post Office is fiction, a suspense novel, but it has much more than just slivers of truth.

I am very grateful to some people. In chronological order, thank you to my son Matthew Phillips who was my first proof reader. Matthew was in a prison where he wasn't allowed to receive books but he was able to get letters that contained the pieces of my book, as it was being written, pasted into the content of my letters to him. Picturing my son in a 5 foot by 9 foot cell 23 hours a day, with no reading material was one of the things that got me writing. I was never as prolific as I was when he was in Elmira prison. In this book, Elmira is spelled backwards and Matthew's name is Michael. Matthew would read my pages, marking typos with his pencil, jotting down suggestions, and then mailing them back to me. By the way, he was the one that encouraged me to plump out the physical descriptions of my characters.

Thank you to my daughter Tara Phillips who was always willing to listen to me chatter about "this book I'm writing" but more importantly, thank you for living this life with me and always being a source of light every time darkness threatened. I might have succumbed to the madness we've experienced if it hadn't been for you.

Thank you to my husband Tim Shipley who gave me the time, space and support to write. He also gave me the idea that resulted in Sally's mistake in Part II. Thank you to my sisters Deb Cruise and Lin Cruise who were early readers along with Matthew. Lin spent hours with me discussing potential story lines, recording our ideas by speaking them into my phone for me. We also spent time sitting in her living room, Lin feeding me fabulous homemade snacks and delicious red wines as we talked about The Post Office. Thank you to my brother Alan Cruise who, as a City of Seattle Homicide Detective, gave me valuable advice for the piece of this book that includes police involvement. That said, any mistakes regarding law enforcement protocol are all mine.

Thank you to Linda Knickerbocker Bassett and Kathy Simmons for reading pieces during my process of writing then later reading the whole manuscript along with Suzanna Prong. You are jewels in every possible way and I love you.

Thank you Heather Proctor; it would be hard to know where to start on this paragraph if I hadn't already set the precedent of chronology. When I had typed the words THE END, Heather was my first phone call and I am grateful for her first words, "Can I read it?" She didn't know I had already printed out a copy and had it in an envelope with her name on it. Thank you for reading it with the speed of an Evelyn Wood graduate; you knew me well enough to know that I would be on proverbial pins and needles. Thank you for meeting with me shortly thereafter to give me great ideas for making it a more complete work. Heather is responsible for my inclusion of the Kate story that ends with "You never know who you touch" as well as the pieces of Earl's story that are about Hope and Hope's mothering of his children, along a few other pieces. Thank you Heather for suggesting that The Post Office was good enough to be read by our shared book club which we lovingly call, Read Between the Wines. And thank you for organizing that reading and subsequent review of this work. Perhaps most importantly, thank you for being involved in my life enough to be witness to Kate's story and hence her validity. I'm writing this paragraph on your daughter Abby's 18th birthday which means we've been close friends for at least 18 years. How very lucky I feel.

In addition to Heather, who is HAP in this book, I have thanks for the other members of our book club: Lisa Fisher, Patti Gates, Kim Yourch, Karen Centonze, and Sandy Pennise. The evening we spent reviewing this book was the fourth greatest day of my life. The only days that were better were when my two children were born, and the day that Tim became my husband. Your love, support, and suggestions are a resource I will always be grateful for.

Thank you to Kim Phillips, Betsy Haines, Chelsie Yourch and Samantha Gates for proof reading for me; Sam: additional thanks for teaching me some rules of writing, including that of the comma-splice. Thank you to a popular Rochester, New York radio talk show host who granted me permission to use his radio name, The Brother Wease, in an early chapter about Kate. Thank you Paul Guglielmo for making that happen.

To anyone who is reading this right now - thank you.

Humbly,

Kim Cruise

Kim Cruise's next book: One Eleven

PREVIEW

~~~~~~

KATE

"Hello Kate? This is Doctor Hockstein, we have your son here." This new voice was on the line as Kate made the right-hand turn that headed her south toward the hospital.

"Hello, what's going on?" Kate wanted details.

"Your son is an adult so I am restricted on what I can tell you, but he is in danger."

Kate: "what kind of danger? Has there been an accident?"

The doctor seemed to be thinking through his words carefully. "Again, I am not privileged to tell you the details, but he is not out of danger. I hope you can get here."

"I am on the road now, it will be another 15 minutes." Kate was impressed with the calmness she was able to fake.

Kate was now on a road that featured small hills, up and down, around corners both small and extreme. Intersections every half mile or so made Kate think of Toni, her daughter. *Toni still needs me - focus Kate! you need to stay safe, no matter what!* Her inner self shouted to her driving self. Kate registered her need to regain some of the control she had lost in the last few minutes. *Okay, breathe in, breathe out, keep your eyes on the road and keep your brain on your driving.* As Kate's rational brain used meditative practices to seek balance; she realized the best thing she could do for herself was to call Tim so that he would be able to meet her at the hospital. In spite of her state's laws that prohibited using a cell while driving, Kate called Tim.

"Michael is in the emergency room in Canajoharie and they tell me I have to get there right away." Kate started crying. Stating the truth made her face it.

"What's wrong with him?" Tim asked, as anyone would.

"They can't tell me because he is an adult," Kate cried into the phone. At that moment the reality couldn't be denied and she realized after all: she should have let Pete drive her. "Please just get there, they say his life is in jeopardy."

"I'm on my way." Thank the goddess for Tim, Kate thought not for the first time.

It had only been six months since Michael's release from shock camp and Kate's greatest fear was becomming reality. When Michael had come home on that proud day in June, Kate thought she didn't really have to worry, at least not until he was out from under the watchful eye - and regular urinalysis- of the staff of the parole office. *Silly Kate,* she said to herself; addiction is so much more powerful than a mother's expectation or a user's interest in getting by when the world - for them - was divided into who was 'using' and who was not.

When Kate finally pulled into the parking lot of the hospital - the hulking entity that knew if her son was alive or dead - she had a hard time interpreting the signs directing her to correct parking lot. The reality that her son may not still be alive was nipping at her brain in spite of her attempts to control her thoughts. She decided to just head to a parking lot with available spaces and pay for any parking tickets later.

Kate walked through the freezing air, she was not aware that tears were running down her face and off her chin, freezing when they landed on her coat, as she headed toward the lighted sign announcing the Emergency Entrance. She made her way to reception desk and told the attending woman her name and Michaels name. Again, the response made her feel that she was being waiting for, and that unnerved her further. The receptionist said, "Oh, okay." Then, as if someone had pushed an unseen button under a counter top or tapped a secret foot pedal under the desk, a different scrub-clad woman appeared, offering to direct Kate into the hiterlands of the emergency department. Kate numbly followed. Kate decided her son was most likely still alive based on this woman's actions.

The stark, clinical acknowledgement of her son's status as 'alive' served Kate on this day, but the price for the containment of her emotions at this time, would be paid a few months later. She would learn that a parent can't ever really be casual about one's child's health status; especially not the ultimate status: alive or dead.

The scrub-wearing woman pointed Kate toward bed number two. Kate entered the curtained area with the number two on the dividing wall. Michael lay in a bed with a mask tightly secured to his mouth and nose and several other machines connected to him in different ways. His eyes were closed. Later Kate would have no memory of how she got to this area of the hospital. Kate put her hand on Michael's arm. "Michael, what happened?"

He stirred and his eyes struggled to open. He reached for the mask as if he wanted to answer. Kate helped him with the latch that was holding it tight against his face. Once it was released she asked again, "What happened?"

Michael struggled for words so Kate stated her fear,"Did you overdose?" Michael shook his head up and down. "On heroin?" Kate asked with incredulity. She had held on to the belief that as many challenges as her son had presented her with, he had never gone past this one line-in-the-sand that Kate felt was the only remaining line; the line that - in her limited knowledge - people didn't return from. Michael shook his head in the affirmative again.

A nurse entered the room, alerted by an alarm that went off when the mask was loosened from Michael's face. "It is very important that this stay on his face." Her words were directed toward Kate.

"I'm sorry. I didn't realize. Can you help me understand what this mask is doing?" Kate was trying to absorb what her son had just told her while trying to be respectful of the poeple who had likely saved his life.

"I'll ask the doctor to stop in to talk to you, but for now, this bi-pap is very important to him." She reconnected the straps and closures so that the mask was visibly tight against Kate's youngest child's face. There would be marks in the shape of that mask for days on the otherwise perfect skin of his face.

A few minutes later a doctor appeared. Kate knew him from years ago when his daughter and Michael attended the same daycare. Canajoharie was a small town by most standards and this type of thing happened frequently to Kate. This was due in a large part to the time she spent serving on charitable boards - like the one at her day care center - and working on many fund raisers, before realizing that her time was better spent staying home with her kids. Kate mentioned the daycare connection as he led her to an area where they could talk, she wanted him to see her as "like him" versus "like them." When they arrived at the private area, he did seem to look at Kate as if she was truly someone he cared to communicate with. After a brief intoduction to the topic, he showed her an X-Ray of her son's polluted lungs. Michael had aspirated vomit as he slept through his heroin high. This is why the mask that forced oxygen into her son's lungs was so very important. His lungs couldn't do it on their own.

DEIRDRE

"Really?" Monica challenged Deirdre. "Tell me about just exactly when you stopped being a good girl."

A truthful answer would have included details about the day a few months earlier, when she found herself in the principal's office facing Monica for the first time. "I don't really feel like entertaining you with stories about my misery," Deirdre offered.

"Oh you're a big fake," Monica knew she was on to something and her need to dominate inspired her to dig in deeper. If she could make Deirdre pick a scab off her own soul, she would do that. Her emptiness knew few boundaries so prices paid by other people had no meaning to her. "You really are a *good* girl, aren't you? A goody-two-shoes actually." She continued, "so tell me, since we are ready to admit your goodness, why do you want to hangout with my friends?" Monica cocked her head and pursed her lips as she waited for her answer.

As much as Deirdre wanted a group of friends to call her own, she didn't feel she wanted to be someone she really wasn't. She wanted to be herself, but she wanted that 'self' to have people to hang around with. This very situation is what put her in the position of accepting friendship from a bully in the first place. "Do I have to be a not-good girl to hang out with you?" She bought some time with her question.

"Well," Monica scoffed, "it would be really cool if we were at least compatible." She shifted in her seat on the school's front steps and turned away from Deirdre. "Jeeeez" she muttered under her breath.

"You'll have to decide if you feel we are compatible. Meanwhile, am I gunna drown kittens or rough up a four-year-old? No, I'm not." It was Deirdre's turn to turn away.

Monica stood up, "Come on, I gotta find a smoke." The two girls walked toward the sidewalk where they joined a group of three others that were heading for the Seven-Eleven. Four of the five teenagers pooled their money so they could buy a pack of cigarettes; Deirdre didn't smoke - yet. The four paying members elected the one who would go into the store by briefly discussing who was the oldest looking member; Monica won this title. The store clerk was a sleepy twenty-something who had dropped out of college during his first semester. He would have sold cigarettes to a 10 year old, but the group didn't know that. She asked for her brand, Newport 100's, and he passed them to her without ever looking at her face.

A few minutes later, the group was standing a circle in far corner of the parking lot behind the row of stores that occupied the business district's one block of Main Street, Fonda, NY. Monica was rapping the pack of cigarettes against the back of her free hand as she got ready to open the pack. As she pulled the cellophane string away from the pack, she asked Deirdre, "Wanna try one? I mean, I know good girls don't usually smoke...."

Deirdre didn't want to fall victim to this type of manipulation but she didn't want to have to explain her way back into this group of friends either. Maybe if she smoked a cigarette, she could blend in better and not fall under scrutiny again. "I don't know," she answered, "my Mom smokes... " she trailed off.

"Then she won't be able to tell if you've been smoking." Monica finished her sentence for her. "Try one, you probably won't like the first one, but it will help you to loose weight. By the time you smoke your third Newport, you'll understand why we like them." Deirdre hadn't thought about needing to lose weight but she let that comment pass as she held her hand out to accept a cigarette between her index finger and her middle finger.

Monica held the lighter to the tip of Deirdre's first cigarette. "Now just breath in gently..."

Deirdre tasted a new unpleasant flavor before she felt her bronchial tubes revolt against this unnatural intrusion. She made a surprised face directed toward Monica. "It's okay, just relax and try again. Just pull a little bit into your lungs."

"This tastes like garbage." Deirdre said. Monica started to protest, "No really. I don't just mean it tastes bad, I mean it tastes like how old garbage smells." She cleared her throat and then put the butt back to her lips. The two of them had moved away from the others. Deirdre wanted to vomit in private, if it came to that. This time she inhaled a bit more smoke, quite a bit more deeply. As she exhaled her head began to swim. She was dizzy and electrified all at once. "It still tastes like shit but I'm starting to understand the appeal."

"Good girl!" Monica laughed at her use of the words which earlier in the day had a completely different meaning. The two girls rejoined the group of others who were enjoying their afternoon smoke. Deirdre smoked her first cigarette modestly, dropping it to the ground and grinding it under her shoe when there was just a half-inch left. She was very queasy but she was smiling.

Six months later, Deirdre was sitting in a lawn chair in her back yard, reading Gone With the Wind for the second time, dragging deeply on a cigarette. A light breeze was blowing her dark hair back away from her face, the smoke from her cigarette was swept away as well. She jumped when she heard the screen door slam because she didn't expect her mother to be home for another two hours.

"When the fuck did you start smoking cigarettes?" Her mother spat the question at her.

"Hi Mom, why do you care?" Deirdre asked earnestly.

"Don't sass me you little brat. Where is your pack?"

Deirdre pulled a half-empty pack of Newports out of her back pocket, and with cat-like reflexes, Shirley Lipton snatched the pack away from her then turned and walked back into the house. She had one of them pursed between her lips before she reached the screen door.

"Oh, that's why you care." Deirdre said to her mother's back.

NATE

Sophie survived the twelve months that Nate was allowed to wear diapers by staying in a state of self-induced semi-catatonia. Handling soiled diapers and diapering accessories was done wearing kitchen gloves, burping the child meant wearing a cape she bought at a hair dressers supply house, and toys were soaked in Lysol on almost a daily basis.   All of this while she shuffled around the house, never opening the curtains.   When Joe would find empty prescription pill containers in the garbage, he did not inquire about it.

At the age of one year, Nate was placed on the toilet and not allowed to get up until he had produced both urine and a bowel movement.   He ate three meals there that first day.   His potty training was supported by negative reinforcement.   His buttocks often displaying red ruler-shaped marks.   By the time he was 18-months old, he was retaining his stools for days.   The side effects of this retention included belly aches, rectal bleeding and self-isolation.

When Nate's elderly aunt gave him a set of dominoes, Nate felt a new emotion: love.   Nate loved his dominoes. He stared at the dots, running his fingers over the white dimples, counting endlessly. He could spend hours happily playing with the dominoes although to him, it wasn't play. It was a job - a job he loved.

Once Nate was in school, he was an excellent student, which always surprised his teachers because he would always appear to be living in his own private world.   He would sit as far back in the class rooms as possible and would stare out the window or off into nameless space. Teachers would start their year with him assuming he wasn't paying attention but since he passed every test and quiz, they ultimately left him pretty much alone.   He excelled at math especially; he seemed to have knowledge of mathematics that weren't even taught to him yet. Theories, patterns and equations never had to be explained to him. It saddened his teachers to notice that he never played with other children nor did he have any friends.   A few times, he was heard humming quietly when the various noises of the classroom would simultaneously end. This led to him being ostracized by the other students, which pushed him even further into his exclusive world.

Nate's world was all about numbers.   As early as he could remember, ones, and in particular, repeating ones would herald something bad, while twos, especially repeating twos, would signal that something good was going to happen.   He felt that most repeating odd numbers were harbingers of doom especially sevens but none were as bad as ones.   The same yet opposite was true of even numbers, with twos being the most powerful and eights being in second place.   When Nate was four, he bagged up all of his dominoes with either one dimple or eleven dimples and pushed the package far down into the kitchen garbage can one day when Sophie was napping.

He carefully replaced the garbage can lid so as not to raise the wrath he knew his mother was capable of.

When Nate was ten years old, he took all of the birthday money that he had fastidiously saved and bought an analogue alarm clock for his room. The digital one his parents had placed on his bedside table had exhausted him. Covering it with a bandanna before it was 1:11 and 11:11 and then uncovering it in time for 2:22 meant a great loss of sleep. Yet he felt his life nearly depended on it. His life felt much more manageable to him when he put that alarm clock into his closet, its face blank. Sometimes in the middle of the night however, he would think that the digital clock was taunting him from its dark corner. So, awake, he would look at the big hand and little hand of his friendly alarm clock to see that it was a tiny bit later than ten after one. It was 1:11 even though the unfriendly clock couldn't display that fact. The comfort his new clock bought him was tempered by this but he was still able to sleep better most nights.

MARYJANE

MaryJane was ecstatic when her pregnancy test was positive. She was a nurse practitioner at a family planning clinic and had given the same result to many other people. Prior to her positive test, she never revealed her fury-laden jealousy. She had been married for six years; a virgin until that night. While she was extremely disappointed when she found out what "all the fuss was about", vis-a-vis, the essential act of procreation, she continued to encourage her husband in bed; she would also encourage him to get done - the quicker the better.

The first year of marriage was easy for her, comparatively. The first night of her second year of marriage, she felt a tingle of frustration over not achieving pregnancy yet. Year three was worse. During year four, frustration turned to anger, concurrently, her husband's interest in her began to decrease. In year five, she actively ignored the signs that he was giving his seed to someone else; she just needed it to work once. *ONCE* she shouted inside her own head.

The irony of the juxtaposition of her role in her profession, and her lack of success at home started what felt like an itchy sweater rubbing against her soul. With every positive pregnancy test she delivered at work, the itch grew greater. By year six, the itch was acidic. There were times when she felt acid was running through her veins when she was at work. She was starting to believe the women she was caring for - pregnant women with no health insurance - didn't deserve to have babies. Her friend and coworker Margo, did her the favor of pointing out that she should keep her attitude hidden while at work. As much as this would seem like unneeded advice, in MaryJane's world, her clients' lack of 'deserving' was simply a statement of fact. Meanwhile, the family planning agency's mission included treating every person as deserving of whatever they needed or wanted. MaryJane needed to fake her support of the clients.

~~~~~~

Made in the USA
Middletown, DE
24 March 2016